CRYSTAL DRAGON

CRYSTAL DRAGON SAGA, BOOK 1

KATIE CHERRY

FALLBRANDT
PRESS

First Edition

Print ISBN: 978-1-949382-90-7

PUBLISHED BY FALLBRANDT PRESS

www.FallbrandtPress.com

BOOKS BY KATIE CHERRY

The Crystal Dragon Saga

Rising from Dust: Companion novella
* * *

Crystal Dragon
Crystal Hope
Crystal Lies
Crystal Curse - June 24, 2020
Crystal Allegiance - July 29, 2020
Crystal Fate - August 26, 2020
Crystal War - September 24, 2020
* * *

Crystal Dragon Saga Boxed Set: Books 1-3

The Dragon Blood Trilogy

Dragon Blood
Dragon Soul
Dragon Heart

DEDICATION

For those who believed I could make it this far.

Thank you!

PROLOGUE

Black. *A mountain of gleaming black scales before him, carrying the stench of death. Paralyzing fear streaming through his body once the gleam of huge golden eyes can be seen. The dragon's lips slowly peel back, revealing teeth the length of a man's arm embedded in the massive jaw. He finds his gaze riveted on a piece of meat caught between two of the fangs, acutely aware that he was about to meet the same fate.*

"Patrick." He flinches at the sudden voice and blinks, the black scales in his vision of the past becoming fabric, cloaked around one of his followers. "...Sir. Are you alright?"

"Yes, yes, I'm fine," Patrick grunts, waving him away with one gloved hand. "What have you discovered?"

"The Queen is in labor," the man reports, straightening and slipping into his role. "The King is currently pacing outside of the door. The man we've hidden inside the room has been able to maintain his invisibility and remain undetected. He's also just informed the mind reader that the Queen is not having one child as we thought."

"What?" Patrick tears his eyes away from a tree swaying in the wind, the notes it sang no longer soothing to him. "She's having twins?"

The man hesitates, then clasps his hands together with resolve. "Triplets."

The word reverberates through the air, piercing Patrick to the heart. His beautiful Pearl... providing another man with not only one, but three children. His heart hardens. This would not stand. "I suppose this calls for a slight change in plans, then," he murmurs, beginning to pace. His footsteps crush the fresh grass on the hilltop.

"Is kidnapping one of them still the plan?"

"Yes. I have no desire to have my castle overrun by children, however. One will be enough of a handful. The other two will simply have to perish," he decides, turning sharply on his heel. The grass tears under the stress; just the beginning of the destruction he would cause in the realm.

The two rejoin the rest of the group, waiting for the signal from the scout planted inside the castle's walls. The sun is just setting when the time comes for the Dragon Hunters to invade.

The stream of black cloaks rushes towards the walls encrusted with gold and precious jewels, slipping in through the now unguarded stone gate. None of them look to the side to see the unconscious guards at the feet of the group Patrick had sent ahead, their gaze focused on their destination. They circle both gleaming entrances, looming just out of sight of anyone inside. Patrick walks silently forward, alone. The King is just coming out of the room where his wife had just given birth, his back to him.

Patrick waits for him to turn, the taste of revenge settling on his tongue, thick and sweet. His hands clench in impatience, the movement stretching the black leather gloves, and release only when the King finally turns. The royal father stumbles back in shock, hitting the door behind him. Patrick remains standing, his back straight and proud, drawing immense satisfaction from the man fallen before him.

The King quickly rises to his feet, turning back to the man. He peers at the face under the hood, straining to remember where he had seen it before, then chuckles. "Trying to give me a heart attack, Pat? There are other ways to announce your presence!" When Patrick doesn't move, the King clears his throat, confused. "So... what are you doing here? I haven't seen you in years!" Patrick ignores him and takes a step towards the door, his gaze focused and intense. The King puts up his guard, although still trying to appear gracious. "Oh, I see. You came to see Pearl," he says, trying to distract him, shifting a little more into his way. Patrick's eyes flash to him, irritated. "Well, I apologize, but she's not seeing any visitors right now. I'll have to ask you to leave and come back another time- preferably when we know you're coming."

Patrick sneers and, before the King can defend himself, knocks him to the ground with a mighty blow to his regal face. His blue-gold eyes reflect the last rays of sunlight streaming through a window as he stares up at the black-cloaked villain.

Patrick looks down on him, contempt in his crooked smile. "You still don't get it, do you, Alexander? I'm not your friend. I never was. I was only using you to get close to Pearl." Encouraged by the hurt and confusion on Alexander's face as well as the blood beginning to drip from his lower lip, he continues, telling the King his story. "I fell in love with Pearl long before *you* ever met her. The problem was, I could never get close to her- those with spectacular Gifts always surrounded her, blocking me out of the picture. The princess never took notice of the little Giftless kid who had been shoved into a corner to be forgotten. Then I had a brilliant idea; since I couldn't manage to get close enough to her to be her friend, perhaps if I somehow befriended someone that she was already close to, she would notice me.

"I tried this for a few years, but I couldn't make friends with *anyone*, let alone someone close to her. I was completely alone. I had actually given up by the time you arrived. But I knew I could get to you since you didn't know any better. You did not yet realize that I was an outcast. As I predicted would happen, the beloved Princess Pearl took a liking to you immediately. It worked fine for me for a while. The three of us were friends, and everything looked brighter in my life. Until I started getting pushed out of the way. So you could have her all to yourself," he says bitterly. "Before I could even have time to make my intentions known, she was set on you and only you, just mere months after the two of you met!" he growls, his voice heavy with years of despair.

"You never said anything... you could have told me, Pat!" The King exclaims to his old friend, standing. Alexander was only a couple of inches shorter than Patrick, but still intimidating.

Patrick doesn't flinch. "That's another thing. The whole 'Pat' nickname was only for Pearl to call me. Since I am no longer pretending to be your friend, you must call me by my real name."

"Pat..." the King starts.

"Patrick!" he abruptly corrects him.

"But Pat," Alexander perseveres, "Where did you go after we got married? You disappeared for over ten years!"

The long-lost friend glares at him before continuing his story. "I was enraged. I left, unable to see my precious Pearl with someone else. I wandered for a time in the wilderness, eventually spending a night in a dragon's cave while it was away. I only learned of my error once it had returned. I tried to run as it approached, but the rocks around the cave were wet from the rain, and I slipped and cut myself many times before I reached the cover of the trees.

"When the black beast landed at the cave, it followed the trail of blood directly to me, paralyzing me with DragonFear. I was completely unable to move. I was as good as dead," he continues, lost in the past. "The dragon started toward me, and I mentally gave up. I was ready to die- it was a better option than crawling back to *you*," Patrick sneers at Alexander, who looks on with astonished eyes. "I waited for my impending doom, but just as the dragon reared back its head and opened its mouth wide, ready to snap me up, I heard two soft twangs behind me. The dragon roared in fury, an arrow protruding from each eye, releasing me from my trance-like state. Unsure of what to do, I merely stood there, completely stunned.

"More spears and arrows were unleashed from behind me, striking the dragon in the mouth, belly, and neck. I was lucky to survive the thrashing that resulted from the assault. Of course, I didn't escape that encounter unscathed. All I remember was something slicing into the side of my head before I promptly passed out. When I regained consciousness, I was among my saviors. They called themselves the Dragon Hunters. They took me in as one of their own and taught me their ways. For once in my life, I wasn't looked at differently because of my lack of Gifts. Now, ten years later, I am their leader," he concludes, smiling smugly.

"That's... quite the story," responds the King, unsure of what to say. "But what are you going to do now? I mean, why are you *really* here? To tell me what happened to you? I have a hard time believing that's all it is if your life is really as great as you claim it is."

Patrick's lips slowly curl into a sinister smile. "Well, I came for revenge, of course. And now is the perfect time... the perfect opportunity."

"Revenge? But why now...?" Alexander starts, confused. His face changes suddenly as the possibilities of what his long-lost friend means to do begin to dawn on him. "What... no! You can't!"

"I can, and I will," Patrick growls, taking a step towards the door. Alexander immediately tackles him to the ground, knocking his black hood off of his face. Shocked at the sight, he scoots back, his mouth open wide with surprise and disgust. As Patrick stands, the King continues to stare, taking in the horrific scar on the left side of his face. His eye was intact, but the area below it appeared to be scraped off, revealing raw flesh and bone beneath it. It had a sickening green sheen that looked diseased. While unhealed, it also didn't appear to be freshly inflicted. "What... what is..."

Patrick grins, enjoying his reaction. "What, this?" he asks mockingly, indicating his face. "This is the injury I got from that dragon. The beast cut me as it turned to flee, the cowardly thing," he mocks. "I suppose either it got infected, or it could simply be the magic of the beast that prevents it from healing, but I decided I don't mind so much. It accents my eyes, don't you think?" he snickers. "Now then..." he continues, his face settling into seriousness. "Stay out of my way and this will all be over with soon."

"Never!" The King cries, standing and using the momentum to send a fist flying into the Dragon Hunter's face while pulling out a knife with his other hand. He holds it to Patrick's throat, panting with anger. "There is *no way* I will *ever* let you take any of my family away from me. I'd rather die! Guards!" he calls, desperation entering his voice as he calls for his absent guards.

"Oh, I know," Patrick replies, his voice cool and cocky as his gaze slowly moves from the door to the King's blue eyes. "Which is precisely why *that* is my revenge. I won't kill you- just your loved ones!" Laughing, he makes a dragon-like roar deep in his throat. Before Alexander has time to react, two of Patrick's men grab him from behind, each taking an arm and twisting it behind his back and toward his head, then lifting him off the floor. The knife clatters to the stone floor.

The King gasps in pain as he's lifted even higher by the brutes. Even as his shoulders pop and his arms start to pull out of their sockets, even as sharp pain is shooting down his spine, he swallows his cries and simply glares at Patrick. Ignoring his glare, the leader of the Dragon Hunters turns to the men in black rushing into the hallway. They stand by, silently waiting for the next command from their leader.

He turns back to Alexander. "As much as I would love to see you dead and the fair Pearl a widow, I'm afraid that's not the punishment I have in store for you. Oh, no... you need to stay alive and suffer." Snapping his fingers, he signals for two men to go into the room that the King was trying so hard to keep them out of. Alexander holds his breath, waiting for the sounds of struggle as the two guards and the doctor defend his wife and children. There's nothing.

Patrick laughs at his confused face. "That's right. I made sure to take care of the doctor and the guards. I had my men subdue them all while we were talking. I also had a man in the room before you even went in. Thanks to his Gift of invisibility and the Gift of another of my men of reading minds, I know all about your three children. Crystal and her... unique dragon eye abilities, Rex, and Hunter, the one you have labeled as the runt of the family. Most likely to become Giftless; is that what you're worried about? ...Perhaps you *should* worry. I hear children tend to take after those who raise them," he chuckles, turning his back to the father, eagerly awaiting his prize.

The King growls and starts to struggle, but someone comes up behind him and drives a needle into his neck, causing him to lose all control of his muscles. His brain fogs up and he can't think clearly. The thin man steps away, a now empty syringe dangling from his long, thin fingers. As the King hangs limply from the two men's grip, he's still aware of what's going on around him, although he can't do anything about it. The door opens and the two men come out; one holding three little bundles, and the other dragging the bound and gagged doctor behind him. Tears run down her face, making evident her fear for the fate of the royal newborns as well as her own.

"No..." the King moans, unable to do anything else.

Patrick laughs, taking one of the babies, and, looking into its sleeping face, announces, "This one, Hunter, will come with us. We will raise him to hate his parents, the Dragons, and we will teach him our ways. He will be the future leader after me and will continue the destruction of *all* Dragons!" His men laugh at the pun made from the royal family's last name.

"Unless, of course, *Alexander* here decides to try anything... in which case, we can always kill him.

"Now, with the other two... I have no need for them, so I suppose we'll kill them? Throw them out and let them struggle to survive before finally dying; abandoned to a world of pain?" The King's anguished cries are drowned out by the many Dragon Hunters cheering.

Something suddenly snaps inside of the King. His brain is clear, and he fills with sudden, immense power. Without knowing what he's doing, Alexander looks at Crystal and Rex with his newly revealed dragon eyes, instinctively knowing he didn't have the power to save all three of the children. The gold stare intensified with emotion and energy. Without stopping to ponder whether it was even possible, moves them both as far away from Patrick as he can- all with his mind. They disappear, to the astonishment of everyone in the room.

The King, now drained of energy, passes out on the floor with a thump as the stunned men holding him release their grip.

Patrick's mind reels at the powerful magic he had just witnessed as he instinctively clutches the last Dragon child to his chest. Leading the Dragon Hunters in a hasty retreat, he glances down at the child, Hunter; relieved that he still possessed the one heir required for Alexander's undoing.

The group sweeps back out of the gate in the wall, their dark capes billowing in the cold wind. With the King and Queen's last baby in his arms and darkness in his heart, Patrick leads his men as they flee the scene. They move swiftly in the dark, and the night soon swallows them up, leaving behind only despair and broken hearts.

1

The sun is hot on my neck as I kneel in the dirt. I examine my fingers in front of me. They're dirty, and a little green under the nails. I sigh and look down at the bucket resting between the plant I'm picking from and me. The peas this year are small and shriveled. I've yet to find much that's salvageable. Groaning, I heave myself back onto my feet, dusting off my faded blue jeans. Lifting the embarrassingly light bucket, I trudge back down the little-worn path through our small farm. Our handful of chickens scatter as I approach and the cow stares at me with heavy eyes as I walk past her. I want to check on how she's doing, but I know better. She's very temperamental now that she's further in her pregnancy and she only lets dad near her.

"Crystal! Back so soon?" Mom greets me at the door, stress and worry deepening the few wrinkles she's been developing.

"It's as bad as we thought," I reply, setting the bucket down. "The peas aren't producing much either." I hesitate before continuing. "I don't know that we'll be able to make it off of just this. If the rest of the summer is this low in yield…" I pause and take one of her hands in mine. "Mom, you know I saved my money from working for the Hansen's last summer. It might be enough for the four of us."

Tears well up in her eyes. "I can't ask you to do that. That money is yours. It's the responsibility of your father and me to take care of you and your sister."

"Mom. We don't have a choice anymore. I know you've been trying, but there's only so much we can do since dad lost his job." I smile at her to let her know it's okay. "It's really alright, mom. I'll go to the store this evening and get what we need. Okay?"

She nods, giving me a sad smile. "I'm sorry you have to deal with this on top of..." her voice trails off and she avoids looking me in the eye.

"Suddenly being told I was adopted?" I give her a tight smile, trying to ignore the pang of pain in my chest at the word 'adopted.' "It's okay. Every family has something, right? It doesn't really change anything." I swallow and step past her into the house. "I'm just going to go shower before I run to the store, okay?" I peel off my work shoes before shuffling up the stairs to the shower.

Once I'm under the cascade of hot water, I close my eyes, letting my body relax. As I do so, a now familiar conversation rises in my memory.

"Crystal... we have something to tell you," dad murmurs as he stops me from going to my room.

"Can it wait until tomorrow?" I sigh. "I'm exhausted."

"I know, sweetheart, but this has already waited long enough." I notice he doesn't meet my gaze. What's going on?

"Okay..." I relent, letting him lead me to the couch. He and mom sit on the couch across from me. Their bodies are stiff with tension. "... Mom? Dad? What is it? What do you need to tell me?"

They hesitate, glancing at each other before looking back at me. My apprehension rises. "Crystal, honey... there's no easy way to say this..."

"Say what?" I demand. "And why are you trying to be so sweet? You never call me 'sweetheart' and 'honey' so often. What are you hiding from me?" Even as I ask it, I know in my heart exactly what they've been hiding for sixteen years.

"...You were adopted," dad finally says. I stare at him, wanting to deny what he said. Surely he meant something else. Adopted? Me? But even as my mind spins, the words settle inside of me and I can feel their truth. All my life I wondered, but I never brought myself to actually consider it. And now, here it was in front of me, put into words.

"I..." I choke on whatever I was going to try to say next. Adopted. I

knew I didn't fit in. I didn't belong here. I always did and said the wrong things... it all made sense now. I wasn't even theirs. They probably regretted their decision to... *adopt* me. That's why they were telling me now. Money was low because dad had lost his job... they were going to cut me off! Send me out on my own at the uncertain age of sixteen! I don't know anything about how to take care of myself. I'm still in high school, after all!

"Honey." Mom's- Janet's- voice pierces through my spiraling thoughts. "Please don't think that this changes anything. We still love you. We just thought you had a right to know, and that you're old enough now to understand and be able to handle it... just because I didn't give birth to you doesn't mean you aren't ours."

I bow my head to hide the tears welling up, trying desperately to swallow them away. *This does not hurt me. I'm fine. Getting too worked up about this is ridiculous. They still love me. She just said so.* Still, the doubt made my heart ache. I stand abruptly, turning away from them. I can't think of anything to say, so I don't. I just flee back upstairs and fling myself onto my bed, the ache in my heart spreading throughout my body.

I blink and realize that tears are again running down my cheeks. I press my hand to my chest, alarmed as always at the physical pain I feel. My thoughts have settled down the last couple of weeks from their announcement, but one nagging doubt continues to eat at me. *I'm not good enough. I never have been, and now... well, I'm not even family. My stay here could be terminated as soon as I'm no longer of use. I have to show them I can be good enough. I can be beneficial. I can help the family. ...The family that isn't even mine.* A sob suddenly escapes me and before I know it, I'm having another meltdown.

After a few minutes, my sobs reduce to shuddering breaths and I'm able to finish my shower. Drying my hair, I pause and peer at my reflection. My light brown hair is dark with water, bringing out my eyes more than usual. The blue-gold irises glint in the light. I want to think they're beautiful, but it's difficult when they set me apart. Especially thanks to the secret they harbor. I blame them, in part, for me being an outcast amongst my peers and even family. "And now I know why," I sigh before turning away from the mirror and heading to my room.

Once I'm dressed, I braid my hair, which still ends up going halfway down my back. I pull at the strands, tempted to cut it shorter. I decide against it. I love my long hair, even if some of the boys at school tease me about it. I head back to the bathroom to put on some makeup to hide the fact that I've been crying before grabbing my wallet and my keys. I open my door to find my little sister, Kiki, staring up at me with big brown eyes.

"Where are you going?" she asks.

"Just shopping," I reply.

A big grin spreads across her face. "Can I come too? Pleeeaaaaassssssseeeeee? I promise I'll be good!"

I chuckle. "Alright, fine. But we're on a tight budget, remember?"

She nods seriously, then pauses. "What's that again?"

"It means we can't buy things we don't need. So we can't get you a bunch of candy like we used to, okay?"

Kiki's face droops, but she nods and agrees to obey the demands of the budget. I smile and lead her to my old car. After prying open the doors, I manage to convince the car to start. It's a bumpy ride, but we survive the trip to the store.

The shopping trip doesn't take long, despite the over-energetic nine-year-old running around the cart. Everything goes smoothly... until I mistakenly take the candy aisle to get up to the front. Kiki stops dead in her tracks, staring down a bag of chocolates. "Kiki... I can't. I don't have enough money," I gently remind her, taking her hand to pull her away.

She looks up at me with devastation written on her face. "Please? There's nothing you can do? You sure?"

"I'm sorry," I murmur, looking up as someone approaches. Immediately embarrassed, I turn, dragging the sad Kiki behind me. A hand on my arm stops me. Startled, I spin around and come face to face with a handsome boy about my age. He's a little taller than me with light brown hair that goes down to his ears. He's wearing gloves without fingers, like biker gloves. They match his denim jacket. His warm brown eyes and charming smile make my heart skip a beat and cause blood to rush to my cheeks. I duck my head, trying to hide the deep blush burning on my cheeks.

"Excuse me." He takes his hand off of my arm and smiles. "Is there anything I can do to help you?"

"H-help me? Why?" I ask, my brain sluggish as my eyes seem incapable of leaving his.

"Well, maybe I have a soft spot for beautiful damsels in distress," he winks, handing me a chocolate bar and twenty dollars.

"What… the chocolate isn't this much…" I begin, but he stops me.

"I know," he chuckles. "The chocolate is for her; the money is for you. But if you feel bad about taking it, perhaps you could pay me back by agreeing to go on a date with me?"

I stare at him in disbelief, mentally going over myself. My hair- nothing special. My eyes, usually off-putting. My worn, sad looking clothes… there was nothing special about me whatsoever. So why was this stunning man even giving me the time of day?

"My bad," he chuckles. "I probably should have started with my name. I'm Brandon." He pauses and looks me over before pulling out a pen and a sticky note. He quickly scribbles on it. "Tell you what. Here's my number. Text me if you decide to give me a chance." He hands it to me, his fingers brushing mine. His piercing eyes lock onto mine one more time. "It was wonderful to meet you…"

"Crystal," I manage. "And it was great to meet you too."

He smiles and bows his head a little before turning and walking back out of the hallway. The world seems to freeze around me and his smile is all I can see. I'm in a daze. I always thought I would be more alarmed once this 'twitterpation' that everyone talks about hit me, but now… it's startling, but also delightful. I can feel the smile on my face making my cheeks start to ache.

That's when I feel the little hand grab onto my empty one and tug. "Crystal! That boy was sooooo cute!!! Do you like him?"

"Oh…" I shake myself out of my haze and face my little sister. "Well, he sure was nice, wasn't he? Now then, let's go buy our food."

After dinner, I finally manage to seclude myself in my room. Climbing onto my bed, I cross my legs and lean forward, staring at the small red phone in my hand. Brandon's number fills the screen. Never before have I second guessed such a small handful of numbers… never before have I been so anxious to type out and send a short text.

Scolding myself, I shake my head and clutch the phone tighter. Even if it wasn't about him asking me on a date, there were still those twenty dollars to repay, and I would much rather repay his kindness how I can. He chose for that repayment to be a date. "That's it," I mutter to myself, clicking on the text box to prepare to type. "I'll think of this as repayment. It's nothing to worry about, I'll just go and have a good time with him, and everyone will be happy."

I blow out a sharp breath, then let my fingers fly. *Hey, Brandon. It's Crystal. I've thought about it and decided that I will go on that date with you. Where and when were you thinking?*

The reply comes within minutes. *That's fantastic! I was worried you wouldn't want to go on a date with someone like me. I'll do my best to show you a great time! What do you like to do? Hiking? Laser tag? Movie?*

Whatever sounds fun to you, I guess. I am a pretty active person, but movies are great too.

Alright. Then how do dinner and laser tag sound? Tomorrow at seven? And could you meet me outside the store where we met? I don't want to make you uncomfortable and feel like you have to let me know where you live or anything.

That sounds perfect. I'll see you then.

Sleep isn't easy to come by that night, nerves racing through my body, electrifying me. My brain won't stop. Around three in the morning, I groan and flip onto my stomach and finally drift to sleep.

When my alarm goes off early the next morning, I'm confused and disoriented. Sitting up after turning it off, I try to blink away the stinging in my eyes. That's when I remember why I'm up so early today. Mostly because Kiki then opens my door and bounds in, looking more refreshed than seven o'clock deserves.

"Crystal! You're babysitting me today! ALL day!" she excitedly reminds me. "Mom and dad won't be back until tomorrow, right?"

"They should make it back sometime tonight," I yawn, swinging my legs off the bed. "You can go and ask them all about it while I get dressed, okay?"

"Okay!" she agrees, leaping out of my room and back down the stairs. Sighing, I pick an outfit for the day before heading to the bathroom to force a brush through my thick hair. Once it's back in its usual braid, I head down the stairs to join my family for breakfast. My parents leave as soon as we're done to investigate a potential job for dad.

The instant the car pulls away, Kiki's attention becomes riveted on me.

"So what are we going to play today, Crystal? Can we go to the park? I have a new game idea! You're a good fairy, and I'm a bad guy who wants to capture you, and…"

"Sure," I sigh. "We can go to the park." Her eyes light up as I grab the keys to the car. Chuckling, I usher her inside, then jump in myself and start the rickety old car. The weather is perfect when we get to the park, and I catch myself eyeing a bench nearby. Kiki begs me to play her fairy game with her, but I manage to convince her to play with the other kids on the playground.

After watching for a while, I decide she's safe and having fun, so I relax and lay down on the bench, closing my eyes against the bright sun. The warmth of the sunlight warms my cheeks and I sigh contentedly. I love the summer. I was looking forward to this warmth for a long time.

Almost without my noticing, the background noise of children playing and laughing and adults conversing with each other slowly fades away. Everything else follows suit until I find myself slipping into a dreamless, peaceful sleep.

I wake suddenly, sitting bolt upright, feeling that something is wrong. I scan the park, but nothing seems to be wrong besides that it's much emptier than before. In fact, everyone seems to have left. I glance at my watch and grimace guiltily when it informs me that I have been sleeping for hours and it was now past noon. I quickly stand up, hastily searching for Kiki. Out of the corner of my eye, I see a black van pull up, followed by a white one. My apprehension rises as I notice the tinted windows.

I race around the playground until I finally find her, curled up in the bottom of a slide, sound asleep. As I approach her, I glance back at the vans. A group of large men dressed in dark leather is pouring out of the vehicles… and begin heading our way. Panicking, I quickly wake Kiki up.

"Crystal? What… what's wrong?" she mumbles, rubbing at her eyes.

"No time to explain," I quickly say, pulling her to her feet. "There are bad guys here, so I need you to run and hide and don't come out until I come to find you, okay?"

"Okay," she replies, still half-asleep as she slowly obeys, shambling off among the slides, ladders, and rope bridges in the playground.

Now to see if I'll have time to hide before they get here... I've only just thought this when I turn and find my world consisting of black leather and the smell of sweat. Scrambling backward, I look up. Right into a big, red, angry looking man's face. Around his neck is a black collar with sharp studs sticking out. Gulping in fear, I turn to run, only to find two more of them have snuck around behind me.

I'm trapped.

Spinning back to the first guy, I first try to talk my way out. "Who are you? What do you want?" I demand, allowing my voice to shake as I speak.

He doesn't respond for a moment, then suddenly chuckles and points behind me. I spin around just in time to see another couple of people grab Kiki and begin to tie her up. She stares at me, her eyes glistening with fear and confusion... and trust. She believes in my abilities to save her- to save both of us. My gut clenches in fear. This was a profoundly different situation than my fighting techniques class.

Taking a deep breath, I steady myself and will my body to stop shaking. My body settles naturally into the stance, my eyes closing for a moment so I can compose myself. When they fly open, I spring into action. Leaping at the man tying Kiki's hands behind her back, I quickly recall how to bring down people- *men*- bigger than me. My foot hits its mark, and he goes down hard, a gurgling yelp caught in his throat.

I want to check that Kiki is okay, but I remind myself that I can do that after I face the rest of these thugs. Turning to the other one by Kiki, I quickly analyze the position he's standing in, preparing to use this against him. But before I can move, I'm grabbed from behind. One big hand is pulling my arm behind my back and forcing my hand up towards my head. His other hand is holding a knife to my throat, the icy blade stinging against my hot skin.

"I wouldn't do that if I were you," he growls. I freeze, pretending to comply. He grunts, pleased that I'm no longer putting up a fight. What he doesn't realize is that I'm merely waiting for a good time to strike. While he's busy tugging me back towards the vehicles they arrived in, I look around and quickly make a plan.

Now I just need a distraction... Even as I'm thinking this, I hear a car coming. *Yes! That should work!* But I'm quickly caught off guard as the thug holding me abruptly lets go of my neck and jumps to the side, ducking behind a large hedge to hide from the approaching car. I fly after him, my arm being pulled so hard and fast it dislocates. The pain is so intense and unexpected that I instinctively start to scream.

The thug immediately clamps his hand over my mouth, pulling back so hard my scream comes out more like a choked gargle. His hand is also covering my nose, so I can't breathe. I struggle to take a breath. I soon feel my body begging for oxygen- my lungs are threatening to burst. I then start to get dizzy, tiny black and purple spots swirling before my eyes. Desperate, I start kicking behind me, trying to hit him, my thoughts focusing on my need for air. With every kick, I get weaker. Now past being merely desperate, I hurt badly enough that I actually believe that I am going to die.

Completely overwhelmed with panic at the thought, I find it impossible to think through the fear of death. Right before I lose consciousness, I swing my head back, hard, in a last, desperate attempt to live. I feel my head hit his, and then there's a sensation of falling.

After that, I don't feel anything at all.

2

Returning to consciousness was a bit like swimming out of thick black water. Sensations return in bits and pieces. The first thing I notice is the soreness in my shoulder. It takes a few moments for me to recall why it would ache. *They dislocated it.* I gingerly move my arm a little, relieved when it responds. *They must have popped it back into place,* I realize. Blinking open my eyes, I'm startled when the black water doesn't go away. No, not water... but I certainly couldn't see much light.

Swallowing the panic that rises in my throat, I focus my thoughts on figuring out as much of my situation as I can. I try to lift my hands to my face to remove whatever is restricting my vision, only to discover that they are bound with rope. They are tied in front of me, however, so I can reach my face. My fingers brush a rough sack which wavers loosely around my head. Attempting to get to my feet nearly topples me face first when yet more rope stops their movement. Ironically the only thing that saves me is the ground suddenly moving in the opposite direction. Straining my ears, I hear gravel crunching beneath tires, as well as two men talking in low voices.

I must be in the back of one of those vans I noticed at the park earlier... Gah! How did I get in this predicament? Where's Kiki? How am I going to escape from a moving vehicle while essentially blind and without the use of my hands or legs?

I try to call out to my captors, only to realize that there is even a gag in my mouth, tied around my head. What comes out is a muffled growl of exasperation. Before I can think of another thing to try, the van stops. An unsettling silence replaces that of the engine and the gravel crunching. I try to slow my frantic heart as footsteps approach the vehicle.

The doors open suddenly, metal scraping harshly against metal. A hand grabs the sack, yanking it and a handful of hair off my head. I immediately look around, taking in all I can through my watering eyes. The soft light of the crescent moon reflects off the back doors of the van, although it is too weak to allow me to see much else. A silhouette stands before me, filling the doorway with his massive presence. I shrink away as I recognize the man who suffocated me earlier. His gaze is accusatory, highlighted by the darkening patch around his right eye.

Peeking past him, I notice another man has a squirming bundle on his shoulder. It takes a moment before the realization of what it is hits me. *Kiki!* She's facing away from me, the man holding onto her by her legs. Before I can move toward her, 'Black Eye' roughly grabs me by the waist, hoisting me into the air. I hardly even have time to scream before my stomach lands roughly on the shoulder of my captor.

Feeling utterly helpless, I watch as the ground begins bouncing as Black Eye starts jogging, holding onto my legs. Slung over his shoulder like a sack of flour, I am unable to see much of anything. My worry increases as I recall that Kiki is in the same position with the other man. *What are they going to do to her? How on earth can I protect her? Those classes I took were supposed to prepare me for this kind of situation... yet I have completely and utterly failed. I've let her down. Poor Kiki.* My mood dips further as the next thought comes. *I wonder if she wishes I wasn't a part of her family. I've let them all down.*

Black Eye then slows. I sigh in relief and lift my head to look around. Unfortunately, all I can see is the long gravel pathway we've just traveled up. Consciously quieting my breathing, I listen to hear what the two men might be doing.

A squeak is the first thing to greet my ears. Metallic... A door hinge. We must be entering an old building, judging from the musty smell that washes over us. Our kidnappers walk down a long hallway, turning now and then. The paint on the walls has long since faded away and chipped off in many places. I strain my brain to remember our path as we go, hoping against hope I'll even be able to use the information to get us both away. I grit my teeth with determination. Even if I don't make it out of here, I'm going to do everything I can to at least get Kiki out. She didn't deserve any of this. Especially since this was far more likely to do with me than a nine-year-old.

We then emerge into a large room. As Black Eye turns and looks around, I have the opportunity to do so as well. The room has a high ceiling and is filled with chairs. Everything is covered in dust and cobwebs, further confirming my assumption of this being an old, abandoned building. Looking down, I see that we've climbed onto a stage. The wood is warped and the nails rusty from water damage. *An old theatre! ... That doesn't help me, though. I still have no idea where we are. I don't know of any abandoned buildings with a theatre in them.*

My heart skips a beat as I suddenly hear new footsteps heading towards us across the stage. Black Eye turns towards the newcomer, effectively facing me away. Frustrated, all I can do is listen as the footsteps come closer, slow and menacing. I shiver- not just from the draft from a hole in the building, but from fear as well. Gulping, I frantically look around for *anything* I can use to my advantage.

When I spot something, I can't help but smile from how convenient it is. Black Eye has a knife in a holster on his belt, and luckily, it's unclasped and can easily be pulled out. It's easily within reach, but still, I move slowly and silently. I don't want to see what will happen if I get caught. I grasp the handle with my fingers and slowly remove it, freezing and holding my breath when Black Eye moves underneath me. After a few seconds, nothing happens. Black Eye continues talking to the newcomer, explaining how they captured me. I don't pay much attention, quickly maneuvering the knife handle around the gag and into my mouth, grasping it with my teeth. I lift my wrists to the knife, moving as smoothly as possible. The rope begins to fray against the knife's sharp edge and soon snaps. I slowly slip them off, holding onto them so no one notices my freedom before I'm ready. Then, still moving slowly and carefully, I reach up and grab the knife before slipping the gag down over my chin, letting it hang around my neck before relaxing and waiting for the perfect time to escape.

A raspy voice interrupts Black Eye. "Yes, yes, I get it. She was difficult. I did warn you that she wouldn't be easy to capture. You aren't getting any more money because she gave you a black eye."

"But sir... we also brought the insurance..."

"The girl? Eh... Kiki, was it? That was your instruction to do so! Had you not grabbed her as well you would be severely incompetent. You will receive what we originally agreed upon. Now toss her and the sister into the waiting room. I don't have the energy to deal with another spoiled brat right now. I'll deal with Crystal Shay in the morning. Alone, of course."

No way am I waiting until morning. We're getting out of here, and we're leaving now! Kicking off the surprisingly loose restraints on my feet, I swing my foot and kick Black Eye in the groin. He grunts loudly and releases me. I spring off of him before sweeping my leg under him, sending him toppling to the ground. His head makes a horrifyingly loud noise as it slams against the protruding nails on the floor. Satisfied that he's unconscious, I quickly spin around to face the man holding Kiki. He backs up a step, surprise and fear inscribed on his face. He slowly sets Kiki on the ground, backing up once more with his hands in the air.

"Listen here," he swallows, fear causing his voice to tremble. "I don't want any trouble..."

"Yes, you do," I growl, stalking towards him. "Why else would you have done all of this?" I finger the knife clenched in my hand but am interrupted by a voice behind me. The leader.

"No, no, he's entirely correct. We don't want any trouble; we simply wanted to arrange a meeting. George, leave her be. Stand guard by the door or something to ensure that we remain alone. Crystal, I assure you, I simply wish to speak with you. No harm was meant to come to you."

As George shuffles away, I race to Kiki and cut her bindings before spinning back to face the boss. I'm surprised at his appearance. He looked like he could be anyone's grandpa, although he did look a little grouchy. As I analyze him, I abruptly notice his face beginning to droop. The rest of his skin follows suit, seeming to liquify and slide off. Horrified, I push Kiki behind me, unable to look away myself as he changes. The melting skin appears to bubble before reforming to him, changing the way he looks like he's wearing some kind of costume. It looks quite painful. The process is soon over, and when he's finished, he looks like a completely different man.

Black hair reaching to his shoulders covers his face until he straightens and sweeps it away. Piercing black eyes stare back at me beneath a heavy brow. His long nose takes up a significant portion of his face. His lips are thin and seem to be always pinching together in disapproval.

He stands from his chair, startling me. I back up a step, then another, before steeling myself and assuming a defensive pose, threatening him while protecting Kiki behind me. With a sudden laugh, he begins to clap. *...This is just getting weirder and weirder,* I notice, waiting for the man's next move. No way I'm dropping my guard on this freak.

"Well done!" he chuckles. "Only one other person got so close to getting away from me, and certainly not as quickly and with beautifully executed maneuvers!" His voice somehow reminds me of a vampire. "I had no idea what you were doing until the moment before you acted, and by then it was too late for me to do anything! Excellent! I definitely have high hopes for you in the Games. Especially if you are paired with that other boy..."

My curiosity aroused, but still cautious, I finally speak. "What? What are you talking about? What Games? What other boy? How many people have you kidnapped? Explain everything, now! Why you captured us, all those things you said, and what on earth happened to you- how you... changed!"

"Changed?" he asks innocently.

"Yes! When your skin was... and then you... how on earth did you change from an old man? Who are you? Tell me! Now! Or you'll get a face full of my 'beautifully executed' punches!" I threaten, desperate to figure out what's going on. However, all this does is make him start laughing again. Frustrated, I growl and advance a few more steps, hoping to drive my point home. At this point, he's roaring so hard with laughter he's doubled over, attempting to recover his breath. Bewildered, I can do nothing but stare as he wipes tears from his eyes and straightens.

"I like your spunk! 'My beautifully executed punches!' That was such a great way to put my words back in my mouth! You sure are a quick thinker. You know," he says, suddenly thoughtful, looking at me so intensely it makes me uncomfortable, "you remind me of the good Queen,

Pearl Dragon. You... look a little like her too," he murmurs, coming closer before suddenly gasping and closing the distance. His dark eyes seem to swirl as they stare into my own. "Y- your eyes," he whispers, shocked.

"What about them?" I demand, backing up and pushing Kiki back with me, keeping her behind me.

"They are like the sky... with gold shining through..."

"Yeah. So?"

"It- it's nothing!" he hastily assures me, scrambling away. I'm confused, but if this guy doesn't feel like talking because of my eyes, I'll just have to change the subject in order to get some answers.

"Fine, don't tell me about your weird obsession with my eyes. Tell me why you kidnapped my sister and me. How do you know who we are? Have you been watching us? How long? And who *are you?*"

He seems relieved that I'm not pressing him about my eyes, which makes me want to ask him again, but I resist the urge- for now. "This will take a while," he warns me. "You will want to sit down. I've told this story three times already- just today! I should know how long it is." Not wanting to let my guard down, I remain standing, glaring defiantly at him. I start at a soft tug on my sleeve. Looking down, I see poor Kiki. She's pale and seems exhausted. Dried tears cover her cheeks.

"Crystal, I'm hungry. Make him give us food," she demands. My stomach rumbles loudly, agreeing with her. It occurs to me that we haven't eaten yet today. I quickly glance at my watch, keeping one eye on the strange man. *Past nine? ...Shoot, today was my date with Brandon! I completely missed it! But even worse, my parents said they would be getting back around ten! I have to get home, and quick!*

I turn back to the man. "Talk fast. I need to get home as soon as possible."

He looks at me, amusement glittering in his black eyes. "I'm sorry, but I think I may have heard your sister wrong. She demanded food from me, and you need to hear what I have to say. I'm afraid I cannot tell you the story that will forever change your life in the time frame you are insisting upon, nor would you want to watch your sister waste away as we talk the night away, am I right?"

I glance at Kiki. She wavers and clutches at my pants to stay steady. The day's events have drained her boundless energy and left her looking worn.

I glance between the man and Kiki, debating what to do. Finally, my curiosity and concern for Kiki win me over. *I guess I can stay long enough to hear what he has to say and Kiki is fed. I could call home with my phone and leave them a message saying I'll be back late. I'll just have to be vague about it… well, I'll think about that later. Right now, food and getting the truth out of this guy are the pressing issues!*

"Fine," I say, turning back to him. "You win. We'll eat first. Then we'll see just how long and 'life-changing' your little story is."

3

_____

We follow our strange captor away from the theatre, cautious and wary yet also unable to help looking forward to the prospect of food. Kiki, always quick to trust others, is jumping up and down with excitement. It doesn't last long since the day's events sapped most of her energy. I'm ready for food as well, but not prepared to trust this shifty character.

He leads us to a small wooden table and pulls out three sandwiches; all wrapped neatly. I hesitate to take a bite, but Kiki doesn't share my concern, and I'm slow to stop her from devouring hers. Licking her fingers, she smiles up at me before her eyelids suddenly droop and she falls onto the table, her head hitting the old wood with a soft thump. Dropping my sandwich, I rush the leader and am behind him in two steps, slamming his head forward onto the table and holding the knife I have yet to relinquish to his throat. He doesn't resist or flinch at the icy bite of the steel blade. Filled with anger and desperation to save Kiki, I demand to know what he had done to her.

He laughs. "Oh, you needn't worry. I simply gave your sister something to help her sleep."

"If you're lying to me..." I seethe, the threat heavy in my desperate voice.

"Check for yourself. The girl is breathing just fine," he replies calmly.

Not yet willing to release my captive, I look over to Kiki. Her eyes are closed, her face peaceful. Looking closer, I can see her chest rising and falling with every breath she takes. Relieved, I release him. He sits up and resumes eating as though nothing had happened as I return to my seat. I don't touch the sandwich. "How dare you? How could you *drug her?*" Lifting a finger, he slowly swallows before answering me.

"Put the knife down first, if you please." I glare at him, but he doesn't waver. Standing, I pull back my arm and fling the knife towards the table. It burrows in a few inches before stopping. He raises an eyebrow at me as I sit back down, then sighs. "Well, why do you think I would do so? Come now, you're a smart girl. Clear your head of all those emotions clouding your thoughts. *You* tell me why I would put your sister to sleep." Frustrated, I do as he says, taking calming breaths as I look back on what I know of the man.

"Because you wanted to talk to me alone?"

"Close enough. The child needs sleep, uninterrupted and without fear. I also wanted to spare her from my story, as it is not for young children." Glancing at my untouched sandwich, he continues, saying, "However, I *didn't* put anything in your food. The only thing it will do to you is keep you alert and your head clear so you can stay awake and pay attention as I answer all your questions."

My gut decides that his answer is good enough, so I choose to trust him for now. If things got ugly, I'd need my strength up, after all. I tentatively take a bite. A pleasant yet unfamiliar flavor flows over my tongue, then continues and fills my body with a delightful warmth. Soon after I swallow, the feeling dissipates, but my hunger is already fading, and I am more alert. I quickly finish, trying to place the flavor the whole time but end up unable to. My mind is unusually clear, just like he had promised. I then realize that my weariness has dissipated as well as any aches and pains I had. I feel… perfect! Feeling refreshed, I turn back to the man. *I should learn his name,* I realize.

"What's your name? I need something to call you if I'm going to sit and chat."

"My name is Vladimir, but you may call me Vlad," he replies.

"Okay then, *Vlad*. Before we get on with the story, I need to call my parents."

"Oh? And what would you tell them?" he inquires, raising an eyebrow. "That you and your sister got kidnapped, but not to worry, you'll be home as soon as you finish finding out why their leader can shapeshift?" I don't reply to the mocking tone in his voice, unsure of how to respond when that was what I had been wondering myself. "Might I suggest convincing them to stay the night elsewhere and go on a nice, relaxing date tomorrow to give you the time you need to get home? We are, after all, hours away from where you live."

I frown. "I guess that's what I'll have to do, then," I sigh before standing and walking a short distance away for privacy.

She picks up on the third ring. "Hello? Crystal? What's wrong, honey?" she asks, concerned. I never call when I'm babysitting unless something's wrong, so she's worried.

"Nothing, everything's fine, mom," I assure her, swallowing. I hate lying. "I was just calling to tell you that things are going great, and I think you should take a day off. Stay the night in a hotel to celebrate dad's birthday and go and do something fun tomorrow. You have been so worried lately, I felt like you need a break. Kiki and I will be fine." I try to sound confident so she won't catch on to anything being wrong.

While I'm talking, I'm watching Kiki and Vlad. Kiki is still resting peacefully against the table and Vlad, having finished his sandwich, is now leaning back in his chair, his eyes closed. "Oh... I don't know..." Mom hesitates, unsure. "Are you sure that it's fine with you? You don't want us to come straight home?"

"No!" I gulp and scramble to cover up my outburst. "Uh... no. You deserve a break, mom. I can take care of Kiki."

"Well... if you're sure..."

"I'm sure."

"It *would* be nice to get away from everything for a while... okay. Thanks, sweetie! We'll be back tomorrow before dinnertime, okay?"

"Sure! Of course! Have fun!" I reply, relieved.

"You too! Bye, honey. I love you."

"Love you too," I reply before hanging up. Walking back to Vlad, my steps feel lighter as the stress of hurrying home lifts off my shoulders. It's only a few more steps before I'm brought back down to earth as I remember that for all I know, Kiki's life, and mine, could still be on the line with this nutjob. Swallowing a lump in my throat, I slide back into my chair opposite Vlad. When he looks at me expectantly, I inform him of the result of the call. "Okay, I stalled them. Now answer my questions."

"I think I'll begin with the story, then see what questions you have left. It should answer most of them." I nod my assent, crossing my arms and leaning back into the chair a little. "Now, don't knock this off as a false story. It's true. What I'm saying is not fantasy, although to you it will sound like it. This is my life, whether you believe it or not, and it affects you and, if my hunch is correct, has been influencing you your entire life," he begins, looking at me with seriousness in his eyes. I hold back a scoff, knowing if I wait quietly he'll get through this quickly and I can be on my way home.

"I come from another universe... another realm, if you will. An alternate realm. Now, before you interrupt, I must insist that you only listen. If, while you are listening, you are closed to what I am saying and trying to disprove everything, you will gain nothing from this. Just listen and believe. Fight against it later, if you must.

"There are seven parallel realms, including this one, the one we call Second Earth. Each is similar, though none the same. We believe they all originated as a singular world, then split into the seven we know today. They are named: First Earth, which is just like this one, but more technologically advanced; Quagon, which is made up of ninety-eight percent water. They use the other two percent of land for farming and have built floating cities to live on. Ponorama is mainly a desert with many huge and violent creatures living there. Lii is beautiful, and so are the people that live there. The grass is blue and the sky is orange, and the colors are more vibrant and beautiful than anywhere else. Zelon is much like your Earth, but the sun is larger and red, and they have more oxygen, resulting in bugs closer to the size of Second Earth's dogs.

"And, finally, there is Zilferia. Zilferia is the central realm that all others are connected to. This is where I am from and where the good King and Queen live. Unique creatures are there and the days are much longer than they are here. We have thirty-two hours a day rather than your twenty-four. Temperatures are more moderate as well. And most recently, it is where the Games take place!"

"The Games?" I ask, recalling what he said earlier. "That's what you seem to expect me to participate in, right?"

"You *are* smart!" he chuckles mockingly. "They told me to expect such, but…"

"What? Who's they? Why were you spying on me? And if you just wanted to talk to me, why did you kidnap my sister and I to do it?" I demand, earning a glare from him.

"Didn't I say to save all questions to the end?" he sighs. "I suppose I will answer these, but please, learn to contain yourself!

"I had some people- it doesn't matter who- spy on you so I could see if you could be the one. I had you and your sister kidnapped so I can see what you're capable of in certain circumstances. I don't intend to harm either of you."

As I start to ask what he meant by me being 'the one,' he stops me. "No more questions! If they aren't saved until the end, I'm not answering them. I'm too tired for this to drag on all night," he sighs. When I don't say anything in response, he continues. "The Games are designed to find each person's magical ability- 'Gifts,' as we call them- in each of the contestants. There are fourteen contestants, two from each realm, put into seven teams of one boy and one girl each. This is chosen randomly, so the pairing has nothing to do with bribery or threats. This year, there are three from both Ponorama and Lii because there are none from Zilferia."

"What are the Gifts?" I ask, curious despite myself.

"I was just getting to that," he responds, glaring at me. Despite this, I catch an amused and pleased twinkle in his eye, revealing that he's glad I am beginning to take an interest in his story. "Each person has a Gift or two, except for the very rare few who happen to have none. Although it's been said that the ones destined to be King or Queen can have up to four Gifts.

"There are quite a few Gifts that one could possess, such as flying, reading minds, extraordinary fighting skills, the ability to disappear and reappear at will, shapeshifting, the ability to befriend and communicate with all creatures, controlling the weather, super speed, super intelligence, being able to remember every detail of everything you see and hear, charm- which is generally used for manipulation, super strength, and telepathy. Gifts are received thanks to the amount of magic woven into the realm- which is why there aren't really any Gifts here on Second Earth. Second Earth doesn't have much magic at all left in it. Very few have a diluted version of a Gift here, but that's all."

Caught up in it all, I can't resist asking, "What Gifts do you think I would have?"

He frowns and studies me, looking me up and down, and, finally, staring deep into my eyes. After a few minutes, he shakes his head. "You're a tough one. I can see you having almost any of the Gifts. However, my best guess would be extraordinary fighting and logic, just from what I've seen of you so far. Although, you seem to be very special and I'm betting you have another one or two... especially because of your eyes. But I can't even begin to guess what they might be."

"Whoa, wait a minute. You mentioned my eyes again. What does that have to do with anything?" He hesitates to answer. "If you don't tell me, then I am not attending these Games you apparently are wanting me to win. I doubt I would anyway, but you have a much greater chance if you tell me *everything.* Including and especially your strange obsession with my eyes."

He frowns for a second, then laughs. "You don't have a choice, my dear. But I will tell you, I suppose... if you promise not to tell anyone else- especially not your little sister. It would only put her in danger."

"Okay, I promise," I reply. I probably wouldn't tell anyone any of this anyway. No one would believe anything this guy's said already. I don't even believe it, and I'm pretty gullible.

He looks relieved. "Alright then. The King and Queen I told you about earlier had triplets about sixteen Second Earth years ago. Two were boys, and one was a girl. These Games are actually to find those who can aid the King and Queen in finding their lost children. The winners from last year took their prizes and went home, no interest in helping the King and Queen; thus necessitating another year of Games. Although...I have reason to believe that you are the Princess Crystal Dragon." He observes me, waiting for my reaction to the news.

I laugh. I laugh hard, for a minute or two. Then, wiping my eyes, I say, "Ha! That's a good one. Me? A princess of some non-existent universe? Wow! If you were trying to convince me that your story is true, you just blew it with that one. Some people eat that kind of stuff up, but not me. I believe in what's real, what's right in front of me. Besides, why would you think I'm the Princess just because of my eyes? My name may be Crystal, but that doesn't mean I'm this lost Princess of yours."

His voice deadly serious, he replies, "Because your eyes are exactly how the King described them to me." He leans forward and lowers his voice. "Your eyes can turn into dragon eyes, can't they?"

I stare at him in disbelief. *How… how on earth does he know?! I haven't told a soul, and I've been careful not to do it in front of others. I haven't even done it in… nearly a decade! In fact, I'm not even sure that I still can…* What I actually say to him, however, to hide how much he unnerved me, is, "Are you insane? Dragons don't even exist! Let alone someone with dragon eyes as well as normal eyes!" The words slide easily off my tongue. I've been repeating them to myself for years. "Look at them, if you want. They're *normal.* In fact," I add, standing and pushing my chair back, "I think it's time for me to go. I don't want to be spending the night with a lunatic."

The instant I stand and say this, two guys come in through the doors on both sides of the room, blocking me off. Looking back at the table, I see Vlad standing next to Kiki, yet he smiles calmly at me like nothing is happening. "First of all, I am not a lunatic. Secondly, if you fight your way out, which I have no doubt that you can, then I will have to keep your little sister here with me until you come back. Lastly, and I'm sorry to say this, but I am under strict orders to get you to Zilferia so you can participate in the Games. That does not mean I have to be nice to you. I would rather not be harsh, but I can and I will. If I have to, I will force you to come back with us to Zilferia. Your parents came up with the idea of the Games before they… well, slipped into their coma. They may not be around right now to enforce the games, but they left me, Thaddeus, Zelda, and Y'vette in charge, and I will not let them down. Especially not when I'm fairly certain *you* are the daughter they've been searching for."

Thinking hard, I can't see a way out of this. Sighing in defeat, I ask, "How long will I be gone? I may go along with this, but my parents would freak out, and you would be arrested. Luckily for you, they just might put you in the mental hospital rather than jail," I say, subtly mocking him.

He smiles knowingly. "Oh, don't you worry about that. When we go to Zilferia, your realm will be frozen in time. It will remain just like this until you get back. But this may take over a month, depending on if you win or not. Your little sister may come with us if you wish, but if we leave her here, she will be exactly the same when we return. You may not want her to travel with us. It is dangerous in Zilferia, especially for contestants and those with them. Plus, you would be put into separate buildings anyway. We have special lodging for you and the other contestants set aside. So, decide. Do you want her taken into danger, or suspended in time where no one can harm her? It is your decision."

He's backed me into a corner. I don't want Kiki to get hurt, of course, but I can't just believe Vlad that no one will be able to get near her until I get back. I can only guarantee that she will be safe by taking her with me, but according to Vlad, that is dangerous- and not just for me, but for Kiki as well. *Ugh! I don't know what to do!* But then I realize that I have a backup. *I can leave Kiki my phone, so she can call the police when she wakes up if I don't come back!* Turning to Vlad, I say, "Prove to me that she will be safe… and I'll leave her here. ….I don't want her to get hurt."

He smiles. "Good choice. Trust me, your sister will be safe here, and you will be back before she knows it. To Kiki, it will seem like nothing happened. Now then, would you rather sleep here tonight, or in Zilferia? If you go to Zilferia, you will get more sleep, for like I said, our days are longer, and so are our nights. Either way, you will sleep alone. We are not introducing the contestants to each other until tomorrow morning. So? Which do you prefer? You and Kiki will be safe no matter what. I'll make sure of that."

One choice seems more logical to me, regardless of if what he's saying is true or not. "I guess I'll go with you to… Zilferia. I'll need my sleep, right?" *The sooner we leave, the sooner Kiki can call for help…*

He smiles. "Correct. In fact, that reminds me." He fishes around in his pocket and emerges with a pill between his fingers. "If you find that you cannot sleep tonight, take this and you will be able to sleep better." I inspect it, although I have no real way of telling if it will do what he says it will. Half is a light blue, and the other half a dark purple. "The blue half puts you to sleep, while the purple ensures that you do not have night-mares," Vlad explains. "Now then," he continues, spinning on his heel and heading out of the door on the right, two of the men following him. The other two move behind me, intending to accompany me to make sure I don't try and escape. I guess it's just for insurance, for I know that I can't get away and leave Kiki here. I'll have to do whatever this lunatic asks me to until I can get Kiki and myself away from him. I follow Vlad into the hallway, slipping my phone and car keys into Kiki's pocket as I pass her.

As we walk, I start out trying to remember the route, so if an opportunity arose, I could race back to Kiki and escape. After a few minutes, I give up on this plan. Our path is too long and winding, and the sandwich I ate is wearing off, so I am no longer alert and clear-headed. As we're walking, I begin feeling very tired. Curious, I glance at my watch to see what time it is. To my surprise, I find it's almost four in the morning. *No wonder I'm so tired! The only thing keeping me awake right now is the fact that I am with an insane man who can somehow change how he looks as well as the fact that I'm obviously still in danger, along with some other 'contestants.' Sure, Vladimir's story is 'life-changing,' but only because he believes it so much himself that he kidnaps people and takes them away somewhere no one will be able to find them!* I growl to myself, my anxiety rising as I picture myself on a news station, a girl vanished into thin air, never to be seen again.

My unease grows with each step as we exit the building at last and walk onto the lawn behind it. The velvety black sky, not lit up much by the crescent moon, looks peaceful and eternal. It makes me feel small and insignificant in comparison. The quiet night does nothing to settle my nerves, however. All it manages to do is make me feel more stressed as well as cause my mind to linger on all that I may be leaving behind to follow this weirdo in an attempt to protect my little sister. *And it may be fruitless, but what else can I do? This Vlad guy has me backed entirely into a corner!*

The thugs now surround me as I follow Vlad into the night. My fear skyrockets as ahead of me I see Vlad turn and wait. Was his 'portal' to another 'realm' actually just death? Was this where I die? Gulping, I force my feet to step up to Vlad, trying to appear strong and unconcerned. My stomach writhes and my throat constricts. When I swallow, it feels like sandpaper. What on earth have I gotten myself into? He smiles at me. "Are you ready?"

"I don't know," I reply, falling back on sarcasm to hide my fear. "I've never traveled to another universe before. How would I know what to expect?"

"Well, I can't tell you exactly what to expect, for it is a little different to everyone who travels through these portals. All I can say is… well, brace yourself." He smiles, then says, "See you in Zilferia." With a sharp turn, he strides toward what looks to me to be a simple wall. Just before he hits the bricks, however, his body shimmers and he disappears.

"Whoa!" I shout, scrambling backward a step or two. "He- he just disappeared!" But before I can ask any questions, someone shoves me from behind.

"Your turn," he grunts. Staggering forward, I fall toward the wall. I instinctively cry out as it rushes toward me. Just before I hit it, there's a flash of light and a subtle tickling sensation. This is followed by an unexpected pain in my gut as though I had been punched. I'm doubled over for about a minute until the sensation fades. Standing, I look around, wide-eyed. A shimmering whiteness surrounds me as I float in nothingness. Then I realize that I hear music. It's very faint, but growing stronger every second. Then I feel as though I've been punched again, so, eyes clenched shut, I don't see what happens when the light fades away. Once the pain fades, I look up and see Vlad standing before me.

"Welcome…" he adds with a grand sweep of his arm, "…to Zilferia!" Staggering to my feet, I am immediately wrapped up in the beauty of the place. Even though it's night, I can see many things by the light of the huge moon overhead, as well as the smaller one that's partially behind the large one. Crouching down, I touch the grass beneath me and feel its soft caress as it seems to slowly reach back, gently twirling around my finger like a greeting. Looking around in wonder, I see big, beautiful trees. And… is it just my imagination, or is that where the music was coming from? In fact, the music sounds oddly… familiar. Looking closer, I see that only when the wind blows through the trees do they sing. That is the best I can describe it, that they are singing a soft, peaceful tune. I feel… at home. Standing and looking past Vlad, who's carefully studying my reactions, I see buildings not too far away. The place is wonderful- impossible, but incredible. Vlad doesn't let me bask in it long. A couple of men we left behind arrive behind me. As soon as they do, Vlad turns and begins walking toward the buildings, suddenly ignoring me. Afraid of being left behind in this strange yet magical place, I hasten after him.

As we walk into the night, I look up to find the moons. The main one is larger than Earth's, but it is the closest thing I have to home, so I hold it in my sight as I walk into this new world, my mind in complete awe and utter confusion, yet filled with a familiar wonder at the same time. So, I walk after the man who I thought was a lunatic just moments ago, pondering my future and how I will ever make sense of the present; let alone the past.

4

I wake slowly, pulling myself from the security that the pill I took last night wrapped me in. I decided that to survive in this insane new reality, I needed to forget everything I knew; which also meant I needed to trust Vlad, and probably others as well, more than I would like. Luckily the pill did precisely what he assured me it would. I blink open my eyes, feeling strangely contented. It almost feels as though I'm where I should be, as inexplicable as the feeling is, for I know I do not belong here. Yet... I cannot deny that it feels like I do. I remember the song of the trees. It was almost as though I'd been here before; heard the trees.

Shaking off these feelings, I turn my thoughts back to my new reality and off of the past. Vladimir told me I would meet the other contestants, making friends as well as potential new enemies. I will meet the other three 'advisors'- Thaddeus, Zelda, and Y'vette. Although they may have something to do with my 'education,' my advisor is really Vlad. Glancing at my watch, I'm surprised to see that it's adjusted to tell the time in Zilferia rather than Earth. I shake my head in disbelief before shrugging, figuring it's not the craziest thing that's happened to me lately.

It's almost nine, and Vlad wanted to meet me outside the building at nine thirty. Swinging my legs out of bed, I quickly dress in the clothes that have been left for me on the bedside table. I'm immediately impressed by the elegant, silky feeling to the threads that caress my body. There are a shirt, jacket, and pants all the same shade of rich, dark green. I smile as I pull on the soft black boots. *These clothes are great! They're light and easy to move around in… they're probably what I'm going to have to wear for the Games,* I realize.

As I exit the clean little wooden hut, I leave behind both my old clothes as well as my past life, stepping into my new insanity that is, supposedly, Zilferia. Looking around, I don't see Vlad, so I sit on the ground and quickly redo my braided hair, brushing through it with my fingers. He still hasn't arrived by the time I finish, so I lean back against the hut and enjoy the perfect weather and the song of the trees. After a few minutes, I get an uneasy feeling that something may be wrong, so I stand and begin searching, although I'm not sure what I should be looking for.

Left with not much to do, I roam through the Village. Although it's quite large, it's also very organized. I am currently in a section of the Village without many people out and about. The huts all look like the one I was sequestered in for the night, except for half of those in this section, which have colored doors- green, black, yellow, blue, orange, purple, and red. I can't see the other sections from here, but it looks like the Village is organized according to function with a more open spot in the center.

Soon I come across a girl sitting in front of another of the smaller huts, looking lost. She is also wearing soft green clothes like mine, leading me to assume she is another 'contestant' recruited and dragged to this strange land.

"Hi," I say, coming up to the girl. She stands and looks at me shyly through her long blonde hair. "Are you a contestant?" Looking surprised, she nods.

"Y- yes," she stammers. "I'm from Earth. Uh- the second one? Vlad explained the differences, but it's all still so confusing."

"I'm from Second Earth too!" I say, a little surprised. "Are you waiting for Vlad?" She nods, her green eyes lowered. "Yeah, me too. But there's no sign of him."

"I know," she sighs. "I've been waiting for him for almost half an hour, I think."

"Well, let's wait for him together," I suggest. She agrees, and we sit together and start talking and introducing ourselves.

"My name is Sierra Davis," she says. "I'm sixteen, and I like to do puzzles and art."

"I'm Crystal Shay," I reply. "I'm sixteen as well. I don't really have any hobbies, although I suppose I also like to do puzzles, like chess and sudoku. ...So, you mentioned Vlad. Did he 'recruit' you too?"

She laughs bitterly. "More like he dragged me here. He had me kidnapped, chucked in a room for a while, then told me an outrageous story about alternate universes and 'Gifts' that I could have. When I told him he's insane, he laughed and said that I couldn't escape, and that I am going to participate in the Games whether I like it or not."

I laugh as well. "Sounds about right. I tried to fight, so he drugged my little sister and threatened me with her. I had to leave her behind and go with him. Vlad sure didn't explain much about the Games themselves, though."

"Yeah... I wonder why that is? Is it super dangerous? I just want to go home! Is that too much to ask?"

"Apparently it is," another voice suddenly pipes in.

Jumping to my feet, I assume a defensive pose. "Who's there?" I demand. A boy walks around the corner of the hut, hands in the air.

"Whoa! Calm down! I'm just here looking for Vlad. No need to attack."

Examining him, I note the green clothes and relax, sitting back down next to Sierra. Peering up at the newcomer, I see that he has hazel eyes, short brown hair, and looks rather strong and lithe as well. I catch my breath. I've been meeting a few cute boys lately, and this one is no different. I feel a blush starting to blossom on my cheeks as I think about what kind of first impression I must have made. I clear my throat and try to cover up my embarrassment. "You must be another contestant, then."

"Yep," he confirms, plopping down next to me. "Either of you have any idea where Vlad got to? Not that I really want to know, it's just that he said he would talk to me outside my hut at ten, but he never showed. When I went to look for him, I came across you two. Did Vladimir drag you guys along as well?"

We both nod. "I thought so," he continues. "Well, now is as good a time as ever to start making new friends, right? My name is Nathan Anderson. I'm sixteen and have a little sister, Anna, who's four. She's at home on 'First Earth' with my parents and Grandma Beryl. So Vlad, of course, threatened to hurt them to get me to come along. Anything like that happened to either of you?"

I nod. "Yes, he captured my little sister along with me and then threatened me with her. So I had no other choice but to come along with that lunatic. She's only nine!"

"We should find him and give him a piece of our minds," Sierra pipes up. Nathan and I agree, standing and looking around.

"Um… any idea where we should go?" I ask. They both shake their heads, as lost as I am. I sigh and continue to look around, finally spotting a tall, gray-haired man strolling just outside the group of huts, a long black walking cane in his hand, although he doesn't appear to need it. "Hey, how about we go ask him? He might know where Vlad is," I suggest. They both agree, so we make our way over to the man. He spots us and stops to wait for us; his hands folded patiently over his cane.

Before we can say anything, he guesses at what we're about to say. "You three are looking for Vladimir, aren't you?" Surprised at his accurate guess, we nod. "Ah, just as I thought. Vladimir must be testing how resourceful you are. He told you he would be at your hut for you, correct? At least tell me he didn't neglect to inform you of today's events?"

We shrug in unison. "All he told us," Nathan answers, "is that we would be meeting the other contestants and some 'advisors' named Thaddeus, Zelda, and Y'vette. He didn't tell us where to go, though, and he didn't tell us any details about the Games or just what we are supposed to do."

The man sighs. "It's just not like him to shirk his duties like that… I'm Thaddeus. I'll show you three to the place where the rest of the contestants are meeting each other and their advisors. Vladimir is, I believe, meeting with someone he doesn't even personally advise." Shaking his head, he sighs again. "He was told not to choose favorites. Oh, well. That cannot be helped right now, of course. Please, follow me," he says before turning and leading the way toward the center of the Village.

After following him for a short while, we enter a clearing in the center of the town; a square area with cobblestone flooring and some wooden tables that are nearly hidden from our point of view because of the large stage at one end of the area. There are a handful of people wandering around, talking to each other. Most of them are dressed in the same contestant outfit we're garbed in. "Welcome to the Town Square," Thaddeus says, waving an arm toward it in a grand gesture. "Feel free to wander, or simply seek out Vladimir and speak with him. He has much more to tell you."

Thanking him, we continue down the slight slope into the Square. Before we can cut our way through the gathering to Vlad, however, a guy with brown hair and stunning blue eyes comes up to us. Walking between Sierra and me, he lays an arm on our shoulders. Annoyed, I shrug it off and continue in my pursuit of our deserting advisor.

"Hey!" he calls, jogging up in front of me, forcing me to stop. "What's the big rush? This time is for meeting other contestants, like me! So, how do you do?" he asks with a flirty grin, his white teeth flashing for a moment in the sunlight. "My name is Jake Elwood, and I'm almost eighteen. I'm from Ponorama, and I love to run, play sports, and wrestle any monsters that come near my village," he gloats, watching expectantly for an impressed reaction. I cross my arms and wait impatiently for him to finish. "Who are you, gorgeous?"

"Crystal Shay from Second Earth. Now go away, I need to talk to Vladimir right now." I'm generally not this forward, especially with a guy I don't even know, but right now I'm not in the mood to play the kind of games guys like him like to play with girls.

He whistles and sounds as if he's hurt. "Ouch! A feisty one, eh? Well that suits me just fine. You'll learn, Crystal. I'm not your enemy, so you don't need to treat me like one. And by the way, I love your eyes. That outfit really makes them pop." And with that, he saunters away, leaving me even more flustered and confused than when I first came here.

Shaking it off, we start heading towards Vlad again, only to find that thanks to Jake's delaying us, he had slipped away once more. Frustrated, I turn to a lady near us with short brown hair and green eyes with a strand of brown in them. "Excuse me," I begin politely. "But do you know where we can find Vladimir? He seems to be avoiding us."

She laughs. "That's probably because he is! Vladimir loves to be that shady character, lurking in the shadows. He must be avoiding you so he can watch and see how well you adapt to new circumstances. But you want some answers, don't you? Well, ask away. I'm an advisor too, you know. My name is Zelda. How can I help you?"

Nathan answers her for all of us. "Could you explain the Games in more detail? We have no idea what we're in for. Vlad didn't tell us much."

"I don't know that I could tell you much more, to be honest," she replies. "It's supposed to be a surprise for everyone but we advisors, but I can tell you that you will go through many Challenges, facing some of the different creatures that live here, or facing other teams. There are a few different Challenges that you will go through, although there isn't a definite number yet known, even to us. I'm afraid I also can't tell you what the First Challenge is. That would be cheating! We strive to have a certain measure of equality in place in the Challenges, so we won't be letting one person know more than another.

"The Challenges are meant to bring out your Gifts. Each one tests one or more specific skills. It may be fighting, logistical skills, speed, etc., so we can attempt to find your Gifts. Your advisor should be beginning to help you develop some of these necessary skills today. Vlad should show his face by then, but for now, go ahead and be social butterflies! Make some new friends! Lunch will be served around noon. If you get tired and wish to take a nap or just relax or explore a little, then you may go into the woods, providing that one of us is with you, so you do not get lost or attacked by any creatures that live at the edge of the woods. Have fun!" she cheers, then flits away to talk to someone else.

"Well, I doubt we'll get to Vlad until after lunch, then," Sierra sighs. We nod, equally disappointed. "So what do we do now? Talk to the other contestants? Because I don't feel like trying to socialize anymore today," she adds. Nathan and I agree.

"What do you think we should do?" Nathan asks me. I guess I've already become sort of the leader of our little group. "Relaxing in the woods sounded nice... being away from all these other people..."

I shrug. "That definitely sounds better than talking about ourselves over and over again with a bunch of competitors." They both agree, so we head towards the trees that we can see to the East of the Village. As we go, I feel someone watching me, so I turn to find who it is. The only person I notice looking our way is a short, somewhat chubby kid with blond hair that's almost short enough to be a buzz cut. The instant he catches me peering at him, however, he turns away.

Hmm, I frown, turning back to face my new friends. *Why on earth was that kid watching us? Not even just watching... he seemed to be staring.* Shaking my head, I banish my worries. *I can figure that out another time. It doesn't matter right now.* Taking a deep breath, I turn and follow Nathan and Sierra to the treeline. Already the trees' song is relaxing me, soothing my fears and pushing them out of my mind momentarily. Sitting down in the lush green grass, I lean back against a tree and breathe in the sweet scent carried in the gentle breeze.

Letting go of all my worries, I finally feel at peace for the first time in a long time. In fact, I don't think I've ever felt this peaceful and relaxed. I was always worried about what others thought of me and the things I had to get done. But right now, I don't have a care in the world.

After about an hour of dozing in the shade of the trees, I snap back to alertness with the nagging feeling of something being wrong. Unable to put my finger on it, I lay back down and try to relax, but I can't seem to be able to. My muscles are tense and my mind won't stop racing, trying to figure out what was making the hair all over my body stand on end. *Something is definitely wrong.* Sitting back up, I look around, but there's nothing in sight but trees and the near edge of the Village. Suddenly the words Zelda said to us come back to me. *"...You may go into the woods, provided that one of us is with you, so you do not get lost or attacked by any creatures that live at the edge of the woods."*

Creatures in the woods? I think, feeling panic bubble up in my chest. *What- what kind of creatures? What would they do to us?... It's probably best not to find out the hard way!* I hurriedly conclude. Standing, I walk over to my sleeping companions and shake them gently. They are completely out. *Are they just sleeping... or are they literally knocked out? What happened to them? Why won't they wake up?!* I wonder, my panic deepening.

I shake them harder, but there's no response. Something suddenly rustles in the woods just a few steps away from us. I tense, preparing to defend my new friends from this unseen threat. However, the only thing that emerges from the rustling bush is a cute little bunny. Relieved, I bend down and pick it up, rubbing its long, floppy ears. I sneeze, and for some inexplicable reason, I begin feeling drowsy again. My eyes are sliding shut, and I can't seem to stop them.

Just before they close entirely, however, I turn towards the sound of a shout, coming from the direction of the Village and catch sight of the guy who was watching us earlier. Seeing me, he breaks into a sprint.

And then, my eyelids slam shut and I black out.

"Please... please wake up... please be okay..."

Startled by a voice I don't recognize, I instinctively react as my self-defense teacher has always taught me and jump up, defending my torso and preparing to attack. I quickly fall back onto the bed, however, my body not entirely obeying me and my head thumping in time with my heart. The person standing before me is the blond boy I last saw running towards me before I blacked out. He looks startled, scrambling back a few steps, before letting out a puff of air between his lips.

"Oh, good! You're alive!" he exclaims, clearly relieved. This statement strikes me as odd. *Alive? Of course I'm alive, why wouldn't I be?*

"What- what happened?" I groan, holding my head between my hands, trying to get the deep, throbbing pain to go away.

"What happened is that you three went into the woods alone, even though Zelda specifically warned you that it was not safe to do so," a familiar voice lectures.

"Oh, well how nice of you to finally show up, *Vlad*," I respond, unexpected bitterness entering my voice. "Way to be a supportive *advisor*. Great job advising us! Don't tell us that you will be there and then not show up next time! We're supposed to rely on you, yet you haven't proven yourself able to do anything but drag us to this terrorizing land. You're supposed to tell us about things that could kill or harm us, not disappear until we're *in the hospital!*" When I finally finish my tirade, I notice that not only did I get back on my feet, but my voice had also risen louder than I intended. Maybe I shouldn't have yelled, but I'm just too upset and fed up to hold back the outburst. His *job* is to help us and teach us, but so far he's done anything but that.

The blond kid glances back and forth between our faces, looking rather frightened as I unleash my anger at Vlad. As for Vlad... well, his face is turning red, and the veins in his neck are beginning to bulge. It feels almost as though he is a completely different person from the Vladimir I met yesterday. But then again, I've only known him for a few hours. His reaction scares me, but he then calms himself- after a brief struggle with himself- and says, "Consider yourself without an advisor, then. I will not advise someone like you. I refuse. Good luck finding yourself another one! After I tell them all of your insolence, none of them will take you in and teach you," he says with a calm madness in his voice. His mouth twitches upward into a small smile, clearly satisfied with his actions.

"Fine," I respond, the reality of the consequences of what he just said not quite hitting me just yet. "It's not like I really even *had* an advisor in the first place."

This seems to make him even more furious, stripping away the cool face he had managed to put on. He storms out of the room without another word, slamming the door behind him. The blond kid looks at me, surprise and awe in his blue eyes. "Wow. I cannot believe you just stood up to Vladimir like that." I shrug, sitting back down on the bed with a wince. "No, seriously. That guy is way scary. And not only that, but now you have next to no chance of winning the Games. Advisors are necessary in order to win- honestly, they're needed to even survive on a Realm that's new to you."

Again I shrug. "Oh, well. I'm better off alone than trying to lean on someone who's not there and end up being hurt and let down. Besides, I'm sure I can get one of the other advisors to help me out, despite what Vlad might say. I've already talked to Zelda, and she seemed to like me well enough. Plus, they said that we would be put into teams, right? Well, I'm sure if I need to know something, then my team member will teach me," I say with a confidence I never knew I had.

The boy's stare increases in disbelief. "Wow. I want you on my team! You're so strong and confident! I wish I could be more like that... By the way, my name is Ham Jacobson. I'm from Ponorama. I was actually taken here on my seventeenth birthday," he sighs.

"Oh my goodness! That's rough," I sympathize. "I'm Crystal Shay from Second Earth. Um... soo I was wondering... is there any way you could explain what happened?"

"What are you referring to?" he asks jokingly. "You probably have a million questions for everything that's happened recently! I know I would."

I laugh. "You know what I mean. Why were you watching me as I made my way to the woods? Why did that bunny put me to sleep? Why did you say that it's a good thing I'm alive as if you didn't expect me to be? And if you're that concerned about me, how are Nathan and Sierra?"

He fidgets a little, not looking me in the eye. "Um… well, I was watching you three because I wondered where you were going, and… well, I don't have many friends, even though I've been here the longest. I got here a week ago. You three just met, but you all seem pretty tight. And that- bunny, you called it?- is a Sietta. It's a creature that lives on Ponorama and Zilferia. Everyone on Ponorama, even the small children- and probably everyone here as well- knows that it puts people to sleep and drags them off to their dens. The thing is, the people they put to sleep don't usually wake up. That's why it was such a relief that you did. As for Nathan and Sierra, I brought them to the hospital. I would have brought you first, but they seemed to be in even worse condition than you were. I had just come back for you when you woke up."

I try to nod in acknowledgment, but this sends waves of shooting pain through my skull. Groaning, I hold my head. "Don't worry, the after-effects are temporary," Ham assures me. "Left alone, the pain would be gone by tomorrow morning, as well as any weaknesses you feel in your body. But if you can get something from the doctors here, it should fade within an hour or so."

"Alright, then let's go," I say, slowly standing up. I stagger to the door, realizing as I go that I am in a hut similar to the one I was staying in- it's probably Ham's place.

"Um… are you sure you can get there yourself?" Ham asks nervously. "I mean, I can probably get some nurses to come here and get you instead."

"I'll be fine!" I insist. A few steps later though, and I'm no longer so certain. "Maybe… you should be ready to catch me, just in case." He nods and moves a little closer to me.

We make it to the medical building, but only just. As I walk in the door, my legs finally give out and I collapse. Luckily, the nurse at the door catches me just in time. Embarrassed, I try to pull myself up, but the nurse won't allow it. Calling two other nurses, she tells them to get a stretcher. Once I'm settled into it, they take me up to a room and help me into a bed before leaving to get a doctor. Ham comes up to the side of the bed.

"They act like I can't do anything for myself!" I exclaim in frustration, still feeling a little confused over the nurses' swift and controlling actions. "I feel fine, except for this massive headache and my body doesn't seem to want to cooperate. They act like I shouldn't be moving around at all!"

Ham chuckles a little, looking at the floor and shuffling his feet. "Um... honestly, you probably shouldn't be. Especially after being that close to a Sietta. I probably should have just taken some nurses back with me to get you in the first place."

"I would have walked here anyways," I state. "I can't stand not being able to move around. I wouldn't be able to just lay around in bed all day- I think that would drive me insane!"

He nods. "That's what I thought. I figured it should be fine, but I guess the nurses think otherwise."

At that, the doctor enters the room. Before I can say anything, he looks me up and down and says, "Well, well, well. Already we have three contestants in the hospital, and the Games haven't even begun yet! For you to have the nerve to *pick up* a Sietta... well, you're lucky you're still breathing, girl."

"Yeah, well do you have anything to get rid of the side-effects? This headache and a weakened body are starting to bother me," I say. The doctor nods expectantly and reaches into his pocket, pulling out a needle. I shrink away from it as he shows it to me.

"This has the medicine you need in it. Now, please roll up your sleeve." At my hesitation, he smiles kindly. "Trust me; this will help you."

Still eyeing the needle unhappily, I cautiously roll up my sleeve, then turn my head away and close my eyes. Just after feeling it pierce my skin, I instantly feel tired again. "You... you didn't tell me it would put me to sleep again!" I accuse him with a yawn. "I- I don't want... to sleep..." The last thing I see before I fall asleep once more is Ham standing guard over me. The sight comforts me as I slip into unconsciousness.

5

"Hey, Crystal..." The voice pierces through my foggy thoughts, causing them to clear and gradually focus, seeming to come out of darkness. It drags me back to alertness, although not fully. "Crystal, you need to wake up! The Games start tonight, and you still need to be put into a team! ...Come on; they're drawing for the teams in less than an hour!"

"...Ham?" I murmur, still drowsy.

"Yes," comes the reply. "Nathan and Sierra are here too. We can all go together if you get up in time. Do you think you can?"

"Of course!" I hurriedly assure him, opening my eyes. It takes a few seconds for them to focus, but eventually my three friends' faces swim into view. "Let's... go..." I slur. They all look at me disbelievingly.

"Are... are you sure you can?" Nathan asks, concern in his voice. "I mean, you need to be there... at least, you usually do. But we might be able to get them to make an exception for you this time..." he starts as I unexpectedly jump out of bed. I land just fine, but then sway and fall. Luckily, Nathan catches me. "...and we just might need to," he continues, letting out the breath he had been holding. "Just look at the state you're in!"

"I'm fine... let's just go," I insist, carefully standing again. I make it to the door on my own, although I'm frustrated with my weakness. Leaning on the door frame, I look back and see the three of them quietly conversing with each other. Talking, I suppose, about me and all the problems I seem to be causing already. Sighing, I humble myself and say, "We need to go now, but I am- unfortunately- not quite strong enough at the moment to go anywhere on my own. Will two of you help me?"

Sierra and Nathan quickly come up to me, and I put an arm around each of their shoulders. In this way, the four of us travel to the center of the town in the bright sunlight of mid-afternoon. By the time we get there, I can walk by myself. I can tell instantly that we are the last to arrive. The contestants are all lined up in one straight line, facing the five adults in front, on a small stage. I recognize Vlad, Thaddeus, Y'vette, and Zelda- the advisors. The last person I've never seen before, even in passing. Everyone there seems to be waiting- a little impatiently- for someone. Us.

We quickly take our place in the line as the person I don't recognize takes a step closer to us. I'm surprised she doesn't even wobble in such towering stiletto high-heels. Behind her, Thaddeus and Y'vette also step up and stand on either side of her, each holding a small black container. I quickly deduce that they contain our names- girls in one, boys in the other. Everyone around me suddenly becomes agitated, although they try to hide it. Swallowing a lump that suddenly forms in my throat, I wipe my palms on my pants to dry them.

Clearing her throat, the mystery lady addresses us. "Welcome, one and all! My name is Nehru, and I am this year's announcer for the Games! But before they can begin, we need to have the teams! Each team will be assigned a color, which I will announce as I pull the names." She pauses, smiling and letting us feel nervous for a little longer. Looking down the row, I can see the anxiety written on almost everyone's faces, even the cocky Jake Elwood, although he hides it well by promptly grinning and giving me a thumb's up. I don't smile back, instead turning to look back at Nehru. I understand why everyone is so nervous- whoever is on their team will pretty much decide if they will win or not. It may even determine if we *survive* in this realm or not.

Gulping, I return my attention to what's going on- just in time to hear, "The red team will be... Sierra Davis, sixteen years old, from Second Earth." Looking over at her, I see her trembling. Walking dramatically to Thaddeus to draw the boy that will be Sierra's partner, Nehru draws out a slip of paper, looks at it, then at us. The suspense is building- and I think one of the boys is about ready to yank the paper out of her hands if she waited any longer. But, after a seemingly long time, she clears her throat and clearly says, "and Sierra's partner is… Ham Jacobson, seventeen years old, from Ponorama!"

The two immediately lock eyes, their relief evident. They already know each other and know that they will get along well. They are told to stand apart from the rest and are led to stand to the side of the advisors. Nathan and I are abruptly left alone, not knowing anyone else. I suddenly regret not making more friends when I had the chance.

Nehru then pulls out another girl's name. "The blue team will be… Roxane Hernandez, eighteen, from First Earth." Looking down the line, I see a thin girl wearing all black chewing gum, looking completely unconcerned. Her partner, Lloyd Jewkes from Lii, catches my eye. He's… beautiful. He's close enough to me in the line that I can clearly see his shining blue eyes, which seem to accent his blond hair, which is a more vibrant color than Ham's, whose hair is almost white it's so lightly colored. He smiles a little out of exasperation of his partner choice. I don't blame him. They seem to be total opposites, not to mention she doesn't seem to care much so she probably won't be of much help. They join Sierra and Ham at the other side of the square.

"Green team! Star Hansen, seventeen, from Lii." Star also has an otherworldly sort of beauty to her. She has short, blonde hair and is about six foot four. "Drake Kingston, eighteen, from Quagon." The match seems to be perfect. They are both not only attractive, but confident as well.

Next is the yellow team- Odette Hansen, seventeen, from Lii. She's obviously Star's twin sister as they look the same, except Odette has longer hair and green eyes rather than blue. They are both very intimidating. Her partner is Frazer Hill, sixteen, from Zelon. He is about six feet tall with short, spiky black hair and dark brown eyes. He looks stout and fearless.

I'm starting to feel a little hopeless. There was no way I could beat either of those teams so I can go home. I've been trying to remember each person, but there are too many, so I give up on it. There are only six of us left. I can feel Jake trying to catch my eye, but I don't respond. So, I could either be paired up with Nathan, Jake, or the other guy. The last one is about five foot nine with brown hair and green eyes. I don't remember seeing him talk to others much, but thinking back I think someone may have called him Felix.

Nehru smiles at the six of us. "Well, we're almost done! Only three more teams to go! And next up is the black team... Norachai Young! She's sixteen, from Zelon, and I'm sure, a great competitor!" Norachai looks Chinese with shoulder-length black hair. She seems friendly, although a little shy.

"And her partner is... Felix Evergreen, who is seventeen and from Ponorama!"

I feel the tension building. There are only two guys left. Which one will be my partner? Secretly, I'm hoping for Nathan, but I try not to get my hopes up.

"Purple team... Crystal Shay, sixteen, from Second Earth!" I wait impatiently, my hands clenched, as Nehru snatches a paper from the boys' bowl.

"...Nathan Anderson, sixteen, from First Earth!" *Yes!* I rejoice. I'm not entirely sure why, but I really didn't want to be with Mr. Flirty over there. Looking back at him, though, I feel bad at the thought as I can see he's disappointed. Until he sees who his partner is, at least.

"Finally, the orange team! Kat Pierson, seventeen, from Quagon!" Kat is about five foot two. She is also very charming. Jake takes to her immediately.

"And, last but certainly not least... Jake Elwood, eighteen, from Ponorama! Congratulations, all of you! You have five minutes to get acquainted with your partner before we assign team advisors. Have fun!" she says, then leaves and stands in a group with Vladimir, Thaddeus, Zelda, and Y'vette. They begin talking in lowered voices. Vlad seems to be speaking the most, and I catch the others glancing at me now and again.

Nathan and I look at each other with relief. "Well, that was close," I say. "I almost got stuck with Jake!"

"So, what? I'm nothing but a better option than Mr. Flirt? I'm just not *as* bad as it could get? Is that it?" Nathan teases.

I laugh. "You know what I mean. I was hoping for you the whole time!"

"Oh, really. Well, that's just because Ham got chosen first, and I was the only other person you knew- besides Jake, of course."

"No!" I protest. "...Well, okay. That was part of it. But I truly think we can make a great team."

"Really?" he says, cocking an eyebrow at me, disbelieving.

"Really. Although, while we may be great, there are other great teams- and I'm afraid I don't have what it takes. But if it means securing my return home, then I will do everything I can to get out of this messed up world," I vow.

"Yeah, I know how you feel. My little sister Anna will be missing me. I'm not quite sure I buy Vlad's story of stopping time. Although he *did* get us here... I also need to help my parents take care of my grandma Beryl. So, what do you say we try our hardest to win this thing?"

"I say let's do it!" I respond, high fiving him.

"How touching," a voice says behind me. Spinning around, I see Vlad.

Sneering, I say, "I hope you're here to apologize." Nathan gasps, looking at me like I'm crazy. Maybe I am, but I'm frustrated with this whole stupid thing- especially Vlad, who dragged us here; so I take it out on him, not considering the consequences.

I'm astonished, however, when he clears his throat, looking embarrassed. I notice him shooting a quick glance at Thaddeus, who gives him a heavy nod. His face red, sounding strained, he says, "Y- yes. I am."

"And..." I say, urging him on. He glares at me before pressing on.

"And... I'm... sorry for behaving so rashly. I will still be your personal advisor... if you will have me," he says, gritting his teeth and acting like every word hurt coming out of him. I glance over at Nathan. It's his turn to nod me forward. Now this is the hard part for me. I *really* don't want Vlad to be my advisor, but it's apparent that I need one, plus I promised Nathan I would try my best to win and get us home. Unfortunately, that means I need Vlad.

Sighing, I turn back to him. "It will be *your* pleasure," I say, rubbing it in his face. This could be dangerous for me, but I don't care, as swept away as I am by all the emotions I had cooped up inside me for a couple of days.

Glaring at me, he spits out, "Good," then stalks away. I can tell he's going to have a few angry words with Thaddeus. I glance at Thaddeus gratefully. He nods back with a smile.

"What were you *thinking?*" Nathan explodes the instant Vlad is out of earshot.

"What?" I say, surprised. I thought I had done the right thing accepting his help.

"What do you mean, *what?!* You just made yourself a powerful enemy! And that won't affect just you anymore! Don't you get it? Now that we're partners, it affects me too!"

I gulp, suddenly feeling remorse for what I had done. "Sorry," I say weakly. But Nathan continues his tirade. I can see he's carried away by the stress of the day as well, or else he wouldn't be acting like this. ...Would he?

"No, you're not sorry. You just don't get it! Look!" he says, gesturing over at Vlad, who is talking avidly to the rest of the advisors. "Look at him! You know what he's doing? No, I don't think you do. He's trying to get the advisors not to help us! He may have to teach us individually, but that doesn't mean he'll teach us what we need to know to survive! And that means we need another advisor! But now we can't even have that!"

I shrink back, weakly repeating, "I'm sorry... I didn't think..."

"No, you didn't. That's the problem." He shakes his head wearily. "Never mind. What's done is done, and there's nothing we can do about it now."

I'm about to respond, try to apologize somehow, but I'm interrupted by Nehru.

"...And, welcome back! The advisors have chosen whom they will mentor. Now, there are seven teams, and only four advisors, so, of course, that means that three of them will mentor two teams. The team that gets one advisor all to themselves should count themselves very lucky! Now, I'll let them tell you whom they have chosen. We will first go to... Vladimir!"

Vlad steps up, scowling, and quickly gets to the point. "I will advise the yellow and blue teams- Odette, Frazer, Roxane, and Lloyd."

He steps back, and Zelda takes his place. She starts with, "As much as I would love to advise all of you great contestants, I am limited to only two teams. It was a hard choice, but I decided on the orange and red teams- Kat, Jake, Sierra, and Ham!" She steps back, smiling.

Thaddeus steps forward, winking at me. Before I can figure out what he means by it, he announces, "I have chosen to advise only the purple team- Crystal and Nathan." He then steps back. It takes a moment before I realize what just happened. *Whoa... not only did we manage to still have an advisor- but we also get Thaddeus all to ourselves! And that sets us at an advantage! The* turn of events is incredible and wonderful, but I must share this unexpected relief with someone else. My new partner, Nathan.

Turning to him, I can tell by the look on his face that he's shocked. He thought we were done for. He had just given up when suddenly the tables turned for us. "W- what? Thaddeus? We get Thaddeus? ...All to ourselves?!"

I chuckle. "I guess my stunt didn't hurt, but helped," I say, grinning at him and winking.

"Wow... I'm sorry for getting so mad at you," he replies. "I let my emotions get the best of me. Can you forgive me?"

"Of course," I say with a smile. "After all, we need to be a team. We can't be if we hold grudges."

"So... friends?"

"Friends," I agree. Our exchange made us miss the last group, but it's obvious anyway since there were only two more teams to assign. Norachai and Felix, as well as Star and Drake, were assigned to Y'vette- the green and black teams.

"I will leave you now to get back with your advisors and arrange training schedules," Nehru says, beaming at us. "During your training tomorrow, your advisor will inform you about your first task and the rules as well. Good luck, and remember- have fun discovering and growing into your Gifts! It may be grueling, but I know that you can all do it!" With that, Nehru steps back and leaves the square, leaving us alone with our advisors.

Nathan and I make our way toward the wise-looking Thaddeus, avoiding the angry, jealous stares surrounding us. Sierra and Ham come running up to meet us. Sierra is beaming. "I'm so happy for you two! Isn't it great that we all got put together? And you guys- getting wise old Thaddeus all to yourselves! That's awesome!"

"Yeah, I guess it is," I say, still a little unnerved by the envy of those around me. Ham reads the look on my face and realizes what's going through my mind.

"Hey, it's okay," he says in an effort to comfort me. "It doesn't matter what these other people think. The only thing that matters is the fact that you now have a better chance of winning this thing and getting us all home."

"But… you guys don't care that we have an unfair advantage?"

Sierra laughs. "No! Why would we care? We're all friends now. We care more about that than these people's stupid Games. We're happy for you! Plus, they say the whole point of this is to 'grow into our Gifts,' right? Well, I think I'll try to concentrate on doing that, as well as having fun. If we have to be here, then we might as well make the best of it, right? … Anyways, I guess we should let you guys go. See you tonight for dinner?"

"Sure," Nathan agrees. "If we can, of course," he adds after a moment of thought. "We still don't know what Thaddeus's schedule will be. But we'll try."

"Right. See you guys later," Ham says. The two of them make their way over to Zelda to talk with her once she's done with Kat and Jake.

I take a deep breath. "Are you ready?" I ask Nathan. He nods.

"As ready as I can be, I suppose."

When we reach the stage, Thaddeus greets us, his eyes twinkling with amusement as he waits for us to speak first. I'm not great with words, but luckily Nathan takes the initiative. "Thank you, Thaddeus, for choosing us to train- and us alone. It truly is an honor."

"Yes, thank you," I add, feeling that I have to say *something*.

He gives us both a slight, regal looking nod. "I am glad that you are grateful."

"Yes, we are grateful…but we were wondering… why us?" I continue. "after all that I've done wrong since I got here… and you still picked us for this privilege?"

"Why you? Well, why do you think?"

"I… I don't know. Because you took pity on us? Figured that we're the ones that need the most help?"

"No, it's because I see a lot of potential in you two. I truly believe that you can win- if properly instructed."

"Really?" Nathan says, surprised. "Do you really mean that?"

Thaddeus chuckles. "Is it so hard to believe? I mean it! Not only can you both survive, but you also have a lot of… spunk."

"Spunk?" I question.

"Yes! Spunk! You two are exciting and different from the rest. Best of all, you're both prepared to do anything to win! And with that drive, you just might be able to. However," he adds, getting serious, "you need to learn to *think* before you act. If you can't think, you can't win. You have to outwit the others. Knowledge is your greatest tool in the arenas. The others will most likely go for brute strength. While you do need to be strong, you need to be smart to survive- and both to *win*. So, we will meet outside of the tallest building tomorrow morning at sunrise so we can begin your training. For a while before and after lunch, Vlad wants you two- first Nathan, then Crystal- but the square will be open after that, so we can train your bodies. We will need to work fast, for the First Challenge will begin in two days. We only have tomorrow to prepare. Then you have to do your best and… try to survive the First Challenge.

"We can make more progress after that- we'll have more time, plus you will have more experience with both your competitors as well as some of the creatures that live here. That is, of course, providing you survive the First Challenge." I glance at Nathan. That was the second time he mentioned the First Challenge like we would be lucky if we even came out the other side alive. What have we walked into, exactly? Just how dangerous are these Games we'd been roped into?

"Vladimir will assess your abilities individually tomorrow and come to me with a report so I can see what to help you with so you can, at the very least, survive," Thaddeus finishes. "Have a good night, and make sure to get some rest- you will need it," he adds as a farewell before turning and walking away.

We don't say much to each other as we leave to find Sierra and Ham. As we sit at one of the wooden tables that were pulled out from behind the stage waiting for food, Sierra and Ham don't say much either. We're all brooding over the new reality that now threatens us in a mere two days. Once the food is brought to us, we eat mechanically and stumble back to our huts. I say goodnight to my three friends and collapse into my bed, falling asleep almost immediately despite my worries about the Games. Reality just hit me in the face.

This is really happening.

6

I'm awakened by a sudden knock on my door, jolted out of my tortured dreams. I jump up, shouting. When I calm down and realize what's going on, I shuffle to the door. I slept in my clothes, and I can tell that Nathan had as well. He stands there wearily, bags under his eyes and his clothes wrinkled from spending the night in them, but he's a welcome sight. It's better to spend the day with a friend rather than complete strangers. Although technically I had met him only the day before. And now we must rely on each other to stay alive in this crazy place and make it back to our families.

He smiles at me, stifling a yawn. "The sun will be up soon, and I figure it can't hurt to be a little early. So, are you ready to go?"

"I guess so. I'll just do my hair first," I reply, letting him into the room. He sits on the bed as I grab a brush and guide it through my tangled hair. I then quickly put it into its uniform braid down my back, making it a little tighter than usual so it won't fall out during the quite possibly rigorous training we have ahead of us.

"Alright, let's go," I say, leading the way out the door. I spot a small plume of smoke coming from a nearby building and head toward it, curious. As we near it, my stomach growls, demanding the breakfast that's being made there. As luck would have it, she's preparing food specifically for the contestants, and we're first in line.

After eating, I fish for something to talk about as we walk towards the tallest building Thaddeus would meet us at. "So… it looks like you didn't sleep very well last night," I observe, then grimace. *I could have worded that in a nicer way…*

"No," he confirms, shaking his head. "I didn't. These 'Games' gave me nightmares. Let's just say, I hope whatever is out there isn't as bad as what my brain came up with last night. I kept waking up. …How was your night?"

"Well, I had nightmares as well, but I couldn't escape into the real world. They just went on and on until you came." Silence follows this as neither of us knows what to say after that. I clear my throat and change the subject. "So what do you think our training will be like?"

"I have no idea," he sighs, staring straight ahead. "But I'm sure it'll be pretty tough. Think you're up for whatever they're going to throw at us?"

"Maybe. I'm pretty fit from working on our farm and from taking Martial Arts and self-defense classes. How about you?"

"Well I certainly didn't do anything like that, but I think I'm pretty well off, considering. I'm not all lazy and fat like most people on First Earth, but compared to what you can probably do… I don't know. I'm pretty fast- I took first place in our school's distance running competition. I even finished third at state. So I can run- hopefully that will help. I've never really tried 'exercising my brain,' so I'm sure Thaddeus will have to help me a lot in that area," he sighs.

I'm about to reply but fall silent as we arrive at the majestic building that looms before us. The rays of light from the rising sun cause the glass to sparkle. I focus and try to peer through the glass, but can't since it's tinted a dark blue. The building is substantial and we have to crane our necks back to be able to see the top of it. The silver walls gleam spectacularly against the dark blue of the windows. I search for doors, but I can only see one at the bottom, which stands closed a few feet away from what appears to be an outdoor elevator. We admire the building for a short time, then continue forward. Thaddeus isn't there yet, but that isn't too much of a surprise, seeing as we're pretty early. Looking around, we see that some equipment has been set out. There's a variety of weapons- spears, longswords, rapiers, maces, knives, shields, bows and arrows, and even a small object similar to a gun I can't identify.

Spotting a person nearby, we head over to her. She's just a few inches shorter than me and is wearing a grey suit jacket, a matching skirt that goes to her knees, and a plain white button-up blouse. She has a necklace made of white gold with dark blue glass- even darker than the glass on the building behind her- which is clasped tightly to her throat. Her dark brown hair is up in a tight, professional bun and she carries herself with an air of authority and belonging. When we ask her who she is, she says that she's Thaddeus's assistant- although she doesn't know why he isn't there yet. She explains that he is at a meeting finalizing the details for the First Challenge and it must be running long.

"Until he gets here… can we try out the weapons?" Nathan asks.

She hesitates, then agrees, provided we are quick and careful.

Returning to the pile of weapons, I select a small, light shield and a rapier. Nathan chooses two slim swords that can fit together into one. They are long, but light and I can tell it's not too problematic for him to adjust to them. After carefully swinging my sword around, getting used to the feel of it in my hand, I eventually get to the point that it feels more like an extension of my arm. Turning to Nathan, we decide to try and carefully attack each other. We start slowly, not really knowing what we're doing, but soon we glide into a smooth rhythm and just let our instincts take over. Our little duel turns into a deadly yet beautiful dance of steel. Neither of us is concerned, too focused to be thrown off track.

I'm not sure how long we fight, but by the time we stop, I'm slick with sweat and panting lightly. Nathan is too. When we start heading over to put the weapons back, I stop in surprise. Standing before us, calm and relaxed as always, is Thaddeus. I don't know how long he's been watching us, but I can tell by the look on his face it was long enough to be impressed. We put the weapons back and walk up to him.

"I'm sorry," I start, shading my eyes with one hand to avoid the brightness of the sunlight. "We didn't know what we should do since you weren't here yet, so we just… tried out the weaponry. I'm sorry if we've disappointed you."

He laughs. "Disappointed me? After watching only the last few minutes of your duel, it became clear to me that both of you are more talented than I would have guessed. Your Gifts are already coming in. Have either of you battled with these weapons before?" We both shake our heads. "Well, then! Isn't that a surprise! To an observer, it appeared as though you had been studying this style of art for quite some time!"

"...Were we okay, then?" Nathan asks, surprise on his face and in his voice. I don't blame him- I'm surprised as well. *Were we that skillful? To deserve Thaddeus's praise? We managed not to get hurt, but I don't really think that's worthy of this kind of recognition. Actually, I don't remember much of that fight at all. Strange... I must have been too focused at the time to absorb what was happening.*

Thaddeus chuckles, shaking his head before waving us inside. We follow him through the door and find ourselves in front of a massive spiral staircase. He continues to chuckle as we begin climbing before stopping suddenly. "Do either of you remember that duel? Any details? Did you think about anything you were about to do or did you just... allow your body to take the reins?"

"How did you know?" I ask, surprised. "I don't remember much of it, nor did I think about anything I was about to do specifically. ...Why do you ask?"

"Same here," Nathan murmurs thoughtfully. "I kind of just let my body take over, I guess. Why? Did we do something wrong? Because if we did..."

"No, no," Thaddeus laughs, waving away his concern. "You didn't do anything wrong- although you two might pose a bigger threat to the other teams than anyone- even the advisors, including myself- could have ever guessed. Yet you don't even know how you were able to do that without any training!" His face softens as he thinks, quickly going quiet. Confused, Nathan and I concentrate on climbing. The stairs don't seem to ever end, although I know that they must. My legs are starting to burn. I try to convince myself that this may help get me ready for the First Challenge somehow, but the thought only keeps me going for about fifty more steps. Luckily, Thaddeus resumes talking, so I can focus on something other than the pain in my legs.

"Well, we may as well work on your brain as we climb. We've already lost some time because of my meeting this morning. So, for your first test... who can provide me with the answer?"

"…To what?" I ask, having forgotten the question already, my thoughts having been too focused on the trial before me.

He chuckles. "I want you to figure out how you two did that with the weapons. *Why* you were able to do it. It shouldn't take too long for one of you to come up with an answer. Plus, it gives you something to do besides thinking about the climb. We can work on both the brain and the body at the same time!" he concludes happily, continuing his steady climb ahead of us.

Glad to have something else to do, I reflect on everything I've learned about this strange place. Something Vlad told me before I even got here pops back into my head. *"Each person has a Gift or two, except for the very rare few who happen to have none. Although it's been said that the ones destined to be King or Queen can have up to four Gifts. There are quite a few Gifts that one could possess, such as flying, reading minds, extraordinary fighting skills…"* Wait a minute! I think, excited. *Gifts; extraordinary fighting skills… Nathan and I must have the Fighting Gift!*

"I think I know!" I suddenly gasp. They both look at me, surprised.

"Really?" Thaddeus says. "I didn't think you would figure it out so quickly! Well, go ahead."

"Well… Vlad told me that there are different Gifts we could develop here… and he mentioned extraordinary fighting skills. So… do Nathan and I have that Gift? Or am I totally off?"

Now Thaddeus seems surprised. "No, no, you're just about exactly right! Considering what little you've been told… It's incredible that you were able to come up with that, honestly. However… perhaps I should clarify before you get ahead of yourselves. This may not be your actual Gift. Before you receive all of your Gifts, your body will go through… let's call it Zilferian puberty. Your body will try out different Gifts, sometimes with more success than others. You may have one Gift for over a week, but another may only linger for a few hours should your body reject the Gift.

"Judging from what I just saw of the two of you, and how you were both equally matched… I thought that maybe you both had already completely grown into that Gift, but since you don't remember what happened… well, that's how you know it's not your actual Gift yet. You won't know if a given Gift has settled on you until you see everything crystal clear- both during and immediately after you use it. It's like your senses are all heightened. You will also feel more powerful for a few hours after receiving your new Gift- like a substantial dose of adrenaline- but you will then feel a drop in energy for about an hour. You will be quite weak. After that, you will then feel normal and be in complete control of your new power. Using it will be like second nature to you, unlike during your Zilferian puberty."

He stops and looks at us a little sheepishly. "I'm sorry, was that too much to absorb at once? I just get so caught up... I forget that you know next to nothing about all this and that it is all very sudden and strange to you."

I shake my head. "No, I think we're alright, but the meaning of what you just said may not sink in for a while. But you might as well toss everything on us at once since we need to know as much as we can before the First Challenge."

"Speaking of which," Nathan adds, "what *is* the First Challenge? Aren't you supposed to tell us? You need to get us ready so we can have the best chance possible. You know what it is, right? You were just at a meeting to finalize everything for it!"

"Oh, calm down," Thaddeus soothes, waving a hand at us. We must have climbed hundreds of stairs by now, yet we are still not at the top, although I think I can finally see it. We are both very winded now, although Thaddeus seems to be fine. He may be old, but he's very fit. I don't ask for a break, determined to do what I must to win this thing, just as I promised Nathan. Even and especially if that means doing anything and everything my advisor asks me to do- without complaint. Nathan does the same, although he secretly gives me a look of despair at the pain we're putting our bodies through. So we struggle silently, not complaining- although we can't do much about our heavy breathing, which becomes continually more ragged as we climb. My lungs begin burning and it's a struggle for them to continue to expand. I start taking smaller, shallower breaths- which only causes my muscles to burn even more from the lack of oxygen. As I run out of energy, my lungs feel as heavy as rocks- not to mention my legs. How on earth does Thaddeus do it? Perhaps he has a Gift of Stamina or something?

"I'll tell you *about* the First Challenge- but I can't tell you every little detail of everything you can expect to find or do. I can simply teach you about the bigger threats that you will almost certainly encounter and how to deal with them. I cannot tell you every little detail that is restricted from the rest of the contestants. We try to make this so that everyone has an equal opportunity to win."

Nathan looks a little frustrated at this long explanation, but he stays calm and pants, "Okay... fine. Teach us... what we have... to know."

"We'll get to that," he replies, a knowing twinkle in his stormy eyes. "For now though, please go ahead and ask away at any other questions on your mind. I will do my best to answer them."

I already have a question on my mind. Quite a few, actually. So I start with the simplest one. "How many... Challenges... are there?" The pain in my legs is starting to drive me to distraction, but I know that I must know everything I can, so I don't waste time crying over the pain that intensifies with each step, but listen to Thaddeus instead.

"Hmm... since this is only the second year we have done this, we aren't entirely sure. It will depend on how long it takes for all but one team to drop out- either voluntarily after one team wins three Challenges in a row, or from injuries too severe for them to continue. Last year it took almost an entire year to finally have a winning team. We went through a lot of Challenges then- about one every week or two, but some lasted about that long as well. This year, we are mostly planning them as we go, but we have a rough idea of what is coming. So far, we have begun planning for about twenty... but again, we don't finalize anything until we know that there is a need for another one. I'll tell you this much, however," he says with a knowing glint in his eyes. "I personally don't think it will take that long this time. They're all much more dangerous since Vlad is in charge- for the most part- this year. Now that's all you're getting out of me about that!"

Now it's Nathan's turn to ask a question. "What... happens... after each... Challenge... when you win... or lose? And how do you... win... or lose?"

"Well, each Challenge has a goal. It may be to find or kill a specific creature, defeat someone of your choice in a skill, which can be riddles, flying, fighting... anything that involves any of the Gifts. I would advise you to pick one to work on that you either *know* is your Gift or you have a feeling about so you can develop it fully. There could be many goals to accomplish, which is why I need to train you both at the same time in the skills you will both need to work on while Vlad works on you both individually to work on your major weaknesses. Although today will just be to find out what your strengths and weaknesses *are*.

"After each Challenge, the top three teams receive prizes, and everyone resumes training for the next Challenge. So all those involved in the Games will not be disturbed by the observers, we have microscopic cameras set around the arena. I can't tell you what the prizes will be- I don't know myself anyway. ...Any other questions?"

"Yes," I say. "What will I... be doing... while Nathan is... with Vlad? Can I... go and... watch?"

"No!" Thaddeus gasps, shocked by the mere suggestion. He's so surprised, in fact, that he stops climbing. I sigh in relief. He stares at me with concern. "Heavens, no! That's *why* we train you each individually as well- the pressure from another person will affect the test. It is also just in case you have some special talents that you may want to hide, in case you have to fight one another in a Challenge, or if you are captured- in the Games, of course- and quizzed about your partner's special Gifts. It's just extra security. But to answer your question," he continues as he resumes climbing, "you can train with me one on one if you would like, or I could arrange for someone else to join us and teach you while Nathan is with Vlad. The same goes for you while Crystal is with Vladimir," he continues, turning his gaze to Nathan.

We're getting very near the top now, and I can see that Thaddeus is pretty much done answering our questions. However, I am desperate for him to clear up something that has been bugging me since I first met Vlad. "Thaddeus... stop for... a second... please. I have... something to... say before we... continue... and I... need to breathe... first..."

Looking at me strangely, he stops. Nathan shoots me a grateful glance as we both lean forward, hands on our knees, and pant until we can get our breath back. As we do, I can feel my muscles beginning to tighten into stone, and I can immediately tell that I will be very sore in the morning. In fact, I will probably barely even be able to move. *What a great way to kick off the First Challenge- barely being able to move without pain! That won't be good no matter* what *the Challenge is!*

Pushing this out of my mind for the moment, I straighten to see Thaddeus patiently waiting for my question. "Just remember," he comments, "that this will take time away from your learning."

"I know," I say. "But it's worth it. I have to know something- here and now."

He raises an eyebrow at me, clearly surprised. Nathan looks at me as well, intrigued now. Swallowing the lump in my throat, I forge ahead with my question. "When I first met Vlad, he... mentioned something about my eyes. He said something along the lines of 'my eyes are just like the King's.' ...Can you *please* explain that to me?" Confused, Thaddeus steps closer and peers into my eyes. He jumps back, choking down a startled exclamation. I'm nervous, but I have to continue. "He... he said that my eyes are just how the Princess's eyes are supposed to look."

"Can... can you turn your eyes into... into dragon eyes?" he asks me, shock and excitement in his voice. Sighing, I decide to try. I haven't done it in a long time, but I must get complete answers out of this guy. So, I roll my eyes back into my head and will my gold dragon's eyes to appear. I can instantly see greater detail of everything around me, although everything is tinted amber- which gives everything a magical look and feel.

To my surprise, there's something new that I notice this time. I can see... the color of Thaddeus and Nathan's thoughts and emotions. Looking at Nathan, I can see an aura around him. It's dark green, which I instinctively perceive to be inquisitiveness and curiosity. I also detect a light gold- wonder and devotion to something- as well as black with anxiety or fear. I pick out a very light rose color ringing it all, which I take to mean love. Although there's not much of it, so I don't know what he loves, and I doubt he knows it either it's so slight.

Nathan's colors are all a bit dull, except for the green, the prominent one. Thaddeus's, however, are bright and almost hurt my eyes. There are so many thoughts flying through his brain that all I can see at first is a swirling, multicolored aura surrounding him. After a few seconds of focusing, I can pick out the major ones. Light green- surprise, grey- he's hiding something and is conflicted, gold- wonder, a little bit of black- anxiety, magenta- wariness, and so many more that can't be put into words.

"Whoa!" Nathan exclaims, leaning back from shock at first, and then forward with interest. "I had no idea... that's... um... wow."

"Yes, this is quite... interesting," Thaddeus says, looking at me like I'm some dangerous new threat to be carefully examined before he dares approach me. "This... confirms a lot of things... as well as makes everything much more complicated."

"So, wait," Nathan says, looking confused. "Does this mean... that she's the Princess?" I look at Thaddeus, switch my eyes back to normal, and wait for his verdict. It takes him a while to reply.

"I... would say so," he confirms, sounding like he's in shock. "But this doesn't change anything. Yes, we are looking for the King and Queen's lost children, but even when we find them, they need to have grown into their Gifts to rule. Oh, and by the way, Crystal, members of the royal family have more Gifts than the others- three, sometimes four. And I'm sorry, but the Games aren't off- for anyone. Besides, Crystal can't just leave you alone, Nathan. So you're both still in this together."

"Wait... what?" Nathan responds, looking even more lost and confused than ever. "*That's* why we're having these 'Games?' Because the King and Queen lost their kids? So they're risking all of our lives... to find Crystal and her brothers? No offense," he adds to me.

"None taken," I reply. "I was thinking the same thing. But what makes you so sure I *want* to be this Princess?" I ask, turning back to Thaddeus. "What makes you think I'll just go along with anything you say?" He looks stunned. "And how come we haven't seen the King and Queen- who are *apparently* my parents- yet? How do we know they aren't just your puppets? Or are they just some figurehead no one's ever seen because they *don't actually exist?*"

I mean for the words to sting, and they do. I don't know why I'm being so harsh to Thaddeus. I guess I'm just taking out my frustration at all of these secrets on him. I've finally accepted that this place exists and that this is all actually happening, so I care about how things run and that I should be adequately informed about everything involving me, so I'm getting frustrated because I'm *not* being properly informed- about *anything*.

Nathan glances at me, surprised, and it looks like he's about to go off on me again about making our helpers mad and decreasing our chances of survival, but then he just gives me a small nod, indicating that he's on my side. I'm shocked, but grateful.

"What... how could you... how dare you?!" Thaddeus exclaims, suddenly shaking with anger. This is the first time I've seen him anything but cool and collected, so now I'm scared and worried and wishing I hadn't said anything. I may have pushed him a little too far. "How dare you take out your anger on Pearl and Alexander Dragon! They are the best King and Queen we have had in centuries- and they are your *parents*, no less! They have fallen into depression, sickness, and now even a coma. They don't even know that their backup plan, the Games, are now under way so we could recruit people to help find their children for them... let alone know that their daughter is now *here*. We have no idea how to help them."

Gulping, I feel remorse for my harsh words. "I... I'm sorry... I didn't know..."

Sighing, Thaddeus calms himself down. "No, you didn't know. I'm sorry as well. I keep forgetting to put myself in your shoes and realizing that you know next to nothing of this world and our lives. You're just frustrated, and I understand that. I'm sorry. I won't snap like that again," he promises. He pauses and takes a deep breath before giving us a small smile. "Now then, are we ready to continue? We are almost there, and we really *must* begin your training. After all, it wouldn't be good to finally get our Princess back and then get her killed, now would it?"

Nathan and I don't comment, opting instead to trudge after him, our sore legs screaming out in pain with each step, but neither of us makes a sound. I feel Nathan's eyes on me almost the whole time, but I pretend not to notice. When we finally reach the top, we get to a door made of dark, rich wood. Thaddeus opens it and directs us through. We emerge and feel a fresh breeze on our faces, cooling the heated skin. Once our eyes adjust to the lighting, we look around, wide-eyed.

The height at which we are at in the sky takes my breath away. A small flock of beautiful, colorful birds fly overhead, singing and filling the air with joyful music, harmonizing with the song of the trees. The landscape is so beautiful and alive, it's a welcome change from Earth's streets and cars gunking up the air. Under and all around is the Village with the King and Queen's palace to our right, shimmering a little in the growing daylight. A vast forest stretches as far as I can see from the left of the village and before it as well. To the right of the forest lie huge, majestic mountains, and on the other side of those is a plain field, empty and barren. Or so I think at first. Switching my eyes into dragon eyes, I look again. Everything is still tinted gold, but I can see both farther and clearer with my eyes. This gives me an idea, and without thinking about how it would be possible, I zoom in with my eyes- almost as though they were cameras. I can now see the plain with much greater detail, so I can also view all the wildlife running around in there. A lot of them appear like they do on Earth, but I've learned not to trust how something looks in this place.

Switching my eyes back, I turn to Thaddeus, who is also gazing out at the terrain, but not with peace and admiration on his face. He looks anxious, like the whole world rests on his shoulders, crushing him, and he can't take it anymore. I feel a pang of sympathy. Walking over to stand next to him, I lean against the railing, pretend I'm looking out at the land, and quietly say to him, "I'm sorry if I'm causing you any extra stress. I'd like to help you in any way that I can."

He turns slowly from the view to look at me, letting the sorrow in his eyes show. "No, you aren't causing anything," he responds, his voice low. "It's just… I'm Pearl's uncle, and I'm concerned about her. Not to mention all the things I must take care of now that she and Alexander are no longer physically able to run Zilferia. The responsibility shifts to my shoulders, since there are no other members of the royal family alive and here right now except for you, and you are not yet ready to run anything. I thank you for the offer, but *I* am the one who needs to help *you* right now." He takes a deep breath and pushes his anxiety down again. "We need to get you two ready to win these Games!"

We sit at a table with three chairs around it and he waves Nathan over. He sits beside me and we face Thaddeus. This is when our training truly begins. He starts by informing us about 'just a few of the creatures you may encounter here,' but there are so many, I get them all confused. *Hopefully, it will all just come back to me when I need it… because there's no way I'm going to remember all of this!*

One creature in particular that I do remember, however, is dragons. Apparently, not only do they exist here, but they thrive and are seen often. They grow to be as large as mountains- although that takes hundreds, sometimes thousands of years- and they don't typically come anywhere near the Village. As for the obvious- they have scales, wings, forelegs and hind legs, and breathe fire. I learned something new about them, though. Fully grown dragons can look into a person's heart, although no one survived it- that is, until my many-times-great grandparents, James and Sally, came along. Their last names were then changed to Dragon, a gift from the old dragon that saw into their hearts. They were made dragon friends, and the dragon then made them rulers over Zilferia.

"Wait," Nathan interrupts, a little confused. "Dragons can *think?* And talk?"

"Of course they can think! They are wiser than all of our Kings and Queens. And in a way, they can talk," Thaddeus responds. "They communicate by touching your mind with theirs and then sending you their thoughts. The younger ones can't form words, so they use pictures and feelings such as hunger or surprise." He proceeds to tell us about the history of Zilferia- *my* history, apparently, although I'm still having a hard time buying into it.

"From then on, the Dragon family was to bring their children to the dragons and have them judged. Every now and again, there was a 'bad seed,' but for the most part, the children were all just fine. When the children married, the fiancé would be judged and made a real part of the Dragon family if they were deemed worthy. As a benefit of being Dragon-Friend, the family grew gradually more in-tune to the dragons' magic, and it became interwoven into their very being.

"Six generations after James and Sally, there was a child born who had a particularly strong connection to the dragon magic. Her name was Alexandra, but she went by Alex. She was kidnapped soon after birth, and then lost in the wilderness. Fortunately, there was an old hermit who lived alone in the forest who found her and raised her until she was eight. The hermit died of old age, leaving Alex alone once again. She tried to find food, but being so young, she didn't know what was and wasn't edible and eventually ate some berries that put her into a coma. She was found by a young dragon just as she crumpled to the ground. His name was Jack. This particular dragon had been there when her parents were judged, so he didn't harm her since he recognized her as a member of the Dragon family. He quickly took her to his cave to try and revive her.

"She wasn't responding to him, so he flew over to the Dragon Mage and asked for his help. When told that the girl was a DragonFriend, the Mage came quickly. But the only way to save the girl was to turn her into a dragon- a feat only possible because of Alex's strong connection to dragon magic. So they made the decision and transformed her into a dragon, although she could also turn back into a girl at will. Alex soon revived, and, to make a long story short, after a few years she and Jack fell in love and were married. Shortly afterward, Jack asked the Dragon Mage to enable him to turn into both a human and a dragon as well so he could be with Alex and help her find her family in human form to attract less attention to himself.

"The spell was unpredictable, however, and worked differently for him. He was part dragon and part human. He looked like a human at first glance, but he had dragon eyes and claws as well as a pair of wings that he could make disappear at will. But he could not take the form of a full human or a full dragon. The two were successful at finding Alex's parents, and they were reunited. When the parents learned that Jack was a dragon, he was very respected.

"They had six children, each with draconian characteristics, although they all faded with each passing generation. Even down to today, most of the Dragons still have dragon eyes they can hide or reveal whenever they wish. The dragons believe that there will be another like Alex, able to turn into both a dragon and a human at will. They say the ability will not show up until a time of darkness and peril for all the land is on the horizon." Thaddeus and Nathan both look at me, and I can see in their eyes the question.

"It won't be me!" I quickly assure them. "I don't *want* to be a dragon, and I don't want to rule this Kingdom- I don't even want to *be* here! I just want to go home!"

"…We'll have to see if you change your mind on that or not," Thaddeus murmurs, inspecting me. "For now, we won't force you to do anything."

"Except enter the Games," I mutter. Thaddeus pretends not to hear me, continuing instead to lecture us about different creatures until my brain feels like it's going to split open. The only things that caught my interest were dragons, phoenixes, and vampires, but not much else. There were a few other creatures as well, but I had already forgotten what they were called. What gave me a chill, though, is that there are werewolves here. They were known for their bloodthirstiness and lack of mercy, as well as the stories of what they do to girls before they kill them.

Finally, it's time for Nathan to meet Vlad- and time for our instruction on creatures to end, which I can't help but be elated about. The sad part is that does not necessarily mean that I am free to do whatever I wish. I want to try out the weapons again, but Thaddeus has other ideas. As Nathan rides an elevator to the ground, he turns to me.

"Let's exercise your planning and strategy." He reaches behind his back, eyes glinting. I brace myself for a big book he'll quiz me on or something. But what he pulls out is something completely different. "...And the best way to do that... is to play chess!" I blink in disbelief, staring at him.

He smiles. "I know what you're thinking, but it really does help you to both formulate a plan ahead of time as well as improvise when things turn out differently than you might expect. Plus, it's fun- arguably the most fun you will have today. I will be white, and you can be blue. I will not go down easily, I warn you," he adds with a twinkle in his eye. "I have only ever been beaten by two people- your parents. Even then, I still beat them as often as not."

"Well, let's just see what I can do, then," I say, swallowing back the grin that's trying to creep onto my face. I love chess. I started playing when I was a toddler, and I have rarely lost. *Thaddeus has no idea what he's getting into, challenging me... I haven't lost at this game in years!*

Thaddeus lets me start. I'm pretty confident I can beat him. I have an arsenal of strategies to win due to my years of playing. I have planned for every possibility I have ever seen, as well as a few I haven't. Even if I don't beat him in the first game, afterward I will know his strategies and the way he thinks. I will be able to anticipate his every move.

After more than half an hour, I think that I finally have him set up how I want him to be. Confident that he has no moves, I grin after moving my final piece. "Checkmate."

Not looking concerned at all, he contemplates the board. For five minutes. I'm about to snap at him and assure him that he has no chance of winning now, when he looks up at me and says, "Patience is a virtue." This rubs me the wrong way since I've heard that all my life and I'm thoroughly sick of it. Frustrated, I look at the board once again, and something I didn't notice before stands out to me. *Oh no! I... I can't believe I left that pathway open! Then again, I guess it couldn't really be helped since my few remaining pieces are all occupied. Still... I hope he doesn't notice...*

Just as I'm thinking this, however, Thaddeus reaches out his hand and takes advantage of my lapse. Using his king, he kills my queen and then *he* says, "Checkmate."

Astonished, I look at the board, only to find that it's true. There's no way around it. "How... how on earth?! You turned that completely around! I had you!"

"I admit, that was a little too close for comfort," Thaddeus concedes. "But luckily for me, I eventually found your mistake and exploited it. Don't be too disappointed, however! You had me worried there, and as I said, the only ones to ever beat me were your parents. You are still an extraordinary chess player." He stands, pushing back his chair. I follow suit. "Looks like it's time for lunch, my dear."

We ride the elevator on the outside of the building, going slowly so we can look out over the land as we descend. The sparkling castle catches my gaze once more. "Hey, Thaddeus? Why does the castle sparkle like that?"

"Ah, the Dragon castle," he begins, holding his hands behind his back as he gazes at it. "It was built with the dragons' help. They gathered the stones from their mountains. They have gold and other precious jewels throughout. That is what you see catching the sunlight."

"The whole thing is like that?"

"Indeed."

"Wow," I murmur, gazing at the beautiful, priceless castle before us. When we reach the ground, we walk to the square and eat with the rest of the contestants and advisors. I can't help but notice that Nathan and I are the only ones walking around with winces. *Great. I knew being this sore would put us at a disadvantage,* I groan to myself. Nathan and I eat together while Thaddeus heads over to talk to Vlad.

We're both ravenous, so not much is said until we are done with our food. It's a simple sandwich, like the one Vlad gave me when we first met, so it doesn't take long to finish.

Swallowing my last bite, I ask Nathan, "So, how did it go with Vlad?"

"Not too bad," he says, leaning back. "He didn't say much, just asked me some questions to test for a logistical Gift, I guess. He also had me run, try to fly, read his mind, and disappear... just tried to see which Gifts I might have, I suppose. What did you do with Thaddeus?"

"Oh, we just played chess," I respond nonchalantly. I immediately laugh at the confusion on his face and explain. "He said it would help with logic and planning and stuff."

"Oh, okay. Did you win?"

"No," I sigh. "But I was so close! I had one little mistake that he somehow found after *five minutes,* so he had me in a checkmate right after I thought I had him in one! Ugh, it was frustrating! That was the first time I've lost in years. And yes, I did play during that time," I tell him before he can ask.

After that, we can't think of much to talk about except the First Challenge, but we don't want to talk about that, so we simply sit in companionable silence. After a while, I spot Sierra and Ham coming over to us.

"Hey, guys! What's up?" I greet them.

"Oh, you know. Training and stuff," Sierra replies matter-of-factly, sitting down next to me as Ham sits next to Nathan. "Not that I know why they even bother," she adds. "There's no way we're going to win. Not compared to Kat and Jake, Odette and Frazer, Star and Drake... well, we don't have a chance against any of them, honestly. Except maybe Roxane and Lloyd. Lloyd will probably be awesome, but I can bet you that Roxane will hold him back." She stops and blushes. "Sorry, we just spent the morning going over the teams, I guess my mind is still lingering on it."

"Come on, guys!" Nathan protests. "Don't talk like that! If you think you will lose, then that *is* what will happen! For example, I thought that I would never make it to state at Track and Field for my school, so I didn't. But the next year, I told myself that not only could I make it to state, I would be in the top three. So I ignored the other runners and just did my best, and I won! So, I'm trying to do that here as well. I have to, for my family."

I nod, touched by his little speech. "So do I. I owe it to my little sister, and to Nathan and his family. But that doesn't mean that you guys can't win as well. We should all protect and help one another, and they won't have a choice but to make it so that all four of us win!"

"Yeah..." Ham slowly agrees. "Sure. I'll go along with this. We'll try our best."

"That's the spirit!" I cheer. "So, how's Zelda?"

"Oh, she's great!" Sierra says, smiling. "She's very understanding and... well, not like Vlad. She's not pushing as hard as I thought she would, luckily. How's the special treatment with Thaddeus?"

"It's a little tough," Nathan admits. "But I can already tell it's worth it. And you're right; he's also much better than Vlad. Then again, Vlad just seemed to have it out for us. I'm sure it would be nice to be his favorite as well- he probably gives them inside information. I just hope he's not telling them secrets about us..."

"Oh, I'm sure he would love to," Ham comments. "It's just too bad it's against the rules- if he did cheat, then he would be replaced, and he would hate that. But you can bet he's doing what he can, giving his teams little 'hints' under the table so no one knows. It's a little unfair that he's the only one doing the Gift testing instead of spreading it out or having someone who's not an advisor do it if you ask me."

Looking up, I see that Vlad is coming towards us. "Speak of the Devil," I mutter. "Here comes Vlad." The three of them turn and look. I have a terrible feeling he's here for me.

"Greetings," he says when he reaches our table, inclining his head a little to acknowledge Ham and Sierra. "May I have a word with Crystal?"

The three look at me, concerned. Touched, I tell Vlad, "Sure." As he begins walking away, I quickly assure my friends, saying, "Don't worry, I'll be fine. He can't do anything to me, especially not in front of everyone. Be right back!" I quickly hurry after Vlad. Once we're out of earshot, he stops and turns back to me.

"As you know, you need to train with me alone right after lunch. I will attempt to assess which Gifts you may have or receive. Although this is difficult to do while you are going through Zilferian puberty. So, and I'm just warning you, your assessment from me may seem harsh. Do not be a baby and whine about it or make my job harder in any way, or else I might 'accidentally' arrange for an accident to happen in the arena. I am in control of the Games this year, so I can do anything I want to you."

"Not necessarily," I bite back. "I don't think my parents would be too happy with you if you 'accidentally' got me killed."

"Don't play the Princess card on me, *Crystal Dragon*. You don't rule over me, and your *parents* aren't alert. They can't save you. You have no power over me, whereas I have all power over you."

"Not for long," I can't help but retort. Vlad reddens, getting angry.

He lowers his voice, coming closer to me. I stiffen and will myself to not back away. "I would watch where you step, *princess*. And that means coming to your assessment, no matter how much you and I dislike each other." He comes even closer, his mouth next to my ear. "But you've pushed too far. I will have my revenge. Let's just say… I hope you aren't afraid of werewolves."

Thanks to my newfound knowledge of werewolves, this sends a shiver down my spine. Backing away, Vlad sends me a crooked smile, satisfied that I am now terrified of him. "See you in a few minutes back here, in the square. Try to run away and it will be worse for you." And with that, my newest and most powerful enemy stalks away.

7

"What did he want?" Nathan asks with concern as I slowly walk back to my friends, hiding my feelings behind a nonchalant smile. *He should be concerned,* I think to myself. *I have now made a powerful new enemy... and it doesn't affect just me, but him as well!*

"Oh, nothing," I reply, sitting back down. All three look at me disbelievingly, but I'm not ready to tell them about Vlad's threat just yet. So I continue with, "No, really. He just wanted to remind me to meet him here after everyone leaves. That's all." Ham and Sierra look relieved, but I can tell that Nathan doesn't quite believe me. He doesn't argue in front of the other two, although I can tell by the look in his eyes that he's going to question me about it later. I notice people beginning to leave the square just as Thaddeus comes over to our table.

"Greetings, Ham, Sierra," He nods to each of them in turn. "I believe it is time for you to go- lunch is over, and training resumes immediately afterward." They nod and leave, waving goodbye to us. Thaddeus now addresses Nathan. "If you will come with me. Crystal needs to be assessed by Vladimir." Nathan nods, giving me a supportive thumbs-up. I return it, trying to look confident even though I'm anything but confident at the moment. My whole world is crashing down around me- isn't that a good enough reason to be wary of everything?

Everyone clears out of the square within minutes, and I'm alone but for the cleaners who are swiftly moving the tables out and sweeping out the square. Soon enough, they're gone as well, and I'm left alone with my thoughts, waiting for Vlad to return and make my life even more miserable.

He arrives shortly with a clipboard, paper, and pencil. Apparently, he's taking notes, just waiting for me to screw up. I sigh. *Here goes nothing.* A handful of people are following him. They've brought weapons, chess games, books, weights, cages with animals in them, and various other objects. *That's right… he's going to judge me and try to see what Gifts I may or may not develop. Well, I can't make anything much worse with Vlad, now can I? Whatever I do won't matter much. Even if I try to fix what I've done, he won't forgive me- he's even more stubborn than I am.*

Once everyone leaves and I am alone with Vlad and one guy by the weapons, he jumps right into it. His voice doesn't betray any emotions as he tells me to try to move one of the books with my mind. Thinking that it's stupid, but not wanting to fail, I concentrate hard on the nearest book. I then picture it moving, jumping into the air and hovering there. It moves about an inch and falls back onto the table. Vlad doesn't say anything, but I can tell by the look on his face that my effort was pathetic. Next, he tells me to bench-press some weights- as many pounds as I can manage. I'm not too great at that, either.

He then looks me up and down before telling me to try and 'charm him' into doing something for me. I try, but when I do, he raises an eyebrow and jots something down. I can't help but feel down about it. What if I end up having no Gifts? What a failure 'princess' I would be. Next, he has me read a passage from one of the books and then repeat it to him. I try to tell it word for word, but I can't help but paraphrase.

We play chess so he can see my level of logic next. I beat him easily. He then has me run as fast as I can around the square four times- just over a mile. I do better than I ever have before- by about a minute- but he just shakes his head and writes on his paper. I'm frustrated by the time he tells me to control the weather, so I imagine a bolt of lightning hitting the ground between us, feeding my frustration into it. Suddenly the air is filled with electricity, and a bolt of lightning actually hits the ground in front of him, surprising me. I didn't think it would really work. Vlad looks charred black, and his hair is sticking straight up. I begin laughing, then realize that my hair is behaving the same way, ripped out of my neat little braid, although *I'm* not all charred with tiny bits of electricity still running between my fingers and strands of hair. The paper, however, is history. It's all but disappeared. He goes to a table, muttering the whole way, and retrieves another paper and clipboard. He writes quickly, covering the previous tests as well as the most recent.

Now, grinning with satisfaction, he instructs me to talk to and attempt to pet a tiger. He backs away hastily when it roars at me, but I hold my ground. Talking to it soothingly and assuring it that I mean it no harm, the tiger calms. It even lets me pet its snout, which is softer than I expected. I then tell it to relax and rest. It lies down and puts its head on its paws, looking up at me sorrowfully. Swallowing, I force myself to turn and walk away without freeing it. Behind me I see Vlad scrambling to hide his surprise and awe. He looks away from me and writes down my results for befriending creatures.

Then, face expressionless, he tells me to focus on the tiger and 'put myself in its shoes.' He tells me to think of how it would feel to be that powerful creature. What I would feel, hear, and smell. So I do. It's surprisingly easy. Next thing I know, I'm on all fours and flicking a tail around. A sudden barrage of smells assaults my nose. There are so many, I can't sort them out. Sudden, feral thoughts fight over control of my body. I feel like I'm on the line between being a tiger and a girl. Finally, my thoughts overrule the tiger instincts and can focus on Vlad, who seems to be yelling at me. I flick my ears back, annoyed at the harsh noise.

"…Now! That's long enough! Concentrate on how you are as a human! Change back, or you may be a tiger forever!" He's panicking, I can tell, but I am calm. *Yeah, I don't think so. I'm stronger than you are. I could do this all day.* Then I remember that I'm trying to get on his good side- if he even has one- so I do as he says, and suddenly I'm me again, my clothes thankfully reappearing with me. Sighing with relief while simultaneously trying to hide it, he scribbles on his paper. I have a feeling I got a perfect score on shapeshifting.

Once he's finished, he tells me to picture myself invisible, completely unseen. I try, but don't disappear entirely. I can still see my body, only I can see through it as well. It's disconcerting, so I quickly imagine myself visible again, and it works. Vlad again takes notes.

Now we finally go over to what I've been looking forward to since I practiced with them that very morning with Nathan- the weapons. The guy there bows to me, and I awkwardly bow back. He invites me to choose a weapon, assuring me that it won't affect the Gift working or not. I choose the rapier again, so the other man does as well. Before we begin our duel, he warns me that Fighting is his Gift and that he won't be holding back much, although he promises not to harm me. We will fight for only five minutes. I agree to this, then settle into a defensive pose, preparing myself for his first strike.

It's a good thing I do. The instant I settle into my pose, he attacks, swinging his rapier at my head. I duck, and then, thinking quickly, I punch the back of his leg with my free hand as I sweep under him, giving him a dead leg. He recovers by the time I get back to my feet, so I am again on the defensive. I make sure to stay light on my feet, just like my teacher back on Earth taught me- and again, it's a good thing I do, because I can barely avoid some of his attacks.

I even get in a few strikes now and again during our duel. By the time we stop, we both have minor cuts, even though we started out trying not to hurt each other. As we return the swords, he asks if I can remember the duel. I reply that it's no better than usual, although it's a little better than that morning when I first attempted to use the Gift. He nods thoughtfully. "That surprises me. The way that you've been fighting, I thought that this was your Gift- you're almost my match, even though you had no one to teach you how to fight."

"Well, I've never fought with weapons before today, but I have fought before. It was just hand-to-hand combat and self-defense," I explain.

"That must explain it," he decides with a satisfied nod. "Plus, just because it isn't your Gift yet doesn't mean it won't be in the future. Your body certainly isn't rejecting it, at least."

"Yes, perhaps it will be," I murmur, having a hard time picturing myself being in control of any Gifts, despite my practicing with them for over an hour. It's just too surreal. It's magic, and magic just hasn't existed in my world before, and it's difficult to accept it now.

Returning to Vlad, he has me throw my thoughts at him and try to pierce his mind and read his thoughts. I try, but I'm tired, and he has a wall of defenses around it, so all I get from it is a feeling of his growing dislike of me. What else is new. He does seem to be impressed, however, with my overall scores for the Gifts.

The last thing I have to do is attempt to fly. So, leaving the square behind, he has me climb a tree as high as I dare so that if I can't manage it, I won't kill myself with the fall. He stands underneath me, ready to catch me should I fall. Determined not to have to touch him, I fearlessly jump into the air and push myself forward with my mind. I start out slowly, but as I realize that I'm not going to fall, I have some fun with it. I shoot upward, make some loops, and simply enjoy the feeling of flying through the warm air. I then decide to scare Vlad a little- and to have fun, but mostly to scare him- and zoom downwards, pulling up just before I hit the ground. He shouts at me to stop showing off and land. Sighing, I do as he says, touching down lightly in front of him.

Scowling at me, he says that I can go.

"What about my scores? Aren't you going to tell me?"

"No," he growls. "I tell that to Thaddeus. *You* need to figure out your Gifts yourself. Besides, these tests aren't exactly reliable. It's not good to rely on them when, if it is not your Gift and you try to use it, and it fails... well, let's just say, your partner in the Games is likely to find themselves without a partner. Now go away! Go back and give this to Thaddeus," he says, handing me the paper after he folds it into thirds. "And DO NOT look. I'll know if you do, and it's just not worth it, trust me. Now get out of my sight!" And with that, he storms off back to the square. Deciding to fly back to Thaddeus and Nathan and rest my exhausted legs, I push myself into the air with my mind and take off in the direction of the tallest building in the Village.

The feeling of flying is amazing... indescribable... the closest I can get is to describe it as a mix of skydiving and riding a rollercoaster, but calmer, slower, and you're entirely in control. It feels... like freedom. I reach the building all too soon and land on the roof next to a startled Nathan and calm Thaddeus. I hand him the paper, watching his face anxiously as he reads it, but I can't read any emotions on it. He just nods thoughtfully and puts the paper in his back pocket.

I'm dying to know what Vlad said, but I know that if Thaddeus wanted to tell me, he would. Begging wouldn't help my cause. So I sit down instead, looking at their chess game. I can clearly see a path that Thaddeus had left open for him, but I don't say anything, sitting quietly on the chair and urging him with my mind which move to take instead. He apparently doesn't see it, though, or the trap that Thaddeus also had ready for him, for he plays right into it. The game is over with Thaddeus's next move.

Sighing, Nathan leans back in his chair. He looks at me, mirth playing in his eyes. "He's beaten me three times already. Did he ever beat you that fast?"

"Well… no, but he *did* beat me. I thought that I was really good, but he somehow avoided all my traps. I think that Thaddeus is the best there is!"

"Your parents too," Thaddeus replies, chuckling. I wonder why they are both in such a good mood, but brush it off. "Although you are the closest to my equal that I've ever seen," he admits.

"Really?"

"Yes. But let's get down to business. I need to tell you two about the First Challenge." Nathan and I lean in, anxious to hear this life-preserving knowledge. "The goal is to find and bring back the egg of a Zyloff." His voice is heavy with meaning, but it goes right over my head.

I blink. "Um… what is that again?" I ask sheepishly.

Thaddeus sighs. "It's essentially a giant snake, only with feathers and wings and, when full grown, can kill you instantly with a mere glance, and it can kill you both with a single bite."

"…Oh," I say weakly. "I guess we should avoid the mom, then."

Nathan jumps in with a question. "You said we have to bring it back. Back to where? To the Village?" An excellent question.

"To your starting place. Each team will start an equal distance away from the nest of eggs, although you may be far from the next team. There are three eggs, so whoever finishes first is the winner, the other two in second and third places respectively. You must bring the egg back to that spot, and then the Challenge will end. Until then, others may take the egg from you. So avoid any other teams, any other creatures you come across, and, well, try to stay alive. And don't get lost; although you should be fine in this Challenge since each starting place is glowing the team's color. You two are dark purple, which also means that you wear an outfit with your color on it," he continues, leaning down and picking up a box. Opening it, he pulls out a new set of clothes for each of us. They appear to be the same as the ones we are already wearing, except it's black with purple on the outside of the pockets, sleeves, around the outside of the soles of the boots, as well as the inside of the hood on the jacket.

"Since you two are now an official team, you will share a building to sleep in. There are two beds, of course, but you will now be living together. I will show you to your house after dinner. First, are there any questions? I probably won't be able to answer any specific ones about the Challenge, of course, but we shall see."

Nathan speaks up first. "I've been wondering... I guess this might be a dumb question, but why do people here have Gifts? And why can we get them, even though where we come from no one does?"

Thaddeus slowly smiles. "That is certainly not a dumb question, and I'm more than happy to answer it for you. Would you like the long version, or the short?"

"Long," we both respond at once. Clarity is essential and hard to come by in such a vastly different world. Being late for dinner is nothing compared to knowledge.

He chuckles. "Very well. In that case, I must also explain to you about the realms. You see, they used to all be one countless millennium ago. No one knows what caused it to happen, but something split it apart into the seven realms we know today. The original realm, Aroidu, had powerful magic woven throughout the entirety of it. But when it split, the magic was unevenly distributed. Lii has the most, while First and Second Earths have almost none- which is what led to such great strides in technology there.

"We call the Gifts such because it is from the realm that we receive it. A person must have a connection to the magic woven into the fabric of every-thing around us in order to receive their Gift. That is why some never get a Gift, and the Dragon family tends to receive more. Their dragon part makes them especially sensitive to that first and oldest of magics."

We sit silently for a moment, absorbing this new knowledge. I stare at my hands, anxious to ask Thaddeus something but unsure if it would be wise to do so. It builds within me until it finally just comes out. "Will there be werewolves?" The two stare at me, a question evident in their eyes.

"Why?" Thaddeus asks. Sighing, I finally tell them of Vlad's threat.

Nathan's eyes widen. "What? I thought I said... never mind. What's done is done. I just hope we can avoid them."

"Oh, you should be able to avoid them, alright," Thaddeus assures us. "Because they won't be in this Challenge. It's too late for Vladimir to change anything to this one. I cannot guarantee, however, that they will not be in the Second Challenge. I would try to get on his good side, that's for sure," he adds. I wince.

"I don't know that I'll be able to. He hates me. I have no chance of that anymore. Nathan might, but I think the best thing for me to do is just to avoid him."

"Why?" He asks, leading to me explaining about reading his mind and feeling his feelings of jealousy and hatred, which the feelings of him being impressed with my skills certainly hadn't touched. "I suppose there's nothing to do if he just has his heart set against you," Thaddeus consents, sighing. "I will still try to reason with him. After all, you are our next ruler, and we can't have you getting killed just because Vladimir is being stubborn." I bite my lip to keep from protesting. I still plan on going straight home after this madness, not leaving my family- the one that actually raised me- for the one that everyone says I belong with. I especially don't want to *rule* this insane place. I'm only sixteen! I can't lead an entire land!

I snap out of my thoughts to hear Thaddeus say, "Alright then. If there are no other questions, then we will head back down." As I step towards the elevator, he adds, "...on the stairs." I groan inside, but don't complain despite my already very sore legs.

"Hey, Thaddeus," I begin as he opens the door to the stairs. "Are you going to tell everyone that I'm the Princess?"

He doesn't respond for a few steps. "Not yet," he finally says. "We don't need that complicating the Games for everyone. Perhaps after the Games." He thinks for another moment. "I'll do what I can with the cameras throughout as well, though you should probably refrain from mentioning that there is anything unusual about you if you can." He warns.

Relief sweeps over me. I didn't want to deal with everyone thinking I'm their ruler on top of everything else. Nathan and I let Thaddeus get a little ahead of us so we can talk as we descend. He turns to me, and I can see that he can barely keep from laughing. When I ask why, he replies, chortling, "You… your hair…" Reaching up with my hands, I feel that my hair is still sticking up all over the place from the lightning. I start laughing too as I picture how I must look.

When he catches his breath, he asks me sarcastically, "What did you do? Play with lighting?"

"Yeah," I laugh. "You should have seen Vlad's face! His hair was worse than mine- it even had sparks running around in it! It was hilarious!" He laughs as well, but it soon dies away as we fall back into our own thoughts. Unsure of what to say, we walk down the rest of the stairs in silence. I eventually get so tired that I slip and fall into the open air. Luckily, I react quickly enough to fly off to the side and land on the stairs. I pant, trying to catch my breath and calm down after that sudden wake-up call. Nathan hurries down the stairs to see if I'm alright.

After that, the trek to our new house is uneventful. We stop to have dinner, where Thaddeus adds a flavorless powder to our soup that's supposed to help with soreness. We eat alone since we missed the designated dinner time for the contestants. When we reach our new house, we both just collapse on one of the beds, not caring who gets which, and fall asleep.

8

I don't get to sleep long. There's a loud knock on the door a few hours before dawn and I hear Vlad shout, "Rise and shine! Make yourself some breakfast and then come down to the square. Be there in an hour and a half- no later! We don't want to wait around for you!" He then walks away, chuckling to himself. I can tell he enjoys torturing us all. Rolling over in bed, I fall asleep again even though I know I really shouldn't.

When I wake up again half an hour later, it's to the smell of eggs, bacon, and blueberry muffins. One of my favorite breakfasts growing up. My stomach growls at me, but before I go over to the kitchen, I head to the shower to freshen up really quickly. Once clean, I change into my new black and purple outfit, find a brush, and detangle my hair before rebraiding it with a new elastic since the other one got... demolished.

Heading down to the small basement I find Nathan dishing out scrambled eggs onto two plates. He looks up at me with bloodshot eyes and smiles wearily. "Hey. I made us some breakfast. I figure we'll need our strength for the First Challenge, right? Plus, who knows where we can find food in there? So eat up, I made plenty."

Feeling guilty, I sit down across from him at the small round table. As we start to eat, I apologize for not waking up when I was supposed to and for making him prepare breakfast, but he interrupts me partway through.

"Stop. Don't apologize. You don't need to. I *wanted* to make breakfast for you, and I figured you probably wouldn't let me if you were awake. So I'm glad you slept a little longer. Besides, it's better for at least one of us to be as alert as possible today, right? If you got up when I did, then you would be just as tired as I am and we would be at a disadvantage. So don't apologize, just shut up and eat."

We laugh a little, but the nerves don't let it last, and it cuts our laughter short. Soon we are just stuffing our faces with as much food as we can eat. We barely finish it all, but I sure do feel a lot better with some hot food in my stomach. Glancing at my watch, I see that our time is almost up. I warn Nathan, and we head out the door together and toward the square. The Village seems unusually quiet today, but that's just fine for me. I don't feel like putting up with Jake's flirting or any of the other contestants' confidence any longer than I have to. Wanting to fly again, I jump into the air and think myself forward, but nothing happens, and I fall back to the ground, landing on my feet. Nathan looks at me, curious. I casually resume walking before explaining that I had attempted to fly. "But it isn't working anymore. I'm not sure why."

"I think I might," he responds. "Remember how we're going through 'Zilferian puberty?' Well, that means that our bodies are just trying out the Gifts. So your body must have moved on to trying another Gift." I nod, feeling stupid that I didn't remember that.

When we get to the square, I realize that something is wrong. I was expecting us all to meet here and be transported closer to the Zyloff together. What faces me, however, is a completely deserted center of the Village. A bad feeling causes my guts to churn. I'm just starting to tell Nathan that we should go back when I feel a sharp prick in my right arm and fall into darkness.

I don't feel groggy when I come to, which surprises me. Blinking my eyes open, the first thing I notice is the bright light. I quickly shut them again, waiting for the burning to fade. I slowly open them and wait for them to adjust. After that, I notice many things as I frantically try to take in everything around me. We are in a forest- obviously the one Thaddeus mentioned as an 'arena' for the Games. Nathan is sitting up next to me on a raised platform, looking around in a panic. There is a purple light surrounding the platform, a few inches wide that emits a column of dark purple that extends into the air, rising above the treetops. We're alone, facing the sun, which is already out and over the mountains. It appears to be about ten o'clock.

Noises come from the woods around us, indicating that there is life here. It comforts me at first, but then I remember that nothing here is as it seems. I jump up, instinctively getting into the defensive position that I was taught long ago. Nathan joins me, and we stand back to back. I can feel his heart pounding as hard as mine. How is this our life now? How did it come to this- being sedated and dragged into the woods to try and survive amongst creatures that should be fantasy?

"So... here we are," Nathan murmurs, his voice cracking under stress. "The First Challenge."

I give a shaky nod in return but am unable to say anything in response as a voice booms out of the surrounding woods. I jump, my nerves on edge. I then realize that the voice is familiar. I finally place it as she continues- it's Nehru. Apparently, she's the announcer for our 'Games.'

"Hello! Contestants! This is Nehru speaking! I know you may be a little confused and disoriented..."

"Yeah, maybe," I growl sarcastically. Nathan does his best at a chuckle.

"...So I will let you know... you are in one of our largest arenas, competing in the First Challenge! So sorry about the sedation, it just helps with the equality of the Games, you know. Anyways, you will be permitted to leave your platforms only once the gun goes off. After that, it's basically a free-for-all- but killing other contestants is not allowed. I hope you each have at least one of your Gifts, or you may have quite the fight on your hands! For the moment, just sit still and... ponder, plan, or just procrastinate!" With a giggle, Nehru's voice disappears. Nathan and I look at each other, eyebrows raised. I shrug, and we sit down again.

"We should spend this time coming up with a plan," I suggest to Nathan.

He nods. "I think we should make our way toward the middle. They're all about making everything fair, right? So the eggs should be the same distance away from everyone."

"Um, yes, that's great… in theory," I reply, groaning in frustration. "The only problem is… where's the middle?"

He looks thoughtful for a moment before responding. "I know! How about once the gun goes off, one of us can climb a tree and look around for the other teams' lights. Remember, Sierra and Ham are red. We can see if we can meet up and help each other."

"Right," I nod, looking around for a good tree to climb. I then notice that I overlooked something earlier. Leaning against a large rock close to us are two black and purple backpacks. Finally, the anxiously awaited and equally dreaded gun fires and Nathan and I sprint toward the bags, pulling them on without looking through them first. *There's probably just food in it*, I say to myself while racing toward a tall tree near me. *Besides, a head start is probably the most useful thing for us right now. We need to get with Sierra and Ham so we can all try to survive this… besides, it's also a race. And the Challenge will end the sooner we get to those eggs. I just hope we can sneak an egg away from their terrifying mother…*

I reach the top of my tree. Nathan is in one close by, but I'm higher up than he is. He yells up at me, asking what I can see. Scanning the treetops, I can't see much, but to our right, barely within my sight, is a thin yellow strip of light erupting from the surrounding green. And on our left, exactly as far away, is a small white strip. *White? There's not a white team… oh, but I guess light can't be black, so that must be for the black team.* I tell this to Nathan. He sighs. Neither one is Ham and Sierra's light. He then suggests that I use my dragon eyes to try and find them. When I do and look straight ahead, I still have to zoom in with my eyes and am finally able to see a protrusion of rock, and beyond that, a thin blood-red strip of light. Switching them back, I climb down the tree and meet Nathan on the ground. I report what I saw.

"What? They're the *furthest* away?!" Nathan exclaims.

"I assume so," I reply, urging him to begin walking with me as we talk. "The Zyloff lives on rocky outcroppings, right? So that must be the 'middle' that we need to get to."

"But that means that our enemies completely surround us! And we don't even know *who* is on the black and yellow teams! …Or do you remember?" he asks me hopefully.

"I don't," I reply, "But I think that yellow was being advised by Vlad."

He groans. "Even better."

As we walk, my feeling of anxiety only increases. With no help from anyone else, we're alone in a world full of creatures that want to kill us. I start getting frustrated as I think about the distance we have to cross to even reach the Zyloff in the first place, knowing that every minute we're here is another minute we're in mortal danger. I can't try the running Gift unless Nathan happens to have it right now as well since I can't leave him behind. I can't fly anymore... unless manipulating the weather would be able to get me to fly?

"Hey, Nathan," I begin. "I just got an idea. I could manipulate the weather and carry us with some wind or maybe try something else... we just really need to hurry through this as fast as we can," I explain.

He nods thoughtfully. "Well, it can't hurt, right? Just... don't accidentally strike us with lighting," he laughs. I laugh as well, then concentrate. I stop walking to better envision what I want to happen before I will the weather to obey and make it happen. My first try isn't great. As soon as I will the wind to blow from behind us, it does, but so strong and sudden that it slams both of us into a tree before stopping just as suddenly.

"Uh... sorry," I say weakly as we stand back up. "Maybe I have to *keep* thinking about what I want to happen- and be more specific, I guess," I gasp, still trying to regain my breath. Still winded as well, Nathan just nods. We walk into a clearing and try again. This time I hold my thoughts and continue to concentrate. I will the wind to come a little slower and gentler than before and to push us up as well as forward. Luckily, it works.

Soon we are in the open air and flying toward the rock. Our ride is a little sporadic as I want us to go faster, and I lose my concentration for a second. We fly for about an hour with the hot sun beating down on us, and the rock doesn't get much closer. I gently guide us down to a soft landing in a large clearing. My stomach is growling and I'm exhausted. Who knew concentrating so hard for so long was so draining? Or maybe that's just how the Gifts work during our 'puberty' period- they take a lot of energy. Either way, I need a break.

Nathan seems to hear the rumbling from my stomach. Telling me to rest, he guides me toward a shady tree while he goes and prepares lunch. I lay down on the soft grass, too tired to protest. I close my eyes and relax, feeling the breeze play with the few hairs that have come out of my braid.

I don't exactly sleep, but I do feel more rested when Nathan calls for me. I open my eyes and just lay there for a moment longer, staring into the branches above me. I suddenly realize that there's a figure in the tree- a human-like shape. My hairs stand on end. I can feel it watching me. I don't move, observing it to see what it will do first. It isn't another contestant; I can tell that much. The person looks at me a little longer, but flees once Nathan's footsteps approach. It jumps to the next tree, barely rustling the leaves, and then the next and the next- and then it's gone, not leaving the slightest trace of its presence.

Except for a feather that drifts down and lands next to me. Sitting up, I reach over and grab the feather. It's beautiful. It looks blue at first, but when I move it and the light hits it, it shimmers and looks green. I quickly slip it into my boot so I don't lose it and so Nathan doesn't ask about it. The person didn't seem to want Nathan to know that it was there, but it left this feather on purpose. So until I figure the encounter out, it's just easier not to tell Nathan about it. Besides, we have plenty to worry about at the moment anyway.

We eat lunch silently. It's a can of soup he warmed over a small fire, but it tastes great and helps restore my energy. Afterward, Nathan looks at me, pondering. I nervously wonder what he's thinking about.

"I don't think you should do that again," he finally states, his voice calm. When I start protesting, he stops me and continues. "Look how drained you were after an hour- and we haven't even gone as far as we would have hoped. I can't let you do this without my help. So I will try different Gifts and see which one works and will get us there the fastest. And when I get tired, you can take your turn. Then we'll eat and restore our strength, and do it again. Me, you, eat.

This makes sense to me, so I don't argue. "Alright. We'll take turns cooking, too." I stop him as he begins to protest. "If you did all the cooking, it would make it so *you* do more work than I do, and that's not fair. And don't say anything about being a girl and not being able to do as much as you or something just as stupid. Just don't even try. Don't say anything about protecting me, either. I could easily beat you in a fight; I'm stronger and faster than you are." Shocked, he closes his mouth.

He nods. "Of... of course..." he stammers, thrown off track by my tirade. "I... wasn't thinking any of that... I think of you as an equal."

Now I'm surprised. "Oh. Really?"

"Yes, really. I just like to cook, and would like to... I don't know, treat you to something nice. My mom taught me to be a gentleman... although I don't have much to work with out here anyway," he explains. A moment of silence passes before he changes the subject. "So, I think I'll try shape-shifting first. I did pretty well at that with Vlad. In fact, he was probably pretty jealous of me," he adds, winking at me. I laugh, appreciative of his ability to lighten the mood.

Concentrating, his body shimmers and then he is a magnificent white horse. His transformation was utterly different from Vlad's, that's for sure. Much faster and less gross. Nathan whinnies and shakes his head, sending his shimmering white mane rippling through the air. I gasp. He is the most beautiful horse I have ever seen, strong and majestic. I hear his voice in my head. *"You'll need to wear both backpacks- I, obviously, can no longer wear mine. Now hop on! Let's go for a ride!"*

I race over to grab his backpack before jumping straight onto his bare back, holding onto his mane to keep myself steady. I'm used to riding horses bareback, so I'm comfortable with that. I sit back and enjoy the ride as he trots away, leading us toward our goal. I empty my mind, the rhythmic movement under me lulling me to sleep.

When I wake, everything is different.

Opening my eyes, the first thing I notice is how dark and cold it is. The next is Nathan laying next to me, eyes closed and chest barely moving with each shallow breath he takes. Crawling over to him, I find that his face is caked with blood. Upon closer examination, I find that it's just a minor cut on his temple. Blood is leaking into his right eye. Leaning forward, I place my ear on his chest. His heartbeat is normal, but his breath is coming out in rasps. I don't know what to do.

Not only that, but I have no idea how we got here, where here even *is*, or what on earth happened to Nathan while I was asleep. *How did I even manage to stay asleep in the first place?* The thought nags as I scramble to retrieve our backpacks. That's when I realize that I have a headache- just like I did after I picked up the Sietta, although not nearly as severe.

Whatever happened, I must have been sedated somehow, so I wouldn't wake up... and then they attacked Nathan... whoever 'they' are.

As though summoned by my thoughts, I hear rustling in the distance and wild, rough laughter. There are lots of them, so I know it's not any of the other contestants, but that doesn't mean they won't attack us. Swallowing my rising panic, I try desperately to rouse Nathan, but to no avail. He is profoundly unconscious and oblivious to the world. And since he can't escape, that means I can't either- and I can't carry him very far.

But that doesn't mean I can't fight! The group gets closer. I hear one say, "Hey, guys, shh…" I then hear sniffing, followed by the voice continuing with, "I smell someone… two humans… and one is hurt! I can smell the blood! We're going to have a feast tonight!" He shouts, obviously not trying to be quiet any longer. This exclamation is followed by shouts of excitement, sounding strangely like wolves howling. "Of course, if there is a woman among them, then we will have to take them both to Wolf. But *then* we can eat!"

No! I think, finally finding something in my backpack that might suffice as a weapon. *They… they're… werewolves…* real fear begins rising in me, and my hands are shaking so badly, I drop the thing I had just grabbed. Bending down, I scrabble around in the dirt until I'm able to retrieve it. Standing back up again, I face where the howls are coming from. *Not… not werewolves! Anything but them!* Everything I know about werewolves rises in my mind; none of it pretty. I recall how they slowly torture their male victims before finally killing and eating them. But what they do to the women is worse.

They make the girls watch the guy being tortured and eaten, all while bound and helpless. After that, they would all fight over the girl- often to the death. The nastiest and most vicious of the pack is usually the victor. The victor is usually the leader of the pack, who is always named Wolf- it's a title as much as it is a name. He then takes the girl and… well, uses her to do his work and lead others to them to kill or turn into werewolves themselves. She couldn't escape from them because after there is a victor, he would memorize her scent. If the girl failed to get at least one victim a week, she would be eaten alive. Until then, she would be kept at their camp. Werewolves are all male and can't procreate, but they sure loved to try- unfortunately for the women they capture.

These are the things of my nightmares of late. And now my worst fears have come true. Finally focusing on what I have clenched in my hand, I inspect it as well as I can with my hands since I can barely see anything. It feels like the hilt of a sword. Probing it with my fingers, I fumble across a button and push it. A blade pops out, glowing a light blue. It lights up the surrounding forest about five yards in each direction. The blade is sharpened on both sides, like a sword, and is only about two feet long. I lightly touch the edge. It's sharp as well as surprisingly strong and sturdy. I grin, relieved to have a way to defend myself against the approaching monsters.

If I'm going down, I'm taking a few werewolves with me! Maybe if I kill enough, they'll even back off and leave us alone… Nathan and I will be safe!

The woods around me then seem to erupt, spitting out more werewolves than I can count, reaching beyond the light of my sword. We're surrounded. Glaring, I slowly pace in a circle around Nathan, protecting him from the drooling beasts. Each one takes a turn trying to sneak past me, but they stop when I wound a good number of them. They stand and walk like men, but are mostly covered in hair, more like a wolf. None of them are wearing clothes- nothing but the fur hides their vulnerable bodies. They snarl angrily at me, displaying their fangs.

I realize that they were toying with me when they were going one at a time. Laughing, five of them attack me at once. I manage to get one across the eye, block another one lunging at my arm, and slash the forearm of another. One of them managed to get behind me, however, and grabbed me by the hood of my jacket, yanking me to the ground. The sword flies out of my hand from the force of the impact, and my head is ringing.

Once I can finally focus again, I realize that another one joined him on all fours, dragging me away with their fangs. My vision fades as I hyperventilate. *This cannot be happening! I have to… I have to do something… lightning?!* Nothing comes from my begging the heavens for help, so I frantically scramble for the zipper on my jacket. Stripping it off, I jump back to my feet. The werewolves glare at me, snarling as they rise back to two feet as well. *Come on come on come on… PLEASE!* This time, I am able to get a bolt of lighting to hit the ground, starting a fire. They look even more ferocious in the light, but they back off for a second, whining at the heat and the sudden intense light. I spot Nathan being dragged away past the wolves circling me. Gritting my teeth with determination, I manage to get past them. I don't quite make it to him, though, as one of the wolves notices my approach. He stands, and with a mighty sweep of his arm, his leathery paw hits me hard against the head. I spin, falling to the side. My head hits a protruding root with enough force to knock me out, leaving my now limp body utterly helpless to my foes.

When I come to, it's still dark and I'm standing, tied to a tree. The only thing I can freely move is my head. A few yards away, I see both of our backpacks, half spilled onto the ground. One of the items in the pile is my glowing mini-sword. *Ha! Idiots! Now as soon as I get free, I will be able to kill them all...* But as much as I wiggle, I can't get loose from my bonds. If anything, they seem to get tighter. Growling in frustration, I suddenly hear someone- or some*thing*- laugh at me. It's a rough werewolf's voice. My heart jumps in fear as if trying to escape from my chest and run away.

"Ha ha! Yes, the lovely lady is awake now," the voice growls. "Now we can have fun with the boy, here!" I hear moaning and recognize it as Nathan's. A spark suddenly jumps to life and catches on a pile of wood, causing a bonfire to suddenly erupt not far from me. I can feel the heat washing over me, but the best part is the light. Now I can see. ...Although that might not be as great as I thought it would be.

I can now see the pack of werewolves around the fire, their fangs shining in the light of the fire. Two of them are holding a now conscious Nathan between them. Standing next to them and looking at me is the most prominent, toughest looking werewolf among them. I can only assume he's the leader. He grins at me, hunger and lust raging in his eyes. I almost throw up.

Looking around at his pack, the leader grandly announces, "Tonight, we feast! And we will have this woman to be with us. Our fortunes have turned for the better!" He pauses to let the happy howls of the pack die down. "So, since we are sportsman-like werewolves," he chuckles, "we will let the boy choose his demise- to become one of us, or to die."

Nathan finally catches my eye. His face is filled with even more terror than I myself feel. Swallowing, he says as loud as his rasping voice can choke out, "I would rather die than become as hideous and disgusting as you!" The leader laughs.

"Very well, then. Our pack is large enough as it is. Far better for you to be food. But we will, of course, let you have a sporting chance before we eat you." The two werewolves drop Nathan, and he falls to his knees in the dirt. Another one kicks my sword over to him. He looks at it, his eyes now finally gaining a spark of hope. "You will fight ten of my pack. If you can defeat them, you may leave. But you must fight them all at the same time-to the death."

Nathan shakily rises to his feet, clutching the sword like his life depends on it. Which, it does. "...No. If I can fight twenty, then you will let *both* of us go." The leader laughs. He figures it won't matter- no one can take on twenty werewolves at one time. So, chuckling, he begins picking out the ones that will fight.

Once the twenty are picked, the rest of the pack back away and form a circle around them. I'm on the edge of the ring, able to see every detail of the fight about to ensue. Nathan wastes no time. Leaping forward, he cuts down three with very precise and powerful swipes before the rest can react. When they do, they jump into action and attack him one at a time. I immediately recognize the tactic. I shout to Nathan that they're trying to wear him out and then they'll strike at once, desperation causing my voice to crack. He doesn't acknowledge me, so I can only hope that he heard me.

A wall of fur-covered muscles suddenly impedes my view. Craning back my neck, I see the leader of the werewolves, Wolf. He grins greedily at me, making me wish I could trade Nathan positions. "No helping," he growls at me. "Not that it will matter. Knowing our strategy is one thing, avoiding it is another. He will die, and you will be mine! ...Enjoy your front row seat to your boyfriend's demise." Laughing, he saunters away to a better spot to watch the fight.

There are only twelve werewolves left, but I can see that Nathan is about to drop. He's lost a lot of blood. Thinking quickly, I cause a large gust of wind to blow burning embers onto the wolves, the flames licking at their fur. Howling, half of them concentrate on putting out the flames, making them easy targets for Nathan. Six left. He starts slowly backing away from them- towards me. I swallow the fear rising in my throat and try to trust him. I desperately hope he can win. While backing toward me, he stumbles, and I scream as a werewolf leaps at him. Luckily, he kills it, but I can see that he's exhausted. Then I look down and see the hilt of a sword lying at my feet. It looks just like the sword Nathan is using. *What? How... oh. Nathan must have kicked it over to me while he was fighting... it must have been when he stumbled. Good thing they dumped out our backpacks. But what does he expect me to be able to do? I'm tied up and can't get loose...*

Nathan is now very close to me- bringing ravenous werewolves with him. As I watch, Nathan suddenly spins on his heel and swings the sword. It severs the ropes around my arms, freeing them. He then continues to fight the werewolves, finishing the spin with fluid movements. Wolf hasn't noticed that anything happened yet. Leaning down, I scoop up the sword, press the button, and slice through the ropes around my legs. I'm free! Jumping forward and using the element of surprise, I help Nathan kill the other six. Swinging around, though, I unexpectedly come face-to-face with Wolf. Gasping, I back up a step and stand back to back with Nathan as the rest of the pack closes in on us, completely encircling us.

His voice calm and cool, Nathan says, "There. I killed them all. Now let us go, or we'll be forced to kill the rest of you as well."

Wolf growls angrily, taking a menacing step towards us. I force myself not to move. "I don't think so." He smiles; a gruesome thing with yellow fangs. "You see, we never let our prisoners go, regardless of what we tell them. Not to mention that you cheated. But we see that the girl is too much trouble, plus you alone will hardly fill our bellies tonight. So we will kill and eat you first, letting her watch, as we always do. But then we will eat her alive."

I almost pass out from the overwhelming fear rising in me, but I force it down and think. *What Gifts might be able to help me here? Ugh, I don't even remember all of them... my brain just isn't functioning... Most of them probably wouldn't do the trick, not with how many of them there are in the first place.* I then remember that Charm is a Gift, and it seems to me to be the least likely to cause terrible backlash if it fails, so I give it a shot. Ironically, it's easier than trying to Charm Vlad.

Lowering my sword, I step forward and smile winningly, trying my best to be like Jake. Nathan notices. "What are you doing?" he hisses.

I ignore him. Batting my eyelashes and lowering my head submissively, I whisper to Wolf charmingly, "Are you sure you want to eat me? Just think of what you would be doing. Don't you want me to stay here, with you?" My soft, calming voice causes Wolf to visually relax, the tension going out of his muscles. He grins like an idiot and starts nodding. One of the other werewolves steps up to him.

"Yeah, I want that girl! Let's just eat the boy!" But this angers Wolf- he wants me for himself. The thought almost makes me throw up, but I hold it back. That would certainly ruin the Charm I somehow have been able to create. The jealous pack leader pounces on the other werewolf and cuts his throat with one swipe of his mighty claws.

Looking around at the rest of the pack, his claws and hand/paw covered in blood, he growls, "Anyone else want her? She's mine!" A fight then ensues, and Nathan and I are able to sneak away, avoiding attention. We grab our backpacks, scooping as much as we can back into them, and begin running. We run for about a mile before we stop to breathe. Once we stop panting, Nathan looks at me and starts laughing. I join in as well, the sweet relief of not getting killed and eaten by those things making me giddy.

"That was brilliant!" Nathan gasps, sitting on a rock. I sit next to him, still laughing lightly. "I had no idea what you were doing at first, but holy cow it worked! You almost had *me* fighting for you too! I didn't even think of trying to use a Gift- I was too panicked! I didn't know you had the Charming Gift! That's amazing!"

"I don't- well, it's not my actual Gift," I explain. "I just tried it and hoped it would work. I almost threw up, though, so I can't believe they bought it!" We laugh for another moment before continuing into the forest. To cover our scent and move faster, we both shapeshift into panthers and run through the woods, our backpacks held in our jaws. We go until we're too exhausted and have to change back, then collapse just as the sun starts to rise.

I wake up around noon. Hungry, I decide to make breakfast even though it's past that time. Just as it's finishing, Nathan wakes up. Seeing the food, he starts to protest, but I stop him, and he apologizes and thanks me for making a meal for us. We eat, then continue to move toward the rock. We are quite a bit closer than when I fell asleep on Nathan's back when he was a horse, plus we need to talk, so we walk for a while.

"What happened after I fell asleep yesterday?" I ask him. He grimaces.

"Well, about an hour or so later, as far as I could tell, there was suddenly this sweet smell carried on the wind. I didn't think much of it at the time, but it made me drowsy. It affected you worse, though. You didn't wake up, even after you fell off of my back onto a rock. Then I knew something was wrong. I tried getting you to wake up, to get on my back, anything. You didn't respond, and your breathing was shallow. I turned back into myself and tried to wake you up, but the only thing that happened is… your heart stopped." He swallows, his voice cracking. "I… started it again without too much trouble, then looked around to try to find something or someone to help. All I found, though, was a rock flying at my head. I ducked under the first one, but another followed right behind it. Behind the flying rocks, I caught a glimpse of yellow, but that was all."

I stare at him. He stops and looks at me. "What is it?" he asks, confused.

"It all makes sense now," I murmur, continuing to walk. Nathan follows. "The yellow team- whoever they are- set us up. They knew the werewolves were nearby- thanks to Vlad, I'm sure- so they made sure that we couldn't escape!" Anger fills my voice. "They tried to kill us!" Nathan tries to calm me down, but it takes a good twenty minutes for my blood to stop boiling. It's only then that I can finally get my thoughts together.

"Wait… the other teams! They could be almost to the Zyloff! We have to hurry!" Since it's my turn again, I try to use the weather, but nothing happens.

Nathan looks at me. "I guess you're done experimenting with that one. Here, I'll do it."

"No! I'll try something else." Deciding on shapeshifting, I try to think of the fastest traveling animal. *Well, flying is faster than running… but what animal is large and strong enough to carry Nathan too?* The only thing that comes to mind is a dragon. I've only ever seen drawings of them, but I'm hoping it will be enough. Concentrating, I feel my skin hardening into scales and wings sprouting from my back. Next, a tail erupts from my tail-bone, spikes grow from my spine, and claws from my fingers and toes. Next thing I know, I'm a proud, mighty dragon.

I leap into the sky, reveling in the power of my new body… and getting lost to it. I only remember who I really am and what I'm supposed to be doing when I look down and spot Nathan, far below. I catch his words. "Crystal! Come back! You aren't actually a dragon- don't lose yourself to it!

We have to go!" It all comes back to me at once, and I am in complete control of myself. I suppress the draconic instincts and dive back to the clearing where I left him. I land beside him and crouch so he can climb on with the backpacks. I never realized how small people are compared to dragons, but I realize as Nathan clambers up my scales that I could hold him in my hand without a problem.

He doesn't seem to weigh much, either. I barely notice him on me with my new strength. Soaring through the air, we get rapidly closer to the jagged cliffs. It only takes about twenty minutes to fly there, although had we been walking, it would have taken the rest of the day. I land about halfway up and turn back into myself since the dragon instincts were threatening to take back over. Looking around, I don't see anyone, but when I switch my eyes into dragon eyes, I can vaguely see four teams gaining on us. Two are flying with their partner, as Nathan and I had. Another group is a blur as they race towards us. I catch a glimpse of red between the trees as well. Ham and Sierra. But one team is missing. I don't stop to wonder what happened to them, concentrating on climbing after Nathan instead. When we get close to the top, I smell blood.

Finally cresting the ridge at the top, my head is almost taken off by a gigantic tail flying past. Nathan is already flat against the rock, so he avoided it as well. My eyes instinctively follow the tail up the feathery body. Before I can stop myself, my eyes lock onto the Zyloff's. I'm instantly paralyzed and I can barely even think. I vaguely remember Thaddeus saying to me, *"When it's full grown, it can paralyze and even kill you with a mere glance..."*

I wonder if I'm dying... I can barely finish the thought. I suddenly feel myself starting to... float out of my body. I still can't move. I cast out with my thoughts, groping to find something to hang onto. I latch myself onto the mind of the Zyloff, of all things. I then find myself not in my own body, but in the Zyloff's. I fight it, but it's like being pulled into a whirlpool. I can't resist it.

I realize then that I can control the Zyloff's body- my will is stronger. Looking down through its eyes, I see myself, slumped and lifeless on the rock. Nathan is kneeling next to me, shouting. I can't hear his words through the Zyloff's ears- they're too weak- but it's clear he's devastated. While I'm distracted, the Zyloff takes back over itself and turns and attacks a person dressed in blue. I recognize Roxane Hernandez, the goth girl. The Zyloff bites her, one of its large fangs piercing her stomach. She doubles over, blood gushing over her hands. Horrified, I find myself powerless to do anything. Luckily, an outraged Lloyd *does* do something. Rushing forward, he stabs the mother Zyloff in the heart as it's still bent over the dying Roxane.

I gasp and find myself back in my own body. I look up and see Nathan leaning over me, tears in his eyes. His look of utter loss is replaced with wonder and joy as he witnesses my return to life.

"How…" he stammers, confused. I sit up, wobbling, and almost fall off the edge of the cliff. Luckily, Nathan catches me and gently pulls me away from the edge. The dying screams of the Zyloff screech in my ears, immediately giving me a headache.

Looking back up at Nathan, I see the question and disbelief in his eyes and simply say, "I'll tell you later." Looking even more confused, he finally nods, accepting this.

We both look up as Lloyd shouts, "Hey! Look out!" and see a great wall of feathers bearing down on us. Nathan shoves me out of the way, but isn't quite quick enough to escape the body of the Zyloff himself.

"Nathan!" I scream, lurching forward. Because of my weakened body, I fall, but I pick myself back up and keep moving regardless. It's slow going, so Lloyd gets there first. He glances at Nathan, then looks at me and shakes his head, implying that he's dead.

"No… NO!!!" I shout, unable to believe it. Finally reaching the great feathery serpent, I crawl over its wings to the other side. I find Nathan's limp hand sticking out from under the body. "No…" I whisper, feeling the world close in around me. I begin weakly trying to pry the beast off of him, but it doesn't budge. I look to Lloyd, desperate for aid.

He sees my pain and decides to help, though it's obvious he thinks it's futile. He transforms into a rhinoceros and strains against the gigantic body. He is finally able to push it off the cliff. I reach forward, trembling, to grasp one of Nathan's hands in mine. It's already beginning to grow cold.

"No… Nathan…" I am then lost for words. My mind shuts down, and all I can do is look at his face and cry. My eyes turn into dragon eyes, as they sometimes do when I lose control of my emotions. My tears splash on his face. I close my eyes and change them back to my normal ones. I can't do it. He's gone.

A rasping voice then says my name. Opening my eyes, I fix them on Nathan's face. His eyes flicker open and his hand grows warm again. I watch, amazed, as he groans my name again. He then sees me and smiles painfully. I smile back, tears still in my eyes. I hear a disbelieving gasp behind me. "That's... that's not possible," Lloyd stammers. He comes up and kneels beside me. I don't even turn my head, soaking in Nathan's face- his alive, smiling face- instead. "He... I swear he was dead..."

"Really?" Nathan rasps. "Then it's good to be back. ...Roxane?" He inquires.

Looking at Lloyd, I see pain clearly in his eyes. "She's... gone. For good." His voice breaks and he looks away, hiding tears. It seems the two had grown close after all. I help Nathan to sit up. He looks at me.

"Now I know how you feel, coming back to life. It really takes it out of you, doesn't it?" I nod, laughing a little. He chuckles weakly in return.

Something large, round, and white is then placed in front of me. Looking up, I see Lloyd. His smile is more of a grimace. "Let's finish this thing before the other teams come. I hate it here. We got what we came for- let's go. ...I'll help you two get down and away from the other contestants, seeing as you were both dead. But beyond that, I have to help myself."

"I understand," I say to him gratefully. "Thank you. I don't know how we'll ever repay you..." He shakes his head before transforming into a giant black bird.

"You'd better get him on me, and climb on yourself. Please grab my egg as well. The others are almost here. Let's avoid as much bloodshed as possible, shall we?" I agree. After struggling to help Nathan get on his back, I climb on myself, an egg in each arm. Lloyd jumps off the cliff, soaring into the air just as the yellow team, Odette and Frazer, arrive at the top. They stare at Nathan and me in disbelief. I guess they thought the werewolves would kill us. I glare at them, although we've already moved out of their sight.

We fly through the night and get about halfway to our platform before Lloyd finally stops. He falls asleep almost immediately after he changes back, and Nathan does as well. It's not so easy for me, since my mind was still racing from what happened in the last couple of days. First werewolves, then I 'die,' witness Roxane dying, Nathan dies... it's a lot all at one time. All I know for sure is that I now hate these 'Games' more than ever, and can't wait to go home.

Leaning back against a tree, I try to calm myself down. Reaching down to my boot, I pull the blue-green feather out and hold it in my hand. It's miraculous that after all that commotion, it stayed intact, lodged in my boot. As I study it, I wonder what kind of bird it might have come from. It's a very large feather, so I can only assume it came from a giant bird. Almost without noticing, I slip into sleep. My dreams are filled with large blue-green birds and human-like shadows riding them.

I wake up before the other two do, so I make breakfast. After eating, we split up. Lloyd flies off toward his light, and we go to ours. Nathan transforms into a giant bird himself, and off we go. We reach the place that we started from just as the sun is setting once more. Cradling the egg, I step onto the platform with Nathan right behind me. The instant we're both on it, a gun goes off; probably the same one that got us started. A few minutes later, it goes off again, and I can only assume that means that Lloyd got back to his platform safely as well.

Half an hour later, it goes off one more time. I hope it was for Sierra and Ham, not the jerks on the Yellow team, Odette and Frazer. I briefly wonder how long they'll keep us here now that they have their winners.

A sharp sting answers my question.

9

"Crystal? Nathan?" I hear a voice piercing through the darkness, bringing me back to alertness. The voice sounds vaguely familiar, but I can't seem to place it. Opening my eyes, they slowly focus on a boy's face looming over me. It takes me a second to put the name with the face.

"Lloyd," I murmur. He looks relieved.

"Oh, good, you're awake. There's someone here who wants to talk to you." He steps back, and I sit up to locate my visitor. Thaddeus stands at the door of the hospital room. He comes up to me with a big smile on his face and puts a hand on my shoulder. "Well done! You behaved magnificently. Although, looking into the Zyloff's eyes was a huge mistake that by all rights should have gotten you killed."

"I know," I say ashamedly. "I didn't know what I was doing until it happened... and I honestly don't really know what happened after, either." So I describe to him, Lloyd, and Nathan what happened after I looked into the creature's eyes. All three stare at me, disbelief written clearly on Lloyd and Nathan's faces, although Thaddeus's thoughts are difficult for me to gauge without the help of my dragon eyes. "It's true," I mutter, looking down at the sheets clenched under my hands.

"I believe you," Thaddeus says, looking into the distance with a strange look- one hiding something. "It's just... I have only heard of one other instance in which that happened- to the Queen, actually. And she only told two people- the King and I. I suggest that you don't share this with anyone else, as it will only make you a greater target. Especially don't tell Vladimir." He turns to Lloyd. "Please do not tell anyone either, young man." He nods solemnly, promising to keep my secret.

"Wait, why not tell Vlad? I mean, I'm not complaining, but wouldn't I normally have to tell him about such things since he's my advisor?" I ask. Thaddeus shakes his head gravely, sighing heavily.

"No, I don't think that you should in this case. Normally he would need to know, but..."

"But what?" Nathan asks, sounding concerned.

"...It's nothing that you should be concerned about; it's just... I have noticed that he hasn't been himself lately. Ever since... well, the first day you were here. Do you remember how he didn't show up as he promised?"

"Yes, of course," Nathan responds. "But what does that have to do with anything?" Lloyd watches us, both confusion and curiosity on his face, but he doesn't interrupt, opting to listen silently instead.

"Well, I saw him just a few minutes after I sent you off to the square, and he seemed... confused and disoriented. He asked me what he was supposed to be doing. It was... strange. I've been watching him closely ever since, and he's been acting differently. I have a feeling something happened to him early that morning or the night before, but he refuses to tell me anything." There's silence for a few moments as we all ponder this.

"So, what happens now?" Nathan asks. "Will they let us recover before we have to keep training?"

"Yes," Thaddeus responds. "In a way. You have the rest of the day to recuperate, and then you three will go to the square to receive your prizes because you are the winners of the First Challenge. Then you will have two weeks until the next Challenge, during which time you will be training with Vladimir and I. The details won't be finalized until next week, however, so in the meantime, we will focus on general preparations. Any other questions?"

"Yeah," Lloyd finally chimes in. "Can I hang out with Crystal and Nathan today? I don't have anyone to hang out with anymore... provided you'll have me, of course," he adds to Nathan and I.

"Of course!" I respond with a soft smile. My heart hurts for him, having just lost his partner in an unfair and bloody Challenge.

"And," he continues, "What will become of me in the Games? I'm out now that my partner is... gone... right?"

"Yes," Thaddeus replies, sympathy in his voice. "I'm afraid you are now disqualified. You will, however, still be required to stay here and observe the rest of the Games and continue to work on finding your Gifts, although it seems you have already discovered one. Congratulations on your shapeshifting abilities! Ah, and you are, of course, welcome to do whatever you like for the rest of the day, the contestants are not required to stay separated."

After that, Thaddeus leaves, and we get dressed and head out into the Village. We get far more attention than we'd like, so we quickly escape to the woods. I promise myself that I'll leave if anything suspicious happens or if we get too drowsy this time.

We find a patch of trees to sit under, and for a while, we just lay next to each other in companionable silence. The grass underneath us is soft and green, the trees above us tall and beautiful, and the sky is free of clouds. Birds dance above our heads, singing happily. Everything is peaceful.

It feels too perfect and surreal after what we've now been through, and it sets me on edge. Before what happened in the arena, I would have no problem relaxing, but now... I just can't let go of my worries. I can tell that my companions feel the same way- especially Lloyd.

We soon get up and begin moving deeper into the forest, exploring since we can't seem to sit still anymore. None of us have the heart to explore, though, despite Nathan trying to cheer us up. He brings me some flowers he finds and gives Lloyd a cool looking rock as well. We smile and thank him, but we are still numb from the traumatizing experiences that we went through just the day before. He gives up after a while.

Around noon, we get hungry but have no desire to go back to the village. Luckily, Lloyd thought ahead and had brought a backpack with food in it, so we have a little picnic. While we're eating, some birds fly down and begin harassing us for food. We toss pieces of bread at them, calming them momentarily- until other birds flock us, fighting to get the bread. Laughing, we quickly put the rest of the food back into the back-pack and run from the birds, hands over our heads. After a minute or two, they leave, resigning themselves to the fact that they wouldn't be getting any more food.

Turning, we find ourselves at the mouth of a vast cave. We impulsively decide to explore it. It's dark inside, but I brought my glowing sword, so we can at least see immediately around us. Feeling reckless, Lloyd begins yelling into the cave, daring anything living in it to come out and face us. Nathan and I soon join in. When we stop, it takes a while for the echoes to finally come bouncing back to us. The cave must be enormous. The light from my sword doesn't hit any walls or a ceiling, so we can't really tell just how big it is.

A few minutes later, an animal's cry comes echoing from deeper inside the cave. We don't know what it is, but we're ready to find out. The sound comes again. It sounds like something is wailing and mourning. It also sounds young.

After a while, the sounds suddenly cease. I'm then abruptly knocked onto my back as something hard flies into my stomach. My sword spins away and my breath comes out of my lungs in one massive gasp from the impact. Lloyd grabs it before it slips into a hole in the floor of the cave. I hear Nathan saying something, but I'm busy with whatever just rammed into me. Cautiously reaching up with my hands, I feel something scaly, yet soft; similar to a snake. I then hear the mourning sound again, only much softer. It's coming from the creature on my chest. I call Lloyd over to me. When the sword is close enough, I can make out the figure in my arms; and so can Nathan. He gasps.

"It's... it's a baby dragon!"

I nod, looking at the poor thing. It's so small, I figure it must have been born not too long ago- maybe even as recently as the last day or two. It seems to be heartbroken; devastated. I sit up, taking it off my chest and setting it in my lap. The light of the sword sparkles off the dragon's bright blue eyes as it gazes up at me. My heart instantly melts. It's adorable, and clearly in need of help.

Lloyd then speaks up. "You know we can't keep that thing, right? You can't exactly march back into the Village carrying a dragon in your arms. Not only would Vlad never let you keep it; it's a dragon. It's not a pet in the first place. In fact, knowing how Vlad has been acting lately, he would probably put it to death right in front of you just to spite you."

"Well, what am I supposed to do?" I plead, holding tight to the baby, which croons as if agreeing with me. "I can't just leave it here to die!"

"Sure… but maybe it wouldn't die," Nathan says, joining the conversation. We look at him, confused. "It has to have a mom, right? I know the dads don't always stick around to raise their kids, but Thaddeus said the moms do. So, let's find the mother."

"Yeah," Lloyd agrees. "She's probably just a little further in."

I sigh, reluctant to let the baby go. "Wait," I say, realizing something. "If the mom's close, then wouldn't she have attacked us by now?"

"Maybe she didn't notice us yet," Nathan suggests unconvincingly. "… Or maybe she can't for some reason. Maybe it's stuck somewhere."

"Either way, we should find it and give that dragon back," Lloyd says, settling it. I stand up, cradling it in my arms, and join my friends as they begin walking again. The little dragon settles into my arms, rubbing its head against my arm happily. *I should name it so I don't keep calling it… well, it.* I think for a bit, going through names until I think of one that fits. Finally, I decide to name him Eric.

We find the mom only a few yards away from where the baby tackled me. As we draw closer, the light from the sword reveals the huge, unmoving heap of scales. Fearlessly walking forward, I gently lay my hand on her side. Nathan and Lloyd gasp, taking an instinctive step towards me. Her side is rapidly growing cold. She couldn't have been dead for long. A terrible smell then reaches my nose. Gagging, I look to the right and see a bloody heap of raw meat.

"What is that?" Lloyd asks, covering his nose and mouth with his hand. "That doesn't smell like fresh game should."

"Maybe it was poisoned somehow?" I guess. "Whatever is wrong with it, it's probably what killed the mom."

The saddest part of the whole scene, however, we see only after moving around the body and take note of what she's curled protectively around. Lying close to her belly are the two unmoving bodies of Eric's siblings- they are different shades of green, although both are pretty close to Eric's dark coloring. Distraught, I look away. Poor little Eric. He must have survived thanks to being the runt and being the last to get any food. He leaps out of my arms and races over to one of the small bodies, nudging it with his snout. He turns and looks at me pleadingly, but there's nothing I can do. I pick Eric back up and gently pull him away from his dead family.

When we leave the cave, we see that the sun is nearing the horizon. I still have baby Eric in my arms, although I don't know what to do with him since, as pointed out by Lloyd earlier, I can't take him with me.

"I know!" I suddenly exclaim. "I'll find a smaller cave closer to the Village where I can hide Eric. I can come and feed him, take care of him, and everything! I'll come every morning, afternoon, and night!"

"Eric?" Nathan questions.

"I don't know…" Lloyd slowly says, contemplating. "You could easily be caught. Not only that, but do you really think that the drag- Eric- will stay put? Plus, you don't even know what it'll eat."

"Oh, stop being so pessimistic," I laugh. "I'll figure it out. And don't worry, I'll make sure that no one follows me when I leave. No one will even notice."

"Yeah…" Nathan adds, slowly nodding. "And I'll cover for you when you leave."

"Really?" I say, pleased and surprised.

"Really," he smiles at me.

Lloyd looks back and forth between Eric and I. "Sure, but that's the easy part. How are you going to get him to stay in the same spot until you come back?"

"I've been thinking about that," I reply. "And the only thing I could think of is that I could try to talk to him with my mind." They both stare at me, but I block them out, focusing on the dragon in my arms. Kneeling, I set Eric on a rock in front of me. He cocks his head and looks at me curiously with his big blue eyes. Smiling, I send my thoughts toward him like I had when I had transformed into a dragon and couldn't speak with my mouth.

I'm not sure if it will work, but I try anyway. *"Eric?"* I think to him, hoping he with both hear and understand me. *"Eric, can you hear me?"* His eyes widen and his wings flutter. I feel his thoughts in my head. Since he's a baby, he can't talk with words yet, but I can feel what he wants to tell me. He's happy with his name, and glad that I'm here with him. I then feel a sudden, intense hunger. It takes me a minute to realize that it's Eric's hunger that I'm feeling.

Turning to Nathan, I ask him to get me a strip of meat left over from our lunch, as well as the water bottle with milk in it. He pulls them out and hands them to me, looking more than a little skeptical. With meat in one hand and milk in the other, I extend both hands to Eric and offer him the strip of meat. He sniffs it, then pushes it away. I thought he might do this, since he's probably too young to have meat, so I show him the bottle of milk.

Putting this beneath his nose, he sniffs at it, then licks it, trying to get to the milk inside. Laughing, I ask Lloyd to get me a plate. When he does, I fill it with milk and set it in front of Eric. It's warm now, but he begins licking it up just the same, much like a cat. When he finishes, he happily climbs back into my lap and falls asleep. His thoughts tell me that he's content and happy. Looking up at my companions, I see that Lloyd has given up. He sighs.

"Alright, fine. Maybe you *can* do this. ...At least until the next Challenge. What are you going to do then?" I look at him, pleading with my eyes. He catches on to the question I'm trying to ask him.

"What? No! No no no no no! I'm NOT going to take care of that thing while you go on the Challenge! I'm not going to risk getting in trouble for a wild animal!" I continue to plead with him with my eyes. He finally gives in, sighing. "Huh. Fine, you win. But ONLY until you get back from the next Challenge. After that, we'll have to see."

"Thank you!" I exclaim, jumping up to give him a one-armed hug while still holding Eric in the other. He sighs again.

"Well, let's just find a new home for the little guy- and fast!" I look up and see that the sun has almost touched the horizon. We have less than an hour left before we're supposed to be back at the Town Square. We dash down the hill and through the trees. A five-minute walk from the edge of the trees, I finally find the perfect little cave. Setting Eric down, I wake him up and tell him, *"Don't worry. I'll be back in the morning. Okay? Will you stay here until I come back?"* To make sure he understands, I also send an image of me walking towards him once the sun has come up. With a sleepy yawn, I sense from his thoughts that he will wait.

Running with Nathan and Lloyd, we make it back to the Square in the nick of time. Panting, I stop before entering the crowd, attempting to fix my frizzled hair. Then, taking a deep breath, I plunge into the crowded

Square with Nathan and Lloyd right behind me. The Villagers instantly identify me, and they all start talking at once, offering congratulations and asking questions. I ignore them, seeing Vlad coming up behind them. The crowd parts for him. Luckily, right then, Jake and Kat walk into the Square and are mobbed, leaving no one to pay attention to us.

Except for Vlad, that is. Coming up to me, he reaches into my hair and pulls out a leaf. Gulping, I look him in the eye. "I see that you went into the forest, although you have been specifically told to stay away from there, am I right?" He smiles sickeningly.

"I... um... I didn't go very far, plus Nathan and Lloyd were with me..."

"Perhaps," he sneers. "But now it's time for you to get your prize for winning the First Challenge," he says, leading Nathan and I up the stairs on the far right of the stage. Lloyd sits next to him, then Kat and Jake. On the other side of the stage, Vlad, Thaddeus, and Zelda sit down. Stepping up to the front of the stage is Nehru, dressed all in dark purple- the color of the winning team. Looking over at the advisors, I see that they are all color coded to their team as well. Vlad is wearing blue since he advised Lloyd's team. Thaddeus is wearing a dark purple suit, and Zelda is wearing orange. *So Kat and Jake must have gotten the third egg. And their color is orange... I'll have to remember that.*

Clearing her voice, Nehru silences the crowd. "Welcome, one and all, to the First Challenge Rewards Assembly! We will start off by introducing your three winning teams! Please come up here with me... Crystal Shay!" My legs wobbling, I stand and walk over to stand next to Nehru. Smiling, she puts her arms around my shoulders comfortingly. She smells strongly of lilacs.

"Well, Ms. Shay. That was very impressive out there, I must say. Especially with the werewolves! You were so brave! Please, tell us. How did you feel? Were you even scared at all? Because it sure didn't look like it!" she chuckles.

I swallow hard, trying to find my voice. "I... well, I certainly didn't feel fearless. I was scared to death. I just did what I had to do, I guess." Nehru smiles.

"You sure did, and you were, once again, very impressive. I'm sure all the girls out there would love to be as brave as you were- am I right?" At this, there's a surprisingly loud cheer from the crowd. I can't believe that many people look up to me. "And boys... who wouldn't want her? Pretty as a flower, smart, brave, talented, determined, and loyal." At this, there is an even louder cheer. I'm blown away. I've never been liked before, but here... everyone seems to. They don't even know that I'm supposedly their lost Princess, either. I'm overwhelmed for a moment, but shove it down so I can concentrate.

"Thank you, Ms. Shay. You may have a seat. And will your partner now come up? Nathan Anderson!" I stumble back to my seat as Nathan stands and does pretty much the same thing I had to with Nehru. After him, Lloyd goes up. I was too numb to really hear what was going on with Nathan, but I'm a little better now, so I listen to what questions she asks Lloyd. "Well, Mr. Jewkes. That was quite an amazing performance there. I'm sure you also have many admirers now. Am I right?" The crowd explodes even more than it had for me. When they quiet down, Nehru continues. "And when Miss Hernandez died right in front of you... that must have been so hard."

"Yes," he responds, looking at the ground. He speaks so quietly, the mic has a hard time picking up his voice, so everyone goes silent and leans in, trying to catch his words. "Yes, it was hard. I had grown to know Roxane better than I thought I would in such a short time. We had even become friends. And I thought... I thought that maybe, after this whole thing was over that we could... still be friends." His voice diminishes even more, and we all strain to hear. "But then... that *monster*... it attacked while I was distracted by what happened to Crystal... and it..." he breaks off with a sob. Nehru lets him return to his seat.

Next, she calls for Kat. I don't listen closely to what she says, but there are some wolf whistles from the crowd. She tells Nehru that one of her Gifts had indeed grown in while she was in the Games. I discover that it was Charm. I'm not surprised. The same thing happens with Jake, and he tells her he predicts that one of his Gifts would be Strength once it officially grew in. Looking over at Lloyd, I see that he has collected himself and is no longer crying softly- which is good, because our advisors are now done being interviewed as well, and have each been given two packages- except for Vlad since there's only Lloyd left on the blue team. The advisors place the containers in a group before us. Thaddeus comes up to us.

"Now you pick. As the winners, you two get to go first. You each will pick one package, and then sit down and wait for the rest to select theirs. You will all open them at the same time. Okay? Oh, and be careful with it," he adds with a wink. We nod, stepping up to the packages. Not knowing what to grab, I close my eyes and take the first one I touch. When I pick it up, it seems to shift a little- though it may just be my imagination. Nathan follows me, selecting the nearest box. We sit and watch as Lloyd goes up and picks one, followed by Kat and Jake. At Nehru's signal, we all begin opening our packages. It's a box with holes in it. Curious, I lift the lid and am stunned by what I see inside. Reaching in carefully, I pull out my gift. I hear a collective gasp from the crowd as the red-tailed hawk on my arm flaps its wings and lets out a cry. I suddenly feel its thoughts enter my mind. I'm surprised by how intelligent it feels.

"Greetings, Crystal Dragon. I can see that you are confused. Allow me to explain. I am your reward for completing the First Challenge. My name is Nora, and I am here to help you on all of your future Challenges- in the Games or otherwise. I am trained as an advisor, message carrier, spy, and hunter, although I can and will do anything else that you are in need of assistance with."

...Wow, I think, amazed at the bird on my forearm. Looking at it with my eyes, it seems normal, but talking to it with my mind, it's evident that it's not. No ordinary bird is that smart. Looking over at Nathan, I see that he has a large rat. Lloyd has an adorable puppy, Kat has- go figure- a cat. And surprisingly, looks exceptionally dismayed by it. Jake is just pulling out a flying squirrel. It appears we all have a new pet.

"We are not pets!" I hear Nora's voice echoing indignantly in my mind. *"We are here to help you, not entertain you! We are called Familiars. Most of our kind aid witches and wizards of high status among the realms, but my companions and I volunteered to aid you in your quest to discover your Gifts. And I am most pleased to have the opportunity to aid you, Princess Dragon,"* she adds, bowing to me, her wings outstretched for balance. I blush, aware that others are watching with dumbstruck, confused, and envious looks on their faces. *"I did not dare to hope that I would one day have the privilege to serve one such as you. But there are some things you are not to ask me to do, and one of those is to attack another Familiar."*

"All... alright..." I think back to her, still overwhelmed that I have a hawk- and one that can talk, at that! I look at Nathan. He seems even more confused than I am.

"I... I have a rat... that can talk..." he stammers.

"What's his name?" I ask, trying to get him to calm down. It seems to work, a little.

"Greg," he replies, glancing at my hawk. "What's your hawk's name?"

"She's Nora," I respond proudly. "Isn't it awesome that we have Familiars to help us out now?" I say, excited and happy. He nods, still a little overwhelmed. Looking over at Jake, I see that Kat has convinced him to trade her Familiars. I start laughing as I realize that Kat doesn't like cats. Nathan, after realizing what I'm laughing at, begins laughing with me. Turning to the audience, I see that quite a few of them are chuckling as well.

Finally, Nehru bids us goodnight and lets us go home. Nathan and I gladly head back to our house and get some sleep after our long day.

10

I force myself to get up before sunrise. Groaning, I roll out of bed and wake Nora. She stretches and seems perfectly fine with being awake so early in the morning. I'm jealous. My eyes are burning, begging me to climb back into bed. Resisting, I head over to the window and look out. The sky is getting light, but the sun hasn't come up over the mountains yet. I quickly get dressed and go to the bathroom, splashing some cold water on my face to help me wake up. I then put on my boots, noticing Nathan stirring while I do so.

"Morning," I greet him.

He opens his eyes and looks at me inquisitively. "Up so soon?" He swings his legs out of bed, his body spinning to face me as he does so.

"Yep. I need to check on Eric before we go train with Thaddeus."

"Are you taking Nora with you?"

"Yeah, I figure she'll want to stretch her wings and hunt for something for breakfast."

"And what are *you* going to do for breakfast?" he asks.

"I'll go see the cook near the square that we've gone to before. She seems to cook mostly for the contestants, so I'm sure she'll get me something."

"Alright," he sighs. "I guess I'll stay here and cover for you in case somebody comes looking for you. I'll probably say something about you getting to know your Familiar, and maybe throw in that you had nightmares to explain why you're doing it so early."

"Thanks," I say, grabbing my backpack. "It really does mean a lot to me. ...I'm forgetting something..." I murmur, slowly spinning in a circle, trying to identify it. "Oh! Milk for Eric," I suddenly remember. I quickly head to our kitchen, pulling out a water bottle and filling it with milk, like before. I also grab a small bowl so Eric can feed himself and put everything into the backpack. I wave goodbye to Nathan as I head out the door.

It's chillier outside than I expected, but I just pull my jacket closer and keep walking, heading toward the pillar of smoke coming from Paula's cooking stand by the Square. When I get there, I am greeted by the happy chef.

"Crystal! I see you're up early," she says, chuckling merrily as she dishes steaming hot eggs and sausage on a plate.

"Yeah, I couldn't sleep," I respond, accepting the plate.

"And getting to know your new Familiar as well, I see," she comments while flipping pancakes. "A fine one you've got there, too. I know I'm jealous!" she chuckles.

"Yeah, I'm a lucky girl," I mutter, fighting the urge to remind her that I only got the bird because I managed to not die in the stupid Games these people were forcing me to go through. Lucky wasn't really the word I would use to describe my life-or-death situation. I head over to a table set up beside the stand and wolf down the food before the wind steals away its heat. After returning the dishes, I head towards the woods.

"Who is Eric?" Nora asks, riding on my shoulder.

"You'll see," I respond. "...Would you be so kind as to see if I'm being followed? I... want to be alone."

"Of course, Princess," she replies, launching into the air. After a few minutes, she returns. "No one is near. You will be able to slip into the woods completely unnoticed."

"Thank you."

Ten minutes later, I reach the cave where I hid Eric. Nora hops off my shoulder and follows as I crouch and enter Eric's new home. I blink as my eyes adjust. I feel another mind touch mine and I can sense joy at my presence. Smiling, I kneel down and scratch under Eric's jaw. He wriggles with pleasure at my touch.

Reaching back, I pull the bowl out of my backpack and place it in front of him. He sniffs it curiously, then reels back in surprise as I pour in some milk. He licks some off his snout and gets excited, thrusting his face into the bowl. While he's eating, I explain to Nora how I came to find Eric.

"So you're raising him?" she asks, disbelieving.

"Well, yes. What else could I do? Just let him die?"

"No... I just think that perhaps a wiser choice would be to tell Thaddeus about him and let him help you return him to his own kind."

"Well... I'll do that eventually, but right now he needs me, and I can't be sure what Thaddeus would do if I told him. I'll take care of him until he can take care of himself. After that... I'll see what I can do about returning him," I reply, my thoughts shadowed by fear of what the adult dragons would do to me if they saw me with a dragon baby. They would probably kill me without taking the time to question me.

"Very well. I'll not argue with you, just help you to do what you believe to be right."

"Thank you," I respond, relieved to have a friend who won't fight with me about all of my decisions.

Eric, having finished eating, is now nuzzling at my hand. Smiling, I tickle him under his wings. He rolls around, cooing happily. I continue to play with him for a few minutes, but soon enough my time is up. Putting everything back in my backpack except the bowl, I try to explain to Eric that I will be back around noon. He's not pleased, but he accepts it and lays back down on the rock, closes his eyes, and begins his waiting.

I feel awful, but what else can I do? I quickly jog back to the house, Nora flying above me. I leave the backpack there and head out with Nathan to train with Thaddeus. At lunch, I eat as fast as I can before running back to the hut to retrieve food for Eric. Back in the woods, I play with him and feed him, managing to return in time for training with Vlad. That part of my day isn't as unpleasant as I expected it to be, since he just coldly instructs me on how to properly care for my Familiar.

Then it's training with Thaddeus and Nathan again. We do weaponry, and I do reasonably well, especially considering my thoughts are elsewhere. After that is dinner and feeding Eric again. Nathan is already asleep by the time I get back.

This is my life for the next week- and it's starting to get to me. Nathan brings it up as we are heading to train with Thaddeus that morning. "This isn't good for you. You're exhausted!" I start protesting, but he stops me before I can even get going. "No, don't try to argue. It's true, and you know it. If you keep this up, you're going to drop soon."

"It's true," Nora chimes in. *"I'm concerned about you. You aren't well. You need to take a break and get some sleep."*

"Gosh, thanks for the vote of support," I grumble. I'm in a bad mood as well- too much stress, I guess. Nathan walks in front of me and stops, forcing me to halt as well. He puts his hands on my shoulders and looks me in the eyes.

"I *am* trying to support you," he says. His hazel eyes convey his concern for me, softening my stubborn heart. "I just want to help you. You shouldn't have to do this all by yourself. Let me take the morning shift, at least." I hesitate. "Please. You need to rest. I'm not saying you have to get rid of him or anything, I think- I know- that you need help."

I sigh and give in. He's sweet to want to help, but it's hard to give up some of my time with little Eric. "Fine. I'll let you help. But only in the mornings. Okay?"

He looks relieved and releases me. "Good. Another thing, though," he continues as we resume walking. "Your head isn't in the training anymore. I need you to pay attention- no offense- so we can win the Second Challenge. The Games can be over if we can manage to win three times in a row. Remember your little sister. You need to return to her. What would she do without you?"

That makes me feel horrible. I've been so preoccupied lately that I hadn't even had a spare moment to think about Kiki. I had completely forgotten about her. "Right. I'm sorry. I'll get my head in the game."

"Good. I need you, and so does Kiki." I nod gravely, my eyes on my feet as we walk.

Thaddeus is late again, so Nathan and I battle it out with the weapons once more. This time, I win easily. He seems to have lost his grace with the sword- his body must have moved on past that Gift. When Thaddeus arrives, he ushers us to the top of the building again. As we climb, he informs us that he had just been at the meeting to determine what the Second Challenge would be.

The point of this one is to reach the 'finish line.' From the way Thaddeus is talking about it, it sounds to me to be some kind of maze. At specific intervals, there will be a creature that will ask us a riddle. If we answer it correctly, we will be able to continue on the correct course. If we answer wrong, then we will be sent on another path that is longer and has an extra riddle as well.

"So basically, in order to win this Challenge, we need to be able to think outside the box," I state thoughtfully. Thaddeus nods.

Exactly. So we will concentrate on your mind for most of the next week. But you will still have to face the rest of the contestants. You will all be starting at different places around the arena, but there is only one finish line, and your paths may cross others' paths multiple times. We will need to make sure you can fight them off."

"Is there anything *else?*" Nathan asks sarcastically. I chuckle, but Thaddeus doesn't catch it.

"Well, yes," he replies seriously. It is also a race of who can get there first, so you will need to be fast. Your bodies will need to be able to endure exhaustion and keep on going strong, especially if you get into any fights."

When we leave for lunch, not only do my legs hurt, but my head as well from having to think about many different things in tons of different ways. After wolfing down my lunch and avoiding the other contestants, I head to the woods once again. Partway there, I am stopped by Jake. He's holding his cat- his Familiar. He grins at me slyly while his Familiar hisses at Nora, who's riding on my shoulder once more.

"And where are you going?" he questions, glancing at my backpack. I swallow, thinking fast.

I nonchalantly answer, "Oh, nothing that would concern you. I'm just taking Nora into the forest so she can catch something to eat. She prefers fresh meat, of course."

"...Of course," he slowly replies, implying that he doubts that I told him the full story. His cat moves its glare to me and hisses again. "Oh, don't mind her. Brianna's not in a very good mood today. Anyway," he continues with a wink, "I guess I'll see you around, Crystal." With that, he walks away. I breathe a sigh of relief, then continue towards the woods.

"I'm relieved he didn't insist on coming with me." Nora agrees.

When we reach the cave, I spot Eric crouching on top of it. Before I can say anything, he leaps off and into the grass. I hear a tiny squeak as he lands, and when I get closer, he looks up at me, grinning a toothy draconic smile. A small mouse is dangling from his jaws by its tail, dead. I'm speechless. As he leads the way back into the cave, I realize just how much he's grown. When I found him, he was about the size of a house cat. He is now double that, with more muscle in his legs and wings.

He takes the mouse and drops it at my feet, looking up at me with a proud look on his face as he waits expectantly for my reaction. I kneel down and scratch under his jaw, just like he like me to.

"Good job, Eric!" I congratulate him. "You're such a good dragon!"

I feel in his thoughts that he is pleased he impressed me, and suddenly, he forms a word in his mind and sends it to mine.

"Kysta…" I look down at him, astounded. He had almost gotten my name!

"Yes, Eric. It's Crystal."

"Er…ic?"

"Yes, that's your name. Good job, Eric!"

"Eric!" He bounces around the cave happily. He continues repeating our names. *"Eric! Kysta! Eric! Kysta! Eric!"* I laugh. Glancing at my watch, I see that my time with him is up. I pour him a little milk and start to leave.

"No! Kysta!" I sigh, sad to leave him. Maybe I'll ask Thaddeus for a break tomorrow so I can come and spend more time with little Eric. Scratching him under the jaw, I promise him that I'll be back tonight.

He pouts. *"Kysta no go!"* He insists. Downtrodden, I tell him to stay in the cave until it's dark so no one will see him. I then force myself to leave. His bright blue eyes follow me intently as I walk through the forest.

After training with Vlad and Thaddeus, I finally bring myself to ask him the question. Walking up to Thaddeus after he dismissed us for the day, I clear my throat. He turns around, looking surprised. "Yes?" he asks.

I swallow hard. "Um… I was wondering if I could take a break from training tomorrow?" My voice quivers from fear that he will say no or get mad at me for suggesting such a thing. Instead, he looks thoughtful.

"Yes, I suppose a short break is in order. I can see that you haven't been yourself for the past few days. I suppose you need a little time alone, yes?"

"Oh, yes! Thank you!" I beam, relieved. He smiles.

"Just make sure to be back the next morning. We have less than a week until the next Challenge."

"Of course!" I say, catching up to Nathan on his way down the stairs. "Thanks again!" He chuckles and watches me go.

When I've caught up to him, Nathan looks at me and says, "That's great and all, but remember that you aren't going early in the morning. I am. Just make sure to warn him first, okay? I don't want him attacking me."

I laugh. "Of course. But I'm not so sure he'll need you to come." He looks confused, so I explain about the mouse.

"So he can catch his own food, then? That's great! Does that mean he can eat meat now too?"

"I don't know," I say thoughtfully. "I would think so, but I didn't see him eat it. I guess I'll check tonight."

Sure enough, Eric ate the entire thing and drank some of the milk as well, although not all of it. I refill it and watch as he dances around, showing me again how he caught the mouse. I laugh, enjoying my time with him. I soon have to leave again, which makes him sad until he hears that I will be able to play with him all day tomorrow. Then he's quite excited, and I go home happy as well, looking forward to tomorrow for the first time since I got to Zilferia.

When I wake up, the sun is shining brightly through the windows. I sit up, feeling better than I have for weeks. Nathan has already left to train with Thaddeus, so I have some breakfast and prepare enough food for both Eric and me to last us the whole day. That way, I won't have to come back to the house until tonight. I don't grab anything for Nora since she prefers to hunt anyway.

I stroll to the woods, not hurrying, just enjoying the beautiful day and pleasant weather, which has cooled a little since I arrived in Zilferia. Nora takes off, searching for breakfast as I walk. When I enter the woods, I'm startled by a figure moving swiftly through the trees. Before I can react, there's an arm around my waist, pinning my arms down, and a hand over my eyes. I'm trapped in place and I can't see or move, but I don't panic. I simply wait for the personage to identify themselves. I hear a laugh from my attacker.

"Well, I expected you to lash out at me, at least. I see you've been working on controlling your emotions and patience. A handy thing for the Games, since you have to fight other human beings as well as wild, vicious creatures."

"Who are you?" I ask. The voice sounds a little like another I know... but I can tell they're disguising their true voice. He laughs again, and I figure it out. "Lloyd?" I cautiously probe. With another laugh, he releases me. I turn and discover that I was correct. He smiles at me, and it hits me once again how cute he is, with his blond hair and bright blue eyes. Now that I am closer to him, I see that his eyes have a thin gold outline around the pupil. My heart unexpectedly does a flip and I'm lost for words for a moment. Luckily, he talks instead, switching back to his normal voice.

"So, how's it going, Crystal? I see you got a break from training for a day. What are you planning on doing with it?" His happy voice hints at something and his eyes twinkle with eagerness.

"Well, I was going to spend the day with Eric, but you're more than welcome to come along as well. After all, we need to get Eric used to you before the next Challenge."

His eyes shine and I can tell he's pleased. "Sweet! I would love to spend the day with you." I notice he doesn't mention Eric. Smiling, I turn away so he doesn't see my blush. As we near Eric's cave, a dark green blur flies from the entrance and knocks Lloyd onto his back. He gasps in surprise.

"Who's afraid now?" I laugh, teasing him a little. I gently pull the snarling Eric from his shirt. He winces a little as his claws scrape over his skin again. His claws have pierced right through his shirt and he's bleeding. Now it's my turn to gasp. "Oh, I'm so sorry! I should have come before you and warned him..." Lloyd cuts me off, sitting up and holding up a hand to stop me.

"No, it's fine," he winces, his other hand on his wounded chest, trying to stop the bleeding. "It's alright. They're just scratches; it's nothing I can't handle." I'm not convinced, however. After setting Eric down and explaining to him that Lloyd's a friend, I turn my attention to his wounds.

I gently pull his hand off so I can examine it, but it's now covered in too much blood. I go to my backpack and grab a small washcloth, getting it wet with water from my water bottle and gently dab at the scratches, washing away the blood so I can see how bad it is. Lloyd grits his teeth from the pain, but he doesn't make a sound. "They're pretty deep, but they should be fine," I decide. "The only thing I'm worried about is them getting infected…"

He stands up and smiles at me, then reaches down, grabs the bottom of his shirt, and pulls it over his head. Getting what he's doing, I wrap it around his chest and tie it so it won't come undone. I try to ignore his lean, muscular body, but I can still feel my face getting red. Turning away from him, I return my attention to Eric. I sense from his thoughts that he's sorry he hurt Lloyd. I smile and suggest that he go over and apologize.

He walks toward Lloyd, trying to look as non-threatening as possible. I can see that Lloyd is still nervous, although he doesn't move away from the dragon. Eric stops and looks up at him, cocking his head to the side as if he's contemplating him. He then ambles forward and nudges at his hand with his head. A small smile starts creeping over Lloyd's face as he rubs Eric's head. Eric starts rumbling- his version of a purr, I guess, and leans into his hand.

After a couple minutes, Eric decides that he's had enough and stalks back to my side. Lloyd grins at me and stands. I do as well, little Eric perched carefully on my shoulder. It doesn't hurt, though, because he retracted his claws. *Hmm…* A sudden realization strikes me. *Eric is more like a house cat than a person would think. He has retractable claws, he 'purrs,' he eats like a cat, and is friendly and curious like most cats.* This is interesting, but I decide to think about it later.

"Okay, I guess he's not so bad," Lloyd admits. "…When he isn't attacking me, that is," he adds, scratching under his jaw, just where he likes it. He coos and wiggles so much that he falls off me. He's quick enough, however, that he manages to open his wings, so he glides to the ground rather than crashes into it.

He then runs around in circles and says to me, *"Come on, Kysta! Come!"* His language expands every day. Laughing, I follow him, Lloyd right beside me. I let him lead us, so we don't go anywhere fast since he keeps chasing birds and butterflies, among other things. I suddenly remember that Nora is hunting. Sure enough, I soon hear an indignant squawk as a red-tailed hawk lifts from a nearby tree and wings its way toward me. I hear Nora's voice in my head, protesting.

"Stupid dragon! Hunting birds for fun! I was just about to catch a nice, fat mouse, too! Ugh! You need to train that thing better, Crystal!" I laugh as she settles on my shoulder, her feathers all ruffled.

"Yes, I know. Sorry about that, Nora. He's just young and excited; this is pretty much his first time out of his cave." She mutters a bit more, then settles down. She starts preening herself, getting her feathers to settle back down, as Lloyd and I continue after Eric.

We follow him for about two hours when he finally gets tired. Lloyd and I sit down on a large boulder and Eric climbs into my lap and falls asleep. Nora takes advantage of this and takes off, looking for another mouse. Lloyd and I are then left alone. We snack on some of the food I brought along, the awkward silence between us growing.

"Um... how are your scratches?" I ask.

"I don't know. Let's check," he says. I carefully untie the shirt and slowly peel it away from his skin. It's stopped bleeding.

"Ah, good," he says. "I get to put my shirt back on! It's a little chilly walking around shirtless," he laughs, pulling it back over his head.

After a while, Lloyd points out a peculiar bird sitting in a tree nearby. I notice that its feathers are the same color as the feather I got on the First Challenge from the tree person. It then suddenly turns and cocks its head at us. It locks eyes with me and seems to take an interest in me. Taking wing, it soars over and perches on my knee, inspecting every inch of my face. I freeze, and so does Lloyd. It glances at the sleeping Eric and tilts its head like it's puzzled about something. I suddenly wonder just how intelligent this bird is and get a little nervous. Leaning down, it opens its beak and plucks the feather from my boot. It drops it in my lap, stares at me once more, then suddenly turns and flees before I can do anything. Lloyd stares at me with curiosity.

"What was that about?"

"I have no idea," I respond softly, watching as the bird disappears among the trees. *I hope he doesn't ask me about that feather...* I think as I tuck it back into my boot, worried that I wouldn't know how to respond to the question. Luckily, he doesn't, just continues looking in the direction the bird went, a thoughtful look on his face.

Without saying a word, we both stand and begin walking after the bird. It's intrigued us and we want to try and find out more about it. It's not like we were heading in any particular direction anyways. I carry Eric for a while, but he soon wakes up and is ready to go again. I laugh and put him down so he can run around some more. Lloyd and I sit under a tree covered in blue-green moss to get some shade as we wait for Eric to tire himself out again, which I figure won't take too long.

Lloyd watches him, a slightly puzzled look on his face. He turns to me. "How old is Eric now? Is he older than two weeks?"

"Yeah, it's probably around there," I respond. "Why?"

"Well... it's just that baby dragons begin learning to fly at about his age. I'm just wondering why he hasn't even tried to fly yet. Normally he should be launching himself off of everything he can find, trying to fly," he comments as we watch Eric crouch and crawl along the ground toward a rabbit. "I mean, it usually takes a few days to figure it out, but he should still be *trying* by now."

"Hmm... yeah, you're right," I realize. "I wonder why that is... do you think we should try to teach him? I mean, we can't really do it ourselves, but if we get him in the air, his instincts should take over, right? That is, if he doesn't panic and fall... maybe we should start out low- not too high or anything."

Lloyd agrees, so I go over to the unhappy Eric, who is returning without his prey. I kneel in front of him, scratching him in his favorite spot, which cheers him up. *"Hey, Eric. I have a surprise for you!"* I sense interest from him.

"What? What is it, Kysta?" I smile at his excitement.

"We're going to teach you how to fly!" I sense his excitement disappear, only to be replaced with anxiety. *He hasn't ever seen anyone or anything flying except birds,* I realize. *So he's afraid... but the ground is no place for a small dragon. Or even a big one. Dragons rule the sky- it's where they belong. The only problem is... Eric doesn't want to learn. He's satisfied with the ground. He doesn't know his true potential. ...I need to figure out how to teach him about the joy of flying... but how?*

Sighing, I pick him up and walk back to Lloyd, sitting down beside him. When I tell him about the problem, he frowns.

"I might be able to show him how to fly if I turned into a dragon myself... but there's a problem with that."

"What?" I ask, surprised. "What problem? Is that not your actual Gift?"

"Oh, no," he laughs. "That's not it. That *is* one of my Gifts. The problem is that in the form of the dragon, I would almost definitely lose myself to the power and strong emotions that all dragons feel. It is the single most dangerous form for a shape-shifter to take," he says, his face and voice conveying just how serious he is. "Very few have ever mastered it and returned- but they were all eventually driven mad by the need to have that power and freedom again. ...So obviously I don't think that would be a good idea for me to attempt."

"Oh." I frown. Eric squirms out of my arms, impatient and wanting to run around some more. I watch as he begins stalking a squirrel. *But... that doesn't make any sense. I did it. I turned into a dragon and was fine... it was just as easy as the tiger... and I'm nothing special.* Confused, I search my feelings to see if I can locate any obsession to return to that form. All I find is an exhilarating memory of the power and freedom. I would love to be a dragon again, but not... not so bad that I can't resist it. It was just a fun experience. *However... that experience did seem to change me. Not drastically, but I am still a different person now. In fact, I haven't even noticed it before now. But now that I look back... mastering the dragon's emotions helped me to conquer- for the most part- my own. I also seem to look at nature and... everything... differently. Everything just seems a little more... beautiful, precious, and unique. Interesting... but how am I so different from all those other people?* This is a question I don't have an answer to, so I shake off the questions and return to myself. Lloyd is looking at me, an intrigued and slightly concerned look on his face.

"What?" I ask, confused now myself. Could I have been too deep in thought for too long? What if he's now wondering what I'm hiding?

He clears his throat uncertainly. "Um... it's nothing. It's just... you completely zoned out for a couple of minutes there. What were you..." He stops, looking down at the ground. "I'm sorry. I shouldn't pry. It's just... you reacted kind of strange when I told you about shapeshifting into a dragon. Have you... actually done it before? You don't have to tell me if you don't want to," he adds hastily, looking up at me. I smile and decide to tell him. Maybe he can help me figure it out.

"Well, I tried shapeshifting during the Challenge so we could travel faster, and I figured a dragon would be something that could move quickly and carry Nathan as well. So... I just pictured one and turned into it, I guess. I was distracted by the feelings for a while, honestly, but... I don't know. When Nathan called out to me, it wasn't difficult to snap back into myself. In fact, it might have even been easier than when I shapeshifted into a tiger when Vlad was judging my aptitude for Gifts."

He listens attentively the entire time, not interrupting or even reacting at all. He just patiently waits for me to finish. When I do, he frowns, looking into the distance, pondering. He does this for a few minutes before I interrupt his thoughts.

"Um... so what do you think? Am I a freak or something?" I ask, unwanted desperation creeping into my voice. He turns and looks at me, surprised.

"Of course not!" He grabs my shoulders, looking into my eyes. "Listen to me," he says, his voice so intense and full of emotion that I can't not obey. "You are not a freak. That is a negative word, and you are anything but something negative. You are special- that much I could tell the first time I saw you."

"Really?" I whisper disbelievingly.

"Really," he affirms, holding my shoulders more gently. "Everyone noticed, actually. There were envious whispers about you from girls the instant you showed up. All the guys... well, let's just say they were all hoping that you would be on their team... myself included. It seems the only one who didn't realize it was you."

He waits for me to absorb this information. "But... I'm not. I'm not special. I haven't done anything extraordinary... I can't do extraordinary things... I'm just a normal girl that couldn't ever get anyone- especially a guy- to notice me in any sort of positive aspect!" I break off, my throat tight from trying not to cry. *The only guy who even got close was Brandon*, I think as the tears start to flow and I can't hold them back anymore. *And I only saw him for a few minutes... I missed our date...* Sudden sorrow overwhelms me, and I start sobbing uncontrollably- something that has never happened to me in front of another person before, especially since coming to Zilferia and putting up the front that I was strong and unfazed.

Lloyd seems to be at a loss for what to do. He eventually puts an arm around my shoulders and guides me into his embrace. I put my head on his shoulder and just let it out. Lloyd keeps his arm around me as he leans back against the tree. He lays his other hand on the back of my head, doing everything he can to try and comfort me.

"I... I'm sorry," he whispers softly. "Maybe I shouldn't have brought it up... but it's true. All the girls want to be you, and all the guys want to be with you. Which makes me a pretty lucky guy," he adds thoughtfully. "To be here, spending the day with you. But mostly I'm lucky to be your friend. I'm the one who doesn't deserve you." I pull back a little so I can see his face. My eyes are still red and watery, but I don't care. I smile at him.

"No, it's not your fault. It's just... a little overwhelming to think that someone actually... likes me. In fact, I don't think my family even likes me very much," I confide, gazing into his sympathetic, deep, blue-gold eyes. "So *I'm* lucky to have *you* as my friend."

He smiles at me, and I smile back. My emotions finally let out, I feel exhausted all of a sudden. I can tell Lloyd feels the same. We lean back against the tree together and close our eyes. My muscles are completely relaxed. Both Lloyd's presence and the soft smell coming from the tree comforts me. As I drift to sleep, I hear a distant voice. It sounds worried, but I am too tired to focus, so I ignore it as my mind slowly shuts down. Then, I am no longer aware of anything around me, least of all the pestering voice.

<<<Nora>>>

Nora arrives just in time to watch them both fall asleep. She's instantly panicked. *Oh no!* She thinks as she nears them. *Princess... didn't she realize what this tree was?! How could she not know about the Hausdorff tree?* She's disbelieving as she realizes that the boy, Lloyd, didn't recognize it either. *Thaddeus told her about this tree less than a week ago! Well, it's obvious that she was kind of out of it then, but still! Just look at what trouble she's gotten into now because of it!*

She flutters around them, not daring to get too close. She calls to Crystal again. *"Princess! Princess Crystal! Please, wake up! You are under a Hausdorff tree! It has sedative properties to put anyone who comes near it to sleep by exhausting them emotionally! You should know that! Please, get up soon or else you might not get up at all!"* Crystal doesn't respond, but continues her deep slumber, her head resting on Lloyd's shoulder.

Frantic, Nora flies high into the air and cries out, magically sending the distress signal echoing through the forest. Since she is a Familiar, any animal that heard her call will have an impulse to help her. And through magic, the one that is most likely to be able to help will arrive first. Nora settles down on a rock close to Crystal and continues trying to wake her as she waits for help, but there is no response.

"Greetings, Familiar. I see that you are in need of some assistance." Nora looks around for the source of the voice, but is unable to detect where it came from at first. She then zones in on an exotic looking blue bird. She notices that when it moves, its feathers appear to be green. She wonders about this strange bird, but decides she has no choice but to ask for his help.

"Yes. My companion is stuck in the Hausdorff tree's trap. Could you please help me?" The bird flies down beside her. She's surprised at how little noise he makes, but doesn't show it. He's bigger than her, but she isn't too intimidated. He tilts his head to the side as if thinking about it.

"I could…" he replies, a teasing note in his voice. *"But why would I want to?"* Sighing, Nora decides to use the only reason she can think of to convince this cocky bird to help.

"Because she is Crystal Dragon, daughter of Pearl and Alexander Dragon, King and Queen of Zilferia; and she needs your help. Please. I will repay you if I can, as I am sure Crystal will as well."

Now the bird really is quizzical. Finally, he responds. *"That does not matter to me, nor to my companions. We have nothing to do with the King and Queen. We have our own leaders. So, if that is your only reason, I'll be on my way."*

Nora panics and flaps up in front of the bird as he begins to leave. *"Yes?"* he asks, surprised.

"Wait," Nora insists, hovering in front of him. *"I don't know what will convince you. But I still need your help. So, if it pleases you, I will show you*

everything that I know about Crystal. I know more about her than she knows herself. Maybe something about her will convince you that she is worthy of your help?" She pleads desperately. Every minute wasted is a minute closer to Crystal's death. She has no time to waste, so she tries her best to get this strange bird to stop and assist her. She hopes it will be enough to save her.

This offer seems to intrigue the bird, so he agrees. The two land again and look deep into each other's eyes. Nora transfers all the information, not holding anything back that might help Crystal's case. The whole process takes less than a minute. Nora gets fidgety when he doesn't immediately reply, but forces herself to stay still and wait for the bird's decision. Finally, he responds.

"Very well. My people and I will help. I have already contacted them. They are on their way." Nora is shocked, but grateful and relieved.

"Thank you! Why did you decide to help us, though? If you won't have anything to do with the King and Queen?" she asks, curious.

"Because she is the chosen one. A Dragon-human with immense power and yet is kind... it is foretold that she will save the Sohos from a... problem we have. You will find out later. For now, don't ask. Zeke will want to tell you at a later time." Confused, Nora nods her understanding and acceptance.

"So," he says, turning away from Nora and looking into the forest. *"What is your name? I haven't met many Familiars. The few that I have were devious and evil. You do not seem to be evil, which makes me curious. My name is Ty, by the way."*

"I'm Nora," she responds, following his gaze. As she does, her trained eyes see flickers of movement through the trees, but for some reason, she's unable to see what's moving clearly. A human-like shape flickers in and out of focus as it runs swiftly toward them, six others behind it. She spots two more blue-green birds flying alongside them. *"I assume those are the Sohos?"* she asks Ty.

He looks at her, surprised. *"You can see them?"*

"Well, yes. Kind of. They flicker so sometimes I can't, but I can tell that they are there, if that's what you mean," she responds. He looks even more surprised.

"Really? Interesting... usually only the 'river birds'- as we are called in this language- can see the Sohos when they camouflage themselves. You are special indeed. Yes, very special..." he contemplates, watching her with renewed

interest. Uncomfortable under his gaze, she lifts off the rock and flies over to the leading Soho. He looks up at her, surprise on his handsome face. Then he smiles.

"Ah, a Familiar. I should have guessed as much," he says. Nora's surprised that his breathing is normal despite his swift pace. "Please, lead us to your companion," he says as he continues rushing forward. Grateful, she does so. When Nora lands in front of Crystal and turns back to the man, she sees that the whole group stayed with her. *Wow,* she thinks, amazed. *These humans are extraordinary, that's for sure.*

The leader finally stops flickering, the rest of the group following his lead. Nora's relieved- they were beginning to hurt her eyes. The leader, who Nora assumes is Zeke, walks up to Crystal. Without saying a word, he bends down and picks her up, lifting her with ease. When he turns and begins walking back the way he came, Nora is confused. *"Wait. What about the other one?"*

"What about him? He doesn't have anything to do with us. Only this girl can help us. Nothing is said of the boy in our legend. Why should we waste time on him?"

Deciding to take a chance, she boldly says, *"Because if you don't, I seriously doubt that Crystal will help you later if you don't help her friend now. She is very caring and concerned about others. She will be distraught if you let this boy die."*

Zeke raises an eyebrow at her. "Oh? You cannot vouch for what she will or will not do."

"I know her well enough to know that she will not be happy that you let her friend die. If I were you, I wouldn't risk ruining your prophecy by not including another person to help. If you rescue him as well, she will be much more impressed and more likely to help you," she bites back. She knows she's taking a risk pushing him, but she has a feeling these people are in desperate need of help and will do next to anything for it.

She's proven right as Zeke turns and tells another member of the group to take him with them. Then, without further delay, they take off, practically flying across the ground as they speed back the way they came. Flying up by Ty, Nora asks him a few more questions. *"Where are we going? Why can't they help them now?"*

"We are going to the Sohos' Village. The medical attention those two will need

they can get only at our Village or the King and Queen's Village. And before you ask, we will be there shortly." Nora can tell from his tone that he doesn't want to talk, so she doesn't ask anything else. Winging her way over to Zeke, she flies above them, watching over her companion. Suddenly she hears a sad, confused voice in her head.

"Kysta? Where Kysta? And boy? Birdie?" Concerned, Nora thinks, *Oh no! I forgot about Eric! Poor little dragon. I guess I'll go get him. Crystal wouldn't be too happy with me if I lost him,* she decides, turning away from the Sohos to find Eric. They don't even notice, continuing to run at their breakneck pace. She hurries so as not to lose track of them and be lost in the forest without her companion.

When she reaches the dragon, he jumps up, relieved. *"Yay! Birdie! ... Where Kysta?"*

"Follow me, little one," Nora responds, heading back toward the Sohos. *"I will explain on the way."* He's confused, but follows anyway, as fast as he can. Luckily, his fastest is enough to keep them from losing sight of the Sohos. It's a good thing Eric is intelligent enough to listen and understand, otherwise he would have no idea what she was saying. He grasps the situation quite well. Nora is impressed, but doesn't express it. They have finally caught up with the group- just as they are stopping. In the middle of nowhere.

What? I thought they were going to their Village, not to some random, uninhabited spot of the forest! Why stop here...? Nora's wondering is put to rest by Zeke.

With Crystal now over his shoulder, he steps forward and away from the rest of the group. The one holding Lloyd steps up and stands next to him. With a nod to the other one, Zeke then shouts something strange- possibly a magic spell- and jumps straight up into the air, the one with Lloyd following closely. Before Nora can even squawk, he lands on the back of a gigantic, silvery-white dragon as it pulls up from its dive. Nora is caught so off-guard that her wings still and she barely catches herself before hitting the ground. This thing is not only big enough to carry an elephant in each paw, but is apparently also very old and powerful. *So that's what a full-grown dragon is like,* she thinks, glancing down at the oblivious Eric. *To think that something so small as this little dragon could turn into something as deadly beautiful as that creature... I don't think Crystal realizes what she's gotten herself into.*

The dragon pulls out of his dive and flies straight up, zooming into the treetops high above. After waiting for a few minutes, Nora begins getting nervous. Just when she's about to try and follow the dragon herself, it returns, landing in front of the rest of the Sohos. The group begins climbing onto the beast, so Nora follows them, Eric following her lead. The little dragon's eyes grow huge as he finally notices the dragon ahead. His eyes then get unfocused, and she can tell he's talking with the big silver dragon. She leads the way, perching on one of the dragon's horns beside the river birds as one of the Sohos grabs Eric- per Nora's request- to keep him from falling off once they get started. A couple of river birds stay behind, seemingly to guard the spot from any intruders. Nora realizes the necessity of this as she looks around and realizes that the clearing had been disguised by magic to appear to be full of trees.

The dragon's muscles ripple as he crouches, preparing to take off. Realizing that it may be a rocky ride, Nora tightens her talons around the horn- just in time. The initial leap off the ground is so fast that she is almost ripped off the dragon. After he extends his wings and begins to flap, however, it isn't so bad. The dragon doesn't shoot straight up as it had with Zeke. This time, it spirals upward, ensuring that no one falls off. Finally, they pierce the canopy and zoom into the open air.

Looking around, her eyes wide with wonder, Nora is amazed. *This green... it seems to go on forever in every direction. But... how can that be? No forest on Zilferia is this large. Which poses the question... Where are we now? What kind of magic could hide a forest within a forest?* Something seems different about it, but she can't place what it is. There's just something... different in the air. The dragon begins flying East, covering vast amounts of land with each wingbeat.

Looking over at Eric, she notices his growing enthusiasm at being in the air. He was afraid at first, but now he has a taste of true freedom- and he's loving it. He starts flapping his wings, then, without warning, he leaps off the back of the dragon. Bewildered and caught off-guard, the Soho who had been keeping a hold on Eric is too slow to do so again before the little dragon begins plummeting toward the ground far below. Frantic, Nora flies off the dragon after him, looking for some way to save Eric. But it seems the silver dragon already had that covered.

Following a happy squealing sound, Nora is lead to the great claws of the dragon. A small green dragon is cupped comfortably inside one of them. Nora can feel the tension leave her wings. She flies down and perches on another one of the claws. *"Eric, don't do that!"* she scolds the excited youngling. *"You can't fly yet! You're just lucky this dragon was ready to catch you!"* Looking up at her, the baby dragon coos and smiles. Her heart softens, but only a little. *"I mean it! Warn me next time, okay? I'm just worried about you."* Eric nods, indicating his acceptance of this rule.

Noticing the dragon beginning to descend, Nora looks around. It still looks like there are just a bunch of trees. But as they get closer and closer to the treetops, Nora realizes that they have arrived at the strange Village. Heading toward a clearing that is still only just big enough for the dragon, the silver beast lands, the wind he creates sending ripples through the grass and causing the trees nearby to bend away from it. The Sohos climb off as the huge dragon gently sets Eric on the ground.

Nora leads Eric after the Sohos as they begin climbing some steps built into a nearby tree. Looking up, she can see buildings, built right into the trees themselves. Bridges stretch between each of the houses, connecting them. The houses are in every tree as far as she can see. The Village is nearly as large as the King and Queen's Village. Shaking off her feeling of awe, Nora flies up to one of the Sohos. He's a big fellow with long legs as well as long hair.

"Where are we going now?" she questions, flapping around in front of his face. He looks at her, bewildered.

"We… we're going to our hospital- that's where Zeke went with your companion." He points at a building with a tint of blue built a little higher than the rest. "It's right up there."

"Thank you," she replies, flapping up to the building with Eric racing up the steps behind her. He keeps up surprisingly well on his little legs, and they are soon at the entrance to the building, the Sohos far behind. Nora can't open the door, but luckily Zeke then happens to open it. He looks a little surprised to see her there already, but he quickly ushers her in, letting out a startled sound when Eric dashes between his legs, nearly knocking

him over. He quickly recovers and leads them to Crystal. Eric climbs onto her stomach and whines with concern. Nora lands on the pillow next to her head. A doctor is working on Lloyd and another working to help Crystal.

Looking at the nearest doctor, Nora can see her mixing a variety of things while also murmuring a magic spell. The finished product is a blue powder, which the doctor holds under Crystal's nose until she inhales. She immediately starts coughing. When Eric turns on her, growling, she quickly assures them that Crystal will be fine. Just after this, Lloyd begins coughing as well. After the coughing fit subsides, Crystal sighs and falls asleep again, as does Lloyd. Nora is concerned that that means the powder didn't work, but the female doctor at Crystal's side assures her that it's just a necessary part of what will heal her. The initial reaction of coughing only started the healing process. She needs a bit more than that because of how long she was under the Hausdorff tree, and, surprisingly, the thing she needed was more sleep. So Nora flies up to the bedside table and perches there, standing guard for her sleeping companion, waiting anxiously for Crystal to wake up.

<<<Crystal>>>

I wake slowly, drawn out of the comforting blanket of sleep by soft voices near me. I try willing them to go away so I can go back to sleep, but they don't leave. Resigned to facing the day, I slowly open my eyes and wait for them to adjust to the bright light. Blinking, I look around without moving my head. I'm in a spacious room with wood walls and bright lantern lights hung on the walls and ceiling. On the other side of the room, I see Lloyd's slumbering body. I'm confused and disoriented and try to force my brain to tell me what happened. It all comes rushing back at once, causing me to groan out loud and hold my head.

"Crystal!" an excited and relieved voice suddenly shouts inside my head. I cry out as the pain suddenly spikes. My hands over my ears, I can barely hear someone else talking.

"I'm sorry, Nora, but Crystal is not ready to speak with her mind yet. It's a side effect of the tree, I'm afraid. She may not even be able to speak with her voice for a few days either since she was under that tree for so long. I just hope the Sohos got to her quickly enough to avoid brain damage," a soft, feminine voice says, worry edging her words.

I remain curled up in a ball with my hands over my ears and my face buried in my legs, trying to escape the pain, escape the strange voice, escape everything! Soon, I feel gentle hands on my arms. They are kind but insistent, and I grudgingly let them pull my arms off of my head. A hand then touches under my chin, gently lifting my face toward the person. I can't help my curiosity, so I slowly open my eyes and look at the person in front of me.

From what I can tell, the brunette woman before me is a doctor. Her clothes gave that away. But what startles me is the kind and caring look in her bright hazel eyes. As if she... knew me. I shake off the feeling that I should recognize this woman and I open my mouth to speak, but she stops me.

Smiling sympathetically, she tells me, "I'm sorry, Crystal, but you... may not be able to speak for a while. Now, I know you want to question me, but please, don't try to talk. If you try too soon, your voice box may never work the same again." I feel my eyes get big at this information and I clamp my mouth shut. I guess she'll have to be able to guess what I want to ask. I look at her, raise my eyebrow, then look around the room with a lost look. Luckily, she catches on.

"Oh, I see. You're wondering where you are and why you are here." I nod, relieved. "Well, after you fell asleep under the Hausdorff tree, your Familiar here called for help. Lucky for you, a river bird decided to help. So, he contacted Zeke, the leader of the Sohos, and he carried you here. I did the best I could to help you, but... well, you may still encounter... problems. Such as your voice."

Looking past her, I see a tall, handsome man. I instantly blush. The doctor glances back, then turns to me with a smile. "Ah, that's Zeke. He's the one who saved you. And I'm Kate."

Zeke walks over to the other side of the bed. "I was happy to do it. I always try to help those in need, if I can. And... let's just say I have a feeling you will help us in the near future. Now, I know you have your questions, but you will have to wait until tomorrow. We don't want to risk you losing your voice entirely. So come see me sometime tomorrow, and I will explain everything I can to you." With that, he walks out the door, meeting a long-haired man in the doorway.

As he leaves, I hear a groan from Lloyd. Kate hurries over to him, leaving me alone. Until, of course, two things jump into my lap. I smile at the sad little dragon and rub his head, which cheers him up. To Nora, though, there is nothing I can do to tell her that I'm alright, and no way to thank her for all that she had done for me.

Before long, Kate returns with a wonderful chowder for me to eat. Once I finish it, I lie down to sleep, looking out the window beside the bed. The sun has gone down. I close my eyes, unaware of what my unexpected absence that night will do to Nathan.

11

___

It turns out to be longer than one day before Kate permits me to try talking again. So, almost three days after Zeke rescued Lloyd and me, I am finally free to go and ask him all the questions that have been burning within me for the past few days. Kate tells me where I can find him. I head over to the house in the highest tree and find him leaning out on the balcony, gazing over the other treehouses and the surrounding forest.

He doesn't say anything when I walk up next to him, so I stand and look out as well. With the sun nearing the horizon, the low light makes the forest look… enchanting. Clearing his throat, Zeke turns and looks at me.

"So, have you finally been cleared to talk?"

"Yep," I say, my voice hoarse from lack of use. "It feels good to finally talk again. So, you said you would tell me everything. Also, I need to get back to Nathan as soon as possible, so you might want to start now."

He smiles. "Alright, then." He grabs some chairs, and I sit down next to him. He gazes back out at the forest. "Oh, where to start?"

"How about explaining why you saved me?" I suggest. "Or about these 'river birds' of yours." I look at the sky as an enormous silver dragon flies by. "Or why you guys have a dragon hanging out with you?"

He laughs. "Well then I guess I'll start… at the beginning. The Sohos weren't called by this name at first. In fact, we started out as part of a group called the Dragon Hunters. I'm ashamed to say I was even their leader at one time. The Dragon Hunters' only goal was to rid this world of Dragons- forever; and this was specifically my life's goal. That is, until something happened that changed my life- and my entire outlook on it."

I listen raptly, enthralled by his rich, emotion-filled voice as it paints a picture of his former life before my eyes.

"I was a young man at the time, about seventeen, and I had taken nearly half of the Dragon Hunters with me on a dragon hunt. We were following a massive black dragon whom we called Giusto. When we found the dragon's cave, we waited near it for the beast to return from its hunt. Some wanderer stupidly went right into the dragon's cave to sleep that night.

"When he came out in the morning, Giusto arrived as well. He chased the man toward us. My people wanted to flee, but I ordered them to stay put. The dragon had no idea we were there, so when it froze the guy in place with DragonFear, it made itself more vulnerable. So, we took advantage of this and attacked it then. It didn't take long to kill it, but one of its claws injured the stranger. He was unconscious.

"I made the decision to take the man into our group. We brought him to our best healer, and he managed to save the man's life. When he came to, he told us that his name was Patrick, and he hated dragons and wanted to help us kill them... so we let him join.

"After a few years, I started feeling more and more lonely. My parents, the leaders of the Dragon Hunters before me, were both dead, I had no siblings, and my friends weren't very good friends.

"So one day I just set off into the forest alone. I wanted to clear my head. I wandered, and eventually I found a cave. As I got near it, I could sense the presence of a dragon. I started backing away, knowing I couldn't take on a dragon alone, but it was too late. A red dragon leapt out of the cave and pinned me on my back. It was majestic and... beautiful. I had never seen them that way before. I felt its mind touch mine. It was a young mother, and it asked why I was there.

"Panicked, I couldn't say anything. So she looked deeper into my mind and pulled up all my memories- the dragon learned everything about me. I was confident that she would kill me, but she didn't. Instead, she invited me into her cave to see her hatchlings. I didn't dare disobey her, so I let her lead me into the cave. The small dragons all pounced on me. I was frightened at first, but I then realized that they were trying to play.

"That moment changed my life. Before, I had always thought that all dragons were evil creatures without souls… but not after that. So I went back to the Dragon Hunters and told my friends about it. They thought I was crazy. One of them believed me, and even let me lead him to see the dragon. He gained an appreciation for dragons as well.

"After a while, we got quite a few people to change their view on dragons. But Patrick didn't. He swayed the people into thinking that all dragons are evil and bloodthirsty and should be disposed of. He took over and kicked the 'dragon lovers,' as he called us, out, saying that if the dragons wanted us, then they could have us.

"Unsure of what to do, I went to see my dragon friend. She took us to the dragon council. The head member, Asoka, was also the wisest and oldest dragon. He agreed to help us find a new place to live, as well as teach us how to live off the land. The dragon council then used magic on us. We were changed. We were then able to use magic, although none of us had the ability previously. We also aged slower.

"And thus, the Sohos were born. 'Soho' is actually what the Dragons call us. It translates to Dragon Friend. We lived side by side with the dragons, and all was peaceful for years.

"Until just five years ago, when Patrick discovered that not only did we not perish in the wilderness, but that we were coexisting with the dragons. Lusting for revenge, he decided to attack us. At first, we just tried to run and avoid him, hiding behind our magic wards, but eventually we had to go on the offensive to get him to leave us alone.

"One dark night, we attacked their castle. We discovered that Patrick had taken many prisoners from the King and Queen Dragon's Village, so we rescued them and burned part of their main building. It was there that I met our new doctor, Kate. She was your parents' doctor in the past. They took her at the same time they took Hunter- your brother- and tried to take both you and your other brother, Rex."

"Wait, what?" I interrupt, surprised. "They tried to take me and… my brother? But they took the other one… Hunter… well, where is he now?"

Zeke grimaces at the question. "I'm sorry to say that Patrick raised him not knowing who he really is; I assume; and… he is actually in line for being the next leader. I fear that because of Patrick's influence, he will lead the Dragon Hunters just as Patrick does now- killing everything, having no mercy, nor patience..."

I sit stone still in the chair, trying to absorb the fact that not only do I have two brothers, but that one is lost, and the other is a power-hungry maniac. It's a little much to come to terms with, so I decide to address it later.

"So why did you save me? You still haven't answered that," I say.

Zeke smiles a little. "I was just getting to that. ...After we rescued Kate and a few others, Kate told me that Patrick was planning to attack us full-on with everything he's got, and that would destroy us. Not only that, but they would stand an even better chance against us because they found a way to steal other people's Gifts- and use them themselves."

"What?!" I exclaim. "No! That's... that's impossible! Isn't it?" I startle myself with the outburst. I didn't realize that I had accepted that Gifts were real in the first place, but not only that, I finally decided that his whole *place* was real. Most startling of all is that I actually now believe that I am the Princess. I mean, there are way too many things pointing out the fact. And now... now, I am even defending these people that lost their Gifts that I don't even know.

I have changed a lot since arriving in Zilferia.

"Yes. It is possible, I'm afraid to say," A voice behind me whispers. I turn and find Kate standing there. "I saw the machine with my own eyes," she continues, walking up next to Zeke and looking into my eyes. With a shock, I realize that hers are glittering with pools of fear. "Of course, it wasn't quite finished yet, but I'm sure they've completed it by now." She shudders. "I urge everyone I meet to avoid that group of villains and their... *Gift Stealer* at all costs." She stops suddenly, staring at me; her eyes wide. Her eyes then fill with tears, and she runs off into the night.

I peer at Zeke, feeling a little unnerved. "What was that about?"

He sighs. "I guess I'll have to tell you. Just so you know, you don't have to help. You can leave us to fend for ourselves. No one could blame you." He takes a deep breath while I wait anxiously. "After I found out about this new threat, I went to the dragons for help. The Dragon Mage told me a prophecy.

"When all seems dark, devoid of the light of hope, there will be one

who comes. A Dragongirl. You will help her, and she will help you. She will attack your shared enemy, and cripple them in a way no one will see coming. She will lose much, sacrifice more than anyone else would, but it will be worth it. And after her work is done, you will be left alone. However... there will be new threats looming on the horizon. New threats... against more than just the Sohos. Threats aimed to destroy more than you can imagine."

Zeke looks at me, seriousness in his eyes, as well as a kind of pain. "As I said, you don't have to do this. Although... I have a feeling you are the Dragongirl- which means you will save us. But please, don't feel pressured to help us just because of the prophecy. In fact, we may not need you yet anyway. It said when all hope is lost, and we still have hope. After all, we haven't heard of anyone getting their Gifts taken away, so I doubt that their machine even works. Plus, we still have the dragons on our side. They don't exactly want to be destroyed either." He pauses to let this sink in.

"I..." I don't know what to say or do. I want to help these people, I do, but that Gift Stealer and the prophecy... 'she will lose much and sacrifice more than any other would...' well, that doesn't comfort me at all. After a few more minutes of wrestling with myself over my decision, I finally have to follow my heart.

"...I will do my best to help you when the time comes," I declare to Zeke, trying to keep my voice steady and confident. It wavers despite my efforts. I'm scared to death, but I feel like if the prophecy is indeed about me, then I have to help them... somehow. Zeke looks extremely surprised.

"Really? You... you'll help us? Even though..."

"Yes," I nod, sealing my fate.

Zeke clears his throat. I realize that the sun has gone down long ago and it's getting late. "Well. Thank you. We are in your debt. However, I assume that you will want to go back to your Village now?"

I nod. "Yes, there are still things I need to do there." I'm nervous that I missed the Second Challenge, but I don't know for sure. I've lost track of the days.

Zeke accepts this. "Well, I would like you to keep that River Bird feather as a reminder of us," he says, indicating the feather just sticking out of my boot. "I don't want you to forget us and our need, nor your promise. For without you, we may all be lost. Of course, we don't know that for sure yet... but when we need you, we will send word. Now then, you need to get some rest. I will take you and your friend back in the morning."

"Goodnight," I tell him, feeling overwhelmed with responsibility.

"Goodnight," he murmurs in response as I walk away. As I return to the hospital in a nearby tree, my thoughts rush ahead to the next day, trying to predict how everyone will react to my return after being gone for so long.

Lloyd and I meet Zeke at the clearing that the silver dragon is usually resting in. Nora rides on my shoulder as Eric races circles around us. He greets the magnificent dragon, his tail wagging excitedly. After climbing onto the dragon, I grab Eric and hold onto him tightly, not willing to let him jump off like Nora told me he had on the way to the Sohos' Village. The silver dragon flies shockingly fast, and we are back at the Hausdorff tree in less than an hour. The sun is just coming up as we land. We say goodbye to Zeke and start walking back to Eric's little cave.

Lloyd, although he had also been cleared to talk, doesn't seem to be in a chatty mood. I don't press him. We walk in silence.

Eric isn't happy to have to wait for me in his cave once more, but I'm able to cheer him up a little by telling him that Lloyd will play with him sometimes while I'm training and in the Challenges. After Nora grabs something to eat, Lloyd goes his own way, giving me a brief hug as he leaves. Meanwhile, I head back to my hut to try and find Nathan. He's not there, so I change clothes and head to the town square, hoping to see him there, possibly training with Vlad.

He is. As I near him, I can tell he's tired. He doesn't hear or sense my approach, although Vlad does. As does Nathan's Familiar, Greg. He sniffs the air and alerts Nathan, who immediately spins around, disbelief evident in his eyes. They then fill with relief and he charges at me, wrapping me tightly in his arms. I'm startled and caught off-balance.

"I'm so glad you're okay," he whispers, pain in his voice. "I... I thought I lost you. I mean, who knows what's out there in that forest? I..." he breaks off, his voice beginning to crack.

"It's okay. I'm here now. I'm sorry I had you so worried." I decide not to tell him all that happened- he seems overwhelmed already. Looking over Nathan's shoulder, I see Vlad stepping up to me. I stiffen and Nathan turns to see why.

"Well," Vlad slowly says, glaring at me. "Look who decided to crawl back here. Have a nice trip in the forest?" Something in this voice tells me he knows what I've learned. I scold myself. I'm just paranoid.

Swallowing my ever-present fear of him, I reply, "Actually, I had a hard time," I say, looking him in the eye. "I ran into some dangerous things in there. I was lucky to come back alive."

He smiles. I can tell he thinks I'm lying. "Well, you caused quite a stir here. Everyone was searching for you for five days."

"Five?"

"Yes. Oh, did you not realize what day it is? Tomorrow is the Second Challenge," he sneers.

"Then I guess I'll go get ready for it," I bite back. I turn to Nathan. "Are you done training with him?"

"Yes," he confirms. Not saying another word to Vlad, we turn and walk away. I can feel the heat of his enraged gaze burning upon my back.

On our way to Thaddeus, Nathan tells me how worried he was and how he didn't sleep at all while I was gone except when Thaddeus made him take pills to make him sleep. I feel awful about it, but he tells me not to. He says it's not my fault. I comfort him some, though, by telling him that Lloyd went with me and helped me out with the 'wild creatures,' as well as Nora and Eric. I feel bad lying to him, but I know that he probably wouldn't be able to handle the truth right now. *I'll tell him what really happened later,* I promise myself.

Thaddeus is relieved to see me as well. "It wouldn't be good if we lost our only Princess, now would it?" is all he says about it. Even though he doesn't come right out and say it, I can tell he was worried if I was okay while I was gone.

When we break for lunch, Thaddeus tells Nathan to go on without us so he can talk to me alone. Once Nathan's out of earshot, he requests that I tell him everything that happened while I was gone. He's surprised at the existence of the Sohos, but he's not surprised at all to find out about the Dragon Hunters- or what I tell him about my brother, Hunter. He explains that Patrick had already told the King about those things before he left with Hunter, and the King relayed the information to Thaddeus. Although they had never before heard of the Gift Stealer, he is concerned about it.

I continue with my story. It's a relief to tell someone. Maybe Thaddeus can help me make sense of it all. He is shocked, though, when I relate Dragongirl Prophecy to him.

"What? The Dragongirl? You think that *you* are the Dragongirl? Why is that?" I hesitantly tell him about not falling prey to the dragon form. "That doesn't mean that you're the Dragongirl."

"Why not?"

"Thanks to your family being part dragon, it's not too surprising that one exposure didn't drive you insane, for one thing," he explains. "Not to mention that the Dragongirl is both creatures at once- equal parts dragon and human. It's not so much that she can *shapeshift* into one, but that she *is* a dragon!"

"Oh." I shrink away from him in embarrassment. "That can't be me, then," I admit. "But I promised to help the Sohos however I can- so help them I will- even if I'm not in their prophecy. They need help."

"Yes," he admits, stroking his beard thoughtfully. "But don't give them false hope, and especially don't give yourself to them. You don't need to sacrifice yourself for naught. I'm sure they can fend for themselves, especially if they are as close to the dragons as you say."

After that, the rest of the day is uneventful, aside from the reactions of everyone who sees me. The contestants themselves are both surprised to see me, as well as unhappy that I've returned in enough time for the next Challenge. I guess I might actually pose a more significant threat than I first thought.

This time, I wake up before Nathan and *I* make breakfast. When he gets up and sees the food ready, he has to bite back a protest before he breaks our agreement of taking turns for everything. Besides, I had plenty of sleep.

That's pretty much all I had to do the past week while I was recovering from the Hausdorff tree. He was the one who needed more of it.

My insistence that he needed rest is only confirmed by the bags still under his eyes. He looked a lot better than he had yesterday, but obviously still drained. I just hope he got enough sleep to be able to do this Challenge. After all, he was the only one here for most of the training. Even when my body was here, my mind was not, so I didn't provide much help for this one.

Thaddeus told us to meet him where we usually do before the Challenge. He's already waiting for us by the time we arrive. "There's been a slight change of rules for this Challenge. This time, you can pair up with another team. Who would you like to work with?"

"Red," we say in unison, knowing that there's no need to discuss it first.

"Of course," he says with a small smile. "Good luck in the arena!" Before I can react, there is once again a prick in my arm and I'm out cold.

My cheek suddenly tickles as a drop of moisture runs down it. Shivering, I sit upright, wiping at my face. It's damp. Opening my eyes, it takes a few moments for me to recognize what I'm seeing. Fog dances slowly before my eyes, difficult to discern due to the lack of light.

"Nathan?" I whisper into the darkness.

There's movement beside me as I speak. "Man I wish they wouldn't do that," Nathan groans as he sits up beside me. I look over at him, but in the dark, he's just a darker patch vaguely shaped like a man.

"It's so that you don't know where the arena is or have a glimpse of any part of the maze before the Challenge has begun. Everyone wakes at the same time. It's fairer that way," Nora states.

"Ugh! I don't care; it's not a fun thing to suddenly wake up and think that you can't see," a familiar voice says.

"Sierra?" I question.

"Who else?" Ham replies. "We are all going to be one team this time, which means that Sierra and I finally have a chance."

I laugh. "Trust me; this will be much more beneficial to Nathan and I.

You're giving *us* a chance. Nathan's sleep deprived, and I basically missed all of the training." Just as I finish speaking, I hear a voice echoing from the surrounding fog.

"Hello! Contestants! This is Nehru speaking! Just so you know, you are in another arena, competing in the Second Challenge! Once again, you will be permitted to exit your starting platform only once the gun sounds. After that, it's basically a free-for-all. With no killing, of course. Find the end of the maze first, and you win! The end will be glowing white. This time, there will be four winners, since each of you have joined teams, and only one can get there first. I hope you each have one of your Gifts, or this may be a little more difficult. For the moment, sit still and… ponder, plan, or just procrastinate!" With a giggle, her voice disappears. I raise an eyebrow, although no one can see it.

"Does she have to say that every time?" I complain.

Ham laughs. "Apparently. Maybe it's her catchphrase or something." We laugh, then get down to business.

"So," Nathan begins once we've settled into a circle. We're close enough to see each other's faces now. "I guess we'll figure out which way to go as we get to each crossroad. I suppose the first thing we should do is figure out what each person's strengths are. So, Ham, do you have any of your Gifts yet?"

"Yes, actually. But it's a dumb one."

"What is it?" I ask. "No Gift is dumb- any one of them can help us," I assure him.

"Well… I have the Gift of extraordinary memory," he confides.

"Awesome! That'll be a huge help with this riddle one!" Nathan says. "How about you, Sierra?"

"Um… I have the Gift of Speed, I think," she timidly responds.

"Wow," Nathan looks back and forth between the two of them, but it's too dark to read his facial expressions. "You guys are perfectly suited for this Challenge! Not only do we need to speed through this maze; we also need to answer some pretty tough riddles!"

Just as he finishes saying this, we hear the blast of a gun. This time, there aren't any supplies for us, so I suppose they either don't think it will take very long, or that we can take care of ourselves and food can be found another way. So we walk cautiously through the fog with no idea where we're going.

After a few moments, we bump into a large hedge. It appears that we are outside... but the question is- why is it so dark? I couldn't see the stars, either moon, or the sun. Getting an idea, I ask Nora to fly as high as she can and see if the fog thins out; maybe see the way to go. She does so, but before she can get very high, she stops dead in the air and can't seem to go any higher.

She returns with her report. *"The arena seems to be enforced with magic. I would assume that they made it so one cannot just fly above the whole maze. I would also wager that the hedges are enforced with magic as well so we cannot just force our way through them."*

"Now what?" asks Sierra. "We'll never get to the end at all, let alone first if this is the best we can do!" We all murmur with agreement.

"Hey, Crystal," Nathan suddenly turns to me and murmurs. "How long can you use your dragon eyes at one time?"

"Without stopping? I don't know... I've never done it for very long. I haven't needed to. It doesn't seem to be all that difficult, though," I reply.

"Wait... what?" Sierra exclaims, astonished by what she just heard. "Crystal has... she has... *dragon eyes?!*"

"Um, yes," he replies. "You know what, I'll explain it as we go, okay? Crystal, will you try using your dragon eyes to see through the fog?"

"Of course," I reply, rolling them forward. They help me see almost perfectly through the fog. "Follow me," I say, grabbing Nathan's hand. He takes Sierra's hand, and she catches Ham's, so no one gets lost or left behind. Nora flies above us while Greg rides on Nathan's shoulder. I start through the giant hedges that I can now see to either side of us for about three hundred yards before it splits. As we walk, I hear Nathan explaining everything to Ham and Sierra. I don't bother to listen in.

I stop. "Okay, there's a split here. Do you think we should go right or left? They both look the same."

"I don't know," Nathan says. "It's up to chance anyway. We could all take turns choosing. Ham, why don't you go first?"

"Um, okay," he responds. "Let's go... right." So I lead them down the path to the right. We walk for about another two or three hundred yards until we come to another split.

"Okay, Sierra. Straight, right, or left?"

"Um... left?" Again, another two hundred yards out, we run into another split. I'm beginning to think that maybe we'll be lucky and we won't have to do a riddle or anything when Nathan decides to go right at the next split.

We get in about one hundred feet before I see something ahead. Looking closer at it, I can see that it's a minotaur- a tall man with horns and hairy goat legs. He's holding an axe and is waiting patiently for us. I swallow as I take note of his bulging muscles.

Noticing that I have seen him, he bellows, "Now that you have seen me, you may not go back. You must answer my riddle- without the help of your Familiar. Answer correctly, and you will go on a faster, less dangerous route. Answer incorrectly, and you will have to fight me. The person given the riddle will be the only one permitted to fight me. If they win, then you can move on, using a longer route with wild creatures and other contestants on it. Lose to me, and you will have to backtrack. So come closer, and pick who your spokesperson will be."

"What is it?" Sierra whispers, shaking from the strength of the Minotaur's call. I quietly tell them what it is as I inch forward, pulling them behind me.

"Ha!" Ham laughs, seeming relieved. "Minotaurs are so dumb. This will be an easy riddle."

"Well then," Nathan says. "Who thinks that they are the worst at riddles? Everyone should be able to try, so we'll save Ham for some harder ones."

"I'll do it," Sierra quietly volunteers. "I'm horrible at riddles. I can't seem to think outside the box."

"Okay," I say, continuing on toward the Minotaur. "But fighting it will be difficult in this fog especially, so take your time in trying to answer it right," I caution. Even as I say this, the fog thins until its almost entirely gone and the others can now see the Minotaur. He stands head and shoulders above us, although it seems like more because of his massive muscles.

"Who will challenge me?" he roars, trying to intimidate us.

Swallowing, Sierra steps up to him, trembling. "I... I will," she stammers, shooting a glance my way. She immediately grimaces and turns back to the Minotaur. I'm surprised until I remember that my dragon eyes are still out, which she had never before seen. I'm relieved that the disgust coloring her aura quickly fades away as she returns her attention to the task at hand.

"Excellent. Now then, are you ready?" He flexes his massive arms before leaning against an axe as large as a person.

"Yes." The reply squeaks out of her, and as hurt as I initially was from the look she gave me when she saw my eyes, my heart goes out to her. *I hope she can do this...*

"Then let us begin. There are six copycats on a boat. One jumps off. How many are left?"

Sierra replies with barely a hesitation. "None, of course. If they're truly copycats, they copy whatever the first one does."

The Minotaur deflates at her words, heavy with disappointment. He steps to the side of the path and gestures for us to go through. "You have passed your first riddle. At the next fork, head left. That is the safest path."

"Thank you," I say, bowing nervously to the creature. He straightens back up, beaming with pleasure.

"But of course, Princess. Anything to help one of the Dragons. ...You remind me a lot of your mother, by the way," he adds.

"Oh," I say, surprised. "Well, thank you."

We hastily move on. The instant we're past the Minotaur, the mist closes in once more. At the next fork we head left, as directed. This time, it's about three or four hundred yards to the next split. It divides into four paths. It's my turn to choose, so I lead everyone down the one furthest to the right.

I was unlucky in my choice. One hundred yards in, there's a fox sitting in the middle of the path, tail wrapped neatly over her paws. We walk up to her cautiously. "My rules are the same as the Minotaur's. Who will challenge me?"

I turn to my friends. "Well? Who thinks they can outwit the fox? Foxes are sly, so she will probably try to confuse us by making an easy riddle sound hard. So... who's up for the challenge?"

All three of them look at me. "I think that you can," Nathan says. "You're pretty witty yourself." The others agree, so I take a tentative step forward, offering myself as the recipient of the riddle.

"What walks on first four legs, then two, then six?" she asks, not wasting any time once we've decided.

I think for a while, going through animals in my head. Before long, it finally clicks and I almost laugh at myself for nearly missing it. "The answer is a human. When they are young, they crawl- using four 'legs.' Then they learn to walk- using two. But then they get old and have to use a walker- making six legs."

The fox looks surprised. "Well done. You may move on. At the next fork in the path, take the middle path. Have a good day, Princess," she adds.

"How do you know that I'm the Princess?" I ask. She grins, intelligence in her eyes.

"For one, your dragon eyes are still out. Plus, you are a lot like your mother, who saved my babies years back. I'm just repaying the favor, helping her offspring through this strange Challenge."

"Oh… thank you," I reply, glancing back at her as we move on. *They keep comparing me to my mom… How did she get on such good terms with such creatures? There sure is a lot I still don't know about my own family. …I hope I'll get to meet her one day.*

At the next fork, we take the middle path, as the fox instructed. Nothing happens after Ham's choice, but when Sierra decides to go left, we run into another creature. This one is a tiger. Nathan steps up.

"It takes six men three hours to dig ten holes. How long would it take for one man to dig half a hole?"

Nathan looks confused. "But… that's so easy. Is that *really* your riddle?"

"Yes," the tiger growls, clearly irritated and looking like he would very much rather eat him.

"Then the answer is that you *can't* dig half a hole!"

"Correct. You may continue. Take the path on the right at the next split."

Nathan's choice doesn't lead us to another creature, but mine does. This time it's a Gryphon. Ham claims it, saying it's his turn anyways. The magnificent creature before him causes Ham to tremble with awe. Finally, he looks at the ground so he can concentrate.

"What is greater than God, and is more evil than the Devil; the poor have it, the rich need it, and if you eat it, you die?"

Ham continues to stare at the ground as he thinks. I see beads of nervous sweat forming on his face. Just as I'm getting worried that he won't get it, his face suddenly relaxes and he stands up straight, looking right at the Gryphon.

"Nothing. Nothing is greater than God, and if you eat nothing, you die."

"Very good. Please, go on. Head straight at the next split. Good day," it says, laying down and waiting for any other contestants to come.

As we walk through the mist, Sierra's hopeful voice pops up. "I think we're going to win!" We all turn and look at her- although I'm the only one that can actually see her. "What?" she continues defensively. "Can anyone else get through this fog as easily as us? No! And not only that, but we have answered every riddle correctly! We're flying through this Challenge!"

"...There's just one thing," I slowly respond as we start moving again. "Isn't there supposed to be paths that will make it so the contestants have to run into each other eventually? We haven't seen anyone else the whole time!"

"Yeah... that is strange," Ham agrees. "Maybe the paths only collide when you go the slower way if you lose a fight with a creature."

"Yes, that must be it," I decide. After a little longer, my stomach begins rumbling hungrily. I ignore it for a while, but then I notice the others' stomachs as well. *It wouldn't hurt to look for food as we go, right?* So I begin searching for berries growing on the branches of the hedges- anything edible.

By the time we arrive at the next riddle master, I haven't found anything. This one is a house cat. Unlike the others, it doesn't let us choose who will answer the riddle. "Come forward, Crystal Dragon, and answer my riddle- if you can."

I share a concerned look with the others and step forward, switching my eyes back to normal. After having them out for so long, it seems strange not having everything all golden.

"Are you ready?" It asks me, eyes narrowing. I swallow hard, nodding.

"Very well then. I give you a group of three. One is sitting down, and will never get up. The second eats as much as is given to it, yet is always hungry. The third goes away and never returns. What are the three?"

I think for a long time. I ask the cat to repeat the riddle, listening carefully to each word. I think again. The second one sounds like a black hole, or maybe a fire. But I can't figure out the other two. Finally, I decide that I am wasting too much time. The slow path would be faster than this. So I tell the cat what I think the second object is.

"Is that all? What are the first and third objects?"

"I don't know," I reply.

With a snarl, the cat swells to twice the size of a tiger. "Then you fail. The answer is a stove, a fire, and smoke," it growls as it jumps at me. I'm ready, however, and leap to the side. It barely misses as it's faster than I expected. The giant cat swings around to face me again, its eyes narrowing in anger. I barely have time to duck and avoid the brunt of the attack, but I don't escape completely unscathed. Its claws rake my shoulder and take out a fair chunk of flesh. With a scream, I fall to the ground.

Before I can get back up, the cat's large paw is resting on my chest, pinning me down. Holding my right arm to immobilize my shoulder, I struggle to get out, but the cat's too strong. My eyes water from pain and the fur above me swirls and twists, slightly mesmerizing.

"Crystal!" I hear Nathan yell. I turn my head to see my three friends rushing towards us. They suddenly stop, frozen mid-step. Even Nora is held still in the air. I blink to clear my vision, sending tears rushing down my face, burrowing into the hair by my ear, turning the dust to mud.

"No," the cat growls, looking over at them. "No one interferes. Don't worry; I won't kill her- just wound her enough that I can declare that she has lost this battle- and you all have to go back." As the cat finishes talking, I kick it in the stomach, as hard as I can. It grunts, retreating. I don't let it. With a determined, adrenaline filled leap, I fly onto its back and hold onto the fur on its head. The beast starts kicking, trying to knock me off, but I've got too firm of a grip. Its convulsions cause my injured shoulder to twinge and burn, rivers of blood flowing down my arm. I refuse to loosen my grip, gritting my teeth so hard my jaw hurts as well. After a few minutes, it finally gets tired.

"Fine," it growls, settling down. "You are the winner. Go through the path on our right." I turn my head and notice a path that was not there before. I climb down and walk toward it, my gaze set determinedly forward, avoiding my friends. The cat shrinks back to size and begins licking my blood from its fur. My friends follow me into the path in the hedge, which closes behind us. I switch my eyes back, although the mist is thinner here. I start heading in the direction we were going before we were stopped by the cat. I hold back tears at the pain in my shoulder. I glance at it, then quickly look away. My stomach churns at the site of so much missing muscle and skin. I don't dare touch it, letting the blood flow slowly down my arm instead.

The others don't say anything, opting to tread carefully around me. They follow behind me silently. After a while, Nathan catches up to me. "Hey," he says softly. "It's okay. I wouldn't have gotten that riddle either. That was a hard one. And that cat would have torn me to shreds. You got away without a scratch! You did great, so don't beat yourself up over it. Okay?"

I duck my head, hiding the tears that erupt from the intense pain in my shoulder. I don't dare say anything. I don't want to be seen crying in front of him. Or Ham and Sierra, for that matter.

"Crystal?" he probes. He puts a hand on my good shoulder, stopping me. I still refuse to look at him, thankful for the mist hiding my tears. "What's wrong?" He puts his other hand on the wounded shoulder. I gasp in pain- barely not screaming- and jerk away. I collapse on the ground, and now there's no stopping the tears.

I sit there sobbing as Nathan kneels in front of me. He holds his hand close to his face and notices the blood. He grimaces as he realizes what happened. "I'm so sorry!" He exclaims. "I didn't notice your wounded shoulder! Please, can you forgive me?" The pain is so intense I can barely nod, but this only gives him some relief as he realizes just how much pain I'm in. I hate letting him see my burden, knowing there's nothing he can do about it.

He gets an idea and quickly tears off part of his jacket. "I'm going to wrap this around your shoulder so you don't bleed out. Okay?" I nod slowly and manage to choke back most of my scream as the cloth comes in contact with the raw flesh. Nathan then shifts into a midnight black horse, telling Ham and Sierra to help me on. Once I'm seated, we head out again, moving as fast as they dare. I tell him when to turn, but I don't do much other than cry and try to stay seated on his back.

This is the state I'm in when we're attacked.

I'm in a haze of pain and can barely move when I see a flash of green and yellow in front of us. I open my mouth to croak out a warning, but it's too late. Before I can form even one word, a huge gust of wind sends me flying off of Nathan's back and against a hedge. Unfortunately, it doesn't knock me out, and I'm still very much aware of my pain. I slowly push myself up with my left arm and look around. Nathan is standing, shaking the dust from his mane. Lying next to him is Ham and Sierra. She's just stirring, but Ham seems to be knocked out.

Rearing up, Nathan rushes at the nearest contestant. Nora joins him, as well as Greg. They all charge at a guy in green- Drake Kingston. He dives out of the way just in time, so the three of them continue, heading straight for a girl in yellow. Odette Hansen. Her eyes get big with fear. Suddenly a swarm of thorns fly off the hedge and attack Nathan. A lot of them pierce his broad neck. Blood starts flowing, and he fades into his own form. He wavers and falls to the ground in a heap. A thorn pierces Nora's wing, sending her to the ground as well. One hit Greg in the side and he falls over, motionless. I hear laughing and see Frazer standing next to the hedge, grinning.

Now I'm angry. I push myself away from the hedge I had been resting on- and almost fall over from fatigue and blood loss. The yellow and green team notice. I hear them laugh.

"What happened to *her?*" Star mocks. "If I didn't know any better, I would think she's drunk!" They all laugh. I growl and stagger toward them, barely remembering to hide my dragon eyes. This brings on more laughter. Sierra steps up next to me.

"Don't worry," she says, glaring at the group. "I'll handle this." And with that, she's gone. Looking over at them, I see Star go flying. The rest of them immediately stop laughing, looking around frantically. A red blur then rams into Odette, knocking her into Frazer. The two collapse, and then there's only Drake. Thinking fast, he suddenly whips up a hurricane, sucking Sierra up into it. He then redirects the hurricane, and she's thrown into a hedge. She slides to the ground in a heap.

Which leaves me alone with Drake.

He walks up to me, arrogance in his stride. My legs lose their strength and collapse back onto the ground. Drake towers over me. I struggle to get up. He watches, contempt in his eyes. Finally, we are face-to-face.

"I could easily beat you," he contemplates, "but…" I follow his eyes as he looks behind him. His team members are getting up. "…I have a Challenge to win. Besides, you can't do much anyway." With a laugh, he and his team walk away, leaving mine in serious trouble.

It only takes a minute to wake up Ham, but then I pass out from blood loss. It's amazing I lasted this long in the first place, really, considering how much my shoulder was bleeding. I welcome the darkness, eager to escape the pain.

12

I instinctively blink my eyes open before quickly slamming them shut at the burning light. "She's alright," a voice says, sounding assuring. I wonder who he's talking to. "We fixed her shoulder- as well as we could- and gave her a blood transplant. She should be good to go for tonight, and your Familiars should be fully recovered in the next few days as well." I hear the person walk to the door, but I don't open my eyes. The light is too bright- it hurts.

"Crystal?"

"Are you okay?"

"Please talk to us. Tell me you're okay!"

I recognize the voices of my three friends and decide to open my eyes. The light has been dimmed, so I can see their worried faces clearly. Their faces relax with relief. Ham and Sierra have a few bruises, but Nathan looks worse. He has a cloth wrapped around part of his face and his entire neck and shoulder.

I'm suddenly confused as my brain recognizes a gap from what I last remember happening and waking up in the hospital again. "What... what happened? I don't remember anything after I passed out... did we win?"

The three glance at each other, avoiding my gaze. Ham finally says something, but it's not to me. "You should tell her," he suggests to Nathan. "You're her actual partner."

"Tell me what?" I demand, anxious now.

"Well, um... I was knocked out for most of it too, but Ham told me what happened," Nathan begins. "He and Sierra both carried us to the next split, where they had to answer another riddle. Ham got it right, and he moved on and got to the end. The thing is, it teleported us here immediately, so we don't know if we won or not. We won't find out until tonight when they call us onto the stand for the ceremonies. I woke up in here as well just a few hours ago. And they um... fixed... your shoulder."

I sit up, clearly detecting the worry in his voice. Apprehensive now myself, I start pulling the bandages off my shoulder. Nathan quickly steps up, taking my hand to still its movements. He looks into my eyes. "They... couldn't completely fix it," he cautions. "Just... be prepared."

Now I'm really concerned.

I finish peeling them off, feeling the cool touch of the air around me on the sensitive area. Taking a deep, steadying breath, I grab a mirror near me and examine my shoulder. The raw meat has been covered with skin again, but... it's an ugly red scar, and there are still pretty deep gouges through the muscle. I move my arm slowly. It appears they knitted the muscle back together so I can move my arm, but... I can tell it will never be the same. It still hurts, but nowhere near the intensity it had initially.

Satisfied with my examination, I ask Sierra what time it is, now ignoring the ugly shoulder. She tells me it's a little after noon. My stomach rumbles at the thought. As though the sound had summoned him, a doctor then enters the room with a tray full of food. He leaves it with us and hurries off. I wolf down more food than Sierra and Ham combined, although Nathan is a close second in his consumption. When I finally finish, I lean back with a satisfied sigh.

At last, I have nothing to do for the rest of the day but sit and talk with my friends.

It's time to go to the ceremonies. Once we are ready, we head out a little early- we don't want to get there late again. We're instantly surrounded by people from the Village once we arrive. This time, Y'vette saves us and leads us up onto the stand. The other contestants are there as well- except the green and yellow team, that is. I don't have long to wonder about what happened to them because the ceremony then begins.

Nehru walks up to the front of the stage and addresses the crowd. I'm not really listening. I'm too busy worrying if we won or not- or if the jerks on the green and yellow team won, and that's why they aren't here yet- so they can get a grand entrance. Unfortunately, we don't get to find out right away. First, she pulls us all up and interviews us individually as she did before. I'm first again.

"So, Ms. Shay. What a Challenge! I must say that you performed very well, especially considering all that time you missed training. I can't believe you beat that cat! It was so fast! And how you held on through the pain... well, *I* sure was impressed! Anyone else?" There is a fair amount of applause at this- coupled with wolf whistles, of course. I struggle not to roll my eyes. The Games are clearly the only entertainment these people have. I'm sure they would cheer for anything I was to do.

"Tell us, what was your least favorite part?" Nehru continues. "Was it getting clawed by that giant cat?"

"No," I say quietly. The crowd is hushed, straining to hear my words. "No, the worst part of the whole thing was watching as the yellow and green team hurt my friends while I couldn't do anything about it. I felt... so helpless and weak." My voice breaks as my mind replays Nathan getting attacked by all those thorns and Sierra being thrown onto a hedge. Nehru lets me sit down. She says similar things to Nathan, but his response to her question is a little different.

"The worst part of this Challenge," he begins, "was when the cat called Crystal to do the riddle- and then when it... got her... well, at the time, I could barely see what was going on because they were both moving so fast, but... when I saw her in pain and trapped under the cat... well, I tried to help her. But I wasn't allowed to. I... hate feeling powerless to help as another person struggles."

The other teams' least favorite parts were the riddles, the dangerous path, the fog, the maze itself, etc. Finally, after talking to all eight of us, we are told to stand again. We all step forward, and Nehru finally announces the winning team.

"And congratulations to the winners of the Second Challenge... Crystal, Nathan, Sierra, and Ham!"

I'm stunned for a moment and stumble back to find my chair. The others sit down as well. Thaddeus and Zelda come up to us, each with two boxes just a little smaller than the average shoe box. Thaddeus hands Nathan and me one as Zelda hands one each to Ham and Sierra. We are then told to open them.

Ignoring the angry, envious stares of the other contestants, I lift the lid. Inside, I find a pair of sleek, sturdy, comfortable looking shoes. They are black with dark purple lining- just like the rest of our clothes. I look over to find that Nathan has the same thing. Ham and Sierra do as well, although theirs are black and red.

Nehru explains to us what they are. "Those are Lightning Shoes," she says proudly. She sighs at our blank looks, although I hear a gasp of envy from Kat. "They enable the wearer to run as fast as if they had that Gift- but the difference is that these have a limit. If you run all out for longer than ten minutes, the shoes will begin to wear out. Within fifteen minutes, you would wear them to shreds, and they'd no longer work. If you give them breaks of about two minutes, however, then there is no limit to the length of time they will endure. They are waterproof and fireproof as well. It's one size fits all- once you put them on, it will mold to your foot for a perfect, comfortable fit. Once again, Congratulations!" The crowd bursts into applause, and we are told we should head to bed so we can be prepared for training to resume the next day.

Nathan and I say goodnight to Sierra and Ham- both of whom are still shocked that they won a Challenge. Of course, this prize doesn't benefit Sierra much, but she is still very pleased with it.

I pass Lloyd on the way to our house. "How's Eric?" I inquire anxiously.

He shrugs. "The same, I suppose. He misses you, though. Are you going to check on him in the morning?"

"Of course," I say, relieved. "Thank you for taking care of him while I was gone."

"Yes, well, I told you that I would help you out for this Challenge- but Crystal, you need to return him to his own kind. I don't want to babysit him for the next Challenge. I had no idea what was happening during this one since I was in the woods the whole time." I hesitate. "He needs to go back to his own kind," he presses.

"I... I know..."

"Will you take him back, then?"

"...Yes. Not now, of course. I'll just have to find time before the next Challenge, I guess."

He looks relieved. "Good. He seems pretty lonely anyway. See you later?"

"Yeah," I mutter, eyes downcast as Nathan and I continue on to our house.

Nathan looks at me and notices my sorrow. "You made the right choice," he assures me.

"Yeah, I know," I mumble. "It's just... how will the dragons react to me walking around in the mountains with one of their young ones? I doubt they'll just let me explain myself."

Training goes on as usual for the next week, with the exception of Nathan covering the morning shifts for Eric. When he returns, we train with Thaddeus, he trains with Vlad, we have lunch, and switch. I don't go to Eric in the middle of the day anymore not only because he can hunt for himself now, but also because of the increasing difficulty to get away with everyone watching me to ensure I don't disappear again. After I train with Vlad, I finish training with Thaddeus and Nathan before checking on Eric. I notice that he's sad more now than ever. He can talk almost as well as I can, but he still calls me Kysta. He keeps asking me to play with him the next day, and it breaks my heart to keep telling him that I can't. Even though it is now three weeks until the next Challenge, I doubt that Thaddeus will let me go again judging from what happened the last time he allowed me to have time off. Finally, I decide that I have to try. I need to return Eric to his real family- I promised Lloyd. Besides, I just can't bear to see him so sad and lonely.

So, a few days later, I tell Nathan about my plan to return Eric. "I'm coming with you," he says, finality strong in his voice. "So, don't argue. Nothing you say will change my mind."

"I wasn't going to dissuade you. I was actually hoping you would be willing to come with me." He seems surprised, just like I thought he would be.

"What- really?"

"Yes, really. Dragons are powerful and I..." I swallow the words that almost escaped my lips.

"What is it?" he asks me softly, tenderness in his voice and in his touch. "You can tell me anything. I promise I won't make fun of you or think any less of you,"

he reassures.

"I... I'm afraid," I finally squeak out.

"Well, of course you are," he says. "It would be strange if you weren't. With the power of the dragons... if you went out alone, then you would be insane- or suicidal. So don't worry, I'll be with you every step of the way."

When we meet Thaddeus the next day for training, we ask if we can talk to him- before he drags us up the stairs again. He raises an eyebrow quizzically. "Yes, what is it that you wish to talk to me about?" He questions.

I swallow and open my mouth to answer him, but Nathan beats me to it. "Well, Crystal and I noticed that we aren't working together very well," he starts. Thaddeus raises a disbelieving eyebrow at him. I wipe my sweaty palms on my pants. "...So we were thinking that we should take today to train our trust in each other. We really need to be united in order to win so we can go home. So we were just going to ask if... if you needed a break today, and we can take over- if that's alright with you, of course."

Wow, I think, impressed. *I can't believe he came up with that so fast! Let's just hope that it's good enough to convince him to let us go.*

Nora quietly agrees. *"Especially after what keeps happening almost every single time you go off to the woods, alone or otherwise..."* she adds.

Thaddeus looks thoughtful. "Normally, I wouldn't let you, but since you two will be together, you should be fine..." I swallow my guilt and nod. "...Alright. But make sure to take your Familiars with you. They have fully healed, correct?"

"Yes," I say. Nathan nods.

"Good. Be back in time for training tomorrow. I expect a full report of the day's events and visible improvement in your relationship with each other." We nod, ecstatic. I can't believe he's letting us go.

After thanking him, we head to the woods while he goes inside. I stop Nathan before we get to Eric's little cave. He's bigger than when he tackled Lloyd- almost the size of a mountain lion- so he would definitely hurt Nathan more. After I inform Eric of his new visitor, he's happy rather than on edge, and he's careful not to hurt Nathan or Greg.

Nathan and I made sure to wear our Lightning Shoes, just in case, but we don't start sprinting off anywhere. We don't know where to find any dragons, so our best bet is to wander around and hope that a dragon will spot us and, most importantly, let us explain.

After an uneventful hour of hiking, Nora takes off to find some food, promising to return quickly. Greg stays so there is one Familiar with us at all times. We decide to head uphill and away from the trees so we are more visible. The thought still freaks me out, but I am comforted by the two Familiars and Nathan. And Eric, of course. If nothing else, we should be able to escape using the Lightning Shoes. *We are prepared for this, so there's no reason to keep worrying,* I tell myself.

As we climb, the trees thin until they are each far apart from the next. There is room for a dragon to land here if it's not too colossal. I notice large rocks, and it's grassy and not very steep. We slow down and wait in the clearing for a while. Eric sees the large stones as well. He scrambles up one that's near us and launches himself off. He snaps open his wings and glides to the ground. He does this for a while, so we stop to watch him. Nora returns and Greg has his chance to get some breakfast as well. After a few times gliding down, Eric decides to try and flap. So he jumps off and starts flapping like crazy. His right wing pumps a little harder than his left, so he slices to the left and lands on the ground in a heap. I step forward, concerned, but he quickly jumps back up and clambers back onto the rock.

He's unhurt, and he learned from his mistake, too. This time he makes sure to time his wingbeats so they are exactly the same. However, he doesn't stay in the air for long since he doesn't flap often enough. He soon gets the hang of it and is flying in wobbly circles around our heads. I laugh and congratulate him. He gives me a broad, toothy smile and glides down to an almost perfect landing.

I smile too. That's when I notice the air… vibrate around us and hear a faint thumping sound. It quickly gets louder. *Thump. Thump. Thump.* Soon it's almost deafening. I can't figure out what it is, but I have a feeling I will soon. I swallow, but the rock in my gut only grows heavier. THUMP, THUMP, THUMP. It's bone-rattling. I look up and finally find the source of the sound.

Coming toward us are two green dragons, the sun glistening off their scales as they approach. I gasp, which causes Nathan to follow my gaze and see them as well. His mouth drops open. "Wow..." he croaks. The huge, mighty beasts are beautiful as well as majestic, making them even more awe-inspiring. We are rooted in place as we watch them speedily approach.

It's not long before they land in front of us, a whirlwind from their wings sending us back. The darker colored one is also a little larger, so I guess that it's a male. It's filled with power and pride while the smaller, more feminine one is a lighter shade of green and is filled with wild beauty. The male's head dips toward me, stopping just inches away. I can't seem to move a muscle. Suddenly, I remember what I learned about dragons from Thaddeus and realize that the dragon is probably about to look into my heart and judge me. Fail, and I die.

The head lowers the final few inches until I find myself staring into one of his great, glistening amber eyes. It's about the same size as my head. I am immediately lost in their depths. I don't know how long it is before he moves on to Nathan, but if I had to guess, it was probably only a few minutes, although it felt longer than that. When he lifts his head, he glances at the other dragon before turning back to us.

"Greetings, Crystal Dragon and Nathan Anderson. My name is Victor, and this is my mate, Tatiana. I see that you have our lost nephew with you. Thank you for taking care of him. Since my only sister- his mother- passed away, and her babies with her, I thought that all was lost. But I see now that it is not. I presume that you came to return him to his own kind?"

"Yes," I reply. "*...I named him Eric and raised him for a while, but he really belongs with you.*"

"Thank you. I'm afraid that we have to go through the Dragon Council first, however. Anything dealing with humans or the death of a dragon must be dealt with in Dragon Mountain during the council meeting. Luckily, that's where we are headed now- and it's fortunate for you as well. The council only meets once

every other year. Since you are involved with this matter, your presence will be required to make the change of mentors. Are you willing to come with us, Dragongirl?"

I start when he says this. I really don't know that I really *am* this 'Dragongirl,' but apparently everyone else thinks so. *"Um... of course,"* I say, still thrown a little off track by that one word. *"But we obviously cannot fly, so we are willing to come if you are willing to fly us there."*

He smiles. It's a lot more frightening than Eric's, since his teeth are almost the width of my head. *"Ah, but you could simply become a dragon and fly with us. After all, you are part girl, part dragon. You are as much dragon as you are human. It should be easy. ...If you do not wish to, however, then I would be happy to give you and your companions a ride. Eric wouldn't be able to make it there in time, if at all, without us anyway. I saw him trying to fly, and he is learning rapidly, but he does not yet have the stamina to make it all the way there."*

"Thank you," I respond. Greg comes racing back as we climb onto the dragons, squeaking in terror but pressing forward regardless. I decide to ride with Tatiana while Nathan climbs onto Victor. I hold Eric close to me, keeping his head on my lap. Greg scrambles up the dragon's leg and into Nathan's lap just as the dragons crouch to leave. Nora hovers above us, waiting. The two then launch powerfully off the mountain, heading North-East. Nora flies alongside us for a while, but she soon gets tired and lands on my lap to rest.

The dragons fly so fast that we cover hundreds of miles in about an hour and a half, with the dragons creating a pocket of air around us so we can breathe and stay warm. Finally, I see a vast, ominous looking mountain ahead. *"Is that Dragon Mountain?"* I ask Tatiana.

"Yes. It is the only mountain with hollow insides large enough to hold so many of us. I do not enjoy being there, though. It is a dark, joyless place. Nothing grows there, and nothing has for hundreds of years."

"Why?"

"Because Dragon Mountain is a volcano. When it erupts, it causes devastation for miles around. Plants grow back everywhere else, but never on the mountain because of the noxious fumes that come from it."

"Um... is it really a good idea to meet there, then? Couldn't you just meet outside?" I ask, concerned. I don't know much about noxious fumes, but I

163

know that they won't do good things to Nathan and me- or our Familiars.

"*No,*" she says sadly as we prepare to land on the mountain. I can already detect a strange smell lingering in the air. "*We can no longer do something like that.*"

"*Why? Nothing is more powerful than dragons, right? What do you have to fear?*"

"*...The Dragon Hunters. If we were to risk meeting in the open, the large number of dragons would certainly attract their attention. Normally, we wouldn't fear them, especially when we are in a group, but we have recently discovered that they have created weapons of mass destruction,*" she says as we land. "*With these tools, they would be able to take out a large number of the dragons there. There is nothing we can do about the weapons, unfortunately. They are impervious to fire, and are strong enough to endure the power of our claws.*"

"*...Oh,*" is all I can say as I climb down, Eric happily bounding after me. I don't know what to say. I would like to help the dragons, but I don't know that I can. It sounds to me like these weapons are indestructible. What could I hope to do against something like that?

As we walk into the mountain, the strange smell gets stronger. I start getting really concerned. "*Um... Victor? Will these fumes hurt us?*"

"*No, not that I know of. It doesn't do anything to dragons, but it could be different for humans and animals. Still, the fumes aren't as strong as they once were, so you should be fine for a while.*"

"*...How long do you think this will take?*"

"*I don't know. There isn't usually this many things that need discussing. Maybe a few hours, perhaps longer.*" I start feeling lightheaded and my stomach churns.

"*I don't think we have that kind of time. Do you think we can do this any faster?*"

"*No... but I have a solution. Your friends will have to wait outside- including and especially Nathan- then you can turn into a dragon to bear the fumes. They will no longer affect you, and it won't matter so much how long this takes.*"

"*Why especially Nathan?*"

"*Because many of the dragons have begun to assume that all humans are like the Dragon Hunters... it would just be much safer for him to never enter.*"

"*But won't it still affect them while they are outside?*"

"Possibly, but it would at least take longer. Your friends should be able to last all day. They will likely have a fierce headache, if I understand humans correctly, but it's the only way." I hesitate, but it does make sense. I take a deep breath. I guess I'll just have to face all these dragons alone.

"...Alright. I guess that's what we'll have to do," I decide. Turning to Nathan, I tell him the plan. He isn't happy about it, but the fumes are starting to make him feel sick, and Greg has already passed out, his little body overcome by it. Nora goes with him, riding on his shoulder since she's too weak to fly.

My nausea is building as well, so I quickly concentrate on the feeling of being a dragon- I don't picture a dragon this time, because that would make me shapeshift into a dragon already in existence. I want to see, once and for all, if I really am this 'Dragongirl.' So in theory, this should turn me into the dragon I'm meant to be.

I'm unprepared, however, for it to work.

Before I realize what's happening, I am suddenly just a little smaller than Tatiana. I'm surprised to find that I'm not green like the two of them, however. I crane my neck around to take a look at myself. I am differing shades of blue and gold. All my spikes and claws are a bright gold- beautiful but obviously deadly, while my scales are a dark, vibrant blue. I wait for draconic instincts to try and take over, but nothing does. I am myself, yet, impossibly, I am a dragon with deadly power.

It's inexplicable since I've never felt like this before, yet it doesn't feel surprising. It's new and unexpected, yet normal, like this was a part of me that was buried deep underneath, just waiting to be let into the light.

"Wow!" both dragons exclaim, stepping backward in shock. Victor continues, *"I... I've never seen any dragon like you."*

"Really?" I ask, nervous. How was I supposed to blend in with these dragons if I'm so obviously different? *"Are all dragons green? Is that what it is?"*

"No, there are different colors of dragons, but none... I have never heard of a dragon of more than one color. You are unique indeed. No one would doubt that you are a child of Alex and Jack. Do you... feel any different? I understand that humans lose themselves to the power and complex minds of dragons..."

"No, I feel fine. Better than fine, in fact. You were right. It seems that I am indeed part dragon. It feels... natural to be in this form. It's not foreign at all,

although it should be." I look down at Eric. He doesn't seem surprised to see me like this. Maybe he saw the dragon in me before I did myself.

The four of us continue into the mountain, completely unaffected by the noxious fumes. Soon we emerge from the tunnel into a vast open space filled with dragons of all colors and sizes. At first, I am overwhelmed by them all. There must be hundreds, all different shades of red, light blue, sapphire, purple, lots of greens, blacks, and some silver. But like Victor said, there are no others with two colors.

There are some that are many times bigger than me, and very few that are smaller. We must be the youngest ones here. I suddenly feel claustrophobic and tiny. Most dragons are *at least* twice as big as me. Intimidated, I pull my wings up over my head and focus on just breathing for a minute, trying to collect my former confidence that I gained from changing into a powerful dragon. I lower them again and feel a little better. Eric, daunted by both the number and size of the dragons as well, climbs onto my back and tries to hide behind one of the large spikes there. I can hear many conversations raging in my head, but they are all quiet and in the background since none are directed towards me. I can gather, though, that they are waiting for something- or someone.

All conversation suddenly drops as a colossal gold dragon saunters into the room. He stops and calmly gazes around the room. I vaguely notice that all the dragons are bowing their heads to him, but I am too astonished by this dragon's presence to do the same myself. He notices me and begins making his way toward me, dragons parting before him to make room. I can feel the eyes of every dragon in the room watching me. The weight of their stares is suffocating.

As he gets nearer, I manage to bow my head respectfully, although I feel more like I'm hiding than paying my respects. My head to the ground, I can only see one of his enormous claws as he stops in front of me. I take a deep, anxious breath. This dragon obviously has power and strength and can easily affect the rest of the dragons, and I have a feeling it has nothing to do with the fact that he's simply the largest dragon I will probably ever see- even bigger than the silver one with the Sohos. If he wanted to, he could probably order all of the dragons in this room to attack me- if not just take my head off himself with one lazy flick of his paw. Who knows? I don't exactly belong here anyway. This dragon could tell that at a glance-

and judging by the whispers in the back of my head, the rest could as well.

I then hear his deep, rumbling voice in my head, drowning out the whispers. *"Hello, child. I can see that you are new here. What is your name? I have never seen you before- nor any dragon like you. Although your scent is somewhat familiar. Who are your parents?"*

"I... I..." I stammer, unable to form words. I'm so in awe of this dragon that my brain doesn't seem to work right anymore. I force it to work anyway. It's rude not to answer a question- and I certainly don't want to make him mad.

I swallow and force myself to look up at him. It's a long way up. *"My... my name is Crystal... Dragon. And you're right, I'm new here. My parents are..."*

"Pearl and Alexander Dragon," he says thoughtfully. *"I should have known. Those two are some of the most incredible, brave, and caring humans that I have ever met... and I have lived a long time,"* he adds, chuckling. I try to smile, pulling my lips up over the long, sharp fangs in my mouth. *"I should have known that their child would be the long-awaited Dragongirl... how are they? Doing well, I hope. I haven't seen them in quite some time."*

I swallow again. *"Um... well, not really. They... they are in the hospital at the moment."* I quickly explain the whole story to him, about my brothers and I being stolen and my parents' hearts being broken, keenly aware of the dragons still staring at me the entire time.

"Ah. That would explain their absence... Well, it's good to have you with us, Crystal. I thought you would be coming soon."

"How... how did you know that I was coming? I didn't even know until about two hours ago!"

"Because you are the Dragongirl. It was prophesied that you would aid us in our time of need, and that time is now. I should have known that it would be at our council... it all works out perfectly. ...But what is that on your back? Could it be... is that the child that was lost after his mother died?"

"Um... yes," I reply. *"At least, I think so, unless it happened to more than one family of dragons. His mother and siblings died. I rescued him and named him Eric."*

"Well, hello, little one," I hear the big gold dragon say to Eric. Eric, rather than responding, just ducks behind my tail to hide. *"There's no need to be*

afraid. We are all here to help you. My name is Gale the Gold." Suddenly Gale looks up, seeming to finally notice all the dragons watching us.

"I must go, Crystal Dragon. I must start the council- the other members are already here and waiting." I glance over at the highest point in the room, and sure enough, there are four other dragons there, waiting. All of them are the biggest and oldest dragons here. There is a sapphire, a silver, a black, and a white, but Gale is the grandest dragon of them all. *"I will talk to you again soon. Very soon, in fact, since the matter of Eric is the first thing we shall attend to. The matter of you helping us is the other. I will do my best to be fair, but I cannot guarantee what the others on the Dragon Council will decide regarding everything we discuss today. Now then, let's get started, shall we?"* With that, he slowly walks to his place.

Once there, he turns and addresses all of the dragons in the room. *"Hello, my friends, and welcome to this Dragon Council! As all of you know, I am Gale the Gold, the oldest dragon alive- thanks to the Dragon Hunters killing Asoka,"* he adds, bitterness in his voice. *"Our first item of business today is that of Jasmine's lost child, who has finally been found!"* He pauses as the dragons murmur amongst each other. When that dies down, he continues.

"He was found by a human- a member of the Dragon family. Crystal Dragon has raised our lost family member, naming him Eric, and is now returning him to us. The only thing to be decided now is to whom Eric should go. Jasmine had a large family, so more than one dragon may decide to claim him. Victor has expressed his interest to me previously to be his mentor. Victor, please come forward."

His head held high, the green dragon, dwarfed by most of the other dragons, quickly makes his way to the front. He bows his head to Gale and stands behind him and to the left.

"As Jasmine was your sister, you have a right to this child. Does anyone object?"

"Yes," A deep, angry voice growls. I look around, trying to discover the source of the voice. A dark black dragon a little bigger than Victor steps up, a proud look on his scaly face. *"My younger brother does not reserve the right to our sister's child. He has not yet even earned his title. As the oldest, I should be entitled to raising young Eric. It is my right."*

"Very well. Please come forward, Vincent the Proud. We will have to judge who is worthy of raising this child." With a satisfied smirk, Vincent strides

haughtily up to Gale's side. He doesn't bow to him. My wings flutter a little with anger. I notice many other dragons are irritated as well. I cannot believe that this jerk thinks he is so much better than everyone else and everything is his *right*. The air about him just seems... wrong, somehow. All I know is that I don't like this dragon. Not at all.

"Does anyone else make a claim on Eric?" No one says anything. *"Very well, then. Due to time constraints, we will decide after the meeting who Eric will stay with. We may even let* him *decide. But for now, we must move on to our other item of business. We have an extraordinary guest with us today."* Gale turns and looks at me as Victor and Vincent go back to their places.

"Crystal Dragon, would you please join me in the front of the room?" I swallow hard, my wings fluttering with nervousness as the eyes of every dragon in the room once again land on me. I hear hundreds of conversations erupt in my head, almost deafening me. I walk slowly up to Gale's side, barely remembering to bow my head first. My tail swishes from side to side anxiously as I stand there.

At first, Gale tries to wait for the dragons' conversations to die down, but they just get more and more excited as they realize what this must mean- especially when they notice my multicolored scales. So after a few minutes of this, Gale has to roar loudly to silence them all.

"Good. Now that that's over with... I know you have all heard the prophecy of the Dragongirl. It was not specific, but it is obvious that Crystal is the one. Never before have I seen, in all my years, a dragon of two colors. Likewise, I have never seen a human become a dragon and not lose themselves to the form completely. It is an excellent sign that she is here. Our dark days are coming to an end! This dragon-human will help bridge the gap between our two races and defend us against the Dragon Hunters and save our world!"

I quickly interrupt. *"I never... I never said that I will take on the Dragon Hunters for you."* Complete silence. That is what my statement causes. *Shock and anger spreads across nearly every dragon's face.* Glee spreads over Vincent's.

"I knew it!" he exclaims, striding up and standing proudly in front of Gale. *"I told you she wouldn't help us! She* is *a human, after all! Everyone knows how selfish they are! I'll do it! I will save us! I will take on this Patrick guy myself! He doesn't scare me..."*

Gale growls loudly, cutting off his tirade. *"You don't know what you're talking about. You have never seen the Dragon Hunter's power. You have no idea the havoc they can- and do- cause. I understand and respect Crystal's hesitance. She is wiser than you.*

"However," he continues, turning to look at me with one great, golden eye. *"I strongly urge you to reconsider. I appreciate that you do not wish a prophecy to rule your life; govern your every action. I know how that feels. Regardless, I have discovered that eventually, you end up fulfilling that prophecy whether you meant to or not. It is still up to you, of course. What does the rest of the council say?"*

The sapphire dragon steps up and stands on the other side of Gale. *"I think that we should leave this up to the Dragongirl, but before she makes her final decision, we should do what we can to show her how much we need her help. Then we let her decide."* Her head swings around and she peers at me. *"...I trust that she will make the right decision."* She lets this hang over my head, a subtle threat. I respond by dipping my head respectfully to her. She returns the gesture before returning to her spot.

The silver and white dragons agree with her, but the black one does not. He stands and strides to the front. *"I disagree. You are all too soft. I think that the Dragongirl should either help us or get out of our way. She must do as the prophecy says. However, I don't believe that we really need her help. We can solve this ourselves. Since when do we need a puny human to help us? We are the strongest, most powerful race in all of Zilferia- in all of the realms. So help or not, I don't really care, as long as we dragons don't sit back and do nothing. If nothing else, my clan and I can take care of this threat,"* he cockily promises as he sits back down, satisfaction written plainly on his face. I can tell that he's probably related to Vincent- he's so full of himself. But then again, Victor wasn't like that, even though they were brothers.

"Are we in agreement, then?" Gale asks, looking at the council. *"We let her decide, but try to help her make the right choice?"* They all nod at this, looking satisfied at the compromise. Vincent and many of the other black dragons, however, do not. But majority rules, I suppose. Gale turns to me. *"Do you agree to this?"* I nod, grateful that they're letting me add my voice to the decision. *"Thank you, Crystal. You may return to your spot. I will speak with you afterward."* I nod again and head back to Victor and Tatiana, feeling the tightness in my chest finally ease.

They continue talking about their dragon news, but not much of it catches my interest. Gale announces that one of the dragon families had laid some eggs and they are all doing fine. He says a bit more, something about clans. I turn to Tatiana. *"What is he talking about? What are clans? Are they like... families?"*

"Yes, in a way," she replies. *"A clan is a group of similarly colored dragons. We organize it in that way because each dragon's color is correlated to their main characterizing trait; so dragons of the same color generally get along better. This doesn't mean that they are always from the same family, however. Vincent and Victor are brothers, but they are different colors, therefore in different clans while still in the same family. The blacks, as you may have noticed, are the most proud. They never think about what their actions could mean. They rely on their own strength.*

"We have mostly green dragons around here, as I'm sure you've noticed. Greens are kind of timid. We don't speak up very often, so when we do, we have something important to say. We don't really enjoy being the center of attention- unlike the blacks. White dragons are peacemakers, silvers the most curious, blues are the smartest, and gold dragons are the rarest as well as extremely powerful- at certain times."

"At certain times? What does that mean?"

"No one really knows. I don't think that even Gale fully understands it. All I know is that for the most part, golds are just as powerful as the rest of us- most of the time. Yet sometimes, an unknown... substance or entity aids them and makes them more powerful. This may happen to you at some point, since you are part gold.

"The purples grow the slowest, and are the smallest because of that. They are timid like the greens. Reds are the fastest fliers and the most nimble. Sapphires are about the same as the regular blues- smart. But sometimes they seem to be able to see more than the rest of us in a given situation. They detect out of the ordinary things before any of the other clans. Did you notice that no one seemed to detect your presence at first except for a few sapphire dragons?"

"Um... no," I reply apologetically. *"I guess I was too wrapped up with everything that was going on... plus I've never seen so many dragons! Of course... before today the only dragon I'd ever seen alive was Eric, so..."* Tatiana chuckles, but no one notices. They're too involved in an argument over something.

"Don't worry, I understand. It's a little overwhelming at first. But you will

eventually get used to it." With that, she turns back to the debate. I sigh. I doubt I'll ever get used to so many dragons at once. I'm only used to *being* a dragon because it was apparently a part of me all along.

It takes another hour or so to finish up the council meeting. I wonder how my friends are doing. I decide that I should probably head back to them as soon as possible, so once most of the dragons have left through the various exits, I start heading toward the one we entered through. I have only taken a few steps before I am approached by Gale. My wings twitch a little. I'm still unnerved by how huge he is.

"Crystal, may I have a word?" he asks me.

"Of... of course," I reply. Leaving Eric with Victor and Tatiana, I follow Gale as he flies up through the hole in the top of the volcano. We perch on the ring and look out at the forest. I once again feel dwarfed compared to both Gale and the expanse of trees before me. A clean breeze dances past. I take a deep breath, releasing the toxins I've been breathing in.

Gale turns to me. *"Well, young one? Do you have any questions for me?"* I'm surprised for a moment. That's not what I was expecting him to say.

"Um, yes. I... I was wondering... why did you say that you know how it feels to be governed by a prophecy? Was there... a prophecy about you?" He smiles a little, turning to gaze out at the forest again.

"I was expecting for you to ask me that. The answer is a bit complicated, but the easiest answer would be that yes, I was indeed involved in a prophecy. When I was young, maybe forty or fifty."

"Fifty?! That's young?!"

He chuckles. *"You must remember that we dragons can live for hundreds, even thousands of years. Fifty is nothing."*

"How... how old are you?"

"You do not need to know the exact number, so suffice it to say that I am almost one thousand years old."

"...Wow," I think, stunned. A thought then suddenly occurs to me. *"Gale? Do... do you think that... I will live that long? Because I am a dragon... but I'm also a human."*

He frowns a little, thinking. *"I believe that you will live a very long life for a human, but I doubt you will live as long as I have. It also might depend on which form you spend the majority of your time in. Regardless, I've lived a long time, even for dragons. Although I doubt that I will be around for much longer."*

"What? Why? Are... are you ill?"

"No. It... has to do with the prophecy I was and am a part of. You see, it said that I would save the lives of every color of dragon. Of course, it didn't mention me by name seeing as I was not yet born when this prophecy was foretold. It simply referred to me as a young, pure-hearted dragon. With each color of dragon that I helped, it said that I would grow that color of scale. After I helped every color, I would then be filled with power and knowledge and... become gold."

"What, what? You... you weren't always gold?"

"No. I was green, actually. I was completely average- I didn't stick out in any way except that I was unusually obedient for such a young dragon.

"One day, I was alone, wandering through the forest when I came upon a large cave that I had not yet explored. I entered and found a small family of purple dragons near starvation. When I asked them why they had not eaten, they told me it was because of a massive black dragon that came into their territory and ate the food there. I assured them that I would help in any way I could. Then came the hard part- figuring out how I could help them when I myself was small and weak in comparison to this giant.

"I decided to try talking to him. My mother begged me not to- she couldn't stand to lose her only surviving child. I told her that I had to do it because no one else would. I hated to do it, but I disobeyed my mother and left in the middle of the night to go find this dragon. I wandered again into the purple dragons' territory and waited for the black dragon to come. It was said that he hunted at night.

"I finally found him just a little while before dawn. He was feasting on the carcass of a bear. I was quite frightened, but I faced him anyway. When I strode into the clearing, he hardly glanced at me, too involved in his meal. His muzzle was covered in the dark red blood of the beast as he gorged. I swallowed my fear and walked right up to him so he couldn't ignore me.

"He growled at me to go away, but I didn't. In fact, trying to sound as ferocious as I could, I growled back and told him *to go away. He was astonished at this, but he didn't leave. It wasn't going to be that easy. He then got right in my face, washing my small body with hot air and told me to run home before I regretted it.*

"I told him no. He was doing the wrong thing, and he needed to go to his own home. This made him angry, and he attacked me. Fortunately, I was ready for him. I had made sure that a large rock was behind me. So when I jumped out of the way as he leapt for me, he crashed into the rock and managed to break a claw on his

right paw. This just served to anger him more. He turned for me again, but I quickly leapt onto his back and crawled between his wings- where he couldn't reach me with his wings, forelegs, hind legs, or head. I thought I was all set. I thought that I might actually be able to win the fight.

"But then he whacked me with his tail, something that I was not expecting. Dazed, I fell off his back. He quickly put a heavy paw on top of me, pinning me down. I could barely breathe. He then leaned down and put his face in front of mine, hoping to intimidate me. It worked. I was more frightened of him than I had ever been before. I realized that he might actually kill me.

"I was so frightened, I wiggled around like crazy, trying desperately to get free, but I had hardly budged under the weight of the paw. Finally, I blew fire into his eye. He backed away, roaring in pain and anger. I quickly flew home, hoping that what I had done was enough to help the purple dragons I had met. I couldn't find the courage to go back and find out until a week later. I did finally go. I had to find out if I had done any good for the purples.

"And I had. I apparently made the black dragon decide that it wasn't worth it, so he left. The family was so grateful to me that it made up for all the fear that I had felt when I faced him. I went home feeling like a true hero.

"A month later, I grew a purple scale.

"I didn't notice it until my mother pointed it out. I didn't know what that meant, and neither did she, so we went to see the head dragon council member- my father. He was a black dragon, but wasn't dangerously prideful like many of the other blacks. He took me to the Dragon Mage to see if he could figure it out. When I showed him the purple scale, he was so surprised! He then told me about the prophecy. He also said that I was destined to help the members of every dragon clan. I, apparently, was destined for greatness.

"When I went home and told my mom the news, she was ecstatic. My father was as well. He suddenly took an interest in me when he had mostly ignored me before that. I tried to act like I was happy about it, but I wasn't. I didn't want to be forced to help others just to fulfill some stupid prophecy. So one day I decided that I had had enough.

"The Mage was glad to see me again, but what I did was the last thing he expected. I told him that I would have none of it. He was so shocked he didn't immediately respond, but when he did, he warned me that I couldn't just walk out on a prophecy. I couldn't choose to live my life exactly how I wanted. I had to do as the prophecy said. I flat out told him no. He cautioned me against trying to escape it; that it would follow me for the rest of my life until it was fulfilled.

"After that, I tried to ignore the prophecy, but I couldn't. Not with the Mage's words still ringing in my ears and with one of my scales still purple. My mother and father wouldn't stop talking about it either, so I ran away and hid in the mountains for a few years, trying to protect myself from it.

"I couldn't hide forever. During my time in the mountains, a storm hit that lasted two weeks. It was so intense I didn't dare go out. On the eighth day, the storm blew a young red dragon into a tree outside of my cave. I instinctively rushed out to help him. I dragged him into my cave, barely not getting blown away myself.

"I revived him, but at a cost. I couldn't go out and hunt since the storm, so I had very little food left. I gave him what little I had, unwilling to let him starve as well as suffer from his broken wing. I took care of him until the storm was over.

"I then helped him get back to his family. When I saw them all together again, relieved and rejoicing... I realized something. I realized that what the Mage said was true. I couldn't *run away from or hide from the prophecy- it was a part of me. A part that I couldn't let go of.*"

"...Wow," I say, touched by the story. "*So you continued helping all of the clans, then?*"

"*Yes. And I learned and grew a great deal along the way.*"

I sigh. "*I know that you meant for that to help me... but, I... I can't do it. I'm sorry. My prophecy says that I will sacrifice so much... and the Dragon Hunters have weapons that I can't do anything against that you can't do... I'm sorry. I just... can't do it.*" Gale turns and looks at me with his great, sad eyes.

"*I understand. I will not force you. But you have agreed to let us try and change your mind, so I had to do what I could. I will contact you as soon as we decide the next course we will pursue to attempt to persuade you next. Please, do not make the same mistake that I had when I wasted those years of my life running. ...Is there anything else you wish to ask me?*"

"Yes, actually. Did you guys decide who Eric will stay with yet?"

Gale chuckles. "*Yes, we ended up deciding that during the meeting. Young Eric will stay with Victor and Tatiana, both because they are family and because they are of the same clan.*"

"Oh, good," I say, breathing a sigh of relief. Gale smiles.

"*Is there anything else I can help you with, Dragongirl?*"

"Yes, just one more thing," I respond, recalling the First Challenge, when Nathan had died and I had somehow revived him. *"I've been wondering for a while now how I managed to do something... odd."*

"What did you do?" he asks, genuinely curious.

"Well... my friend Nathan... died. And... well, whenever I have a hard time controlling my emotions, my dragon eyes come out. When they were out, I cried and he... well, he came back to life. I know, it sounds crazy," I hurriedly continue before he can say anything. *"Which is why I want to know if you know why that happened? Or how?"*

He looks thoughtful as he ponders this. *"I have a theory to why you have such abilities,"* he slowly begins. *"...When Alex and Jack had their first child, he was extraordinarily concerned with the welfare of others. Before long, it was discovered that he would have dreams and... premonitions about both dragons and humans who were in need of his assistance. He also had a gift of healing. I believe that you may have inherited some part of his abilities."*

"...Oh," I say, unsure if I'm any less confused or not. *"Okay... I guess that makes sense."*

He nods his head to me slowly. *"Was there anything else you needed?"*

"...I don't think so," I say after a few seconds, my mind focusing once more on the pressing need to return to Nathan.

He then bids me farewell, and with that, he flies away, disappearing into the clouds with just a few flaps of his enormous wings. I realize as soon as he leaves that he didn't tell me why he thought he would die soon.

I shrug it off and head back to Victor and Tatiana. We quickly go back out the way we came, hurrying to Nathan. I'm worried because I now realize that we were in there for most of the day, and that means he must have breathed in a lot of toxins by now.

I don't see my friends when I first emerge from the tunnel, so I start panicking. Scolding myself, I stop and think. Looking around, I spot him about a mile away where the tree line begins. He's lying on his back, with Nora and Greg lying still beside him. Worried, I wing my way over as fast as I can, followed by Victor, Tatiana, and Eric.

When I arrive, I see that they are still breathing- although shallowly. I carefully pick them all up and put them on my back. I bid farewell to the three dragons before Eric leaves my life forever. It's a sad parting, but I try and assure Eric that everything will be fine and we can visit sometimes. It doesn't do much to ease the pain. I sadly turn my attention back to my poisoned friends and fly as fast as I dare back to the Village, hoping I can get them help before it's too late.

Two hours later, just after the sun goes down, I land near the edge of the forest. Returning to my human form, I feel small and weak. Shaking it off, I grab my three friends, but I quickly discover that I can barely move Nathan, let alone when my hands are full with Greg and Nora as well. Thinking quickly, I open Nathan's backpack and carefully lay the two Familiars inside. Leaving it unzipped on my back, I can now carry Nathan, although I have to stop and rest every few yards. At first, I blame my weakness on my imagination simply because humans were so much weaker than dragons, but I soon put it together. Changing forms must be draining, and I'm now fatigued from the change. I didn't imagine it; I'm definitely much weaker than I was previously.

I finally reach the hospital around midnight, but I barely make it. I collapse from exhaustion just after knocking on the door.

13

I'm jerked suddenly from my sleep, my eyes flying open. I don't see anyone else in the room. It's dark, but I can still tell that I am in a room in the hospital. I'm filled with relief. *Good, that means I made it and that Nathan, Greg, and Nora got help,* I conclude, sitting up. I feel refreshed. I'm curious as to what the doctors gave me since I've only been asleep for a few hours. I freeze as I finally glimpse something moving in the corner of the room, hoping desperately that they haven't noticed me. I haven't moved much, so it's possible that the shadow hasn't realized that I'm awake.

It hasn't, as far as I can tell. It continues moving slowly from the open window to the door, carefully opening it and slinking into the hallway. I quietly slip out of bed and follow the shadow person into the hall. As we make our way down the hallway, our steps soft and silent, I debate between tackling the person now or waiting to see what they're up to. I decide to wait, mostly due to my curiosity. The person goes into the last door on the right. Now I'm concerned, because I know that's where the doctors keep their information as well as supplies. It's definitely time to confront the shadow-man and stop them before they do something irreversible and damaging. I take a deep breath and step through the open door.

...And come face to face with a tall man in a black cloak. I gasp and take a step back, but I run into something. I spin around and find myself trapped between two men in black cloaks. I glance back and forth between the two, wondering how I'm going to get out of this one.

Deciding to draw upon my Gift of fighting, I pull back my arm and let it fly toward the first guy. He disappears and my fist sails through thin air. Confused, I instinctively take a step back and am grabbed from behind. The man has a crushing grip on my left shoulder, pinching a nerve. My arm suddenly goes dead and I can't feel it. I am now at these people's mercy. ...And I have a feeling they aren't very merciful.

The first man reappears and strides up to me with an air of authority. He leans down and peers into my eyes, then smiles. "Looks like we've got our little Princess," he sneers triumphantly to the other man. My body fills with dread. Who knew that being a princess would cause me so much trouble? It looks like I'm about to be kidnapped again. I'm dying to ask the man what he's planning on doing with me, both for information and so there's a possibility of someone hearing and coming to rescue me, but I can't talk because of the bigger man's hand pressing firmly over my mouth. Luckily, the first man is feeling talkative anyway, so he tells me as he unlocks the window and pulls it up.

"I'm sure you're wondering why I'm here. Well, my mission tonight was simple. I was to look at their patients' records to see if the rumors were true- that the princess was here. If she was, then I was to drug her- you- so that you wouldn't wake up until tomorrow night. Then my companion and I were to return and kidnap you and take you to our leader. Ironically, it seems that my job is made faster and easier because of you, Crystal Dragon!" He steps out of the window. Once he does, the man holding me pushes me out of the window after the first man.

I hook my feet onto the sides of the window, trying to pull away as the first guy pulls on my arms, but to no avail. The man is too strong. Soon I am being tugged into the nearby woods. After a while of this, I finally fight through the panicked fog in my brain and concentrate once again on the feeling of being a dragon. I feel the scales emerge from my skin and wings erupt from my back, clipping the guy holding me. He falls back, landing in the undergrowth.

Before I can finish the transformation, the first guy pulls out a large syringe with a green liquid inside and injects it into my foreleg. I quickly revert to my human state and fall to the ground, devoid of all my energy and unable to control my muscles. I look at the man, wide-eyed. He scowls at me. "I was warned you would try something like that. I didn't believe him when he said that you could turn into a dragon, but luckily, he took precautions and gave me this liquid. As I'm sure you've noticed, it makes you turn back into yourself, and you can no longer control most of your muscles. The best part is that you can never turn into a dragon again, no matter how hard you try."

Disbelieving, I concentrate on being a dragon again. Nothing. I try harder. Still nothing. My eyes widen and a tear escapes my left eye. This means that I can't help the Sohos. I can't help the dragons... I can't even help myself. I am overwhelmed with panic and fear with no outlet. The man laughs. "I see it works, just like Patrick told me it would. He truly is a visionary man. In fact, he had us hide this to make our job easier when we were to grab you tomorrow..." he searches in the bushes a few feet from us. He finally pulls out a sled a little longer than my body.

The second man grunts and heaves himself out of the plants, wiping blood off his forehead before it drips into his eye. He glares angrily at me after laying me on the sled, then grabs the rope in front of the sled and begins pulling. I close my eyes, just wanting to die. I know that these guys want to use me against my friends, or else they would have just killed me outright. I won't be able to stop them from causing great destruction and sorrow- not in this state. I open my eyes and gaze at the sky overhead and am suddenly struck by the beauty of it. As I watch, it slowly lightens as the sun begins to rise, not yet clearing the tops of the mountains.

We stop about an hour later. I can now move my head, but nothing else is responding to me. I look up at them to see what they're doing. They are talking, quietly arguing about something. Finally, the second man turns to me and tells me they will be right back. They are going to go prepare their people to open up the way for us. I open my mouth to say something, but the only thing that comes out is a weak croak. The two laugh at me and walk off.

Now I'm worried about the wild animals in the woods. They could easily walk right up and eat me while I can't do anything to fight back. I start to wish they had been smarter and left one of them with me while only one of them ran ahead. Surely they would be better than being eaten alive by some wild animal- right? So I start trying to yell for them to come back, but again, all that comes out is a weak little croak. As I continue, I get a little louder and stronger. I finally stop and rest my vocal cords.

After a little longer, I can move my arms. Deciding that will have to be enough for me to escape back to the Village, I heave myself off of the wooden sled. I begin dragging my body back the way we came, using my forearms in an army crawl. *I wonder if anyone is looking for me yet. Surely someone has noticed by now! The sun is already up. ...I wonder if they will even bother sending out a search party?* I worry. *I am just an expendable person who participates in their little 'Games.' They can easily do without me.* I sigh and begin despairing. At the rate I'm going, I will quickly be re-caught by those guys again. I'll never make it back to the Village, and no one cares enough to come rescue me, so I'm on my own.

My legs eventually gain a little strength so I can crawl a little faster and my forearms no longer have to bear my full weight. I stop and rest when I reach a large rock. Leaning back against it, I feel my arms screaming out at me in pain, but I don't look. It won't help to see all the blood. As I'm resting, I hear a small group of people, maybe three or four, walking toward me. I freeze, hardly daring to breathe. They stop a short ways from me. I hear them talking, but I can't make out anything they're saying. They continue walking again, slowly. I make out what they're saying as they draw near.

"Are you sure they came this way?" A worried voice asks.

"Yes," a disgruntled man replies. "See the sled marks?" They move on past me.

They don't get far when they stop again and I hear someone gasp, "...Is that blood?!"

Another concerned voice responds, "...Yes. That is definitely blood. I wonder what happened? How much trouble is she in this time?" *Hmm. These can't be the same people that kidnapped me. They wouldn't care what happened to me, much less be worried about it. ...These people must be on a search party from the Village!* Deciding that my best bet would be to contact these people, I call out, even though my voice is still hardly more than a croak. Luckily, they hear me anyway and hurry toward me.

They catch sight of me and gasp with relief, surprise, and disgust. I look down. My arms are almost entirely covered in blood with rocks and sticks ground into them. The blood has been dripping down my shirt and pants, covering them as well. I realize I'm light-headed and swallow as I think about how much blood I've lost. I try to stand, but I sway and fall. One of the guys in the group catches me, saving my head from a meeting with the large rock. He looks down at me, surprise in his warm brown eyes. Those eyes are the last thing I see before I pass out from blood loss.

I wake suddenly. Looking around, I see that I am, once again, in the hospital. I am instantly filled with relief, since that means I made it back safe. I notice a doctor standing near me. He looks relieved that I'm awake. I recognize this doctor. I smile at the thought this puts into my head.

"...Why are you smiling?" he asks me, concerned. "Are you delirious?"

"No," I laugh. "It's just that I'm here so often the hospital is more my home in Zilferia than the house they set aside for me."

He's not amused. I can tell he thinks I'm crazy. I sigh. "Wait... where are Nathan, Nora, and Greg?" I ask, suddenly panicked about my friends' welfare.

"They're fine," the doctor assures me. "Although it seems they had inhaled a fair amount of toxins. However... as far as we know, there are no such toxins anywhere near here." He watches me, waiting for an explanation. I shrug and don't reply, deciding it's far easier not to tell him the truth- or anything at all, for that matter.

He isn't happy about me avoiding his question, but he pretends not to care. "...We saw what happened last night through the security cameras, so we heard what that man said about his plans. We have a theory as to what group those men belong to. ...Did they tell you where they were going? Who their leader was?"

"...Yes," I reply. I quickly tell him what happened- excluding the dragon part- and what they told me. He grimaces at the name Patrick.

"It's just as I thought. They are part of a group called..."

"The Dragon Hunters," I whisper, my voice filled with unmasked dread. The doctor's surprised.

"Yes. How do you know about them?"

"Uh... I just... um, heard about them from people."

"Did you hear what they did to your family?" He continues before I say anything, suddenly becoming animated as he relates the story. "Patrick came with his goons and snatched you and your two brothers away from the King and Queen, and although one of your brothers is still lost, Rex, the other one is with Patrick. Your parents are in a coma right now, so they have no idea that one of their children is back. For a while we thought it was due to stress and lack of taking care of themselves, but now... we can't help but wonder if Patrick slipped them something once he heard of their strategy to use the Games to find you and Rex. He must have known they were close to finding you. Most of the Village doesn't know the truth about them- or about you being the Princess, honestly. Oh, that reminds me..." and with that, he leaves the room. I shake my head, quietly laughing at the strange doctor.

After getting dressed, I find a nurse and ask her to take me to my friends. At first, she tries to make me go back to bed, but I refuse. I've been in bed far too much lately. She finally gives in and takes me to Nathan's room. The two Familiars are there with him as well. I sit in a chair next to his bed as the nurse leaves. I watch him as he sleeps for a little while. I've never seen him look so... peaceful. That is, until his face suddenly fills with pain. I'm shocked and unsure of what to do. I'm about to wake him up when he lurches upright, shouting. After breathing heavily for a few seconds, he sees me next to him. His face instantly fills with relief.

"Oh, good. You're okay," he gasps.

"Yes, I'm fine," I respond. I refrain from telling him about my kidnapping since the nurse told me he was sleeping the entire time and had no idea that it had even happened. I figure what he doesn't know won't hurt him. "Why wouldn't I be?"

He grimaces and lies back down. I notice that he's soaked in sweat. "I... had a dream. It was just a nightmare, really. But... I dreamt that the dragons took you away, and the babies started eating your arms and you were screaming but they paralyzed you so you couldn't escape and... and then... you... you died. Again- just like what happened with the Zyloff and almost with that cat in the Second Challenge. It happened right in front of me and I... I couldn't do... anything..."

I calm him down, assuring him that it was just a dream and that I'm just fine. He believes me until he notices the bandages on my arms. "What-why... your arms..."

"Um, yeah... about that..."

"My dream wasn't true, was it? The dragons didn't hurt you, did they?"

"Well, no, but I was kidnapped by someone else," I say, finally giving in. I tell him the whole story, starting with what happened at the Dragon Council and finishing with me waking up here just a few minutes ago.

"Are you okay?" he asks the instant I'm done. I smile a little at his sweet concern when he's in worse condition than I am.

"Yes, I'm fine. Are *you* okay? You breathed in a lot of toxins on that mountain..."

He starts assuring me that he's good to go when he suddenly starts coughing so violently and for so long that he has to catch his breath when he's done. "Yeah, I'm good too," he finally manages through his scratchy, dry voice. I hand him a cup of water from his bedside table and watch as he hastily gulps it down. His voice is better now, but it still sounds painful to talk. "In fact, we need to go train with Thaddeus. He told us that no matter what, we had to go to training when we came back. If we hurry, he might not find out that anything happened."

I look at him with concern. Not only has it been an entire day since he wanted us back, but it is also late in the afternoon. I feel his forehead and find that it's burning up. It's obvious he has a fever. I shake my head. "No, you can't go in this condition." He starts protesting, but I quickly stop him. "No. You can't go. You have a terrible fever, and you are coughing like crazy. I'll go."

"But..."

"No. I will go- alone. Don't worry, I'll come back and tell you every-thing he says, okay?"

He isn't too happy about it, but agrees reluctantly. Talking to me must have depleted his meager store of energy, because he falls back asleep very quickly. Before I go, I walk over and check on Greg and Nora. They haven't awoken yet. Their breathing is shallow and even worse than Nathan's. I wish there was something I could do for them, but I'm powerless. I just have to depend on the doctors to help my friends. As I head out of the hospital, I talk to a nurse to tell her Nathan's condition. She thanks me, although I can tell she already knew this, and tells me not to worry. They have everything under control. I nod and turn toward the door, but another nurse comes by and stops me.

He insists that I eat something, so I grab a sandwich and head outside. I eat it as I head to the building where we do our training with Thaddeus. When I get there, I see the lady with the blue necklace at the weapons again. I ask her if Thaddeus is here. She replies that he's at the top, meditating. I ride the elevator to the top of the building and head towards him. I walk up beside him but don't say anything.

He sighs heavily, and I can see the weariness on his face. Not looking at me, he stares out at the forest. I follow his gaze, but I don't see anything. "It seems that you get into trouble a lot, Crystal," he begins.

"Yes, but I don't usually seek it out."

"True, the Dragon Hunters sought *you* out this time, but what about the dragons?" There's a knowing tone to his voice. *What- how does he know about that? There's no way... the only one I told was Nathan...* "Of course, you didn't really get into any trouble there..."

"What?!" I exclaim. "How... how did you know about that?"

He chuckles slightly. "Come on. You really think I fell for the 'working on our relationship' thing? I kept an eye on you with magic."

"You... you were spying on us?!"

"Well, I wouldn't call it spying..."

"Then you... you saw the other me?"

He stands and looks at me solemnly. "Yes, and I was quite impressed, both by your actions as well as your skill. I knew you were the Dragongirl. ...Well, alright, I didn't know for sure, but I had a feeling. What I'm truly stunned at, however, is how you were able to raise a dragon right under all our noses and no one knew about it! Not only that, but your willingness to give him away! I saw the bond between you two, and it was strong."

I sigh. "Well, I'm still going to miss him."

"Of course." He turns back to the forest. After a while, he says, "One thing concerns me, though."

"Oh? Just one?" I tease. He doesn't smile.

"Yes. You see, I tried to find you with magic when you were kidnapped."

"Okay?"

"I couldn't see you."

"Um… what does that mean?"

"It means the Dragon Hunters have somehow found a way to not be detected by magic. Which is very bad… that means that they could retake you. We will have to keep people around you at all times."

I groan. "Really? …Can't Nora just look out for me?"

"Perhaps, once she is back to full health. For now, I'll look for volunteers to guard you. Alright?"

"…Okay," I reluctantly acquiesce.

"Good. Now then, it's about time for you to be getting to bed. It's getting late." I look around and realize it's true; the sun is going down.

"But I'm not ti…" Even as I start saying this, I am interrupted by a sudden yawn. This surprises me. I thought that after sleeping so much, I wouldn't be tired again so soon.

Thaddeus smiles wearily at me. I notice that there are bags under his eyes like he hasn't been sleeping. "Don't worry, you'll be feeling better soon. How is Nathan? Is he well enough to come train tomorrow?"

"No, not even close," I reply as we head to the elevator.

"Hmm," he grunts. "Well, I guess I'll just have to tell *you* about the Third Challenge. Now get some sleep, I'll send over a couple of people to guard you. Don't worry about anything. The Dragon Hunters won't be able to get to you again."

I don't reply, deeply annoyed with the idea of being babied- but strangely comforted by the security at the same time.

I wake the next morning feeling refreshed. In fact, I feel so good I completely forget that my arms were previously reduced to hamburger- until I sit up and the blood rushes straight for the wounds in my forearms. I gasp as they burn with pain, instantly causing tears to pool in my eyes. After a couple of minutes, the pain subsides and I can see clearly again. Looking up, I see a guy sitting in a chair next to the door. It's a guy from the rescue party- the one with the warm brown eyes.

At first, I'm confused at his presence, but then I remember that Thaddeus was finding people to guard me day and night. The guy smiles at me heartily. "Good morning!" he says, standing. "I am one of the people protecting you until your Familiar is able to watch out for you again." He steps toward me, covering the short distance between us in just a few strides. He holds out his hand, and I shake it carefully. "My name is Dallas Peterson. Pleased to meet you, Princess Crystal."

"Uh, yeah. Same," I respond, a little surprised he knows who I am. Not that I should be. My guards would have to know who I am and why their job is so important, so it only makes sense. "Before I go and train with Thaddeus, I want to check on my friends," I tell him, sliding out of bed.

He nods. "Of course."

Nathan is still sleeping when I go in, but there's a nurse there this time, so I ask her how he's doing. She tells me that his fever broke and they're still trying to flush out all the toxins he breathed in, but he should be good to go for the Third Challenge. I sigh with relief. The bad news, however, is that neither of our Familiars will be able to help by then.

I thank the nurse, and Dallas and I head to the breakfast area. The hospital has surprisingly good food, but it's still not as good as most food I've had in Zilferia. We then head to train with Thaddeus. I can't help but think how weird it feels to have a random guy following me, as if taking Nathan's place. Without Thaddeus at the bottom making me take the stairs, I opt for the elevator again. When we reach the top, we find Thaddeus in the same spot as the day before, gazing out over the forest. He turns as we approach.

"Ah, good," he says. "You're up and moving. Don't worry, we won't be doing any physical training today- so you also won't have to train with Vladimir- although we *will* tomorrow." Fear flashes across my face before I can hide it. The thought of doing anything in my condition honestly scares me. "Don't worry, it won't be very taxing at all. We will be very gentle at first- although your arms should be much improved by then anyway." I don't believe him. My arms can't improve that fast. Especially seeing the shape they're in now- they just keep throbbing with pain in time to my heartbeats.

"Now then," Thaddeus continues, heading toward the table. "Let's get down to business. I need to tell you about the Third Challenge." Before he does, however, he sends Dallas over to a chair by the elevator. I suspect that it's more so he can't hear us than making sure no one else comes up.

Thaddeus peers at me seriously. "First off, I want to ask how Nathan is faring. Will he be able to train with us tomorrow?"

"No... but," I add, "he will be able to participate in the Third Challenge, luckily."

"Yes, that's fortunate indeed, for he would be put in the arena if he's somewhat stable regardless."

"Wait... what?" I say, disbelieving.

"Yes," he confirms, his voice sad. "I'm afraid it's true. Like I said at the beginning, these Games are rigorous. They are unforgiving, and there's no way Vlad would put them on hold for one boy with a fever. Either he plays in the Challenge, or you are both eliminated and may be kept here even longer than if you were in the Games."

"Wow," I mutter. "What a jerk."

"I believe he is just having a rough go of it lately. He wasn't like this last year... perhaps the pressure has gotten to him."

"I... guess..."

"Now then, about the Third Challenge. It is water-themed this year, so I hope you can swim."

"Yeah, I can swim," I reply. "...Usually. I probably can't really now, because of my arms."

"How well can you swim, though? The entire thing is underwater."

"Pretty well," I say after a moment's thought.

Thaddeus raises an eyebrow. "I suppose we'll find out tomorrow." When he sees the question written on my face, he explains. "We are going to go swimming tomorrow to see how well you can perform in the water, as well as to strengthen your muscles and lengthen your endurance. I suppose since Nathan cannot participate, he will just have to learn and adjust while in the arena. You might have to help him more than ever before during this Challenge," he warns me. I nod.

"What's the goal for this one?" I ask. He grimaces and doesn't answer, refusing to look me in the eye. "What is it?" I demand. "I need to know. I don't care how dangerous it is, we still need to do our best so we can end these Games and we can go home."

He slowly nods, drawing in a deep breath. "You... you have to retrieve... the Mermaid King's Trident."

Apparently, I somehow miss the significance of this. "What? A mermaid? That's it?"

He shakes his head at me. "You don't understand. Mermaids aren't gentle girls with fish tails like the people on Earth have come to believe. They are all- male *and* female- fierce warriors that are masters of the sea and nearly all the creatures that live in it. They are much more dangerous than sharks, moving so swiftly they're difficult to keep track of. When they aren't moving, they are indistinguishable from the seaweed permeating the area. They can only be seen if they *want* to be seen. Some eat any humans that wander into their domain. The King's Trident has the power to control your body. They are all at least as intelligent as you and I. ...Now do you have a clearer understanding of what you're up against?"

It takes me a while to find my voice. "Yes," I squeak out. "But... I thought that the point was not to kill us, but to help us get our Gifts! It seems to me that Vlad is seriously trying to end us all here and now! ... Does he really hate me that much?" I am now genuinely terrified of Vlad now that I know just how far he can go in his punishments.

He shakes his head again and sighs. "I don't know. All I know is that he isn't acting like he normally would. ...Did you ever notice a difference from when you first met him and the next day?" I think about it. I remember he did seem a lot less... uptight when I first met him. In fact, in any other circumstance, he could have even been... nice. Now he's obviously trying to get me killed, no matter the cost- even at the price of other, innocent people's lives! I suddenly remember that night he told me about the Games... he put Kiki to sleep, saying she needed sleep and didn't want to be frightened from his story.

When I tell Thaddeus this, he nods. "Yes, that is how he normally is. However... he has changed so drastically I know something's up. I am simply not sure what exactly it is."

"What are you saying? That... That he's not the real Vlad?"

"Perhaps. Either that or he is being controlled somehow."

"What do we do about it?" I ask, concerned.

"...Nothing. We can't do anything about it until the Games are over. I will, however, keep a close eye on Vladimir and try to protect you from him as best I can."

After that, we grab Dallas and get lunch. Before I eat mine, however,

Thaddeus dumps a powder into the soup and stirs it before handing it back to me. When I ask him what it is, he tells me that it's just something to speed up the healing process for my arms. After we eat, the throbbing is a little better, but Thaddeus says it works mostly overnight.

Since my body can't yet do anything physical, he sends me back to the hospital to rest and keep an eye on Nathan and make sure he's recovering. Dallas, of course. Comes with.

Nathan doesn't wake for about half an hour, so I talk to Dallas while I wait. First I ask him to tell me about himself, but he says that he's just an average guy, nothing special. When I say that surely he's unique in some way, he confides that he enjoys playing chess. Excited, I challenge him to a game sometime. He replies that he'd love to before suggesting doing so now while we wait. I agree, so he goes out and looks around for a chess board.

Soon after he leaves, Nathan wakes up and coughs, and although he still doesn't sound great, it has improved a little. Once he catches his breath, he asks me to tell him about the Third Challenge. So I do, and when I'm finished, he's silent but for the fear on his face.

"...Can you swim?" I ask him.

He nods. "Even better than I can run, but that's not what I'm worried about. Those mermaids sound like real monsters. ...I'm not so sure we should do this."

"What do you mean?" I ask, confused. "What else can we do? We have to get home!"

"Yes, but that doesn't necessarily mean we have to win, right?" When I don't respond, he presses it further. "Right? I mean, they want their winners and everything, but who says we have to win to go home? They just said we can go home once the Games are over. As long as we're still alive, of course."

"Sure, but it only ends if there's only one team left, or if someone wins three Challenges in a row. We've already won the first two. Besides, they won't be letting us just quit. They dragged us here. I don't think they'll let us go that easily."

"No... but we don't have to quit to not get eaten by mermaids."

"...I'm sorry, I don't think I see where you're going with this," I finally say after he pauses to see if I will catch on and figure out his plan.

"We'll just hide," he explains. "In the water, but away from any mermaids or other creatures. We can just wait for someone else to win, and then they will end the Challenge- just like they always do."

I'm about to argue, but then I stop and think about the predicament we are in and agree. I really *don't* want to get killed, especially so far away from home. No one would ever know what happened to me. A nurse then comes in and tells me that I should go back to my own bed so I can rest and heal. I warily agree and say goodbye to Nathan. As I stand to go, Dallas returns with a chess set. We head to my room and play one game. He's tougher than a lot of people I've faced, but I still end up victorious. He seems a little disappointed. I offer a rematch tomorrow. He agrees, then leaves. He's replaced for the night with another guy who doesn't talk much, which is fine since I need my sleep anyway.

The first thing I notice when I wake is that my arms don't hurt anymore. I sit up with a start, electrified. For a moment I don't move from shock, but then I quickly begin pulling off the bandages. A nurse comes in and tells me not to do that, but I ignore her and finish pulling them off. We're both astounded by how much they've improved. Before, they looked raw and bloody- completely disgusting. Now, there are some scabs, but other than that, they look almost like they always had. I carefully touch them and can't keep my spreading grin off of my face when I feel no pain. I'm elated. *I'm healed! Well, mostly. Maybe the water will soften the scabs and they'll just fall off... that reminds me, I need to go train with Thaddeus!* After I get dressed, I start to leave and see that the other guy has been replaced by Dallas. They must trade day and night shifts. After grabbing some breakfast, we go and find Thaddeus for training.

He's not by the building we usually meet at, but his secretary is there, who directs us to the pool. We follow her directions and find Thaddeus talking to another person. As we draw closer, I see that the man's skin, perfectly tanned from the sun, glistens gloriously against the light green of his swimming trunks. Thaddeus introduces us. The tall, muscular man is from Quagon, the watery universe, so he is an *excellent* swimmer. He's going to help me swim and point out ways to better conserve energy in the water.

Thaddeus hands me a swimming suit, and I have to choke back a sigh at the colors. I'm really getting sick of black and purple. After I change,

Thaddeus tells me to do whatever I want in the pool, just warm up and get comfortable with being in the water. The water is clean and cool, and doesn't have chlorine in it like the pools in Second Earth do. It's refreshing, and I feel rejuvenated and better than I have in quite a while. After I swim around for a while, I just float on my back and gaze up at the clear blue sky.

The guy from Quagon then jumps in. He swims over to me and has me do a few exercises, from simple things like staying afloat to doing the breaststroke across the length of the pool four times without stopping. It's exhausting, but luckily, I manage to do everything he asks. He has me do all of the strokes I had ever heard of as well as some that I hadn't, so I have to quickly learn some new moves. They are surprisingly easy, though, and I can tell they were made to reduce the amount of energy spent in the water.

I even learn how to best swim *under*water, since the entire Challenge will be taking place underwater. When I express my concern about being able to breathe, he laughs a little.

"I can tell you are not from Quagon," he says with a light accent that sounds like one I heard on Earth, from a New Zealand tourist. "You may swim like one of us, but you would know about the technology we have if you were there for even a day. You see, we invented a device, small and convenient, to enable you to breathe and see clearly underwater. However, it is permanent. But while you have it, you can breathe air when you are not in the water. It only activates once your mouth and nose are in water. It does not give you gills, but we can do that for you instead if you prefer. The gills would fade almost all the way while you are not underwater. All you would be able to see is thin white lines on your neck. Which would you prefer?"

"Uh, the first one," I choose, still boggled by the concept of breathing underwater. He nods.

"Very well. I will get one for both you and your partner during lunch."

"Do… do you have one?" I ask him.

He laughs. "Of course! Anyone over the age of four in Quagon has one or the other. …Do you wish to see how it works?"

"…Sure," I say. He nods and dives underwater. I peer down and see him calmly sitting at the bottom. It looks like he's breathing normally, like the water is just air. After a few minutes, he comes back up. He's not breathing hard, reinforcing the fact that he was just breathing underwater. "Wow," I say. "That's really cool! ...And you can't even see it?"

"Not easily. Do you see mine?"

"Well... no, but I don't know where to look," I say sheepishly. He smiles and points to the base of his throat, where it connects to his collarbone. I look closely and see a tiny black dot. "Cool," I repeat.

After that, we swim around for a little longer until it's time for lunch. I get out of the pool and change back into my other clothes while the guy from Quagon leaves to grab the breathing devices. I head to the Village Square to eat lunch with the rest of the contestants for the first time in a while. I get my food and sit down with Ham and Sierra. They're both surprised to see me.

"Hey," I casually greet them as I take a bite of my sandwich.

"...Hey," Ham replies. "You're already out of the hospital? I heard what happened, and they said they didn't expect you to be out for at least another week!"

"Yeah, well. I didn't feel like waiting that long, and neither did Thaddeus, so he gave me something to help me heal faster."

"Well, it sure worked!" Sierra exclaims, leaning forward to peer at my arms. "You don't even have any scabs or scars! The doctors said you would at least scar, your arms were so bad."

"Hmm," I grunt. "So, what have you been up to?"

"Oh, nothing much," Sierra replies, taking a bite of her sandwich as well. "Swimming and stuff. But Ham and I don't really care anymore. We *really* don't have a chance on this one. I don't think anyone does, not even you and Nathan. I mean, those man-eating mermaids? Really?! Is Vlad trying to kill us all or something?" She sighs. "So Ham and I are just going to sit back and let the other teams try their luck. If nobody wins, then maybe they'll just have to cancel this Challenge. We figure it's worth a shot, right? Because I really don't want to get eaten or impaled on a giant fork that can control me. That's just *not* my idea of a good time."

I laugh a little. "Yeah, Nathan and I were thinking pretty much the exact same thing." I suddenly feel a hand on my shoulder. Spinning around, I relax as I see the guy from Quagon.

He smiles and hands me a tiny bag with two black dots about twice the size of a freckle inside. "Here you are," he says. "Put one on now, and you can try it out after you eat," he suggests, then leaves to get his own food. I put them in my back pocket.

Ham and Sierra look at me quizzically. "What's that?" Ham asks, clearly burning with curiosity.

"They're supposed to make it so we can breathe underwater," I respond.

"Really? That's so cool!" Sierra exclaims. "…Do you think we'll get one too?"

"Probably. Just ask Zelda for one. I don't see how they'd expect us to do an underwater Challenge without them anyway."

"Okay, we will!" she agrees, excited.

After lunch, it's back to training with Vlad, my least favorite person. All we've really been working on lately is trying to get me to grow into one of my Gifts- I'm the only contestant left that hasn't yet- but it hasn't been going so well. I sigh and wait for everyone to clear out of the Square, wanting them to leave faster while at the same time hoping they'll linger longer so I won't have to be alone with Vlad.

Soon enough, the inevitable happens, and everyone leaves and Vlad comes walking up with some people behind him, hauling weapons. I feel better instantly. That means I'll only have to deal with the weapons person. When they get here, Vlad acts nonchalant and barely acknowledges me, just instructs me, in as few words as possible, to fight with the weapons guy. We choose rapiers again since they are durable and light. As soon as we start to fight, I notice that something is… different about this fight than any other time we've fought before. This time I can almost see what he's going to do before he does it. Everything is… more clear and detailed. It's like everything but me is moving in slow motion. He can't get anywhere near me with his sword. I see surprise on his face and take advantage of it. In just a few more moves, he ends up with his sword on the ground and mine pointed at his throat. We stay like that for a few moments, panting lightly. I then lower my sword and offer my hand to him and help him up.

"Well, looks like you've finally grown into one of your Gifts," he says as we put the swords back. "But you only beat me because when you first get your Gift, you have a rush of energy. Next time, we will be much more evenly matched."

"I see," I thoughtfully respond. "And this means that I'm never going to lose this Gift, right?" I ask, just wanting confirmation.

"Yes. But it won't be your only one. In fact, in your case, you may get two or three more, since you are of the Dragon family. ...Well, good luck in the next Challenge- you'll need it," he adds grimly, turning and leaving, hauling the weapons with him. I walk back to Vlad and tell him that Extraordinary Fighting Skills is one of my Gifts- just like he guessed when he first saw me. I watch him carefully for his response, to see if I can catch him stumbling over something that he should know but doesn't, but all he does is nod and tell me that I can go.

So I do, heading for the pool. I swim around for the rest of the day, although I don't use the breathing device because it doesn't feel fair that I can use it and Nathan can't yet, so I wait until he can join me before I try it out. Fortunately, the doctors tell me that I only need to wait for five more days.

The thing is... that's when the Third Challenge begins.

14

"Ready?" I ask Nathan. His face is ghostly white, his lips set in a firm line. Once again, we are wearing black and purple, although they are not the usual clothes. These are wetsuits that cover most of our bodies to conserve warmth, and are thin and flexible enough that it should be easy to move around in. We are ready to go... although I've never felt less ready for anything in my life.

"...Yeah," he replies, uncertainty clear in his voice. "Let's do this thing. Hopefully these will help," he continues, holding up his 'black speck' that enables us to breathe underwater. I nod and place mine where the guy from Quagon put his- at the base of my throat, just above my collarbone. Nathan does the same. After holding it there for a few seconds, I feel a pinch and it stays. There's no going back now. I take a deep breath, attempting to calm my frayed nerves.

"Let's go," I say, leading the way out of the door. It's still dark outside, but the sky is beginning to gray. We are wearing jackets over our wetsuits because of the chilly, windy air- and because not having pockets drives me a little crazy. We were once again told to meet in the Square, so that's where we're headed.

"Are you sure you're fine?" I ask him as we walk.

"Yes," he sighs. "I'm even better than yesterday, and I felt fine then. The doctors said I'm good to go. The thing is... they left my bed ready for me, and yours as well. I think they know what we're in for better than we ourselves do."

"I don't think so," I contemplate. "You don't need to know much to know we're in trouble. In fact, that might even be their way of being hopeful- that we'll still be in one piece and *alive* because the hospital is better than the alternative." I don't continue. We both know all too well what the alternative is. Despite our plan to avoid the thing altogether, I've still had more than one nightmare with those vicious, bloodthirsty mermaids.

I turn to another topic. "So, who's left in this thing?" I ask.

"Well, there's us, Ham and Sierra, Kat and Jake- the orange team, and Norachai and Felix- team black. Just four teams... but... I have a feeling that this will be the last Challenge." After that, we stop talking, not wanting to dwell on the concept of death. Although it's hard to get it out of our minds when we are essentially walking towards our own.

When we arrive at the Square, we merely wait for the sedative that we know is coming. They always knock us out cold before dumping us in the arena, but this time it doesn't happen. Confused, I look around and spot someone running toward us. I wonder who it is. I don't get to find out, because there is a quick little prick on my neck and I'm out- again.

We've been dumped on a small island. I'm almost blinded by the light when I open my eyes. After blinking multiple times, I can see well enough to realize that all the light is coming from the sunlight reflected off the water surrounding us. The brilliant blue waves sparkle brightly as they slip onto the sand, only to pull back again. Looking around, I can see two more small islands on our right, and one on the left. This surprises me, since they usually put us in a circle with the goal in the middle. This way will be more challenging to find the trident, since we can't just head towards the center of a circle. Behind us, I see a forest on the horizon, but other than that, the only thing out here is ocean water and contestants.

Once again, Nehru's voice echoes around us. "Hello! Contestants! This is Nehru speaking! Just so you know, you are in our very largest arena, competing in the Third Challenge. As always, you will be permitted to leave your island only once the gun sounds. After that, well... I haven't been told what your goal is for this one, so just do as your instructors suggested, I suppose. I hope you each have at least one of your Gifts, and can breathe underwater, because it looks like you're going to need it! For the moment, just sit still and... ponder, plan, or just procrastinate!" She ends her alliteration with yet another giggle. I'm really getting sick of her pre-Challenge announcements. The bright side to this being the last Challenge is we won't be likely to hear much from her anymore.

Nathan and I don't say anything. We've already discussed our plan, so there's no need to go over it now, while the other contestants are listening. So after removing our jackets, we merely wait for the starting gun along with everyone else. Once it goes off, Nathan and I immediately plunge into the water as though anxious to get a head start on the Trident. We do this just to throw off the other contestants so they can quickly get on their way and we can hide.

As soon as we're under the water, we open our eyes and look around. We quickly find an underwater cave in the dirt and rock under our little island. We swim in, still holding our breath, and watch as the other contestants jump in and swim away. I still don't breathe, not quite ready to trust the foreign device, but my lungs finally convince me to try. I slowly let out my breath, tense and ready to rush to the surface if it doesn't work. I watch as the bubbles wiggle toward the surface and carefully breathe in. It doesn't hurt. It feels normal, amazingly.

I look over and see Nathan cautiously trying it out as well. His face is filled with surprise. "This is so cool!"

"Whoa- I can hear what you're saying clearly!"

"I know! It makes it so you almost forget you're underwater!" he grins.

After we get over the shock of being able to breathe underwater, we do what we planned and cautiously head out. We swim slowly because we don't actually want to find anything, but we know that everyone in the Village is watching us, so we pretend we're at least doing *something*.

Soon we decide to have some fun with it. I race Nathan and beat him, but not by much. He has us do a different stroke and we race again, and this time he wins. We have a contest for who can find a purple shell first, and I find one about ten minutes later. We pop up to the surface every now and again to make sure our island is always in sight so we don't get lost. For the rest of the day, we pretend to look for mermaids while really doing our best to avoid them.

Soon it gets dark and we find another cave that we can sleep in. I tell Nathan that I will stay up and watch for mermaids while he sleeps.

"Fine," he says. "As long as you wake me up partway through the night so I can take a turn while you sleep." I agree to his terms, although I doubt that I'll be able to sleep thanks to the threat of the mermaids. After a few hours, though, I find that I was mistaken as I slowly fall asleep without even noticing.

~~~~~The Merman~~~~~

As soon as the girl falls asleep, the merman outside of the cave reveals itself. The green, fishy creature easily blends in with the plants around it, which is why none of the humans that had entered its domain will ever be able to find it. It grins savagely, displaying its sharp, yellow teeth, finding their ignorance humorous.

It then turns and swiftly swims away from the cave to report to its king all it had learned about these intruders, his fishlike tail propelling him forward with almost no effort. After a while, he comes to a wall of seaweed. Undeterred, the merman swims directly through it. There are jellyfish guards on the other side, but they do not attack the scout, for this is his home; this is where he belongs.

As he swims past the homes of the other mermaids, they all come out and silently watch as he passes. He is practically royalty here, for he works for the King directly- although that isn't an enviable job what with the King's mood swings and lack of tolerance for those who disappoint him. He puffs out his slim chest with pride. He has lasted longer than any other servant to the King. He's going on five months now.

Finally, he reaches the castle. It's made of stone, for the humans built it long ago and possessed it until it drowned in the sea after an earthquake. Now *their* King lives and rules within its crumbling walls. The place reeks of fear, but the merman pushes through it and swims up to the top of the building where the King waits for his report. When he arrives, he can tell he is the last of the four scouts to return. He quickly heads to his spot, his head lowered in false humility.

When the King asks for a report, one of the other mermen assigned to watch one of the groups of humans swims forward. "The humans wearing red are no threat to us," he proclaims. "I have observed them all day, and it seems that they are hiding from us. They will not dare approach us."

"Very good," the King says. "Next."

The next merman in line swims forward and delivers his news. "As you told me to do, oh King, I watched the humans wearing black. The girl is timid and scared, but the boy is trying to find us and kill us all, he says. What do you propose we do?"

"Get two others and kill the boy, but leave the girl to warn the humans, once again, that we are not to be trifled with. Go now."

"Yes, sir," he says and swims out of the door.

"Next."

The other merman edges forward, trembling a little. He is the newest of them all- today was his first day. None of the mermen like him much because of the way he talks and because of his constant itching to fight and kill more than necessary. "The- the orange humans I watched, and... the boy respects us, but the girl is angry with us. She thinks that she is better than us. Do I have your permission to kill her?"

The King sighs. "Yes, but only the girl. We just want to get them to leave us alone, so we need to send them a message. Make sure the boy is watching when you kill her," he finishes. The merman bows.

"Yes, my King," he accepts. As he swims away, a sly smile creeps over his thin lips.

"And what do you have to report for the purple humans?" The King wearily inquires of the last merman.

"As far as I could tell, they seemed overly at home in the water. They fear and respect us, and yet are not trying to avoid us... or attack us. They seem... almost... like us," he finishes, flinching as though he expects a blow at the proposed idea. It never comes. When the merman looks back up, the King seems thoughtful.

"Hmm... like us, you say?"

"Y... yes, sir."

"…Bring them to me. Perhaps through these two, we can forge a friendship with the humans and end our constant wars."

"…Yes, my Lord," the merman replies before swimming away to fulfill his wishes, relieved that he had survived yet another meeting with the King.

When I open my eyes, I'm surprised by what I see. I was not expecting to find water over my head. I instinctively start to panic and suck in my breath, holding it. After a few seconds, I remember both why I'm underwater and why I'm not drowning. I release my breath and inhale normally once I remember my breathing device. However, once I remember where I fell asleep, I realize I'm not in the cave anymore.

I suck in a breath too quickly and spin to find Nathan. To my relief, he's here as well, although he's still sleeping. I look around to try and figure out where we are, but all I see is seaweed, swaying gently in the underwater current. The water is far overhead, and I wonder if the breathing device helps to reduce the pressure of the water as well.

I still don't know where we are, so I swim up to the surface and look around. I look as far as I can in every direction, but I can't see any of the islands we started on. I start to panic and swim back down to Nathan, waking him and alerting him to our predicament. He gets up and looks around as well, but we can't see very well through the thick seaweed. I then notice that there are parts of the seaweed that don't move at all; mounds the size of small houses.

I'm about to point this out to Nathan when I see something emerge from one of the mounds. It looks like a large chunk of seaweed broke away and is floating toward me. I narrow my eyes as it approaches. Nathan notices it too. As it comes closer, I blink and it suddenly looks like a small, green child… with a fishtail. My mouth drops open.

"Nathan…" I croak. "Look…" He peers closer at the child and it seems to click for him as well.

"Mermaid," he whispers. We back away as the little mermaid girl comes closer, but she's relentless. We finally decide that surely the children won't hurt us- right?- and stop trying to get away. Behind the girl comes two other children- a small boy and girl. Following them is another small mermaid boy who is waiting and watching curiously.

Nathan and I freeze as the first child comes closer to us, not daring to move. She finally stops just a few feet away and I'm able to see her clearer. She's the size of your average five-year-old human- except instead of legs, she has a fish-like tail. Her neck has three thin slits on each side that open slightly periodically, as though she's breathing through them. I realize that these are gills. Her skin has a green tint to it, but her hair is the color of leaves in the fall- in fact, it seems to... shimmer a bit and fade into different shades of red and orange. When I first saw her, it was more orange, but now it's a deep red as it flows gently around her shoulders. Her bright green eyes are filled with curiosity as she looks me up and down as well. Finally, she speaks.

"You're weird," she states.

I smile a little. "So are you."

"What are you?" she asks.

"We're people- humans," I reply cautiously.

"Do you live near here?"

"...In a way."

"Why haven't I seen you before?"

"Because... I haven't ever come this close to your... people before."

"Oh. Do you like to play games?"

I glance back at Nathan, who shrugs, looking lost. "...Sure." I reply to her.

"Have you ever played 'Bite the Shark?'"

"No."

"Really? What games do you play, then?"

"Um... my people like to play tag," I finally answer, thinking of Kiki running around at a playground, chasing other kids. My heart pangs and I quickly shove the thought out of my head. I had no time to mourn right now.

"What's tag?" she asks, the two other children coming to a rest right behind her. They look identical to the girl, just a little different in the shades of green, and their hair is similar as well.

"Well, you get together with lots of kids and... well, one person is 'it,' and they have to 'tag,' or touch, another person, and then they're it."

"Oh. That doesn't sound like fun," she complains. "Bite the Shark is more fun. You pick five kids to be a 'shark,' and then the rest of us are mer-warriors and we attack the sharks before they can destroy the village. The mer-warriors usually win, and they get medals, but sometimes the sharks ruin the village first. I know, we'll show you!" she exclaims. The excitable little girl then swims around and gathers about twenty other mermaid children. They pick out about six of them to be a shark, and then the game begins. I quickly learn that it's a very vicious game as Nathan and I watch them chase each other around a designated area, biting each other with their small, sharp yellow teeth. Apparently they have thick skin, though, since they don't bleed much if at all.

Nathan and I are at a loss for what to do until some other mermaids come out and yell at the kids to come back in and help prepare their meal. The kids whine and groan, but they do as they're told. This reminds me that I haven't eaten for a while- we only snacked on what we deemed edible the day before. My stomach growls, accompanied by Nathan's. We look at each other and laugh a little.

"We should probably find something to eat," Nathan says. I nod, but am immediately distracted by a sudden swift movement out of the corner of my eye. I turn and see a merman swimming toward us. Nathan and I start backing away and we turn to run- or swim, I guess- away, but we are overtaken by the merman before we can go more than a few feet.

He swims in front of us, halting our retreat. The merman is different from the children we've seen, for he is more blue than green. He smiles at us, trying, I suppose, to appear friendly, but his sharp yellow teeth look more frightening and threatening, so we start backing away again. He quickly stops smiling once he realizes that we're scared.

"Greetings, humans. I am Gorg, leader of the mer-warriors and main bodyguard of His Majesty." We don't reply, just watching him with fear, our muscles tense. "Our King has been most gracious and has invited you to dine with him." *Or dine on us!* I think, panicking. I try to swallow my fear and reply.

"I... I'm sorry if we are intruding," I begin, fishing for an excuse to leave and not meet with the King. "We... we don't know why we're here. We... we'll just leave and not bother you anymore. We are sorry... for disturbing the King."

The merman looks surprised. "You would deny the King of his offer?"

"Um, no," I say, seriously thinking that we're going to be killed now. Apparently not meeting the King isn't a good move. But I'd still rather never enter his presence. "We... mean the King no disrespect. We just... need to be going now." Nathan and I continue backing away, but Gorg doesn't let up.

"I do not think you understand," he presses. "The King is trying to be *nice* to you. He noticed humans in our waters and wanted to learn more about them- you- and how you breathe underwater when most humans cannot. It is an invitation rather than a command, true, but it is always wiser to do as the King requests than to oppose him. Those who do... are never heard from again."

I glance at Nathan, who gives me a slight nod. His face is pale, but his lips are set. He's determined to see this through and try and survive- no matter what. I take a deep breath and turn back to Gorg. "Then... then we will accept his gracious offer," I say, sealing our fate.

Gorg leads us to the King's palace. The whole way there, everything I've been told about mermaids flies through my head. The terrifying images of man-eating fish-people just doesn't quite match with what I've seen so far. Sure, the kids like to bite each other, and sure, these creatures have terrifyingly sharp teeth, but... we haven't had anybody trying to eat us yet, and hopefully that's not what the King intends to do with us either. Gorg made it sound like we were honored guests, so he *shouldn't* eat us, but I guess you never know...

I can tell by the look on Nathan's face, however, that he is still wary of every move Gorg makes- but I guess one of us should be that way. We should be able to make our way through whatever situation comes with me being open and Nathan being suspicious.

Gorg leads us to a large, old stone castle that is completely submerged. It looks out of place down here in all the green and blue. We then enter a spacious dining hall and sit down at a large table. Gorg then leaves to go alert the cooks and we are left alone. Nathan looks across the table at me. I can tell by the look on his face what he's thinking.

"No!" I say.

"But now's our chance!" he insists.

"If we leave, then we will tick off the King, and he'll send a bunch of mermaids after us. We wouldn't stand a chance."

"You don't know that," he argues.

I sigh. "We have a better chance here. In fact, maybe we should make *friends* with the mermaids. Then we wouldn't have any reason to fear. In fact, we would have powerful allies. Not only that, but maybe we could get the King to lend us his Trident so we can end these dang Challenges. I know, I know, it's a stretch, but it's better than just delaying the inevitable! If the King wants to kill us, then he will kill us. If he wants to be friends, then I think we should give that a try first!"

"...You're right, of course," he mumbles. "I'm sorry." He takes a deep breath and runs a hand through his hair. He smiles a little. "I guess I'm just... freaked out. I should be more calm and collected... like you."

I laugh a little. "Ha! Calm? Collected? Not even close! I'm just in survival mode, I guess. My thoughts and emotions are honestly everywhere. Plus I just get the feeling... we should be here."

Nathan raises an eyebrow. "So now you're getting special feelings?" he mocks.

"Well... let's call it a sixth sense. I just feel... like this is where we need to be right now. And it's not just for the Challenge, either... Never mind, I can't explain it."

"Hmm. Maybe it's a dragon thing."

I shake my head. The memories of how I lost the ability to *be* a dragon flash through my head. "No. I... I can't be a dragon anymore, remember? That part of me was stolen away."

"Just because you can't turn into a dragon doesn't mean it isn't still a part of you," he insists. I'm amazed at how much his words comfort me. I laugh a little at myself.

"To think that a few months ago I was just living my life, trying to be normal... and now here I am, wishing I could be a dragon again. I didn't even believe in dragons before I came here!"

"Yeah, it's pretty crazy how much this place has changed us," Nathan comments. "To think that my best friend is part dragon and it doesn't even freak me out at all... I've accepted it... it's pretty weird when you stop and think about it!"

"I agree!" I laugh, trying to ignore the burning feeling I got in my chest when he called me his best friend.

I suddenly hear a deep voice behind me, near the hole where the door used to be. "Dragon, did you say?" I whirl around, but whoever it is is still in the shadows.

"What... who are you?" I demand, my heart pounding in alarm. A tall merman swims forward and emerges from the shadows. The light from the underwater torches reflect off his iridescent scales. They sparkle and I can see little rainbows in every scale on his tail. I gasp. I then notice the beautiful golden crown on his head and realize that this must be the King. I quickly get out of my seat and kneel, figuring that this must be the proper way to greet a King. Nathan rapidly follows my lead.

"No, please. There's no need for that. You are my honored guests. Let us treat each other as equals."

Nathan and I stand and wait until the King sits down in his seat before we sit back in ours, playing it safe despite his words.

"So... how much did you hear?" I ask, a little embarrassed. He smiles, and I notice that his teeth are much whiter than the other mermaids' we've seen here.

"Almost all of it. I heard you say that you feel that you two were meant to be here, as well as everything following that. I had heard whispers of rumors that there was a Dragongirl among us in Zilferia, but no one knew who she was or where she came from... so hopefully, you may deem me worthy to hear your story."

I start to reply, but he stops me. "No, I won't make you say anything now. I must first have someone destroy the little metal things following you, for I do not want anyone else to hear what either of us has to say. Just because they are not recording at the moment doesn't mean they won't again at a moment's notice. Plus, I think it is fairer if I tell you my story first, and you two need to eat- I am quite sure that you are hungry after eating hardly anything yesterday." I stare at him in bewilderment. He can see the cameras that broadcast the Challenges to the Villagers? *Not only that, but he clearly had mermaids following us yesterday. And we didn't even notice!* I shift in my seat, uncomfortable with just how powerless Nathan and I are in this whole situation.

The King claps his hands, summoning a few servant mermaids,

drawing my attention to his fingernails, which look more like claws. I shudder. The servants enter, bearing silver dishes piled high with fish, crabs, and other such seafood. There are also several different sauces they bring out to flavor it all to our liking. These are followed by a huge platter with an even bigger swordfish on it. There is seaweed and other vegetables laid out around the gigantic fish, and they even have dressing.

Nathan and I dive in as the King begins his story. I'm amazed at how much I enjoy the fish- especially since I've never liked fish in the first place. But that's all changed now that I've had this seafood spread. I can't remember ever eating anything quite so good. Therefore, it isn't too much of a surprise when I realize I'm eating too fast. I make a conscious effort to slow down and listen to the King's story as well as eat.

"I don't want to bore you with a tale of my childhood, so I will shorten it considerably and tell you only what I believe is necessary for you to know to understand where I'm coming from. ...Believe it or not, I was not born into royalty as most rulers are, and my life was not an easy one. I got into a lot of trouble and stupid, dangerous situations where I almost died were it not for the help of a creature the rest of the mermaids loathed.

"A human. His name was Alexander, and he was young- about your age."

"Wh- what?" I exclaim, choking on shrimp I had just put in my mouth. I finally force it down my throat and am able to speak. "Did... did you say Alexander?"

"Yes... why? Does this boy have significant meaning to you?"

"Yes," Nathan replies for me. "That... boy... is actually her father." I nod, still shocked to hear that my actual father had been down here, dealing with these dangerous creatures.

"Hmm..." The King says thoughtfully. "That is very interesting. You may have to tell me about this after I am finished," he decides before continuing. "Alexander saved me from a Mako shark and from then on we were friends, although we never told anyone else since it was pretty taboo. He visited me regularly for years. I haven't seen him in probably about... sixteen years. The last I saw him, he told me that he was the King now and he was married, and his wife was pregnant. He was so excited and said he had a lot of places to go to spread the word to all his friends, so he didn't stay long.

"Once he stopped coming, things got worse down here. My grandfather was the leader of the mer-warriors, so when he died, I was put into his spot, since my father had passed previously. I quickly became the mermaid King's closest advisor and even friend. About a year after Alexander disappeared, we began to be attacked by the humans. They threw bombs into the water that filled it with black gunk that clogged our gills, making it so we could not breathe.

"The humans had declared war against us, so we had no choice but to respond in kind. After a few years, the other King, my friend, died and appointed me to reign in his stead since he had no children. The war has calmed down recently, so we were cautious, knowing the humans would never give up so easily. And then, a few weeks later, what do we find but eight humans swimming around in the water talking about finding my people? Everyone demanded that we kill them all outright, but I just couldn't. I couldn't forget my friendship with Alexander, and you eight reminded me of him, for he could breathe underwater as well.

"Unfortunately, I must still show my people that I am strong and will lead us to victory, so... I had to kill at least a few of them, to send a message that we are not to be trifled with."

Nathan looks as sick as I feel. "Were... were any of the ones you had killed wearing... red?" he chokes out.

"No," the King says. We both breathe a sigh of relief. "But I had my warriors kill one of the orange ones and one of the black ones- the proud ones that thought they could take us on. We left alone the ones who either respected or feared us- and your friends, the red ones, were fearful of us. They were no threat."

I try not to think about the two people he had killed. I swallow and ask, "Why are we here, then? You said you left alone those who didn't want to attack you. Well, Nathan and I didn't want to attack you, or even find you! We were just minding our own business. Why did you drag us here?"

"You two intrigued me, as well as reminded me of my lost friend. You acted just as he did when I first saw him here- playing, exploring... carefree. I thought that maybe you two could also be the peaceful solution to our problem- that I could send you back to your people and convince them to stop attacking us. I even dared to hope... that you two could help me forge a friendship between our people, if at all possible."

"I... see," I say thoughtfully. Was this why I felt that we needed to be here? To form a friendship with the mermaids?

"Now then, what is your story?" he asks.

So I tell him the highlights. I tell him about the Games, the Dragon Council, the Sohos, Thaddeus and what he told me about my parents' condition, my Gifts, the Dragon Hunters, and even about me being part dragon- at least until the Dragon Hunters stole my dragon part from me.

When I finish, the King looks thoughtful. "These 'Dragon Hunters...' do they dress differently than the rest of the humans? Do they wear all black and cover all of their body- even their hands?" This question seems a little strange, but I answer that they do. "Ah... that makes more sense. They are the ones attacking us. I should have known that our assailants were not Alexander's people. Hmm. They seem to be the scourges of every race, don't they? But you... promised the Sohos and the dragons that you would destroy this scourge, correct?"

"Well... no," I say guiltily. "I... I didn't ever tell them for sure that I would. I just... chickened out, I guess. These Dragon Hunters scare me," I admit, staring steadfastly at the table, my fists clenched.

"Hmm... it seems to me that you cannot avoid them. This *is* your fight. Think about it," he continues when I glance up at him, confused and scared. "They tracked *you* down, did they not?"

"Well, yes, but..."

"Then they dragged you into this, whether you like it or not. If you do nothing, then they will likely just kidnap you again regardless- next time with more people, so they will not leave you alone. They will have learned their lesson."

"But... I have guards now," I weakly retort.

He laughs. "You really think that one or two measly humans will stop them when they have hundreds? If they wanted to, they could use force to grab you rather than stealth. Therefore, the best course of action you can take is to attack *them* before they get to you and your friends. Do not let what happened here happen there," he advises.

I gulp, fear of them overwhelming me. "I... I... I can't. What do you think I can do that you and your armies cannot? What can *one girl* do against hundreds of men?"

The King looks at me seriously. "Do not underestimate the power of one. One can easily hide amongst the hundreds, and no one would notice. You could sneak into their own home and strike them where it counts."

"What… what do you mean?" I ask, my brain stuck on the image of me surrounded by hundreds of black cloaks.

"Kill the one in charge, and the rest will not know what to do. Of course, you'll likely have to kill the one that is next in line as well, but one girl with the power of a dragon at her command should be able to do that, don't you think?" I smile a little, feeling encouraged and like… I could maybe do this… all for the first time.

"Well? Do you think that you can go back to your people and then on to the Dragon Hunters and strike them at the core?" He presses.

"Well, I… might be able to… but there may be a problem getting back to our people," I say.

"What is it?" he asks, concerned. "Were the two of you outlawed? Cast out from among your people?"

"In… a way," I say. "We cannot return until we've completed the quest they gave us… to retrieve a certain object."

"Oh? And what is that? I am willing to help you find anything you need in order to stop this war."

I glance across the table at Nathan. He looks surprised that I'm going to ask for it, but he gives me a nod, lending me his support. I take a deep breath. "They… they sent us to find the Mermaid King's Trident," I finally say, looking up to see how he will react to this. He looks thoughtful and doesn't say anything for a few minutes. I clear my throat. "Um… do you… have the Trident?"

"Of course I do," he says. "It has been handed down from generation to generation. Each King has used it at least once, to prove that he is worthy to be King."

I swallow and force myself to say what I must. "Would… would you be willing to lend it to us?"

"And let you hand it over to our enemies?" he says with an accusatory tone. I gulp and look back at the table again, every muscle tight; ready to flee. We wait for another couple of minutes before the King says anything else. When he does, it's not what I was expecting.

"…Very well." I jerk my head back up and stare at the King in shock. He smiles. "You may have the Trident. However, there are some things you must know about it. I will be right back," he says, getting out of his seat and swimming out of the room. I stare at Nathan and he does the same, his eyes wide.

"We... we did it," I say. "We got the Trident!"

"Well, I wouldn't go jumping to conclusions just yet," Nathan warns. "You never know, he may be going to get it just so he can kill us with it or something. I mean, doesn't it seem too good to be true? We just ask the King for his powerful weapon and he just hands it over? I wouldn't be surprised if he was lying in order to keep us here while he arranges our deaths."

"Oh, you're such a pessimist!" I say, not giving much care to what he said. "Why would he do that? He seems nice enough, plus he was friends with my father!"

"Or so he claims," Nathan mutters. "Whatever. If he's going to kill us, there isn't much we can do about it anyway."

The servants return while the King is gone and clean off the table. He returns just as they're leaving. When he swims into the light, I gasp as my eyes immediately cling to the magnificent weapon in his hand. The Trident's gold metal glimmers in the underwater light, nearly blinding me for a moment. It's nearly as big as the King himself- about a foot taller than me. The Trident has a dark green glow around it, adding to the feeling of ancient power emanating from it.

"Wow..." I murmur, stunned by its simple beauty and immense power.

The King smiles. "The reason I am not too afraid of you having this Trident is that it won't matter if it falls into the wrong hands. Its power can only be unlocked if you know the... password, I suppose you could call it, and if you are a mermaid friend. I have declared the two of you official mermaid friends, so I will now tell you the password, in case you need to use it- which I hope that you will not.

"This Trident was forged for the first King- King Demeter. The King did not want its power to be used for evil, so he had the smith- the most talented our race has ever seen- make it so that it would respond only to a King or King to be, and only if they were a mermaid friend. An extra precaution was put into place- they also had to say the password. The word which he chose was his own name. Once you say it, and all other requirements are fulfilled, then it will obey you no matter what. Obviously, since none of our enemies are mermaid friends, we have nothing to worry about. However…"

"What is it?" Nathan asks.

"The power in the Trident is great- enough to overwhelm you if you are not prepared. And I'm sorry to say, but the only way to prepare you is to give you a taste of its power. Therefore, I will have to use it on you- with your permission, of course."

I give him my permission, figuring it's better to be safe than sorry, and if I should need to use it, then I should be prepared. Nathan takes a little longer to agree, but he eventually decides to trust me and warily submits. The King has us kneel before him, side by side. He then points the Trident at us and says, "Paralyze."

I instantly can't move my limbs. I can still think and breathe, but it's shallow and automatic. "Release," he says, and we're instantly in control again. The mermaid King gazes at us sadly. "I… I'm sorry, my friends. This one… this is the necessary one. It… it will hurt."

I find that this is an understatement when he again levels the Trident at us and says, "…Torture." My body is wracked with torment, screaming in pain as I throw my head back and shriek. It mingles with Nathan's cry as well. My back arches uncontrollably as every cell in my body seems to burn, and some even feel like they're exploding. Tears roll down my face, and I'm powerless to stop them. I don't care to stop them anyway. "End," I finally hear.

I lurch forward, my forehead on my knees, gasping for breath as the tears come faster and harder. My body still tingles, but it doesn't hurt any longer. Again, the King levels the Trident at us. I flinch. "Heal." I sigh with relief as a wave of calm washes over me. I relax and bask in the comforting feeling. It feels… like a cold shower on a hot day, a cup of hot chocolate when it's cold outside, a warm blanket sheltering from the crisp cold, the feeling of being loved, of accomplishment and compassion, and more that cannot be put into words. "End," I again hear, and it does.

I sit up, feeling refreshed. I instinctively wipe the tears off my face, which I then realize is pointless since we're in water anyway. "You now have a taste of the Trident's power," the King says to us as we stand. "… Therefore, you will be able to use it in case of an emergency, but I would caution you to use it only as a last resort. I know that it works for mermaids, but I have never heard of a human using it. As far as I know, it may not even work," he warns us as he hands it to me. As soon as his blueish skin is no longer touching it, the green glow fades until it is hardly visible.

"Good luck defeating the Dragon Hunters, Crystal Dragon and Nathan Anderson. I wish I could join you, but I would not survive on land. If you ever need help, do not fear to come and ask. I will order my mermaids not to harm you should they see you. And if you can bring the Trident back, then please do. Not only will it help us stay alive during this war, but we will need it to pick our next King if needs be."

"Of course," I reply. "If we can manage it, we will return it to you. Thank you so much!"

He inclines his head to me in a small bow. "You are most welcome, Dragongirl. ...And even though we may not have a prophecy of you, I know that you will help us as well as the other races. Good luck!"

"Goodbye!" Nathan and I call back as we swim out of the castle. When we emerge outside, Gorg is there waiting.

"I am here to escort you back to where we found you," he informs us. We nod.

"Oh, wait!" I say.

"What is it?" Nathan asks me.

I don't reply, grabbing a clump of long seaweed strands instead. Putting the heavy Trident on my back, I use the seaweed to strap it into place. "Now I can swim easier," I explain.

"Very well. Are you ready now?" Gorg asks.

"Yes," I reply. We follow him through a towering wall of seaweed and past some over-sized jellyfish that seem to be guarding the exit. We swim for a few hours before we reach the cave where we fell asleep. Once we arrive, Gorg turns and bows to us, then swims back the way he came, leaving us alone once again.

We rest in the cave for about an hour before heading out again, back toward our little island. We reach it in about an hour. When we climb ashore, we have to drag ourselves out- I feel like I weigh more than twice as much as I had before. It is suddenly hard to move my limbs, and the Trident feels heavier as well. I quickly undo the seaweed and let the Trident thud onto the sand next to me. We lie beside each other on the sand

and rest fully for the first time in days. I hear the gun go off, signaling that we have won the Challenge. I look over at Nathan and smile. He smiles back. We finished! We're alive! Not only that, but it seems that this really *is* the last Challenge! *We're done!* Of course, that doesn't mean that I'm done with what I need to do here, but at least I'm no longer at Vlad's mercy in these 'Games.'

We wait, expecting to be tranquilized again, but nothing comes. We're confused until we see a helicopter-like aircraft coming towards us. It looks like we actually get to be awake on the ride home. Well, we probably won't be awake for long, but at least we get to sleep voluntarily. Our island isn't large enough for both us and the helicopter, so it lands on the other island, and we swim over to it.

When we climb inside, we're greeted by a relieved Thaddeus and an ecstatic Nehru. We sit down across from them as we take off. Nehru immediately starts asking us questions. "What happened after you went inside the castle? Our cameras that were following you went dead once you went inside! We didn't see anything until we could send more out there, and by then you were leaving the castle- with the Trident!" she exclaims, staring at it as I lay it on my lap.

Luckily, Thaddeus comes to our rescue. "Now, Nehru, don't you think that the big reveal should be at the winner's ceremony tonight?"

She frowns but grumpily agrees. "Alright, fine. I guess if I were one of the citizens, then I would want to be the first to know. At least I will only have to wait for a few hours anyway." After that, we are allowed to sleep, and sleep we do. We wake as we're touching down in the Square. Luckily, no one's there to swarm us. Nehru explains that the winners are always swarmed by people, but they wanted to save us from that for at least a little longer. Relieved, we thank her and start heading toward our house, wanting to eat and sleep, but we're cut off by Vlad.

He scowls at us, obviously not pleased that not only are we alive, but in one piece- and with the Trident. "Well, well, well," he says, glaring specifically at me. "Aren't you two full of surprises."

"Yeah, well, we like to keep things interesting," Nathan replies sarcastically.

Vlad shifts his glare to him for a moment, then returns it to me. "Well, hand it over." I raise an eyebrow at him disbelievingly. He sighs impatiently. "The Trident is what you were sent to recover, but that does not mean that you get to keep it. The Challenge is not officially won until I have the object of interest in my possession."

I glower at him and hand it over. He seems surprised by how heavy it is. "Very good," he says. He then turns and walks away without another word. I sigh.

"Let's go home," I say to Nathan. He nods and we head back to our house, where we grab something to eat and crash into bed.

15

My dream starts out like it always does- a random mix of things that I had seen and/or thought of during the day, except nothing is very clear. It's all in color, but it's fuzzy and out of focus. First, I'm playing on the playground with Kiki. Then her friends come over and they're all suddenly little mermaid kids, biting each other. I yell at them to stop, but then Nehru steps up with the Trident and paralyzes me. Nehru then turns into Vlad, and, with an evil grin, he begins torturing me. It goes on and on like that. I fight to escape the dream, but I seem to be locked into place.

Until finally, it all fades away. The pain disappears, Vlad and the Trident are nowhere to be seen, and it's just me. I look around and find that I'm once again at Dragon Mountain, but there are no toxic fumes to hurt me. *How did I get here?* I wonder. *And why am I here?*

I hear a familiar chuckle. I look around, but no one's there. "Who's there?" I call.

"Do not worry, child," I hear deep in my head. I look around once more, and a massive golden dragon flickers into view just in front of me. *"I have ended your previous dream so I could talk to you. Why are you so tortured as you sleep, young one?"*

"Gale!" I gasp with relief. *"I just... I don't know. I can't control it. I guess my brain just plays on my fears... thank you for stopping it."*

"Why do you fear? You are part dragon, and not only that, you have all of our support, as well as that of your own people- Nathan's at the very least. You do not have to face this alone. What troubles you?" So I tell him. I update him on everything since I last saw him. It's a long tale, but it doesn't seem to take very long in the dream. My eyes are filled with tears by the time I finish.

"I... I don't know that I will be able to help you, Gale. I no longer have the power of a dragon."

"Hmm. Even if that's so, you still have us to help you, and what more do you need than friends? It is possible for a few to overtake many, as the mermaid told you. I have also seen it many times over the years. It is what changes the outcome of a war. You can do this. Besides, being a dragon is a part of who you are. You may no longer be able to fully transform, but you still have our power within you, even if it's more difficult to reach. You have since before you were born. You can still change your eyes, can you not?"

"I don't know," I reply. "...If I try now, would it work like it would in real life?"

"I believe so." I try switching my eyes out, and for the first time, they seem to resist. I push harder and they turn around. I look around and find that they work the same as they always have.

"You see, they cannot take away your entire identity. You are still one of us, for better or worse."

"...Thank you, Gale," I say quietly. "You don't know how much that means to me. But how did you know I needed you?"

"I... didn't. I was simply contacting you to inform you that the sapphire clan is planning something to convince you to help us. I was going to ask if you..."

"There's no need for that," I interrupt.

"What?" he says, obviously caught off-guard.

"Yeah... I decided... I'm going to do all I can to help you, the mermaids, and all of the other races destroy the Dragon Hunters."

"Is that so? What changed your mind?"

"It was partially the mermaids, as well as the Dragon Hunters' own fault. They brought the fight to me personally, and I can no longer ignore the harm they're causing- to everyone. That, and I couldn't take the guilt of leaving you all alone. It was eating me up from the inside out."

"Oh. Well, I'm glad. I want to make sure you understand that we are all behind you on this. If you need our help, just call my name with voice and mind, *and I will hear you and come to your aid with all the dragons I can rally. I'm sure the mermaids and Sohos would do the same. We also feel guilt for leaving it up to you."*

"Thank you," I say, touched and reassured. Gale then starts fading before my eyes. *"What… no! Where are you going?"*

"It seems you are waking up. It's alright, I will see you later. Goodbye, Crystal Dragon, and good luck…" His voice fades as his body does and I am alone on the mountain as the dream finishes wrapping up.

I open my eyes and see Dallas's face looming over me. I blink as his face swims into focus. "W- what?" I mutter as I sit up, drowsily rubbing my eyes.

"I'm sorry to interrupt your sleep, but Thaddeus wishes to speak with you and Nathan before the ceremony tonight. He sent me to wake you as well as protect you."

I groan a little, still drained from the last Challenge. "Thanks." He nods, then leaves so I can get dressed. After I'm ready, I wake Nathan, then step outside for some fresh air. The sky is blue, with a few white clouds floating lazily by. A cool breeze dances through the trees, causing them to sing once again. It's a peaceful day, and for once, my mood matches it.

I feel refreshed, although still a little fatigued. All of a sudden, the meaning of the winner's ceremony actually hits me. "Whoa… wait a second… we won?"

Dallas looks at me, surprised. Then he smiles in understanding. "Yep. You are officially the winners of the Games this year!"

"We… we won… we won! WE WON! I… I can't believe it! This… this means that the nightmare is finally over!" I laugh, feeling better than I have in a long time. This is astounding! This is spectacular! I… I can go home soon… But as I'm thinking this, I remember my promise to the dragons, mermaids, and Sohos. I need to first finish off the Dragon Hunters. I feel a sudden urge to run; just run back home and forget all about this freaky place.

No… I couldn't do that to my friends. The Dragon Hunters would kill them and destroy this world if I don't stop them… I have to do my duty. There's no backing down. Somehow, this thought doesn't hinder my good mood. The hopeful feelings I had derived from my dream still linger in my mind and heart.

When Nathan comes out, we follow Dallas to the hospital. Nathan and I go inside to check on our Familiars. They're doing better, but they're not up to full speed yet. Nora's pleased and excited at the news that we won the Games.

"I'm not surprised," she says proudly. *"From the moment I met you two, I knew that nothing would be able to stand in your way."* I smile and tell her that I'll be back to check on her tomorrow. *"Could you bring a fresh mouse? The food here stinks!"* I laugh and assure her that I will if I can catch one.

From the hospital, we head to the Square. Before we get there, Thaddeus catches up to us. "Congratulations," he says, smiling broadly. "I knew you could do it! Now then, the ceremony will begin as soon as you two arrive." He looks us up and down with a frown. "However, first you need a shower and some new clothes. Come with me." We follow him to another building and take a shower. When I come out, there are some clothes laid out on the bed.

I slip on the dark purple sleeveless dress and put the silky black jacket on top. There are some high-heeled shoes and black necklaces and earrings as well. There's a new watch on the bed, which is fantastic since mine wasn't waterproof and was ruined in the last Challenge.

As soon as I'm dressed, two women I've never seen before come in and begin doing my hair. As they do, I admire my new watch. It's the nicest watch I've ever seen. After inspecting it, I see that it is waterproof and tells the temperature as well as the time. I find when I push one of the buttons that there's a map with both my location and Nathan's as well. At the top of the map is the label 'ZILFERIA.'

"That watch actually adjusts to whatever realm you're in. I have one myself. They're very useful." I spin around and find Thaddeus standing at the door. My hairdressers slip past him as they leave, their duty done. "In fact, they actually programmed yours to be able to connect with Nathan's and vice versa. You can talk to him. Go ahead, try it. Just twist the circumference of the watch, then lift it a little."

I do as he says, and suddenly a picture of Nathan's face is projected from it. I watch as he looks at me with surprise. "Whoa!" he exclaims. "How did that happen? Crystal? You have a watch too? Aren't they cool?"

I laugh. "Yep, they're pretty awesome. Hey, where are you?"

"Right behind you," he winks. I turn as the door opens and he walks in.

He's wearing a nice black suit with dark purple lining, just like the rest of our outfits. His hair is done up for the first time since I've seen him. He looks completely different from what I'm used to.

"You look… nice," he smiles. "I'll have to get used to that!"

We both laugh. "Don't get too used to it. I'll be back to normal as soon as I can."

"That's good. It feels weird to be all dressed up like this." I agree.

Thaddeus glances at his watch. "Oh, dear- we're going to be late if we wait much longer! Let's go!" He then hustles us out the door and down to the Square, where we are greeted by a thundering cheer from the crowd. My eyes widen. This is the most people I've seen in one place the entire time I've been here. There's a path cleared right through the middle of them, so I assume that's where we're supposed to go.

Nathan and I walk side by side down the aisle, waving and smiling at the people with Thaddeus right behind us. After several minutes, we reach the stage where Nehru is waiting patiently for us. We climb the steps and stand on her right while Thaddeus stands on her left. The noise from the crowd is deafening, and it continues for a couple more minutes before Nehru can quiet them down.

When it's finally diminished to a few catcalls and whoops, Nehru steps up to the microphone and clears her throat. The crowd finally goes silent. "Welcome, one and all, to the Games' final Ceremony of Winners!" More cheers. "And a hearty congratulations to our winners… Crystal Shay and Nathan Anderson!" I just now remember that the majority of the people have no idea I'm their 'lost' Princess thanks to Thaddeus tampering with the video feed throughout the Challenges. As the cheers die down, I hear a sudden shout from four girls near the stage, "WE LOVE YOU, NATHAN!" I laugh as he smiles uncomfortably and waves at them. They swoon and fall over, and I snort from trying to keep in my laughter.

"Now we will have the audience ask a few questions from either Crystal or Nathan." Hundreds of hands immediately pop up. Some are even jumping up and down to stand out and get called on.

Nehru picks a random guy close to the stage. "Crystal," he begins. "What happened after you went into the castle? Nobody knows- the cameras went out." At this, there's a bunch of boos- as if it was someone's fault. I smile a little as I think that it was indeed, but they don't actually know that.

"Well, when we went in there, the King came in and had his servants feed us. We asked him for the Trident, and he gave it to us."

Another person from the crowd. "Surely it wasn't that easy?"

I swallow. I can't tell them the whole truth. "Uh, well the King just liked us, I guess. He said he saw how... how I was nice to the mermaid kids and he was impressed. Yes, he did take a lot of convincing, but he eventually decided to trust us." This seems to satisfy them on the subject.

Nehru then picks a guy toward the back. "Crystal, will you marry me?" he asks, shouting over the distance. The crowd bursts into laughter and wolf whistles as I blush. Luckily, I don't have to answer since he wouldn't hear me anyway.

Next is a girl. "Nathan, do you love Crystal?" I look over at him curiously and find that he's blushing a bright red. I am as well. He doesn't answer, nor does he meet my gaze.

"Are there any *serious* questions?" Nehru asks. Most of the hands go down. Nehru fights a smile. She picks another person, saying that this is the last question.

"How do you think you two were able to win?" they ask.

I let Nathan take that question. "Um, I don't know," he says. They boo at his lack of response. "All I know is that it wasn't really because of anything I did. Thaddeus helped us a bunch, but it was Crystal that got us through it all."

"What?! No, it wasn't!" I instinctively protest.

"Yes, you did pretty much everything. Remember the werewolves? If it weren't for you, I would have died. And the Zyloff- you died and I couldn't do anything, but when I died, you saved me!" I start to protest more, but he cuts me off. "And at the maze, I got knocked out pretty fast. I was worthless."

"So did I! I didn't do anything spectacular there but be clawed to shreds by a freaking giant cat!" The audience watches with amusement as we argue.

"...But most of all with the mermaids," he continues, as though I hadn't said anything. "You were always in control, you never panicked. You were the one that sweet-talked the King while I just sat there. You were the one who led us through the maze… need I continue?"

I won't just stand here and be complimented when he deserves recognition too! "But you helped too! I kept getting knocked out, and you helped me since I was basically a useless sack of flour. You were the one with the shapeshifting skills. I just *barely* got my first Gift!"

Nehru cuts us off there. "Alright, that's enough. You were both very impressive. You were obviously a great team- you won every single Challenge! And now for your reward!" She has us sit in the two seats in the middle of the stage. Once we're seated, Nehru hands Thaddeus two small boxes about one square inch on each side. He then walks over and hands us the boxes, then moves off to the side of the stage.

We open the boxes to find a silver and gold ring in each. The silver band is sandwiched between two gold bands. Nathan's is the opposite- gold on silver. I look at Nehru, confused. She smiles. "Those are Matter Rings. They enable the wearer to walk straight through solid objects! And anything you're touching when you put it on will become intangible as well. As soon as you're no longer in contact with that object, however, it will become solid again and you will pass through it.

"Those rings do not make you invincible," she cautions. "If you're fighting someone or something that's smart enough to realize why they cannot touch you, then you had better protect that ring, or else they can just pull it off, and you will become solid again. Therefore, the only thing you can touch while you are wearing this ring is either another person wearing one since they'll cancel each other out, or the ring itself. Once it is off of your finger, you will return to normal. So while you're not using it, I would recommend that you keep it in a safe pocket."

I immediately take this advice, slipping it into the jacket pocket. Nathan puts his in a pocket as well. After that, Nehru spotlights Thaddeus. When asked how he got us so far, he responds, "They're just talented kids. I could tell that from the beginning- that's why I chose them to advise despite the rumors. What I did didn't matter much- they never really paid much attention anyway," he says, winking at me. I blush, embarrassed because I know it's true.

After that, we go to a huge banquet where we don't get to eat much because of everyone questioning us. After a while, we decide to take turns with the questions, so we're able to eat something. Thaddeus doesn't have anyone to cover for him so he can eat, but we take the bulk of the attention from him in the first place.

We're finally able to slip away after midnight as some of the people begin to leave. We quickly head back to our house, change, and crash into bed, falling asleep immediately.

There's a knock on our door before the sun comes up. I groan, looking over at Nathan. He's still sound asleep. There's another knock. I sigh and haul myself out of bed to answer the door. When I open it, I'm surprised to see Dallas. He looks at me, worry evident in his eyes.

"Dallas? What are you…"

"No time. Hurry, get dressed. I need your help."

I nod, suddenly alert. I shut the door and quickly get dressed, putting my Lightning Shoes on and making sure my Matter Ring is in my pocket. I quickly put in my hair in a ponytail and head out the door. Dallas doesn't say anything, just starts hurrying towards the woods. I have to jog to keep up. After a while, he stops and I catch my breath.

"What's the problem?" I ask him. He's looking into the distance, ignoring me. "Why are we here?" I demand. He finally turns and looks at me. An unexpectedly evil grin crosses his face. I back up. "Dallas…" Next thing I know, he's dressed in black- a hood, gloves… everything is covered. I feel a rush of fear and turn to run. I have only taken a few steps before another hooded figure runs in front of me. I spin around. I'm surrounded.

"What more do you guys want?" I plead, my voice cracking with fear. "You already took my ability to be a dragon."

'Dallas' steps forward. "We want *you*." He simply states. My eyes widen with fear and for a moment I'm too afraid to do anything. Then I subconsciously switch into my dragon eyes and my fear seems to burn and become power and rage. I feel like a dragon, even though I'm not in the body of one. *Gale was right, I do have the power of a dragon all the time*, I conclude, feeling a fierce joy.

Turning, I sprint towards an unsuspecting Dragon Hunter and knock him down. I try to continue onward toward the Village, but the guy grabs my ankle and I fall forward. I kick him in the face and stand up, but they're all standing between the Village and me now. I grin, looking forward to fighting my way through them. I bare my teeth at them as my tongue probes the ends of my teeth. I'm surprised to find them sharp, like the mermaids' teeth, but the men don't flinch.

I run up to one of them and punch him so hard he flies a few yards and lands with a thump. To my surprise, he starts to pick himself up and dust himself off. Growling, I punch another and another of the cloaked figures. Then 'Dallas' comes up from behind and grabs my arm, twisting it behind my back. Undeterred, I swing backwards with my other arm and nail him in the gut with my elbow. It's like hitting a rock. He isn't even affected. Fear starts to settle on my heart once more, making it difficult to breathe.

"Alright, that's enough," he growls, waving a thin man over. He inserts a needle into my neck, and I fall to the ground as Dallas releases me, no longer able to control my muscles. My brain becomes heavy with fog, and I can barely think. My eyes revert to normal. Dallas then picks me up and carries me further into the woods- in the direction the other two Dragon Hunters had tried to take me. I then fall asleep, utterly devoid of energy. Apparently using the power of a dragon while not actually being one uses an enormous amount of energy.

I wake up on a simple, clean white bed that is not mine. I sit up and look around. I'm in a small room with clean stone walls and no window. There are small torches on the walls with holes for the smoke to escape. I swing my legs out of bed and find a rug on the floor. I stagger to the door and try to open it, my socks protecting me from the cold stone floor. Unsurprisingly, it's locked. Sighing, I shuffle over to the rocking chair I see by the wall opposite the bed and plop down. I just sit there and stare at the wall without a single specific thought rumbling through my brain.

I don't know how long I stay like that before I pull myself out of it and think. The first thing I do is take stock of what I have. I'm wearing different clothes- a basic, black T-shirt and some worn jeans- so they must have taken my other clothes, which means they have my watch, the Matter

Ring, the shoes, and any hope I have of ever escaping from here. I sigh and put my head in my hands.

A few minutes later, the door opens and then shuts again. I don't bother to look up. "I don't suppose you're going to let me go," I say.

There's a slight laugh. "No. Not yet, at least." I slowly look up and see yet another man in a black cloak.

"Not yet?" I repeat. "I have a hard time buying that you are ever going to let me go."

Another chuckle. "Yes, you may be right... although I am actually thinking about it. A few things provided, of course."

"Of course," I sigh. "I figured you would want to use me in your little war. I'm not much of an aid now that I no longer have the power of a dragon at my command, though. I guess that one backfired on you."

He smiles. "You're very smart," he notes. "And calm, I see."

"Yeah, well. I don't see much point in wasting my energy fighting when I have no chance of winning."

"Oh? And how do you know that you have no chance? You fought my people with very impressive strength and stamina. It occurred to me that they might actually fail in capturing you, but I shouldn't have worried. Not with Hunter there." The name rings a bell in my memory.

"Hunter?" I repeat, confused. "Isn't that..."

"Your brother's name? Yes, it is. The one whom you met as Dallas- and Brandon back on Second Earth, actually- is your brother, Hunter." At my confused look, he continues. "Hunter was sent in to retrieve you from Second Earth before Vladimir could, but we were just a little late on that one... which is too bad, really. I could have taught you everything you needed to know- more than those fools did. And yes, we also snuck him into your little Village- shortly before my sub-commander failed to bring you here. I, of course, had him... fired... for his mistake."

"Killed," I state, no emotion in my voice.

"Why, yes," he says, surprised. "How did you... never mind. It doesn't matter. Just a guess, I'm sure. You assume that an evil guy who had you kidnapped would also have anyone inadequate in my ranks killed. ...And perhaps you're right."

"You... you are killing more than just Dragons," I growl, my emotions finally starting to push through my numb indifference. "The mermaids, the Sohos... my family!"

"Yes, well, there is more to our organization than you will ever know," he says cockily.

"Who are you?" I finally ask, although I have a feeling I already know the answer.

"My name is Patrick. I'm the leader of the Dragon Hunters," he says, voice full of pride. This doesn't surprise me at all.

"I see. Why did you kidnap me? To anger and hurt my parents even more? ...Because they don't even have any idea that I'm here. They went into a coma shortly before I came to Zilferia. What you do to me won't affect them."

"Oh, I know," he replies with a smirk. He doesn't continue on the subject of my parents. "I took you so I could... show you a better way."

"More like twist my mind until you can use me as a weapon to destroy countless others," I bite back.

"Perhaps," he says, amusement in his voice. "If I can find a way to control you as a dragon, then I would give you your power back and then we would see. Although you may not even be worth the trouble. It's far more likely that I would grant the power of a dragon to your brother, for I know that he will obey me, without question."

"Does he know who he is?" I demand. "Does he know that he's a prince, loved by his suffering parents? Does he know that I am his sister! Tell me that!"

"Yes," he replies, staring at me coldly. "He does know that you are his sister and that he is a child of those two traitors I poisoned. But he is under no delusion that they love him. Oh, no. I raised him to be smarter than that."

"*They're* traitors? It seems more like *you* are the traitor to me," I state. His face gets red and I can tell he's getting angry, but I don't care. "You've been lying to him; deceiving him. ...I'm going to tell him the truth," I threaten.

"Alright, I've heard enough out of you," he says and shoots something into my neck. Darkness immediately closes in.

I wake up with an awful headache. I groan and hold my head in my hands until the pain diminishes. Once again, the door opens and shuts behind someone. I assume it's Patrick. "Go away," I grunt.

"Why?" he responds. "Don't you want company?"

"No."

"Well, you need to hear the truth." I look up and glare at him.

"I already know all I need to know," I bite back.

"Oh? Do you now? ...Because I thought you'd want to see what happened the day you were born for yourself."

"That... that's impossible," I say. "You can't go back in time."

"No, but I did record the encounter so I could show Hunter the truth. It seems I now need to show you as well." He steps forward and hands me what seems to be a pair of sunglasses. "I had a man turn invisible to observe and record what happened that day you were born. Look at it, if you wish. If you do not, then there is the option nonetheless." With that, he turns and leaves, locking the door behind him.

I put the glasses on the floor and climb back into bed, refusing to look at them. Thaddeus already told me all I need to know. Seeing it for myself would change nothing. I wait for a few hours, expecting food to come at any time. I haven't eaten since I got here, and I figure he doesn't want me to starve to death.

After a while, I realize what he means to do. He wants me to watch his little movie, so he's not going to feed me until I do. He's trying to train me to do as he wants, like I'm a dog! Well, I'll show him. I can outlast him. He has to feed me eventually.

So, still ignoring the glasses, I wiggle under the covers and fall asleep.

When I wake, everything is exactly the same, although my hunger increased from a dull ache to a pain so sharp it's all I can think about. After all, he hasn't fed me even once since I've been here, and I've probably been here for at least two days.

After a few hours, I'm more bored than I think I have ever been in my entire life. I sigh and continue my wait for food. After another hour, I finally give up. What's the point? I'll just watch the video. It doesn't mean I have to believe it- I'll just get food for doing so.

Feeling almost... guilty, I pick up the glasses and put them on. I am immediately immersed in the past. I'm standing in a smallish room next to a woman on a bed. I start as I realize how much she looks like me. *I guess that's my mom, the Queen.*

The door opens and a tall man with an aura of authority walks into the room. His face softens as he sees the mother and her three babies on the bed. He sits down next to her and I can see that his eyes are just like mine. The two talk for a while, naming us.

I watch as my mom hands me over to my dad. I blink and open my little eyes. When I blink again, they're my dragon eyes. I'm astounded, just as they are. I can't believe it. I was *just born,* and I was already using my dragon eyes. My mother says about the same thing, calling me a prodigy and... a useful tool. They then talk about Hunter, calling him worthless and how he will never have a Gift- but if he did, he would likely only have one, and he wouldn't be very good at it, either. Something feels wrong about this conversation, but I can't quite put my finger on it. Could it be just that they are different than the parents I had imagined- loving and accepting of everyone? Kind and gentle and understanding?

I shake off the feeling and watch as the man who wore the glasses takes me after the King as he leaves the Queen so she can sleep. 'We' slip through the door as he says goodnight to her. I see the man in black- Patrick- before the King does. He shuts the door silently and turns. He gasps as if Patrick came out of nowhere- but, of course, he didn't.

I then learn why he acted like that when he says he hadn't seen Patrick in a long time- so long, he was assumed dead. Patrick then asked him if he mourned, and he said no. Again, this does not sound like the parents I have been imagining, or the 'good King and Queen' everyone's been saying they were.

Patrick then tells him a long story about a dragon and meeting the Dragon Hunters. I listen carefully, hoping to learn all I can of this man- my kidnapper. When he finishes, Alexander jumps on him and pins him down. I gasp as his face is revealed. I understand now why he has that baggy hood- he's trying to hide his ugly scar! Alexander is surprised as well, but he just jumps on him again. Patrick makes a dragon-like growl and a swarm of Dragon Hunters come into the hallway and drag the King off of him. They plunge a syringe into his neck, and he loses control of his body, just as I had.

Angry, Patrick sends two guys back into the room. They pull out Kate, the doctor I met in the forest, and three babies- my brothers and I. They hand Hunter to Patrick, and he talks about how great he can be, even though Alexander and Pearl don't believe in him. He says that they can do whatever they want with Rex and me, though. It's only once Patrick says this that the King gets angry. It really does appear that he doesn't care for Hunter at all.

He is suddenly filled with power, and his dragon eyes come around-again, looking just like mine. He stares hard at Rex and me, and we suddenly disappear. The Dragon Hunters quickly recover from the surprise and flee into the night, back to their hideout- where I am now.

Then it's over. I pull off the glasses and find a tray of food waiting by the door. It seems I was correct in assuming that this was what he wanted. The food is actually very good quality, and I'm surprised. He gave me cheesy scrambled eggs, bacon, muffins, orange juice, and even a doughnut. I haven't had a doughnut since before I got to Zilferia. I long to dig into that first, but I force myself to save it for last so I can properly savor it. I take the food to my bed so I can eat somewhere other than the floor.

I'm somehow full by the time I get to the doughnut, so I'm actually able to slow down and enjoy it. It's my favorite kind- a maple bar. When I finish it, licking the sweet glaze off my fingers, the door opens and Patrick comes in.

I laugh. "You are so predictable."

"Oh?"

"Yes. I don't know why you were so desperate for me to watch that, but I did. I knew you would only feed me once I did. I'm not a dog, you know?"

"Oh, I know. That does not, however, mean that you do not need training to obey me."

I laugh. "Obey you? What a joke! I already told you, I'm not going to be a weapon for you. There's no way I will help you hurt my friends. I was actually going to come here and stop you from doing just that. ...You just beat me to it."

"Oh, really?"

"Yes."

"Ha! And how were you planning on doing that when I have hundreds of men at my command?"

My voice diminishes as I respond. "...I was going to sneak in and kill the leader and his second in command."

He laughs more, tauntingly. "Really? Let's just assume for a moment that you actually *were* able to kill me if you followed through on your plan and were able to infiltrate my castle. Who would you kill then? Do you even know who the second in command is?"

"No," I weakly reply.

"That's what I thought. ...The one going to rule after me is your brother, Hunter." My eyes widen in dismay. *No! But... I can't kill him! ... Maybe it'll be enough if I can still...*

Patrick seems to read my thoughts. "But *I'm* still here. I am the leader, so go ahead, try and kill me," he invites sarcastically. I raise an eyebrow at him, disbelieving. I stand and look him in the eye- the only one I can see.

"What trick is this?" I demand.

He smiles. "No trick. I just want to see if you have it in you to kill anyone- even me. Go ahead. I won't even fight back."

Suspicious, I turn away from him. But realizing that if I kill him I might be able to get away, I suddenly turn and charge at him, catching him off guard. I pin his arms and legs to the ground and pull a knife out of his boot. Surprise fills his eyes. "How did you..."

"I'm very observant," I say. "I knew that you would be the type of person to always have weapons on you. People tend to walk a little different when there's something in their boot- or up their sleeve." I reach up his sleeve and pull out a vial. "What's this? Poison?"

He smiles. "It's just a sedative. A large enough dose will knock a person out for a week."

"Hmm, useful," I comment as I lay the blade of the knife on his exposed neck. A drop of sweat rolls onto it. He's frightened, even if he doesn't admit it. "But I think I'll just get to the *point*... don't you think?" His hood was thrown back when I knocked him over, revealing his face, but I'm unaffected. I just saw it through the glasses, so it doesn't startle me, although I'm a little surprised at how much better it is.

Patrick, although he's frightened and staring death in the face, still manages to muster the nerve to taunt me. "Go ahead," he invites, his voice shaking. "Go ahead and kill me. Just a downward slash, right? Easy. And then you could run along back to your mom and dad, who don't even want you anymore. I'm sure they've forgotten all about you."

"No... they care. They're suffering because they have no idea what happened to Rex and me," I say, trying to convince myself more than him.

"Really? Are you certain? Have you seen them since you've arrived?"

"Well... no, but-"

"Have you asked them *why?*"

"...No. But Thaddeus said..."

"Oh, old Thaddeus told you something? How does that make it true?"

I press the knife against his throat, drawing blood. He stops talking, his Adam's apple quivering. "Don't you *dare* insult Thaddeus," I whisper threateningly.

"I wasn't," he assures, despite the knife. "I'm sure he was telling the truth- at least as far as he knows." I swallow. "I'm sure that if you kill me, you can go and find them yourself. ...But where would you go once you realize that you have no friends or a loving family? ...I know Hunter wants to get to know you. Do you want to meet your brother? Or are you going to go on a wild goose chase after Rex to try and find some scrap of family? I..."

I cut him off, again pressing the knife into his neck. I'm tempted, oh so tempted, to just finish him off and go home, but... what he says drives a knife into my own heart. That and... I've never actually killed anyone... the closest I came was watching the Zyloff kill Roxane.

Finally, after a minute of turmoil, I release the knife and get off of him and sit on the end of the bed. He looks surprised as he stands and dusts himself off, but it quickly turns into a gloating look. "I knew it. I knew you couldn't do it." I just sit on my bed, head down, and don't respond. He retrieves the knife and sedative and leaves, again locking the door behind him. As soon as he's gone, I silently cry to myself, despair again creeping over me, freezing my heart until each heartbeat is painful.

I'll never see the light of day again, will I?

16

A fter that, I don't see much of Patrick. He just leaves me alone in my room to feel sorry for myself for the most part, although he still comes in two or three times a week to put me down even more and to destroy all the things I thought I knew. During one of these visits, I ask him how he thinks he's going to keep me here for so long without someone eventually finding this place to rescue me. He gives me two answers.

"Actually, I doubt anyone will take note of your absence," he says casually.

"Ha ha. You should know that *someone* would see that I was missing. If no one else, Nathan would notice immediately."

"Oh? You really think so? Hmm. Interesting. Too bad you don't know..."

"What don't I know? Tell me!" I exclaim, frustrated. He smiles, knowing that would irk me.

"Oh, it's nothing, really... we just had someone watch you since you arrived until the night we kidnapped you to know how you act around others. Then, when we kidnapped you, she shape-shifted into you. She is posing as you even as we speak. That's why no one will ever notice, although we're prepared for that possibility regardless. We used magic years ago to hide this area of the forest- as well as any sounds coming from it. Even someone with very strong magic will not be able to see through that spell. Not even the dragons. You are cloaked from anyone trying to see you with magic- just like the rest of us.

"Anyone who gets close to this building physically will run into our distraction spell and it will send them in the opposite direction. Although if *that* failed, then the next spell causes the sound of a man running away, into the forest, causing anyone close to give chase only to eventually find nothing and be lost." He gets a glint in his eye as he recalls the next one. "The last spell causes them to go blind. I would make it permanent, but I have not yet figured out how. So for now, it lasts for about an hour. And *if* they made it past all of that, they would run into a vicious porcupine-tiger we bred specifically to guard the castle. It would tear them to shreds. Given the remote possibility that they somehow survived the porcupine-tiger, then they still wouldn't be able to get to you, because if they could even locate the correct room, the same type of spells surround your room, which can only be dropped if they have the key- which only I have. Plus, there are two guards outside the door. ...Any more questions?"

I shake my head, overwhelmed and deprived of what little hope I had been harboring of someone rescuing me. He laughs. "I didn't think so." He leaves, and I am again feeling even worse after the visit- just like all the others. I collapse back in the chair and sigh, too weary to cry like I have been for the past couple of weeks. I just don't think I have any more tears to shed.

During his next visit, I challenge him on the impersonator he told me about. He smiles and says he thought I'd say something like that. He pushes a button on a remote that he had brought and a picture appears in front of me. It's my friends and me, sitting at a table in the Square. The image then turns into a video. I watch, telling myself not to be gullible and to watch it while challenging everything I see- just like Nathan always does.

I'm sitting next to Nathan, eating lunch and talking to Ham and Sierra. From what I can gather, none of them realize that the person they are laughing with is not me. What they say next *really* worries me, though.

"I'm so happy you guys won!" Sierra exclaims. The fake me laughs-exactly like I do.

"You've been saying that for the past three weeks, Sierra!"

"Yeah, I know. I'm just so proud of you two! And now I'm even more glad you won, because we can finally go home! The Games are over! They can't keep us here much longer. I don't care what they say. They're lucky we've stayed this long. Thaddeus said we had to wait for the injured to heal first, and so the King and Queen can meet us all. Well, the King and Queen aren't any better, but the rest of the contestants are fine, so we could go home at any time!" The four of them cheer and Patrick ends the video.

"Still doubt it?" he asks me tauntingly. I shake my head, trembling.

"They... they're leaving soon?" I gasp, unable to accept this.

"Yes, within the week, actually. As soon as I have Vlad send them..." he trails off, realizing that he slipped. He shrugs. "Oh, well. It's not like you knowing would make any difference."

"Knowing what? I realized Vlad wasn't acting the same after he brought me here, if that's what you mean. Are you controlling him?"

"...In a way," he says, looking surprised that I even noticed. "I had him watched for a while, figuring since he was looking for the King's lost children then we could just watch him. When he found you, I immediately sent Hunter to collect you, but you never met up with him again, thanks to Vladimir getting to you first. So when he returned to Zilferia, we changed the plan and captured him. Like you, he got a replacement. Unfortunately, we couldn't spare our best impersonator- the one who's you at the moment, so he isn't acting perfectly. Obviously, he's too led by his emotions. I was angry when he put in the werewolves in the First Challenge, but I let it go since I figured you could take them. And if not, then you were of no use to me anyway.

"The mermaids, however, were the last straw. I had no idea you had gotten so under his skin, Princess. I had actually sent someone to kill him when I got the feed of you with the mermaid King. You seemed to be doing fine, so I stopped and watched. ...So now you know that we are, indeed, at war with those fish. It really doesn't matter anyway. But just so you know, your actions prevented the fake Vlad's death."

"...Where's the real Vlad? Is he here?"

Patrick laughs, scolding me. "Is he here? Of course he's here! Where else do you think we'd put him? He's a man with power. We aren't going to put him in our less guarded building so the Sohos can come and snatch him like they did that doctor... Kate." A beeping sound goes off in his pocket. "I've got to go," he suddenly says. "Stay here." Yeah. Right. Like I'm going anywhere.

As he heads towards the door, something else occurs to me. "Wait!" I call, stopping him. "What did your impostor do to our Familiars? She must have done something. They should be healed by now."

"Can't have them telling everyone the Crystal that's there is fake, now can I? I have a man keeping them under. That's enough questions for now," he growls impatiently before turning and yanking the door open, slamming it shut behind him. I listen carefully in case he forgets to lock it, but as always, he doesn't neglect to do so. I sigh, more frustrated and hopeless than ever and climb into bed and try to fall asleep on the stiff mattress.

Just as I'm drifting off, I have an idea for how to get out of here. But I won't be able to do it alone... Next thing I know, I'm dreaming once more. I'm walking around in the woods, looking for something. I can't seem to find it. Frustrated, I call Gale's name. There's no reply. I'm confused, for he's supposed to hear me if I call for him. I desperately need his help, but my plan failed.

The next morning when Patrick comes in again, he brings welcome news. "You have earned a break from this room. It has become clear to me that your body and mind are deteriorating while staying here. Let's go." He grabs my arm and hauls me unceremoniously out the door. The two guards fall in behind us, trying to discourage me from escaping, I suppose. I might actually think about it, were it not for Patrick's iron grip. That and my promise to my friends. Although... they would understand if I just couldn't do it, right? If I just bailed? I'm not doing any good while being Patrick's prisoner anyway.

As we walk briskly through the hallways, I rapidly memorize all I can, but there are lots of turns, so I'm unsure how well I actually do. By the time we emerge outside, my head hurts from concentrating for so long. Not only that, but the bright sunlight burns my eyes. I collapse, ripping out of Patrick's grip so I can cover my eyes. The searing pain eases, but my eyes are still watering like crazy. It's evident that staying indoors in the near darkness for a month affected my eyes as well.

Patrick sighs impatiently and pulls me to my feet. He tells one of the guards to give him a piece of cloth. He pulls my hands away from my eyes. I keep them tightly clenched, fearing the light. I feel a strip of fabric settle over my eyes and around my head.

"Open your eyes," Patrick orders me. I hesitantly blink them open. The black cloth on my eyes is thin enough to see through, but it also keeps out most of the sunlight. It works like sunglasses. I sigh with relief. He then again grabs my arm and we continue into the forest. I stumble a lot in the beginning because my body is so unused to the movement, but I get better as we go along. When we reach the porcupine-tiger, it turns toward us and growls, but Patrick shakes a bell, warning it off. It backs away, wincing as if the sound hurt it. I put this information in the back of my head, storing it away for when I'll need it.

We travel quite a ways, trying to get me some exercise, I guess. We stop right before the trees start to look more green- in fact, there seems to be a prominent line where they begin to wilt. The ones closer to the Dragon Hunter's main building are more stunted in their growth and brown. As soon as we stop, my legs wobble, and I collapse to the ground at the base of one of the trees. I'm astounded by my weakness. *It wasn't so long ago that I had to swim all day with a Trident on my back during the Third Challenge. Just look at me now! Merely walking hardly more than a few miles and I'm panting and weak!*

"Rest," Patrick orders. "I need to check the border. Stay here. We can hunt you down anywhere- not that you'll even get far in that state." Sadly, I think he's right. I watch as he walks along the line of smaller, weaker trees away from me. My two guards stand on either side of me as I lie back against the tree and close my eyes.

I suddenly realize why my idea didn't work last night- Patrick said that the first spell kept in both sounds and magic- and calling a dragon requires both! I open my eyes and peer at the line where the first spell must be. These trees must not be as healthy because they're cut off from the flow of magic. Thinking quickly, I yawn and change positions, laying on the grass and almost reaching the line. *Dang. So close!*

Trying to act like I'm not up to anything, I sit up after a while and look around again. I then stand and take a step toward the line. "Don't cross the line," the younger guard says. "Patrick's orders."

"But..." I turn to protest, but stop in my tracks as I realize he's just a boy- about my age, in fact. "You... you aren't very old," I say before I can stop myself.

He looks surprised and a little offended. "So? I'm seventeen! What, did you think we were all old geezers except your brother?"

I blush. "Um, I actually hadn't thought about it." I bite my lip, unsure of how to act around a boy my age. The only person I'd seen in almost a month was Patrick. The boy's face shifts to sympathetic.

"It's okay. The only person allowed in to see you is Patrick, so I can understand the confusion. My name is Chet, by the way." He pulls off his hood, revealing his features a little better. He has sandy-blond hair, bright green eyes, and boyish freckles. He smiles and I can see that he isn't a bad guy- probably just mislead. My instincts with reading people have always been accurate. *Probably because of my dragon part,* I realize. *Similar to them reading people's hearts.*

"I'm C-Crystal," I reply, shaking his outstretched hand. "...But you know who I am, obviously."

He nods. "Only heard about you, though. It's nice to meet you."

"S... same."

Chet glances over at the other guard, seeming to debate about something. Finally, he says, "Hey, George. She needs more exercise- that much is obvious. And she needs air that isn't tainted. This air is disgusting."

The other Hunter has a glint in his eye like he knows what Chet's planning. "Fine. Take her out. ...Just don't go too far- Patrick will be back in a few minutes!" He calls as we start walking away.

"Sure thing!" he calls back. Chet leads me away from George until he can't see us anymore. He then has me sit on a fallen tree while he sits on a rock across from me. "Now then, what's the real reason you wanted to get across that line? No one even knows you're gone; they won't be looking for you with magic."

I hesitate. "Well, I..." My voice stops and I can't seem to make the words come out. Why should I tell the enemy what I'm planning anyway? For all I know, this Chet person would try to stop me- and it wouldn't be hard to drag me back over the line in my state. But then again... he seems to be trying to help me. ...Maybe if I can make it so he thinks my plan will never work...

"It's okay," he says, understanding almost hiding the pain in his eyes. "I understand. You can't tell the enemy anything." He looks at the ground, hesitating before he continues. "I... I don't have to be your enemy, you know."

I raise an eyebrow. "Really? ...Because when you serve Patrick, that's all you can be. ...I'm sorry."

He looks up from the ground he was staring at, looking excited. "That's just it- I don't *want* to serve him!"

This catches me off guard. "Wait... what?"

"He just enrolled me in his army years ago, threatening me if I didn't comply. So, of course, I did. I did everything he told me to. I was expendable. If I fought him, then he would kill me. What other choice did I have?"

"You didn't," I whisper.

"He... he took my dad and me right from our home. They start with the homes nearest them- the ones not in the main Village- so no one will react much if they go missing. They just think we got dragged off by wild animals or something. ...My dad was killed because he fought. He told Patrick every day that he meant to escape. So he disappeared... I never saw him again. He killed him, to show all of his recruits not to mess with him or try to get away.

"So I've been waiting for an opportunity to escape- I just don't make the same mistake dad did and tell him about it. The only one I told was George- and now you." He looks at me pleadingly. "Please, if you have a plan... please include me? I mean, I understand if you can't. *You* are the important one, obviously. Only you really need to get away."

My heart softens. I may be too gullible for my own good, but I can tell this boy needs help. ...And maybe I can be the one to help him. "Okay," I say. He looks skeptical.

"Really? ...Can you do that? Will it endanger your plan?"

"No," I say. "It shouldn't. In fact, you can help immensely. You see, my plan is to contact my friend Gale."

He looks confused. "Gale?"

"Yeah. He's a dragon- kinda the leader, actually."

"And you think he can help you?"

"Yes. He said that if I need him, then I can just call- with both my voice and my mind- and he'd help. But something else he said stuck with me. He said that a few can go almost unnoticed in a large group."

"Oh, I see," he exclaims, his eyes lighting up with hope. "You're going to ask him to get help- but not from a dragon!"

I'm surprised. "Well, yes. I'm going to ask him to alert my friends to my absence, and I will also give him my memories to relay to Nathan about this place, the spells and such."

"And then they'll come for you? ...You'll tell him that I'm a good guy, right?" he adds nervously.

"Of course. I also remembered the way to my room from the outside, so I'll tell him that too. I'll just need you to take care of the key."

"Wow," he says, impressed. "Were you working on this plan for a long time?"

"No," I admit, a little embarrassed. "Just late last night and this morning."

"Well, go ahead and call your dragon friend. I won't stop you. Just... you're going to have to make it quick. I don't know what's holding Patrick up, but it won't last much longer."

"Right! ...Gale!" I shout, using my mind to push the message out with magic as well.

For a second, I think that it didn't work when I hear his deep, rumbling voice in my head. *"Crystal? There you are! I couldn't sense you for nearly a month! What happened? Are you with the Dragon Hunters?"*

"...Yes. They kidnapped me- and they've been hiding me here this whole time. I need help getting out! Can you contact Nathan in a dream like you did for me?"

"Yes. Why? What do you need me to tell him?"

There's no time for words, so I just shove my memories since the winner's banquet on him at once, not bothering to pick through them. *"Nathan doesn't need to know all of that, but I need to hurry. I don't have much time before Patrick comes back!"*

"Okay. Good luck, Dragongirl. ...Would you like your other two friends to come as well?"

"Yes! Anyone Nathan can get- just don't make the party too big!"

"Hold strong, Princess. Your rescue party will come. Good luck!" With that, he's gone. I look over at Chet, whose whole body is tense with anxiety.

"Done," I declare. He nods, relieved.

"Good. We need to get back- *now!*" He grabs my hand and hauls me back over the line. We get there just in time- Patrick comes striding up just moments after. Chet quickly drops my hand before he gets too close. George winks at Chet, chuckling. I don't think he quite understands what happened, but I need to catch my breath and act like I have no hope at all, not in the entire world. I am once again completely devoid of happiness- at least on the outside.

When Patrick returns, he's flustered. When George asks why, Patrick replies that the Sohos have been waging an attack; as have the dragons and mermaids. He glares at me. "It seems our little Princess has encouraged them; gave them heart again. You undid a lot of my work, girl," he growls as he once again grabs my arm and begins dragging me back toward the building. I stumble after him, unable to keep up with his quick pace. "It looks like I'll have to start from scratch to remove their hope. I even have an idea of how to do just that..." He ends there, letting fear settle in my heart once again.

He takes me back to my room and locks the door behind me. I take off the cloth around my eyes and collapse onto the bed. I'm still shocked at how much weaker my body has gotten while I've been held captive. I just can't get used to it. I'll just have to build my strength back up again. And until Nathan arrives, I guess I'll have to try and stay on Patrick's good side. I won't promise him anything, but maybe I can pretend to give a little and not resist so hard.

Pleased with my plan and full of hope once again, I feel better than I have in weeks. For the first time, I climb into bed and fall asleep with a smile rather than tears.

<<<Nathan>>>

After spending another great day with his friends, Nathan heads home with Crystal. As they walk, she seems to zone out, just as she has for the past month or so. *Ever since we won, she's been acting differently,* he reflects. *Yet... no one else seems to notice. ...Maybe I'm just paranoid. I mean, who says you act the same after the Games as you did before? It's not a drastic difference, so... maybe I'm just imagining things?* He lets out his breath in a huff. *I may* be imagining that, but I am definitely *not imagining this feeling I have that we shouldn't leave. It's real, I'm sure of it... I don't know. Maybe* I'm *the one who changed. I mean, I never thought it was a bad idea to leave before.*

He looks over and sees Crystal nodding slightly with a hand near her ear. This just reconfirms how she's acted differently for the past while. What changed? She'd acted... a little colder to him at times, and then at others, she would suddenly be happy and talkative and stand a little too closely to him... all he knows is that this is not like the old Crystal.

Most of that was after the Winner's Ceremony. Now she's closer to normal, but for some reason, she tries to avoid talking to anyone whenever possible. She would normally seek others out to talk to them- especially him, Sierra, and Ham. She even declined his invitation to join them when they went to visit the other contestants in the hospital. It just wasn't like her to not care about other people and how they're doing.

Crystal notices Nathan watching her and smiles at him. He smiles back, although the pit in his stomach grows. That isn't right. Crystal's highly inquisitive, wanting to know everything that's going on. If she saw him watching her, she would ask why, not smile!

Maybe she's just excited to go home, he decides. Once again, he has a sick feeling about leaving. He tries to figure out what's holding him back, but once they get to their little house and he climbs into bed, the only thing he can think of is that their Familiars are still mysteriously unconscious. But that was nothing new, and Thaddeus said they could send their Familiars through portals to them once they're recovered anyway. Finally, he decides that he will go home. If he can't decide what's holding him back, then there probably isn't anything. Besides, he hadn't seen his family in months. He *needs* to go home.

He closes his eyes and sees a picture of his family in his head. He smiles, eager to go home, and quickly falls asleep. He instantly has a dream. He's confused and startled, for it usually takes a while after he falls asleep before he dreams. Well, that and the fact that standing right in front of him is a dragon so large he feels like he's standing at the base of a vast golden mountain.

He backs up, gasping. He's almost blinded by the sunlight reflecting off of the beast's brilliant scales. The dragon doesn't waste any time. *"Nathan Anderson, your friend is in danger."*

"W- what? What friend? I just barely saw them all- they're fine!"

"The one sleeping in your house is not Crystal." Boy, he sure gets right to the point!

"What do you mean? Of course it's Crystal! Who else could it be?" Even as he says this, he feels like the dragon's right. What he's saying confirms what he's been secretly thinking for the past month.

"The real Crystal was kidnapped the day you two won the Games."

"Wait... what?!"

The dragon sighs impatiently. *"I don't have much time. Time moves faster in your dreams than it does in real life. Here, I will show you her memories since that night. ...Are you ready?"*

"I... I don't know. I guess," he replies. The instant he says this, a torrent of memories floods his mind. He's Crystal as she responds to Dallas's knock and follows him into the woods. He feels her fear and then her power as she retaliates against the Dragon Hunters. He's her when she first meets Patrick, when she cries herself to sleep every night, and when she attacks him.

Nathan feels her suffocating hopelessness after every one of Patrick's visits, he learns about the spells protecting their main building, about Crystal's parents- or at least what Patrick shows her. Through her, he learns about the porcupine-tiger and how to subdue it. He feels how she feels when she meets Chet and how hopeful she is while talking to Gale.

And then, as suddenly as it started, the memories end. He staggers back, gasping.

"Do you see now?" Gale asks impatiently.

"Y... Yes. How long do you think she has? Even with the help of her memories, it will be difficult to get to her quickly. Who else does she want to help? I know she wants a small group so we can slip in and out, but *who* does she want?"

"I do not know how long she has, but I would hurry. Patrick is not a patient man. I have a feeling he will take his anger on us out on her, just because he can. She wants you, Lloyd, Sierra, Ham, and Thaddeus. Anyone else you deem necessary is welcome as well, as long as the group doesn't get too large. You know the castle thanks to her, so you can judge how many would be sufficient. Chet and George will help out in any way they can- count them as allies. You must also plan on taking Chet out of there with you."

"Of… of course," Nathan replies, still reeling. "But… what should I do with the impostor? If we tell her we know what's up, then she will immediately tell Patrick we're coming. We need to be sneaky. Should we tie her up? Take her with us?"

"I… do not know what you humans would prefer to do, but since they are the enemy, we dragons would kill her, no questions asked."

"Oh. Well, I don't think so. I'll come up with something. Maybe Thaddeus can help."

"Yes, very good, but the sun is coming up. I cannot stay with you much longer. Good luck. Remember- do not fall for the spells' tricks. It will waste time and will likely get you discovered. Farewell, Nathan Anderson. Crystal is counting on you to save her… you are her only hope…" His voice fades even as his body does and next thing Nathan knows, he's sitting upright in bed, covered in sweat and panting.

'Crystal' sits up in the other bed. "Are you okay?" she asks.

He nods. "I'm just… going to see Thaddeus. I… might need some… medicine. Don't worry, you can go back to sleep. I'm sure it's nothing." The impostor nods and lies back down. Nathan quickly gets dressed and heads to Thaddeus's place, noticing that the sky is beginning to lighten, although the sun isn't up yet. Luckily, he's there, already awake.

When he knocks on the door, Thaddeus opens it, glances at him, then double-takes and peers at him as if just seeing him. "Wh-what? Nathan? What are you doing here?"

"I… need to talk to you about something. …In private."

"Oh… okay," he says, letting him in and closing the door. He quickly mutters a spell to make it so no one will be able to eavesdrop on them, then sits down at the table. He gestures for Nathan to sit across from him.

Once he's seated, Thaddeus asks him to reveal everything that's on his mind. He quickly tells him about his dream and how he felt about 'Crystal' even before he knew the truth. "The thing is," he finishes, "I have no idea how I felt not to go home. I mean, I'm not a descendant of the Dragons- am I? Could I have dragon powers as well?"

"Perhaps," he muses, his hands folded in front of him. "I do not know, but there is a chance you two are very distantly related. One of Alex's children left Zilferia and went to another realm, likely Quagon. You are likely not closely related- if you are at all. But that isn't important right now.

Rescuing Crystal is, and our most pressing matter is disposing of her impostor."

"Yeah, I know. I don't know what to do with her. Gale suggested killing her outright, but… well, I thought I would ask you first." He says, the idea of killing someone making him queasy. He was fortunate to not have to in the Games, and he certainly doesn't want to now unless it's absolutely necessary.

Thaddeus looks thoughtful. "I don't know. I see a few options, but I know there must be a better option that I do not yet see. …I shall ponder on it. For now, don't let this impostor know anything. Pretend that you are still ignorant. Make sure you continue to address her as Crystal. Try to act normal. …I will take care of the rest."

<<<Crystal>>>

When Patrick comes the next day, I ask him if I can see Vlad- the real one. I tell him I won't believe anything he says until I have proof of Vlad being here. He smirks and seems to find this as a great opportunity to brainwash me- just as I was hoping. He grabs my arm in the same place as before, his fingertips lining up almost perfectly with the purple bruises I received from being dragged behind him the day before. Chet and George follow behind us again. We follow the hallway, then head down some stairs.

It becomes dark and damp the further down we go. I shiver, glad Patrick didn't decide to keep me down here as well. It's super creepy and the walls seem to radiate an even stronger feeling of hopelessness than those of my room. I feel worse and worse for Vlad as we plunge deeper. After a while, there are no more torches on the walls, so Patrick lets go of my arm and grabs the last torch. I wonder how I'm going to get Patrick to leave me alone with Vlad for a while and see if he can help with the escape. I'm sure he's going to want to leave this place as well.

Patrick stops in front of one of the cells and unlocks the door. He turns to me, the torchlight making his sneer more gruesome than ever. "Here you are. This is the real Vlad. You two will have plenty of time to talk since I'm not coming back until tomorrow. Have fun!" he says, pushing me into the cell. I stumble and fall to my knees on the worn stone as he locks the door behind me and walks away, laughing, leaving us in the near darkness.

There's only one torch inside the hallway of cells, so the lighting is horrible. I cautiously call out, "...Vlad?"

A hoarse voice toward the back of the cell replies. "What? Who's there? ...I recognize that voice..."

"It's Crystal," I reply, relieved.

"What? Patrick got you, too? I'm so sorry, poor girl!" he says. I'm startled at the difference between this Vlad and the other one. I mean, I knew there was a difference, but not this severe!

"Yeah, but it's okay."

"Wha... no, that's not okay! You need to finish the Games so you can go home! But before that, you need to meet your parents so they will begin to heal from the terrible wounds Patrick dealt them. They need you. ...Are they out of their comas yet? Do they realize that you're here?"

I smile to myself in the darkness. I hadn't realized how little Vlad knows. I forgot that he had been taken the night I arrived and has no idea of what happened since. So I tell him everything that happened. I spare him most of the details so the telling would go faster. I finish a few hours later. My eyes have adjusted somewhat, so I can see how big his eyes are.

"Wow. That's... that's amazing! You are the most extraordinary person I have ever met. I am deeply sorry for how much my impostor hurt you." Again, I'm surprised. He's apologizing for something that's not even his fault!

"It's alright. I'm sorry you've been down here for so long, and none of us had any idea. But don't worry, I have a plan to get us out of here. Of course, it all depends on Nathan and Gale, but still..." I tell him my plan. He's impressed.

"Well then. You are quite full of surprises! Well, let's just hope this works. But for now, you need to sleep, Princess. You won't be able to help with your own rescue if you are too tired to move." I nod. Vlad offers me his bed, claiming that he won't be able to sleep tonight anyway. I'm surprised at how tired I am after doing nothing but talk all day. I fall asleep quickly.

17

I sit up suddenly, startled. "W... where am I...?" I gasp before I remember. I am sitting in a dungeon with the real Vlad... and it's pitch black. My eyes flicker back and forth, straining to see even a hint of light. I start panicking. I have always been afraid of the dark, especially when the darkness is so thick and stifling. My breaths start coming in rapid, small little wheezes. I hear Vlad in the dark, trying to comfort me.

"Crystal? What's... oh. It's okay. Nothing is in here but you and I. No one can hurt you. There's nothing here..." As he tries to reassure me, I hear his footsteps shuffling over to me and I feel his hands hold one of mine between them. The warmth and gentle pressure helps a little as I struggle to keep myself from hyperventilating. He continues to talk to me, to try and comfort me, but I can't understand what he's saying through my hysteria.

I burst into tears. My heart is racing, sending waves of heat through my body. I start sweating, despite the chilly air around me. My head starts to feel light and I know I need to get more oxygen in with each breath, but that's easier said than done. I fight to slow my heart, but there's no stopping it from racing away. I close my eyes and feel the same panic. It doesn't help; I know that it's dark around me. I soon pass out from the irrational terror.

This time when I wake, I open my eyes and it's dark, but I soon see a light coming toward me. The flickering light reveals Patrick's face. I've never felt so relieved to see the monster. I turn and see Vlad. His eyes are bloodshot, but he smiles at me. "Good luck. I'll be waiting," he says, reminding me of my plan. I nod and follow Patrick out of the cell as he grabs my arm yet again.

I blink as we reenter the light until my eyes adjust. I'm surprised as we pass my room. "Where are we going?" I ask.

Patrick smirks, and I can clearly see that he's hiding something. "We're just going to... test you. I want to see if you can solve a certain... *problem* I give you."

I frown. *Something is definitely off about this...* I shake it off. I will do whatever he asks me. I won't be here much longer anyway. At least, that's the hope. Maybe I'll take as long as possible to do whatever it is he asks me to do so I can buy more time for Nathan. I would do nothing at all to be even more cautious, but that might make things worse because of Patrick's temper. I'll need to tread carefully around him, that's for sure.

We climb and reach a much larger room than the one I had before. The stone is also a lighter shade than the stone in the last room. I walk in and am surprised by the window on the south wall. Patrick seemed to be keeping me away from anything that could make it so someone could see me through before. I shrug. Oh well, the reasoning doesn't really matter to me. I'm just grateful I will be able to look at something other than the wall now. Patrick releases me and walks out the door without another word. George and Chet come into the room to guard me this time.

Neither of them say anything, so neither do I. We wait in silence for him to return. While we wait, I continue to look around the room. There isn't much in it- just a large table and a single chair in front of it, facing the door. There is a rug underneath both of them, but that is all that is decorating the room. There's nothing else but the clean stone walls.

Patrick soon comes back, followed by four other Dragon Hunters. Patrick is carrying a large paper while the four behind him struggle to move a large metal contraption. The four place the... whatever it is, next to the table, then leave. Patrick sits me down in the chair and lays his paper out in front of me. It's a drawing of the plans for the contraption that is now looming over me.

I raise an eyebrow. "What is this supposed to be?" I ask.

"This is the layout for this… machine. There's a problem with it. Your job is to figure it out."

I stare at him. "What? Seriously? …Then you must not know me as well as you'd like to think you do. I'm no good at mechanics. What is this thing even supposed to *do?*"

Patrick's brow furrows as he contemplates how to respond. "I… um… we'll let you figure that one out. It will… be part of the equation." It's obvious he's hiding something, but the question is… what? *Wait a second… this is a perfect excuse to delay until Nathan comes and saves me! How am I supposed to make something work the way it's supposed to when I don't even know its purpose in the first place?* I grin in triumph.

Patrick looks confused at this, but he decides it doesn't matter. As long as I do what he wants, he's content. With that, he leaves me alone with no idea what to do.

<<<Nathan>>>

"Do you know what we're going to do yet?" Nathan asks. Thaddeus holds up a hand, telling him to wait until he finishes eating. He had come back over right after lunch, telling the impostor that he wanted to ask him when they could go home. He fidgets, waiting impatiently. Every second they waste is another second Crystal has to spend with a dangerous maniac. Thaddeus finally finishes his sandwich and takes a drink of milk. Nathan groans. *It's like he's* trying *to take as long as possible!*

He stands and puts the dishes in the sink, then sits back down. He looks up at Nathan, his eyes kind but serious. "Sit down!" he instructs. "All your fidgeting and pacing is making me nauseous."

Nathan swallows hard and forces himself to sit. The very action feels almost like a betrayal to Crystal, like he doesn't care about her enough to rush to her side as soon as he can. He grits his teeth and waits for Thaddeus to speak, at the edge of his seat. He sighs at Nathan's impatience. "Didn't I teach you patience?" He laughs a little and shakes his head. "Well, I suppose your actions are only reasonable."

Nathan then loses what little tolerance he had left. "What is your plan?! We need to get this impostor off our tails!"

He sighs again, and Nathan knows he's disappointed, but he doesn't care. "Very well. There was only one way I could think of to keep the impostor from alerting Patrick to us catching on to his ruse. ...We have to not capture or harm her in any way. All we need to do is simply tell her that you are going home. That you two, as the overall winners, will be able to go home first- that way, we won't have to send Sierra, Lloyd, and Ham away before we can get rid of the fake Crystal. I am quite sure the impostor will then slip off back to the Dragon Hunters, since she does not have a way back here from First Earth. I imagine that the Vladimir impostor will help her to get away. We will then follow her as she heads back to their main building. Hopefully, we can slip in after her when she disables the protective spells and no one will ever know we got in. Of course, getting out may be a little more difficult, but our main concern is getting in quietly. It doesn't matter how much noise and chaos we cause getting out."

Nathan stares at him. That wasn't at all what he was thinking. All he could think of was how to attack the impostor. He smiles a little at his reckless stupidity. *Wow. I can't believe I didn't think of that... or anything even close, for that matter. ...No wonder I could never beat Thaddeus at chess. He truly is a mastermind! Thinking ahead of just what needs to be done now... manipulating something that could cripple us into something that aids us...* He shakes his head in awe, newly appreciating Thaddeus's intelligence.

"Wait... did you say we?" he asks, thrown off guard once again. He figured Thaddeus's part would be helping to plan and to get them there. Not to face the danger head-on.

Thaddeus smiles wearily. Nathan suddenly notices he hasn't gotten much more sleep than he himself had recently. "Yes. I intend to come with you, of course. You might need someone who can use magic, plus I'm not going to just stand by while my niece gets tortured by that fiend." He laughs at the look on Nathan's face at the word 'magic.' "Did you already forget that I can use magic? Not only did I use it constantly to keep Crystal's identity hidden during the Challenges, I just cast a spell not too long ago to keep our words veiled!"

He's startled, then laughs at himself. *I can't believe I already forgot that! I don't know that I'll ever fully grasp the intricacies that this world provides- like magic.* They don't laugh long. Nathan thanks him, then starts to leave. As he steps out onto the street, Thaddeus's hand on his shoulder stops him.

"Don't you want to know when to tell the fake Crystal when to leave?" Nathan chuckles at himself again.

"Yes, of course! Sorry, I'm not thinking." Thaddeus smiles, then tells him to inform the impostor that everyone is leaving in the morning. Nathan thanks him again and heads back to the Square, where he left Ham, Sierra, Lloyd, and the impostor. His heart feels lighter now that they have a plan, and he feels like skipping. He smiles. "Don't worry, Crystal. We're coming for you," he whispers triumphantly.

<<<Crystal>>>

I'm worried. I have no clue as to what I should do, and Patrick's reports say that Nathan still has no idea what's going on, so apparently Gale wasn't able to contact him. Not only that, but he's leaving Zilferia tomorrow morning! *I guess my plan didn't work,* I sigh as I stare at the paper with pictures on it that mean nothing to me. *Now what am I going to do? ...I can't escape by myself, and Chet and Vlad are counting on me to get them out of here! ...I don't know that obeying Patrick will help me much now that there's no reason to stall him...* I hang my head in my hands and close my eyes. The hated feeling of hopelessness once again smothers me in its blanket of sorrow. I struggle to breathe through the pain of disappointment and hatred- and perhaps even fear- of Patrick.

Well, if there is no longer a reason to obey Patrick, then I'll just see what I can do to stop his progress. ...Maybe for starters, I'll tell him I figured out the problem with this machine, and make it so it will blow up or something. I don't care anymore if I lose myself in the process of getting rid of Patrick and his Dragon Hunters. They must be taken care of, and I'm here, so it might as well be me. I take a deep breath and peer at the paper again. They told me the power source was simply magic... but where did they get the magic to put into it? It would have to come from somewhere, right?

My eyes trace the shape of the machine, following a tube that's convoluted and connected strangely. *Something about this has always seemed a little... off to me, but could that really be what's wrong with this machine? No, it's too simple. But... I think that it is!* I grin, pleased with myself. Then I frown. *I don't know how what to tell Patrick to do to make it blow up, though... I really don't know much about engineering. ...Well, maybe I'll find another way to destroy him and his operation... I don't have much choice at the moment anyway. I'll just find another opportunity to strike...* I look up to see the door opening. Patrick storms into the room, his foul mood seeming to darken the very air around him.

"What's taking you so long?" he demands, slamming his hands down on the wooden table with a thump. "It's been two days! Haven't you figured it out yet?"

"Well, why couldn't *you* figure it out?" I bite back, taunting him. "Why are you depending on a sixteen-year-old girl to think for you? Are you really that lacking in intelligence?" Patrick's face gets red with anger. He barely restrains himself from hitting me, although I can see on his face how much he would love to do so.

"I told you," he growls through clenched teeth, "This is a *test*. I want to see what you can and cannot do. ...I already know the answer to the puzzle. The purpose is to see how long it will take *you* to figure it out." With that, he spins around and storms toward the door, apparently fed up with me.

"Wait!" I call out as he reaches a hand out toward the door. Clenching his fist, he stops and turns around.

"What is it?" he growls. Great, now I've put him in an even worse mood than before. I swallow and decide not to try and make anything up to tell him; especially since he claims he already knows what the problem is anyway.

"I... I figured it out," I squeak out uncertainly.

"Well, it's about time!" And with that, he leaves.

"Where's he going?" I ask Chet and George. They both shrug, so I sigh and wait for him to come back. He returns sooner than I thought, with three men behind him.

"Well then, if you really have figured it out, tell my men what it is."

I nod, still confused as to what he's getting at. I point to part of the picture. First I want to check as to what they want each piece to do, even if they won't tell me the purpose of the machine as a whole. "This is supposed to connect these two things, correct?" I ask. They nod. I check with a few other things, but Patrick soon grows impatient.

"Have you figured out the problem or not?" he spits out.

"Yes." Turning to the actual thing beside the table, I point out the over-complicated tube. Disconnecting and reconnecting a few things, I free up the extra tube before taking it and connecting it through the top to what seems to be the main part of the machine, then let it emerge out the front. I take another small tube from a pile of spares they gave me and make it stick out the side, explaining that whatever gunk the machine produces releases here.

I don't really know what I just did, especially since I still don't know what the machine is even *supposed* to do, besides have powerful suction and have somewhere for... something... to go when the device is finished. I back away from it so the three can see what I did. They swarm over it for a couple minutes, and once they're done, one of them gives a slight nod to Patrick. He smiles wickedly and walks out of the room, leaving the three to carry the machine back out of the room. Chet lends them a hand. I watch, dumbfounded, as they go and the door closes behind them.

"What the crap just happened?" I wonder out loud. George shrugs, just as lost as I am.

I sigh and sit back down in the uncomfortable chair and close my eyes. I don't want to sleep, I just... ponder. I try to figure out what I'm going to do now to send word to Nathan before it's too late, but my only plan didn't work, so I haven't a clue what to do. I think of him, already missing the sound of his laughter and even his stubbornness.

<<<Nathan>>>

...I sure hope the impostor really bought my story... Nathan can't help but worry as he lies in bed, unable to sleep. *Crystal really needs my help- I just know it! She's in trouble...* He glances over at 'Crystal' and watches as she sleeps. *Well, I guess I'll find out tomorrow. The only way we can get to the real Crystal is with stealth and surprise. We won't have surprise on our side if the impostor knows we're coming... No. Thaddeus's plan* will *work. It has to.* Still, he can't shake the feeling that the impostor won't act the way they're expecting. Sighing, he pushes these thoughts out of his head. Worrying about tomorrow won't change anything. He rolls over and finally falls asleep.

When he wakes, the impostor is already gone. He smiles a little. She'd been slipping up even more than usual lately. Crystal wouldn't just leave without him, she would make sure he was ready to go as well. They were partners, and they trusted each other with their lives... and that bond was something you just can't duplicate.

He gets dressed and finds his friends already eating breakfast. They're all excited, and he understands their anticipation. People around them assume that it's because they're going home, but it's actually because they can't wait to save Crystal- just like him; although he's less excited than he is nervous and anxious. Still, he sits next to the fake Crystal and starts on his breakfast. Ham, Lloyd, and Sierra still try to act normal by talking about seeing their families again, and the impostor eats it up. Nathan grins a little before quickly wiping it away. *Man, this impostor is so gullible!*

When they finish eating, Thaddeus and 'Vlad' come up to their table and tell them what to expect. "You will go one by one," Thaddeus explains. "The winning team will go first. So the order will be Crystal, then Nathan, Sierra, Ham, and Lloyd will be after the rest of the contestants since he was out of the Games first. You will go with Vladimir to the portal in a few minutes, Crystal. We will leave you now so you can say your goodbyes." Then they move on to the other contestants' tables to tell them the news as well.

The goodbyes aren't very heartfelt since the four of them would be seeing each other again in just a matter of minutes, and the other doesn't know how Crystal would act saying goodbye.

'Vlad' returns soon after they finish and has 'Crystal' go with him. Nathan grins. *This is so perfect! Since they're both actually Dragon Hunters, 'Vlad' will probably just send her into the forest toward the Dragon Hunters' building. This couldn't be better!*

Sure enough, it doesn't take long for Vlad to return for him. Nathan follows him, trying to act like he's excited when really, he's terrified. Thaddeus told him he made it so his portal would just put him in the forest a few feet away rather than sending him back to First Earth, but... what if it doesn't work? How would he get back and save Crystal then? He shakes off the feeling of foreboding and keeps moving. He just has to trust Thaddeus.

They reach the spot sooner than he expected. 'Vlad' gestures to a large tree. "This is your portal." Nathan nods, swallowing his fear. He steps forward and walks through the tree. There's a slight tingling sensation, but it doesn't last long. Next thing he knows, he's standing behind a tree only a few yards away from Vlad. He peers around it and watches as Vlad nods, satisfied, and heads back to the Square to get Sierra.

He tells her to travel through the same tree. She ends up beside Nathan. Her eyes widen with surprise, but she stays quiet. The same thing happens with Ham. Nathan watches intensely as Jake is led to the same tree. He holds his breath, fearing he might pop up there with them. After a minute, he doesn't appear. He releases the breath he had been holding, relieved that it worked just like Thaddeus said it would. As Vlad leaves, he remembers what Thaddeus told them to do next.

"Let's go," he whispers to Ham and Sierra. They nod and start heading in the general direction of the Dragon Hunters. After about ten minutes, Nathan's fear returns that they made a mistake, but they spot a person in the distance soon after. She stops in a small clearing and looks around cautiously. They quickly duck behind some trees.

Satisfied, 'Crystal' crouches down and concentrates. She shimmers and becomes a girl with long black hair, who stands and begins walking away again. She's wearing all black, with even her hands covered- just like the other Dragon Hunters. They quietly follow her again, Nathan's two friends treading carefully right behind him. They travel for a few more minutes before Thaddeus and Lloyd catch up to them. Their appearance is sudden, causing Sierra to yelp, but Nathan stops her just in time. Thaddeus had already warned him that he would create another short-distance portal to put himself and Lloyd right behind them. He releases Sierra, nods to Thaddeus and Lloyd, and continues after the impostor with single-minded determination. The other three exchange surprised looks, but Nathan hardly notices.

The only thing he's concerned about is Crystal.

<<<Crystal>>>

I stare at the wall, biting my lip with frustration. Patrick hasn't come back yet, and Chet doesn't know what's going on either. Not only that, but it's too late for me to stop Nathan from leaving. He left about an hour ago, which I know because the person who was impersonating me reported to Patrick as soon as she left. My impersonator will be back soon, apparently. I sigh and rest my head on the table. I feel like I should be crying, my heart wrenching with sorrow, yet... I'm not. I'm puzzled, but I figure that I'm so sad and so drained, I *can't* cry. When I was on earth, I heard that happens sometimes. The person is kind of just too... numb to cry.

I close my eyes, trying to forget myself, my predicament, but mostly Nathan. Ignoring myself is surprisingly easy, but forgetting Nathan... as hard as I try, he just won't disappear from my heart. He's as much a part of me as my family is, maybe more so. There's just no forgetting him. I sob and feel my heart break at the thought of never seeing him again. A single tear slides down my cheek.

<<<Nathan>>>

I wonder how she's feeling right now... Nathan ponders, suddenly feeling guilty. Since the fake Crystal thought he was gone, the real one must believe that as well. She probably feels betrayed... abandoned. *I'm sorry*, he cries out with his mind, knowing she can't hear him but trying regardless. *It's the only way... if you could know, then I would have told you, I promise! But don't worry, our plan seems to be working... so far, at least.*

He peers around at the forest, trying to find the line of wilted trees he saw in Crystal's memories. He sighs. There's still no sign of it, and it's starting to get dark. Looking ahead again, he notices the Dragon Hunter stop. They slowly creep closer, staying as silent as possible. They aren't quite close enough to catch her words, but it doesn't matter. He knows she just asked for the spells to be lowered so she could walk through. They are getting closer and closer to their goal.

Nathan's heart pounds in anxiety and impatience. He can't wait to see the real Crystal again.

<<<Crystal>>>

When Patrick finally reenters the room, he wears a smug smile. Triumph radiates from him. I shrink back, feeling a rock of fear form in my gut, waves of pain throbbing dully through my body. I stand, trying to ignore the crippling terror.

"Well? What now? ...I passed that test, didn't I?"

"I believe so, but we... need it to be... tested. Yes, tested. And who better than you?" he sneers, grabbing my arm yet again to drag me out of the room. He waves for Chet and George to stay. The looks of concern shadowing their faces don't help to ease my fear.

He takes me down some stairs into a dark room. I squint, trying to see. When my eyes adjust, all I see is the machine with a chair in front of it. A suction cup has been added to the tube sticking out in the front, and the smaller one on the side has a crystal tube similar to a test tube one would find in a Chemist's lab attached to it. Patrick pushes me toward the machine, but when I see the restraints on the chair, my sense of danger shoots even higher. Panicking, I whirl around and try to charge past Patrick, but he catches my arm in a shockingly firm grip.

I scream for help even though I know that no one who hears me will be able- or willing- to help. Patrick then hollers at the Dragon Hunters in the room for assistance, and two more men run up and grab both of my arms in their iron grip. I wriggle around, but I can't break loose. I scream again, frustrated. I kick one in the leg and his hand disappears from my arm. I spin and kick the other in the chin, snapping his head back, but I am soon overwhelmed as four more guys pile on me and haul me to the chair. Now the only thing I can do is bite, so I swivel my head around and clench my jaw around some dude's arm. He yelps and releases me, but it's not enough. I manage to bite another hand before someone hits me in the head with something hard. I slump as my brain clouds. I can't seem to react as they strap me into the chair, trapped watching my own demise.

I look up at Patrick, hyperventilating with panic. "What is this?" I scream desperately. "What are you going to do to me?!"

He's breathing hard, as are the eight other guys standing around me. "We are going to make you an example," Patrick grunts. "After this, you will not be a martyr, as you would if we were to kill you." Fear completely overwhelms me at this, and I couldn't hide it if I tried. I have an idea of what he means to do. He grins at me, and the glint in his eyes reveals just how much of a maniac he is. A dangerous, intelligent psychopath who now holds my life in his hands.

"Prepare to lose your Gifts, *Princess*," he laughs, putting the suction cup on my forehead. He then starts toward the lever to start the machine. I fight to escape the restraints, but it's too little too late. With a mighty yell, he pulls the lever down. My body instantly stiffens and my eyes roll back into my head.

Pain rushes through my body, feeling a lot like when the mermaid King tortured me, but this… is like the torture has been taken from a general sense to a much more focused and intense one. I feel like my nails are being pulled out slowly and my whole body is being stabbed by burning needles that pierce deeper and deeper. My back arches in pain and an unearthly scream erupts from my throat. It's only ended by me losing my voice. I feel four distinct tugs on my heart before I pass out from the pain.

<<<Nathan>>>

"What was that?" Sierra gasps, fear causing her voice to tremble. Nathan can't find it in him to reply, so Thaddeus tells her instead.

"That… was someone in pain. So much pain that it cannot be measured nor fathomed."

"…Crystal," Nathan chokes out, his heart heavy, each beat burning with pain. "No…" He drops to his knees in the grass. They were too late. Tears leak out from beneath his clenched eyelids. He buries his face in his hands and sobs, not caring that his friends can hear. Thaddeus kneels in front of him and puts his hands on his shoulders. He turns away, refusing to be comforted. He had failed her. His best friend… his teammate.

"Nathan. Nathan, it's okay!"

"No it's not!" he yells. "He's killing her! I just know it! And you don't even care!"

"No, he's not," Thaddeus assures, his voice so calm it just irritates Nathan. "He couldn't do that without starting a riot. He wants to subdue our spirits, not inflame them. He won't kill her. He may hurt her, but he wouldn't dare kill her, much as he might like to. She has too many powerful friends."

He shakes his head, but Thaddeus's words somehow find their way through the barrier around his heart. There may still be hope. He stands shakily and glares at him. "Then we will save her," he states. Thaddeus nods, even though it wasn't a question.

It was a promise.

They march on and meet the porcupine-tiger. It growls at the group, but

Nathan growls back, so much hurt and rage in his voice that the creature backs off. The other four look at him, fear and amazement in their eyes, but he doesn't care. He races toward the door leading inside with Lloyd following close on his heels. It's unlocked. The Dragon Hunter they were following had no idea they were coming and didn't bother to lock the door behind her. He grins, but it's the twisted smile of an insane man. And maybe that's what he is now, but it doesn't bother him. As he runs, he follows the path Crystal memorized and ends up standing in front of two Dragon Hunters, panting. They both look at him, fear and surprise in their eyes.

"Let me through," Nathan growls. They nod and unlock the door, then step aside. He walks forward and slams open the door. The unconscious figure of his best friend is sprawled on the bed, her now bleached blond hair forming a halo around her head. Admiration and sorrow almost overwhelms him when he notes the state she's in. Her face is clenched in pain, tears still fresh on her cheeks. He carefully picks her up and heads to the door. The two Dragon Hunters watch him, wide-eyed. The younger one then runs to catch up to him. He pulls off his hood, revealing a freckled face. "Chet," Nathan recognizes.

"Crystal said I could come along." Nathan nods, remembering this. "She... she also wanted to take Vlad with us," he continues, edging away from Nathan, clearly afraid. He glances worriedly at Lloyd, who stands at Nathan's back as the others catch up. He's far beyond caring.

"Fine," he grunts. "Go and get him- *fast!* Or we'll leave you behind." The boy nods and races off. Nathan sits down on a chair near Crystal's cell with her on his lap. He gazes at her face, and a few more tears are released from his eyes as he sees her pain. Her eyes wander beneath her eyelids like she's having a nightmare. He gently brushes the bleached hair off of her face. Her skin is hot to the touch, and her face is damp with sweat. He looks over at the other Dragon Hunter- George, he thinks. "What..." his voice breaks. He swallows, then tries again. "What did they do to her?" he pleads. George averts his eyes and stares hard at the ground.

"Patrick, he... he tricked her. And then... they took away her Gifts. She fought admirably, but... it wasn't enough." Nathan stares at the wall, unable to breathe for a moment. *He... he... that monster...* His hands clench involuntarily in anger. Fury builds in him and he punches the wall, fighting down a scream of fury. George, Ham, Sierra, Lloyd, and Thaddeus back away. Hot tears stream down Nathan's face. Crystal's Gifts were a *part* of her. How... how could they take that away? How would that not kill her?

"She's very strong," Chet says. Nathan looks up and sees him with Vlad's arm around his shoulders. He stares at the boy, not comprehending what he said. "It would take a lot more than that machine or even Patrick to kill her." He nods, feeling his anger cool slightly. He can now control the flame of range, but he knows that it will never die. He would get revenge for what Patrick had done.

Lifting Crystal back into his arms, he stands and heads back out of the door leading outside. His friends follow behind him, keeping their distance. After they pass the porcupine-tiger again and reach the border-line, a cackle of surprise and wicked joy drifts through the air. Nathan shivers as he realizes just how much of a maniac this Patrick guy is. Fear causes his skin to crawl, and it doesn't fade as they cross the border and the laughter disappears.

As they head back to the Village, Lloyd lays a friendly hand on his shoulder and offers to help him carry Crystal, but he backs off after Nathan barks at him that this is his burden, and he is happy to shoulder it. Lloyd nods and falls back behind him. The cool night air does nothing to cool the anger and fear that causes his skin to prickle. In this manner, they return to the Village, triumphant and with their friend back.

Still, he has a feeling this isn't over.

18

The first thing I notice when I come to is a gentle pressure on my right hand. I open my eyes. Nathan is sitting next to me, asleep. I look down at my hand and find his in mine. A slight smile lifts my lips. I don't know why I'm in the hospital again, but... *Wait, didn't...* Everything comes rushing back to me and I suddenly can't breathe. A monitor next to me starts beeping like crazy as my other hand goes to my chest, alarmed at the tightness beneath it. Nathan wakes up and starts to pull his hand away, but I clutch it desperately, needing his support. He nods to me, understanding sparkling in his sad eyes.

Nurses and doctors rush into the room. One of them sticks a pre-prepared needle into my arm and I can breathe again, but slowly and shallowly. The monitor stops wailing and the room falls silent. I pant, struggling to regain my breath. Normally if this happened to me, I would be crying through an anxiety attack, but I'm strangely numb.

The doctor who helped me explains. "I'm sorry, but if you experience fear or any other emotion too strongly, then... your body becomes over-stressed and shuts down." I nod. That explains it. My breathing is still shallow, so I can't ask a question, but Nathan reads my mind and asks for me.

"Why is her breathing still restricted?"

She grimaces. "There's only so much we can do when her heart has been weakened so drastically... but shallow breathing is better than not breathing at all." We nod in grim agreement. "The serum I injected won't last long. It will only hold your emotions in check for another hour. So I suggest you two talk now, but try to avoid causing a panic attack, alright? The serum only works so well," she says to Nathan.

"Of course," he agrees.

"...And you should probably leave within the hour as well."

"What- no!" he exclaims. I shake my head at the doctor, agreeing with Nathan. I need him here with me. "What if those Dragon Hunters come back?" he continues. "What if she has a nightmare or something?"

The doctor shakes her head. "I'm sorry. We all want what's best for Crystal, and you being here will not help. We can guard her ourselves. She will be safe here," she promises.

I decide I need to say something, but I can't find the words. Talking seems to be a struggle at the moment as well. I watch, eyes wide, as the doctor and Nathan stare at each other, a battle of wills raging in their eyes. Finally, Nathan sighs and nods. He slips his hand from mine and stands. I finally manage to croak out one word, "Stay..." The doctor and Nathan both look at me, surprised. The doctor tries to assure me that it's for the best. I shake my head vigorously. I thought I had lost Nathan forever. There's no way I'm letting him walk away from me right now. Her eyes widen and she sighs.

"Very well. Whatever you want, Princess. Just... be careful. Your kingdom needs you." I nod and all the doctors and nurses leave, filing out until only Nathan remains with me. I can't ask him any questions or tell him what happened to me, but he can still tell me what happened on his end. Last I heard, he was gone, headed back to First Earth!

Nathan sits back down in the chair next to me with a heavy sigh. He looks exhausted. Unable to comfort him with words, I grab his hand and hold it gently between the two of mine. He looks over at me, surprised, then smiles. I stare at his face, the face that I had missed so much in the month I was with Patrick, and smile back.

He then tells me everything that happened since the night I had been snatched, how he noticed that 'I' had been acting differently, how Gale told him to help through a dream, and Thaddeus's plan and how they went through with it. I shiver when he tells me about Patrick laughing when he rescued me and how Thaddeus assumes that it was because of two things; that they were too late to save me- with my Gifts intact, at least- and the fact that he took the Gifts to spread the word of his power, and what better way to do that than to have me pulled out of the fire- Giftless? When I indicate my hair color, he says the hypothesis is the magic being drawn from me to fuel the Gift Stealer bleached my hair as well.

As he talks, I close my eyes and focus on his voice- the voice that I thought I would never hear again, except in my dreams and memories. I take a deep breath and try not to dwell on the past so my heart won't give out again from the stress of emotions. "When we got back from rescuing you, we discovered that the fake Vlad had disappeared. We don't know where he got to, but Vlad's fine with it. He says he's not much of one for revenge anyway and good riddance to the spy. He also went around to everyone apologizing for all the grief his 'replacement' had caused. It's weird to think of Vlad as a nice guy now. Anyways, as nice as it is to have him back, it's much better that you're back as well," he adds. "Nothing felt right while you were gone."

After he's finished, I smile and quickly fall asleep, exhausted. His hand is still in mine when I spiral back into the dark oblivion of sleep.

I'm in the hospital for a few weeks before I can both talk and stand upright on my own. It's another week before I can go anywhere past the bathroom, and yet another month before the doctors say I can go. Nathan was by my side every moment during those months, supporting me, encouraging me… even crying for me. He never does it when he thinks I'm watching, but I hear him almost every night before I fall asleep, and soft tears of sympathy linger on his cheeks each morning.

Waiting got harder for me. All I could do was lay in bed. Lloyd, Ham, and Sierra came by every day to tell me stories before eventually, one by one, they all went home to their own realms and families. Vlad came by after the doctors cleared him and thanked me, as did Chet. Nora eventually got better and tried to help me with my boredom as well, but it wasn't enough. I wanted to be out there myself, to feel the wind in my hair, to laugh and to dance and to play… the simple things were the hardest to part from, it seemed.

Finally, the doctors say that I can go- just *'be careful.'* I walk outside without Nathan's help for the first time in months and finally feel the light and warmth from the sun on my skin, warming my heart and lightening my heavy, clumsy footsteps. A cold breeze plays with my hair and I laugh as it dances around my face. I pick a flower and inhale its bittersweet aroma. I feel the grass tickling the bottom of my feet, and I laugh again, pure joy and pleasure bubbling up from deep within me.

I spend the entire day outside despite the cold. I find lizards, climb trees, revel in talking, laughing, singing, and dancing. I even stay there for a while after the sun goes down. I sit on a grassy hill, exhausted, as the sun sinks below the mountains, turning the clouds pink and orange. Nathan sits beside me with Greg curled in his lap and Nora perches on my shoulder. We watch silently as the sun's last rays of light leave the land, plunging us into a cold world of darkness.

The air around us loses its meager warmth almost instantly. I shiver and watch as a leaf falls slowly from the tree above us. Winter seemed to be taking its hold on the land. I suddenly realize that means I've been gone for over half a year, since I was taken at the end of spring. I turn to Nathan. "I need to go home," I abruptly declare. He looks at me with surprise, then nods.

"Of course. But we might want to ask the doctors if that's okay first." I crinkle my nose and frown.

"I guess. I'm just so sick of being in the hospital! I never want to set foot in there again!" He smiles and laughs.

"I understand. I'll talk to them for you tomorrow. Okay?" I nod, grateful.

He helps me to my feet and we head home, back to our little house. I'm surprised at how much I've missed it. Then again, it's much better than the hospital's bleak white walls and demanding doctors- and anywhere that's in Patrick's clutches.

I gratefully climb into bed and fall asleep. In my dream, I go home and find Kiki a year older. She doesn't know who I am. My parents see me and scream and run away, thinking that I should be dead. I sit down and cry because they don't know me. I try to find the King and Queen, but they tell me that I couldn't possibly be their daughter and send me away. I go to the mermaids, but they try to kill me, and their King is dead. I go to Gale, but he tries to eat me. Everyone hates me because of my weakness and inability to stop Patrick. Zilferia is covered in flames, and everyone except the group of Dragon Hunters is dead. I fall to my knees and wait for death to claim me as well.

But then there's a comforting hand on my shoulder. I look up and see Nathan smiling down at me. He helps me to my feet, pulling me into an embrace. Together, we go and kill Patrick and restore Zilferia. But still, no one is there to see my victory but Nathan.

I wake, gasping, tears on my cheeks. My pillow is drenched. I look over at the other bed and find Nathan still asleep. I get up and wash off the tears in the bathroom. The cold water helps bring me back to my senses. I then get dressed in my clothes that I wore during the Challenges. I didn't think I'd miss those clothes, but it felt so good to wear those silky soft pants and jacket again... especially now that the weather has turned. It isn't as cold in Zilferia as it is where I lived on Second Earth during this time of year though, I realize. I also put on the new watch that Thaddeus brought me. After he learned that mine was taken, he took the initiative to get another one to me so he, Nathan, and I could communicate after we all go our separate ways.

By the time I get back to our bedroom, Nathan is already dressed. He smiles at me. "Let's go get some breakfast," he suggests. I nod and Nora and I follow him and Greg into the brisk air. The food tastes fantastic- much better than the hospital food. As soon as my last bite of blueberry muffin melts on my tongue, we head back to the hospital. As much as I don't ever want to see that place again, I know that I should really get permission from the doctors to leave.

Nathan heads into the building while I wait outside with our Familiars. I watch Nora as she does spectacular tricks in the air and Greg as he shows how he would scare off a cat if it thought to take him on. I laugh.

Nathan soon returns with the good news that I'm allowed to go home. "But," he adds, "They want you to do one thing for them first." I should have known. Help is never free. "...They want you to see your parents before you go. They need to know that one of their kids is alive and well, or else the doctors fear that they will fade away soon. They've been comatose for too long." This is not at all what I was expecting.

"Of... of course," I stammer. "Now?"

He nods. "Why not?"

So I follow him back into the building that I swore to myself I would never set foot in again. We meet a doctor and follow him to the back of the building. We head down some stairs and to a door. The doctor turns to us. "The King and Queen are in this room. You can try and rouse them, but there is very little chance they will respond. You are very welcome to try, however," he says. "We've been keeping them alive and have been able to prevent too much atrophying of the muscles," he adds. We nod, and he opens the door and ushers us through. The door gently swishes shut behind us as the doctor leaves us alone.

In front of us are two beds, each with a still, unmoving form on them. We hesitantly walk closer. In one bed is my father, Alexander Dragon, and in the other, my mother, Pearl Dragon. They are both hooked up to a lot of different machines- even more than I had been for the past two months. They're both very pale, but beneath that and added wrinkles and faded hair, they look just as they had in the 'movie' Patrick had shown me. My mom's stunning green eyes are closed, as are my dad's stormy blue ones. I sit on a chair next to Alexander's bed while Nathan waits, hovering by the foot of the bed. Alexander's eyes wander restlessly under his eyelids and he's covered in sweat. He looks just like how Nathan described me when he first saw me after the Dragon Hunters took my Gifts.

I don't know what to do to let him know I'm here, but I try holding his hand, as Nathan had with me. There's no response. So, feeling awkward and out of place, I start talking to him. I tell him about my life on earth as well as what happened after I came here. After a while, I notice that his eyes have stopped wandering.

I keep talking. I tell him about Vlad and the Challenges, the dragons, the mermaids. When I mention Hunter, however, I finally get a major reaction from him. The instant I say his name, Alexander's hand tightens momentarily, then relaxes once more. Confused but excited, I try it again, this time using Rex's name. His hand twitches. I try telling him my name again, and a small sound gurgles up from his throat.

My eyes widen. He's almost talking! "Yes! Yes... dad. It's me. It's Crystal." It's a little weird calling this stranger 'dad,' but I figure it will help draw him out of his coma.

"Cry... Crystal?" he asks, slurring the name.

"Yes! I'm right here!" I'm getting excited now.

"...Crystal?" he repeats, sounding stronger.

"Yes! This is Crystal! I'm here! Please, sit up! You're okay! Come on!" He slowly opens his eyes, but they don't focus on anything. I help him sit up.

"Crystal? Is... no. It... can't be." His eyes slowly focus on my face. His eyes widen and tears begin making their way down his cheeks. He grabs my hand again. "Crystal... it is you!"

"Yes. It's me," I confirm as he puts a hand on my face. I switch to my dragon eyes briefly to back up the claim before changing them back. He pulls me closer and I sit on the bed next to him.

"My... my beautiful daughter... where's Rex? Is he here with you?"

"No. I'm sorry. I don't have any idea where he is," I tell him. His eyes sadden for a moment, but then they fill with joy again.

"But you're here."

"Yes, I'm here."

"Then that's enough." He finally tears his gaze away from my face to Nathan standing behind me. For a second, he's confused.

"...Hunter?"

"No," I quickly correct him, "This is my friend, Nathan Anderson. He's from First Earth."

"Ah," he says. Every second he's up, he seems to gain strength. "Nathan. I see. ...You know, you look a little like a Dragon, my boy. ...A member of the family, I mean," he laughs. I'm amazed by his rapid transformation.

Nathan smiles uncertainly, but I can see hidden pain behind his eyes. "...Thanks," he says.

It's only now that Alexander notices the Queen on the other bed. "Pearl?" he asks, confused.

"Yes, that's Pearl. She's in a coma still, like you just were," I inform him.

"Ah," he nods. "I see." After pulling out everything attaching him to the machines, I help him take the two steps to her bed. He sits on one side of her and I sit behind him to keep him from falling off the bed in case he doesn't have enough strength. He does the same thing I did and holds her hand and talks to her. After a while, I join in and so does Nathan. She soon opens her eyes as well.

"...Xander?" she says. He nods, tears in his eyes, and hugs her. Nathan and I stand back and let them have a moment. When they're finished, Alexander has me come over to them so Pearl can see me. I sit on the other side of the bed. She also puts her hand on my cheek as her eyes soak in my face. Reality doesn't seem to set in immediately, but when it does, her tears start flowing and she hugs me too. Then they're both hugging me, and I feel the love of family again for the first time in... well, ever since I was told I was adopted. But this time, it's with my true family. The family I didn't know existed a year ago. The Dragon Family.

After they release me, I have to tell them the whole story over again, since they didn't really hear and understand anything I said while they were unconscious. Nathan runs to grab me water as I talk. Once I finish, they tell me theirs, although I already know it. I knew that Patrick messed with that video. I already knew that Thaddeus was telling the truth about what happened, but it's still nice to hear it from them.

When they're done, Nathan and I help them outside so they can get some real food. The doctors we pass are awestruck. My dad greets them with a happy wave and a laugh, which just increases their bewilderment. Apparently he hasn't been this happy since before I was born, and everyone who knew him is blown away by the change. I laugh with him, his joy so overwhelming that I just can't help but revel in it as well.

We find the Village cook, who freezes in shock at the sight of her King and Queen. She, like the others of the Village, had only just discovered my true identity after I was rescued from Patrick. Pearl smiles and tells her that she missed her as well. The cook pulls herself together and rushes forward to hug the Queen before hurrying away to grab the only food she had ready- sandwiches. She apologizes profusely, but Pearl just smiles gently and thanks her, assuring her that it's just fine. As soon as we leave, the cook, eyes still wide with shock, runs off to alert the Village to the return of their King and Queen.

We sit at the nearest table and start eating. I didn't realize I was so hungry. I was too preoccupied with meeting my parents for the first time to notice that the entire day had slipped away, the sun already having set. I wolf down the sandwich and sigh with satisfaction. Just as I finish, a group of people come and surround us. I frown, bothered, but Alexander just laughs and waves to the people, greeting most by name. I'm surprised. *No wonder everyone loves them; they love everyone they meet, and clearly care about them individually!* I suddenly feel guilty. I don't act like that. I care about myself more than some stranger. I swallow. *And since they're my family, I'll be expected to be like them!* I feel a sudden wave of panic and am almost overwhelmed, but I force it down.

The crowd slowly disperses as it gets colder. Before we find a place to sleep for the night, Alexander and Pearl want to visit Thaddeus. So Nathan and I help them to his house. After I knock, Thaddeus opens the door, wearing his pajamas. At first, what he's seeing doesn't quite register. His mouth opens and closes like a fish out of water, and his eyes stare as though they'd never need to blink again. "P- Pearl?" he stammers.

She smiles. "Hello, Uncle Thaddeus! It's been a long time!"

He still can't seem to stop staring. I can't help but grin. I've never seen him lost for words before! "Why... yes, it certainly has. C... come on in," he stammers, opening the door all the way and ushering us into his house.

After we're all seated at the small table, he just stares at the King and Queen for a while. I start to feel a little awkward, but my parents don't seem to mind. They just continue smiling as they wait for him to recover. Once he does, the three talk for hours. Nathan and I eventually leave, finding some couches to sleep on.

When we wake the next morning, we find that they had talked all through the night. Alexander and Pearl look much more solemn now than they had before. Thaddeus must have caught them up about the war that the Dragon Hunters are waging in Zilferia. They push the worry from their faces and smile at us as we walk back into the kitchen. The five of us then go back into the Village for breakfast, where we once again have to deal with almost the entire population of the Village. Thaddeus shoos the crowd away, telling them to let the King and Queen get some rest before their attention is pulled in so many directions at once.

We finally introduce Nora and Greg to them formally. Nora tells me after that I am more like Pearl than I think. Somehow, this thought comforts me, as I see now just how amazing and sweet she really is.

After we eat, we head to the Dragon palace- the largest building in the

Village, by far. The closest is the building Thaddeus was always in, which I guess is kind of like a government building, but even that is only about a third the size of the palace. Nathan and I gaze up at it in awe. It's made of stone with bronze and gold throughout, and there are a lot of steeples and stairs. It's built into the side of the mountain by the Village. It has an ancient feel to it, and yet it also seems… almost new. From the outside, it looks like it has probably six stories, but there's probably some of it underground as well. Needless to say, it's impressive.

Pearl notices our stares and smiles, a little self-conscious. "This castle was built with the help of the dragons for Alex when she first came back to the Village with Jack. My family has owned it since then; we just hand it down from generation to generation for the King and Queen."

"Have all the Kings and Queens been part of the Dragon family?" Nathan asks as we start up the stone steps leading to the front door of the castle.

"Well, ever since Alex's time. …Thaddeus told you about her, right?" We nod.

"Of course, I did!" Thaddeus protests. "How could I leave something like that out? I also told them the protocol when someone in the royal Dragon family got married, too! The question is… do they remember?"

"Yes," I reply. "The fiancé would be taken to the dragons to be judged. They would look into their heart and if they were good people, then the dragons would bestow the last name of 'Dragon' upon them. The same thing happened to the children of the Dragons- they would be judged."

Thaddeus nods, satisfied. "Very good. But of course, that story has a special meaning to you, doesn't it? …Since you're now a part of that history." I nod, a little embarrassed. Alexander laughs and we keep climbing.

When we get inside, Nathan and I stop dead in awe once again. I look around in awe at the amazing interior. And I thought the outside was brilliant and ornate! The Dragons' home looks warm and inviting, stylish, open, and peaceful. There are different shades of brown and gold throughout, and the soft beige carpet really makes the place feel comforting and like a real home. Pearl chuckles when she sees our faces. "It's pretty big for our little family, but I think it's nice, don't you?" Nathan and I manage to nod.

"You could fit the whole Village in here!" Nathan finally exclaims.

"Well, yes, we have thrown a few parties for the Village here, but not for a while. That reminds me... I think we have a celebration in order! Our lost daughter has found her way back to us!" At this, they all cheer. The color in my face instantly deepens.

"Not only that," Thaddeus adds, "but the two of you have come out of your comas and are alive and well! That's what the Villagers will really want to celebrate- they've already had an event for Crystal." Nathan and I laugh and it's Alexander and Pearl's turn to look a little uncomfortable. As we laugh, a door opens behind the King and Queen deeper into the palace. A plump, pleasant looking lady steps slowly into the room, a look of surprise and disbelief spreading across her face. Tears well up as she takes it in, staring as if trying to convince herself that what she's seeing is real. I smile. Nathan then notices the woman as well.

I turn to Pearl and quietly inform her of the visitor. She grins and turns to see for herself. She beams as she sees the lady. "Matilda!" Alexander then turns as well. He laughs delightedly. "Matilda, how are you, my dear friend?" Pearl continues. Tears fill Matilda's eyes and she rushes forward and embraces the Queen.

"Pearl! How... you're better! I... I thought that... you..." she breaks off and pulls away from Pearl, embarrassed. "Oh... I'm so sorry. I should... give the returning Queen a more respectful welcome... but oh, dear, you've gotten so thin!! I'll go fix you up something to eat right now!" She then hurries off back through the door, a new sense of purpose in her step. She calls back, "Lunch will be ready in a little while! I'm overjoyed to see that you two are back and healthy... although you could always do with a little more meat on your bones!" she adds, laughing.

When the door closes behind her, Nathan and I turn to the King and Queen. "Who was that?" Nathan asks.

"That was my good friend and personal chef, Matilda," Pearl replies with a smile. "Oh, but where are my manners? I need to show you to your room!" she exclaims, putting her hand on my shoulder and leading me towards a hallway on the right. "I mean, we are a family again, and you should really stay here with us..." She continues, but I let her voice fade away as I think.

A... family? Now I'm concerned. *I already have a family; on Earth. And I love them, even though I know that they aren't my real family. I knew them much longer than Alexander and Pearl, and they are the ones who actually raised me... but these are my real parents, and they obviously need me... but so does my family on Earth! I now have a life in two different realms, and I can't choose between them! I love them both; the simple normality on Second Earth, fitting into the crowd, just being normal... but here, I've made friends with many people and creatures, and the life in the limelight is actually a little appealing... and I have a sense of purpose. My parents missed me so much they almost died, so I can't just leave them... but I also can't abandon the ones who raised me and cared about me...* I sigh in frustration. *I can't do this! I can't choose between two parts of myself!* I clench my fists, a battle raging in my heart.

I swallow and push the thoughts aside as much as I can so I can concentrate on following Pearl as she leads us toward my room. Nathan and Alexander follow behind. We go up another flight of stairs and stop at the top, in front of a wooden door with a gold emblem of a phoenix blazed into the middle of it. Pearl turns back to us and smiles. "Ready?" she asks. I nod and watch as she twists the golden handle and pushes the door open, revealing a room beyond my wildest dreams.

The 'room' is huge- the same size as my entire *house* on Second Earth. A King size bed is on the far wall beside a large window, the frame of the bed made of silver and the posts shooting up above it. A white cloth hangs down from it, surrounding three of the sides, since the headboard is pushed up against the wall, which is painted a warm brown. A large book-case stands next to it.

A table is on the other side of the room with another considerably large window right above it, which sends the golden light of day pouring into the room, which draws my attention to a glass dresser near it. I walk over and find a finger scanner on it. Putting my thumb on it, a light flashes across the bottom and a beep sounds while a green light appears next to the handle. I grab the silver handle and gently pull it down. Looking back at my parents, they smile and nod for me to go in.

So I do. Stepping into it, I find that it's much larger than it appears to be on the outside. Looking around, I see that the walls are all mirrors and there are revolving racks of clothes. They have shirts, jackets, pants, shorts, capris, earrings, necklaces, shoes, socks, sandals, high heels, boots, and makeup. My mouth drops open in shock. Only the richest of girls on earth would even dream of owning all this! I have no idea how I am ever going to wear it all. This is every girl's dream- and then some!

I hear a gasp and see that Nathan had come in behind me. His eyes are bugging out in surprise as well. "You... this is all yours?" he breathes disbelievingly. I shrug.

"I... I guess so. I'm never going to be able to wear it all!" I laugh. He nods and we exit the walk-in dresser.

Pearl looks worried. "Is there enough in there? I asked Taylor to keep it stocked with clothes that she thinks might fit you... but there aren't very many because we weren't entirely sure... well, when you were coming back." She stops there and tries not to cry.

I can't disguise my stare of disbelief. "Are you kidding? There's beyond plenty in there, and I'm pretty sure at least most of them will fit," I assure her. She smiles, relieved.

"Still, if you ever want anything else or something doesn't fit you, just let Taylor know and she'll make you something else. Okay?" I nod, stunned.

"Now then, let's move on to the next room- I'm sure Matilda will be finished with lunch soon."

"Wait... there's another room?" Nathan gasps.

"Of course! This whole level is for Crystal!" Pearl replies, surprised at his surprise. My mouth drops open once more. The whole floor? That's like having my entire high school to myself!

Other than my bedroom, I have a spacious bathroom, a room with a pool in it, a room with a ping-pong table and full sized tennis court, a racquetball room, a snack room where I have my own chef as well- his name is Steve- and, my favorite, the balcony. When we climb the stairs and open the door, a cool rush of wind hits me, taking my breath away. Storm clouds are coming in.

It starts raining while we stand there, but I don't care. I love the wind on my face, the cool rain on my skin, and most of all the view. I can see the mountains, the forest, and the ocean, all of which hold memories for me. The only thing I don't know much about is the dry, desert-like part of the land to the North of the mountains and forest. It looks dead and without life, but I recall that it's not. I decide that I want to explore that wilderness someday. Nathan comes up and stands by me as we look out into the rain-drenched landscape. I look at him and smile. Whatever adventures I have, I want to have them with him by my side.

By the time we retreat indoors, Nathan and I are drenched. Alexander and Pearl had sheltered inside while Nathan stayed with me outside, so they are dry. Thaddeus then walks up, smiling and holding a towel for each of us from the pool room.

When lunch comes around, we're all sitting up to a large mahogany table, Nathan and I swaddled in thick, warm towels. Before long, Matilda comes into the room, followed by six men in suits. They set down trays of fish, lamb stew over rice, chicken, turkey, watermelon, grapes, milk, duck soup, burgers, steak, salad, and more that I don't even know the names of. We dive in. The food is fantastic and before I know it, lunch is cleared off the table and Hot Fudge Sundays are served, as well as banana splits. Afterward, Matilda brings Nathan and I a cup of hot chocolate to finish warming us up. It has a hint of mint. It not only warms me up, but makes me feel a lot better overall. Nathan and I thank Matilda, who blushes and bows before going back to the kitchen to start on dinner.

Then Alexander and Pearl decide that they should get to know Nathan and me better. We play ping-pong while telling stories. Pearl tells me of the time she saved the babies of a new mother fox- the fox that I met in the Second Challenge.

"I was walking in the woods," she begins, "when I came across a den of foxes. The mother leapt out and growled at me, threatening me should I go any closer. I was intrigued because I had never met a talking fox before. Her name was Lola, and she told me that she was able to talk because she had helped the dragons with something. They, surprised by her courage, gave her the gift of speech with their magic.

"I noticed two things as she was talking- she was far too thin- I could see her bones and her fur was dull, and she had three little kits hiding behind her legs. I asked her what the problem was, and she told me she couldn't leave her pups to go hunt because their father was killed by a wild wolverine, but they were starving, and she didn't know what to do.

"So I offered to watch the pups for her. She didn't trust me at first, and I wasn't surprised at that, but she agreed once I told her that I was a member of the Dragon family and was a friend with not only the dragons but to all creatures. ...And that's how I made a red fox as a friend."

"That's really cool!" says Nathan. I agree.

Alexander grins. "Just wait until you hear *my* story," he gloats with a wink. "I was in the mountains, looking for an adventure when I was… oh, eighteen or so when I saw my first minotaur," he begins. "I was overly confident then…"

Pearl laughs. "I'll say, you were!" He playfully glares at her before laughing himself.

"Okay, I admit I wasn't too bright back then. I was a teenage boy trying to impress a girl- and honestly, that almost never turns out right." We all laugh. "Anyway, so I was heading into the mountains, trying to find something to fight so I could impress a girl named Amanda with nothing other than my Gifts to protect me. I soon found a mountain lion. I was about to take it down when what looked at first to be a hairy giant came and completely smashed the mountain lion in one hit from a tree he ripped out of the mountainside. The minotaur- still easily the biggest I've ever seen- then turned to me.

"I ran and ducked behind a tree just before the minotaur's tree struck the ground where I had been standing. I snuck around him and jumped onto his back, holding onto his horns. The beast swung around, trying to get me, but he couldn't reach me. Then he slammed me into a tree and crushed me until I let go. Before I had even finished falling to the ground, he caught my leg and held me in front of him upside down.

"He smiled gruesomely and flung me into the air too quickly for me to get my wits about me and use my Gift of flying to get out of there, so I came back down in a tree and was severely wounded. The minotaur tried to get at me for a while, but then it decided that I wasn't a threat anymore and left.

"Luckily, Amanda, who was watching invisibly, sped off to get help. To my surprise, it was the Dragon family that she brought. That was the first time I saw Pearl, and when I fell head over heels in love with her."

She laughs. "You were delirious with pain! You had no idea what was going on when I found you," she protests.

He chuckles. "Alright, fine. It was when I woke up and found myself in this gorgeous castle with a beautiful girl taking care of me… I've got to say, fighting that minotaur was worth it!" he finishes with a wink.

Then Pearl asks Nathan to tell a story. "Well… I don't really have a story like that," he says. "My life was pretty boring before I came here. I guess… I could tell you about the day Vlad came to get me," he decides.

"Sure," I say, curious myself as to what happened when he was kidnapped.

He nods. "Okay… well, not only was I on the track team for my school, but I was in band as well. And there was a football game- the last one of the year- and our school had high hopes for the team. School was canceled for the day so we could all go down and watch as we played against the Ponies. Well, we all figured we would cream them since we were undefeated for the past two years… that, and we were the wolves, and ponies can't exactly stand up to wolves in a fight." I laugh, but no one else gets it. They all have blank stares and empty smiles as they wait for his story to reach a point that they would understand what was happening.

"Well, the game was really close, but our quarterback scored a touchdown with only eleven seconds left… holy cow! The stadium exploded!" he says, a faraway look in his eyes as he relives the moment in his mind. "The other side was screaming because they were so mad and our side was screaming because we had won, but just *barely*… Anyways, as my friends and I were leaving, a guy from the losing team's school came over with three of his buddies and they had us cornered against a wall. As the biggest guy charged one of my friends, I jumped up and kicked his head. He went down like a sack of potatoes. The others looked at each other and ran, leaving their buddy behind. My friends asked how I learned to do that, and I just shrugged and told them that I had no idea," he laughs as he remembers. "They decided that I must be a descendant of some Viking king or something… it was pretty funny.

"When I started heading home on my bike, though, I was stopped by four guys that pulled up in a black van with tinted windows." I nod, recalling my own kidnapping. "My friends had gone another way, so I was alone. I got off my bike as they stepped out of the van. I knew right away that something was up, but I pretended not to notice…"

"Can I help you?" Nathan asks calmly as his heart stops with fear for a second, then starts pounding like crazy. The biggest one steps forward, looming over him with a permanent sneer drawn across his face. He was wearing leather clothes and stood head and shoulders above Nathan. He

shrinks back, his heart pounding so hard he could feel it in his brain. He swallows hard and gathers his courage to speak again.

"...Can I help you?" he repeats, too terrified to come up with anything better. The man continues to sneer down at him. The fear in him rises as the guy seems to be contemplating something, then it hits its maximum and disappears. He's strangely calm. Looking up at the big guy, Nathan stares him in the eye for the first time. "I said, can I help you," he growls, making it a threat this time. The guy arches an eyebrow. Finally, he speaks.

"You have spirit, kid, I'll give you that," he says in a surprisingly normal voice. "So I will give you a choice, although I would rather do things my own way... you can either come with us quietly, or you can fight and come with us anyway. We have more people than you might realize, little boy," he states as another van comes rolling up beside them. He gulps, but for some reason, his fear remains muted and he's able to think clearly. "So you may fight us if you wish." The glee on his face clearly tells Nathan how much he would rather fight as he continues. "...Or you can go with us willingly- not make a scene, not call for help, just come with us and do exactly as we say. You have one minute to decide."

Nathan's first instinct is to kick this guy's ugly face and then ride off as fast as he could on his bike, but he decides that that would be foolish. *I can't escape these guys for long if they really want to grab me... plus, if I agree, then they might trust me more and give me more freedom than I would have received otherwise... plus, who knows? They may have other people that they captured. I could try and help them...* He reaches a decision.

"Fine. Let's go," he says, walking calmly past him toward the van, dropping his backpack and clarinet by his bike. Everyone stares at him, utterly bewildered, as he climbs into the passenger seat. He leans out the door. "Hey, are we going, or what?" he remarks as he closes the door and buckles up. After standing there stunned for a moment, they all climb back in and the big bald guy starts the engine. Nathan notices that none of them are wearing seatbelts and a small smile begins to creep over his face. *This might be easier than I thought.*

"...So they took me to this old, abandoned building and led me inside.

None of them touched me; I just walked in. Once inside, they led me into this little room at the back of the building. There were two locked doors that we passed- the rest were wide open. I thought that surely there must be somebody in those rooms; why else would they be locked? I began formulating a plan to get us all out of there, but I lost track of my thoughts completely when I saw who they were taking me to. He looked like a serial killer that was famous at the time. Obviously, I was freaked..."

Nathan swivels on his heel, charging past the unsuspecting thugs that brought him there and charges toward the locked doors. He somehow remembers to grab the key ring and swiftly unlocks the first door. Looking inside, he sees a girl about his age with stunning green eyes and short black hair.

"What... who are you?" she demands, stunned.

"No time," Nathan gasps. "Let's go. I'm getting you out of here."

"Oh... okay," she agrees, standing and following him out of the room. They tear down the hallway toward the other locked door as multiple footsteps land heavily on the wood floor, gaining on them. He aches to run faster, he knows he can, but he can't just leave the girl behind to be recaptured. Finally, he stops and lets the girl continue. She spins around, opening her mouth to protest, but he yells at her to go- *now-* and help anyone else she finds along the way. He tosses her the keys and she nods and runs off, tears streaming down her face.

He waits behind a corner for them to come lumbering past. He quickly trips the first, so about three others trip over him and they all tumble. As they fall, he runs. He can't run back the way he came or the way the green-eyed girl went, so he heads a different way. As Nathan runs down this new, unexplored hallway, almost twenty other guys chase him, heavy scowls on their faces. Behind them are the four that fell, limping slightly, but clearly determined to catch him anyway. He puts on another burst of speed and makes a sharp turn into another hall-way. Just like bulls, most of them can't turn fast enough and keep going. Nathan allows himself a small smile as he continues running, glancing back. Now there are about eight- still too many, but much more manageable.

He tries turning again, but this doesn't fool any of them this time. And, unfortunately, he ends up in a dead end. He's in an empty, dust-covered room with nothing but a wooden table in the center. He's trapped.

He whirls around to see if he can get back out the way he came, but the route is already blocked by panting, angry thugs. Nathan gulps and retreats a few steps. They all grin cruelly and run towards him. Before he realizes what's happening, he's grabbed and thrown on top of the table.

"Well, after that, they started beating me up. Vlad rescued me, telling the thugs off. He apologized for their roughness- he didn't want them to go that far. He healed me up and talked to me about Zilferia and the Games. And that's all I've got," he finishes. Thaddeus insists that he has no story, so it's my turn. I tell them about my trip to Dragon Mountain. They are surprised and overjoyed to hear that I am- or... was, at least- the Dragongirl, but that excitement quickly dies once I tell them of my kidnapping when I got my dragon part taken away, as well as a bit about my month with Patrick- just enough so they know that I am now a Giftless, powerless girl that isn't really special in any way.

To my surprise, they are saddened for me, but they aren't disappointed in the slightest- they give me a big hug instead. "Oh, my poor baby!" Pearl cries. "I am so so sorry that happened to you, you poor thing! Don't worry, maybe we can find a way to help... somehow."

"You... you still want me?" I ask, confused.

"Of course!" Alexander gasps. "Why wouldn't we? You are still our beautiful, talented daughter, and we love you no matter what!"

I smile, my eyes filled with tears as I feel the love and acceptance of my true family for the first time. I may have grown up thinking I was a Shay, but while I cared for the family that raised me, they weren't my only family.

Maybe it's time for me to consider myself Crystal Dragon rather than Crystal Shay. The name sits on my heart, making it feel warm, and I know I made the right decision. *Crystal Dragon it is.*

Nathan and I stay with my parents for a couple more days, but he soon gets restless, itching to see his family again. I know how he feels- I want to go home and see Kiki again. I also want to see my 'parents' on earth again, as well as the few friends I have in my neighborhood... I just want to get back to my regular, boring life.

We decide to tell my parents. We have to break it to them gently, however, since they obviously didn't react well to losing me the first time and there's no guarantee of how they will respond to me wanting to leave again.

We decide to break it to them over lunch. As we're finishing off the last tidbits of the meal, I glance over at Nathan, nervous. He gives me a slight nod of encouragement. I take a deep breath. "Nathan and I think…"

At the same moment I start to speak, so does Pearl. "Your father and I have…" We look at each other. "You go first," she says.

I nod and take another deep breath.

"Um… well, Nathan and I have been thinking… and we love it here on Zilferia, but… we have been here for a very long time, and…"

"You want to go home," Alexander finishes. I look up at him, surprised.

"Well… yes. I mean, we can come and visit, but… we have another life besides the one we got dragged into here… and we miss it. Does that make any sense?"

"Of course it does," Pearl replies, her eyes shining with unshed tears. "It would be strange to not want to go back to the comfort of what you have known and loved for the vast majority of your life. Don't worry, I understand… I didn't always want to be queen- or princess, back when I was your age- so I ran away from my responsibilities and worries every once in a while to get back to what I loved first- the forest. …It is alright for you to go, it would be selfish of us to keep you here when you don't want to be here. But there is something we want to ask you two, as the winners of the Games. You do not have to accept this mission…"

"We'd like you to help us find our son, Rex," Alexander finishes for her. "It would involve traversing the multiple realms and going head to head with danger and it will be challenging to find him, since he will most likely have no idea who he really is." He looks at us seriously. "We can't do this, as we are getting too old for such adventures, but you two are in your prime. You don't have to do this; we can continue to use the Games to attempt to find him, although I would prefer not to do so since they are not very productive in anything except hurting you young, wonderful people."

"And you wouldn't have to do it alone," Pearl adds. "We might be able to find others to help you, but you may be on your own for the most part. …You don't have to decide today, but it would be best if you two decided together, and that's obviously easier if you are both in the same realm," she adds with a little humor. "As you two decide, we will go and talk to Thaddeus to make the necessary arrangements for your travel home."

With that, they stand and start to leave. I look over at Nathan. I know what I want to do, but I won't make the decision for him. He smiles at me, and I can read in his smile, as well as the mischievous twinkle in his eyes, his answer. I smile back, already excited for the adventures we will have while looking for my little brother.

19

I bolt upright in bed, screaming. I am covered in sweat from head to toe and shaking. I put my head in my hands and focus on taking deep breaths. *It's alright... it was just another nightmare... it's not real...* And yet it was so *vivid* and realistic... I can still hear the wicked cackling of Patrick and feel his hands grabbing hold of me once again, preparing to lock me up forever and torture me over and over again...

I shudder and stand, swaying. I quickly make my way out of the room, tears streaming down my face between my hands, dripping off my chin and onto my neck, where it traces a small, thin line past my collarbone and into my shirt. I continue to sob quietly as I open the door to my favorite part of the house- the balcony.

I stumble toward the chair next to the edge and collapse into it, my face still buried in my hands. Just as I hoped, the chilly early-winter air helps me to begin to forget about the nightmare. My hot, fevered skin cools and I can see my breath in the crisp, cold air. I slowly pull my hands from my face and look up. The sky around me is filled with the first snow of the year. The big, soft, and perfectly white flakes dance around me, landing on my nose, eyelashes, and lips. I blink them off of my eyes and catch them on my tongue.

A small smile begins to lift my lips. I have always loved snow; been enchanted by it. As the flakes swirl around me, my skin feels cold to the touch, but I don't care or even notice. I slowly begin to join the snowflakes as they dance as soon I am twirling around the balcony in my silky white pajamas, my wet hair sticking to my scalp and neck, a broad grin on my lips.

When I stop, I have to sit down because I am too tired and dizzy. I laugh a happy, stress-free laugh for the first time in more than a year. It feels so good I do it again, listening to it echo off the mountains. By now, the warmth from my skin has melted the snow on me and I am once again soaked. My body finally realizes how cold it is and suddenly I have goose-bumps and begin shivering. I wring out my hair and start towards the door when it swings open, revealing the figure of my best friend.

"Crystal?" Nathan begins disbelievingly as he steps forward into the coating of snow on the balcony. His eyes trace the path in the snow caused by my dancing. "What are you doing out here? Are you insane?" he asks jokingly, blinking as the snow lands on his eyelashes. A light coating of snow highlights his brown hair, making it sparkle from the light coming from the hallway behind him.

I smile. "Maybe. That depends on how you look at it," I laugh. "After all, you came out here as well, did you not?"

He can't help but smile back. "Alright, fine. You caught me red-handed. I am a crazy sleepwalker who likes to freeze to death," he mocks me. "I'm out here because I couldn't sleep, actually."

"Ah," I respond. "I know how that is. I was just about to go back inside, as a matter of fact. It's a little chilly out here," I say sarcastically. He steps forward and takes one of my hands, withdrawing it almost instantly. Eyebrows furrowed, he then puts his hands on my bare arms. They are so warm compared to my frozen skin that I'm a bit startled.

"Wow!" he exclaims. "How long were you out here? Your skin is like ice!"

"I don't know," I contemplate, turning to look at the horizon. The sun is almost coming up. "Over an hour?"

"What?! You're going to get hypothermia or something!" I let him guide me inside, back into the warmth. He runs and grabs me a towel from the swimming room and wraps it around my shoulders. My face feels warmer than usual, and for a moment I am concerned that I really have caught something, but then I realize that I'm just blushing. *Wait… blushing? Why am I blushing? I've spent a long time with Nathan and know him really well… why do I suddenly feel different when he does the same things for me that he always would? He hasn't changed… so how have I?* I shake it off and force the blush to disappear, a talent I learned a while back. This is different than encountering a random cute boy at school, however. I don't know what happened to me over the past little while, but I am acting differently, and I don't like it.

We get hot chocolate from the kitchen and sip it slowly while sitting on the couch, side by side. I feel the blush starting to come on again, but I make it fade away, stuffing my emotions deep inside to sort out later. Now I feel calm and at peace as well as safe, just as I always have with Nathan. I start to wonder if the blush was all just a figment of my imagination.

I don't really want to go back to bed, and Nathan doesn't seem to want to either, so we decide to make the most of our last day on Zilferia together. Without disturbing our Familiars or anyone else in the house, we quickly get dressed and head out into the snow. Nathan holds an umbrella that we both huddle under as we walk through the gently drifting snow. We head toward the woods, not to find anything, but simply to walk.

As we make tracks through the deepening snow, we don't know where we're going, and we don't exactly care. We just walk, enjoying being alone together in the soft silence; in the peace we missed for almost the entire time of being in Zilferia. After walking for a while, I pick a tree and climb, Nathan following right behind me. We go as high as we dare, then turn and look out over the clean white landscape. The sky slowly transfers from gray to blue, almost too slowly for us to notice it. Not long after, the sun is peeking over the mountains, the sky above us a bright, nearly cloudless, blue. The snow slowly stops falling and we watch as the sun slides into the sky, boldly shining over the land made new. The sunlight sparkles and shines on the snow, but it is still cold enough that it doesn't start melting yet.

After a while, we climb back down and continue walking around. I stop as I hear something coming towards us and warily watch as a large bush in front of us rustles as a large, powerful liger steps out to meet us. I had no idea they had ligers on Zilferia; I figured making a tiger-lion was something unique to Second Earth. Apparently not.

The liger turns to face us, snarling. I don't move, just lock eyes with it, even though generally you shouldn't since wild animals take that as a challenge. I stare it down for a few tense moments. Finally, it lowers its head to me slightly and continues on its way. Nathan stares at me, amazed. I'm surprised as well. I thought that being able to befriend animals was one of my Gifts, which were all taken by Patrick and his Dragon Hunters.

After walking around for a little longer, we decide to head back to the Dragon castle since my parents are probably up by now. When we get back, no one is awake yet except the servants, who mostly ignore us and continue with their business. One takes our coats, boots, and umbrella. We sneak into the living room, where we sit down on a couch just before Alexander and Pearl come down.

Thaddeus joins us for breakfast, which is a grand farewell feast that is so large Nathan and I just sample everything and I get really full really fast. I notice that Thaddeus has a surprisingly large appetite as he downs dish after dish, even continuing after Nathan and I have to stop.

After breakfast, we head out with our Familiars, my parents, and Thaddeus. We don't know exactly what we'll do with them once we get home, but we can't just leave them here, so we are taking them with us. It has started snowing again, but it's pretty light and there aren't many clouds in the sky. We head toward the woods. After we get in a ways, Thaddeus stops before a large bush and turns around.

I'm surprised to see tears in his eyes as he says, "Crystal, my little niece, and Nathan, I will miss you both. You are both brilliant, kind, and caring, and have been great examples to me. Thank you for teaching me to be young again." He says, then steps away, filled with emotion. I'm surprised by this since he seemed almost not human because of how smart he was- he was never wrong and he never really talked about anything that didn't pertain to the task at hand- which was keeping us alive through the Games.

Now Pearl comes up to us. She gives me a hug and whispers in my ear that she loves me. I swallow, forcing the tears down before they start to flow. She then puts her hands on my shoulders and tells me that I am always welcome to come home and stay for any length of time. She extends the same invitation to Nathan, saying that he should include himself with the Dragon family and he will be welcome at their house at any time and for any reason.

Alexander then comes up, clearing his throat. He finally gets out that he loves us and will let us make our own decisions although he would rather we be a family now, but he loves us anyway. He has basically adopted Nathan into the family, as has Pearl. When all the goodbyes are finished, Thaddeus tells us that he will give us word about our first realm to search for Rex through the watches, but that it won't be for a while so we can have some time to rest at home.

"Oh, and remember, it isn't winter yet in your dimensions; we froze time there, so it will be exactly as you left it. Alright? So have fun back in your old homes for a few months; recuperate and enjoy yourself. ...Good-bye," he chokes out, walking away.

Nathan turns to me and smiles. "See you in a few months, then?"

"Right," I say. We give each other a quick hug and then, with one last wave of farewell, Nathan walks through the portal, with Greg riding proudly on his shoulder. Swallowing, I stride forward and walk through as well, calling one last goodbye to my parents and great-uncle.

Once again, there is a flash of light and I feel like I am being tickled, before the sudden feeling of being punched in the gut. When I stand and look around, I don't find shimmering whiteness like I had when I came to Zilferia. This time, it's a gleaming silver. There isn't music from the trees in Zilferia, but the sound of wind through normal trees- no music, no singing, just rustling leaves and the call of birds. I suddenly feel incredibly home-sick and am anxious to get there as soon as possible. I can tell I've almost arrived when I double over once again as something invisible seems to punch me. When I look up, I see the thugs that had escorted me to the portal to Zilferia. I stand and suddenly remember how one of them had shoved me into the portal.

Without warning, I lunge toward the man and shove *him* into the wall, which is no longer a portal. He slams into it harder than I expected. I glance down at myself and realize that I'm a lot tougher than I was before I left, despite my time in the Dragon Hunter's castle and the hospital. My arms are actually quite muscular, as are my legs. I strip off my coat and jacket I had on, leaving just a blue t-shirt. I put my hands on my hips and stare threateningly at the other thugs as the first one slowly pulls himself off the ground, glancing at Nora as she hovers beside me.

"Well? You punks need to take me home now, remember?" I glance up at the sky and see the moon- precisely the same as the night I left it. I lead the thugs back inside the building and find Kiki still asleep at the table. I slip my hand into her jacket pocket and sure enough, there's my old cell phone and car keys that I had tucked into her pocket as I was leaving for Zilferia. I put it in my jeans pocket and pick her up. She continues to sleep thanks to the sandwich Vlad gave her before we left.

Wow, this all seems to have happened so long ago… yet nothing has changed here. Meanwhile, I'm a whole new person. …This will take some getting used to, I decide as we walk toward the vans. The thugs cower behind me. They were frightened of me even before Zilferia, and they are quite terrified now. I smirk a little. *Serves them right.* We pass the form of 'Black Eye,' as I called the thug who suffocated me so long ago and I can't help but smile at my handiwork. He's still knocked out, after all this time.

I hop into the passenger side of the white van, Kiki on my lap. I tell him to drive me back to the park where they kidnapped me, and step on it. The man gulps, but holds his ground. "Where's Vlad?" he demands. "I take orders from him, not you. "Where is he?"

I'm surprised. I hadn't thought that any of these thugs would have had an ounce of loyalty- or courage, for that matter. "Vlad stayed in Zilferia," I reply. "He told me to tell you to take me home, and then just continue on with your lives. You are released of duty once I get home."

"Ah," the man says, putting the key in the ignition. "Then I will drive," he declares and starts heading back the way we came… or so I assume, since I was out cold for most of the ride the first time.

Two hours later, we finally reach the park that seemed to have started it all; the change of my entire life and countenance, as well as my strength and experiences. I have grown so much in the past eight months or so that I don't know if my own… 'family' will recognize me. I mean, almost dying multiple times changes a person.

Once Kiki and I are out of the van, the guy takes off at top speed, apparently anxious to resume his life from before he met Vlad. I smile a little, for that is exactly my plan as well- resume my former life. At least, for now.

When we get home, the sun is just starting to come up. I take Kiki upstairs and tuck her into bed, hoping that when she wakes, she'll just assume it was a weird dream she had that we were kidnapped. Then I head to my own bed, finally tired from waking up so early that morning in Zilferia and dancing in the snow. Nora perches on the post of my bed nearest to my head. I feel comforted having her here with me. I fall asleep remembering the friendships I had forged in Zilferia, a smile on my face and feeling thankful for that particular chapter in my life. My last thought is, *When 'mom and dad' come home, they'll sure have some explaining to do… I always knew I didn't quite fit in here. I know they love me, but…* I fall asleep even as I'm thinking about what the future may bring.

<<<Nathan>>>

Nathan grits his teeth as he goes through the portal, once again feeling as though he was suffocating. Once it fades, however, he opens his eyes and realizes that he's not surrounded by shimmering white this time around, but a glistening *black*. He doesn't hear the song of the Zilferian trees either, but the screech of metal on metal instead. It grates on his ears, but luckily doesn't last long.

He pops out of the portal back on top of the old building where he first met Vlad. Nathan looks around the pre-dawn landscape and breathes in the smell of smoke that permeates the area. *Ah, finally. Back home, where I belong. Good old Tanguay… wow, I've missed this place.* He climbs down and meets the thugs that beat him up the first day he was there. His lip curls with disgust and he can barely keep himself from beating *them* up. At least they have the decency of mind to be surprised and afraid that he's back, having survived everything Zilferia had thrown at him. They realize that this means Nathan is stronger than them. It helps that Greg hisses angrily at them as well, he supposes.

He grins, glad at their fear. "Let's go," he says, walking straight through the group. They silently make way for him, then slowly follow, their footsteps cautious. He climbs into one of the vans and has one of the thugs drive him back to where they left his backpack and bike all those months ago. After he hops out, they take off as fast as they can, tires squealing until they launch into the air and rejoin the flow of traffic overhead. Nathan smirks and puts his backpack on. He feels the weight of his clarinet in it; a pressure that he hadn't felt in so long, the once familiar feel of it was now awkward and strange to him.

Nathan climbs onto his bike and begins making his way home, stress that he never realized he had been carrying gradually melting away. *Finally, I'm home.* He's relieved to be back where he belongs, but that doesn't mean he isn't already looking forward to the adventures he'll have in the future with Crystal 'Shay' Dragon while searching for her brother in all the known realms.

EPILOGUE

A dragon's roar echoes through the dark forest as it burns, sending black smoke hurdling towards the already darkened sky. The fire brightens as it greedily devours the trees surrounding the wounded dragon, revealing the dark crimson blood leaking down its side as it wavers, struggling to stay on its feet and continue fighting. The purple beast snaps at the small black figures darting around it, but it is too slow, and for its efforts it gets nothing but another swipe across its muzzle from a sword.

The dragon's dark eyes reflect the fire as the flames of anger and fury erupt in them. The dragon stops holding back, attacking with all its might-no matter what the consequences might be for itself. It charges at the nearest man in black and kills him as well as the man next to him. The dragon then charges at yet another man while roaring at the sky, calling for help. None comes. The dragon must fight alone, for the other dragons that were fighting with the first have been separated and are each fighting desperate battles of their own.

The dragons, known for their wisdom and power, are losing this battle against the evil humans. They are even being slaughtered by the dozens.

Finally, a loud trumpeting call echoes through the woods, calling a retreat for all those dragons who can still flee. The group flaps weakly away from the burning section of the forest, leaving with less than half of the group they began with. The leader of these dragons, a large black dragon, snorts angrily and flames flicker from his nostrils.

We should have won this fight- easily! He rants to himself. *This is just humiliating. We are stronger than those puny humans- and we always have been! ...It's all Gale the Gold's fault. He put me in charge of these weakling purple dragons. They can't fight! He should have let me lead the* black *dragons into battle! We would have been the ones slaughtering the humans rather than the other way around! This isn't right!* He continues ranting and raving as they retreat back to the volcano they named Dragon Mountain. When they finally arrive, more than half of the survivors faint as soon as they touch down, exhausted. The black dragon stalks away from them, into the mountain, leaving them to be taken care of by the green dragons that had been waiting there from the direction of Gale the Gold.

The black dragon's snout wrinkles and he snorts in anger again. *We wouldn't* need *the green dragons to take care of survivors if Gale had either had the blacks join us- or my clan to go alone, themselves! Our clan is the strongest as well as the largest, besides the greens. It isn't right! Dragons are not to be calling a retreat when fighting those puny weaklings- they should be the ones running from us! I don't care if they are led by a man whose name is Patrick! I don't care if one of them suddenly has a ton more power and is his runner-up; I don't care! We should have destroyed them with ease! ...I will have to talk with Gale the Gold about this.*

He stalks towards the council room where Gale and the other council members await his report. When he enters the vast room, he heads directly towards Gale, the largest of them all. The black dragon had been taught to respect him, but he was too proud. Gold dragons were supposed to have immense power when needed, but he doesn't believe it. *If he has that kind of power, then he would use it to protect us, to wipe the humans off the face of Zilferia and rid us of their power-hungry wars forever! But he hasn't. He is a weakling and a disgrace to all Dragonkind.*

It's with this attitude that he approaches the leader of the dragons, the one dragon he resents most. Except, perhaps, the Dragongirl. She had one mission, and she had failed. Horrifically. He would never forgive her for that- or for the council for foolishly trusting her to save them.

Gale lifts his head at his approach. *"Ah, very good. You are back, Vincent the Proud. How did it go?"*

Vincent snorts flames once more to show his seething anger. *"We had to call for a retreat. Half of the attack party is dead. Most of the survivors are out cold and being tended to by the green clan. We lost this battle. ...And it was all because of you, you stupid, weak, pathetic excuse for a dragon!"* he continues, his anger unable to be contained any longer. *"If you had let me lead my clan out into battle, then we would have been victorious. We would have succeeded if the council had fought as well- that is, if you are as powerful as you have led everyone to believe. We lost because the purple clan is weak. They were slaughtered like lambs. It was pathetic, and I am disgusted by your neglect. We cannot win a war like this. The Sohos, despite what you believe, will not be able to help us. They are weaker than us and are weaker than the Dragon Hunters as well. The mermaids may be fighting their underwater war, but they are losing as well.*

"Soon all of Zilferia will be at war with these humans, and we will all be destroyed. We are the most powerful of all creatures in Zilferia, yet we cannot stand up to them because of weak leadership."

Gale sighs wearily. *"What do you mean to do about it? If the Dragon Hunters are more powerful than us, then they are simply too powerful for us. There is nothing we can do."*

"Wrong. We are not weak; we are the most powerful of all creatures! We are only losing because you do not know how to direct an army."

"And you think that you do?" The sapphire dragon bites back.

"Yes. The black dragons are known for their great abilities at fighting."

"Maybe so, but they are not so good at strategizing and planning ahead."

"Well, look at how far that's gotten us in this war! We are losing because you just sit in here and think! *Well, thinking will not be what wins this war. It will be the amount of power and strength we can muster. Thanks to your failures, we won't even have as much force as we had to work with before.*

"...I ask, for the good of our very race, to be a part of this council. I also ask that the council will join us in fighting. The dragons have no heart to fight when their leaders are cowering and hiding. They need someone to lead them. I will lead them, but if you join me, they will be more courageous and therefore have the power and drive to defeat these rebel humans."

The dragons are silent, stunned by Vincent the Proud's forwardness. They then begin arguing among themselves. Grinning to himself, the black dragon lowers himself to the ground, content to wait for them to reach a conclusion. It doesn't take long for them to get back to him. The silver dragon steps forward to deliver their answer.

"Vincent the Proud," he begins, *"We have considered your offer and have discovered that we are divided. Some of us would have you join, but some would not."* Gale, the sapphire, and the white dragon glare at Vincent while the rest of the council glare at the other three. *"We are very sorry, but this will cause a delay until we can all have a more unanimous vote. We would still be very pleased if you would continue to lead a part of the army."*

Growling, Vincent finally manages to lower his head. *"Very well. I trust the council has their reasons for not wanting to let me help. I will continue to lead the dragons into battle on the hopes that we may be able to win this war despite our lack of leadership. Good day,"* he concludes before stalking away from them and flapping up to the hole at the top of the volcano. He perches on the highest section of the rim and gazes out over what used to be a beautiful view. Now it is nothing more than something to inspire him to never give up, or else the future could be even worse.

Vincent looks out sadly at the burning section of the forest where the Dragon Hunters are cheering after yet another victory. The last few rays of light from the sun catch the smoky air and reflect on the metal machines the Dragon Hunters had created to destroy his race. A tear slides out of his eye as he pictures a future with no dragons; no life. He feels an immense sadness weighing on his heart. *I will do all that I can to prevent that from happening,* he promises himself. *I will never let these humans completely destroy the world. If I have to, I will stop them all myself. It shouldn't be that hard. I just have to kill the one called Patrick and his underling, the one they call Hunter. I know that Hunter recently gained strange powers, but they will not be enough to defeat me.*

...I will save all of Dragonkind, even if I have to do it alone. Reaching a decision, Vincent launches into the air and starts toward the burning section. He knows just where to find this 'Hunter.' He had seen him disappear when fighting one of his dragons, and he also saw him talking to a liger that then attacked a dragon- which was completely against its nature. He figures that wherever there is a clump of animals, the boy was likely to be there. He flies around the area until he spots a man suddenly lift into the air and begin moving forward. He is followed by five others.

There he is… Vincent follows them and quickly catches up. He swiftly kills the five in the back of the group. The one in the front spins around, his brown eyes wide with fear. He promptly disappears. Growling, Vincent whirls around, trying to find him. Then he suddenly feels a strange weight at the base of his head. Startled, he quickly dives toward the ground, hoping the strong wind would tear the boy off.

When he lands, he finds that he is still clinging to his horns, panting for breath. Angry, Vincent tilts his head back and looses a torrent of fire which then rains back down on them both. It doesn't affect the boy. *Oh, that's right… these Dragon Hunters have some kind of removable scales that protect them from fire…*

He then hears the boy's voice in his ear. "Be calm, dragon," he soothes. Against his will, Vincent's muscles slowly relax. "Yes, very good. Now listen to me, dragon. I am a Dragon Hunter. That means I kill dragons… in fact, I killed many of your friends today."

"They were not my friends," Vincent bites back.

"Ah… I see. You're a proud one, no friends, full of yourself… did you think you could kill me all by yourself?" Vincent snorts and doesn't answer, trying to buck the boy off of his long neck. He clings on stubbornly. "Calm down, I won't hurt you," he assures. Vincent's mind rolls. He knows the boy is lying, yet he is calming down and relaxing. *What is going on?* "That's better… you know, I *could* kill you… but I think it would be better to keep you as a pet, eh? Sound like fun?" At this, Vincent stands again and roars, shooting fire into the sky.

"Never, puny human! I will destroy you! You might as well surrender now!" The boy just laughs at the threat.

"Yes, I think I will keep you… then I can practice these new Gifts I've received. …My name is Hunter. Tell me, dragon, what is yours?"

Against his will, he replies. *"I am Vincent the Proud, Prince of the black dragon clan. …Get out of my head! I will not answer any of your questions!"*

Hunter laughs. "Oh, but you will, Vincent, you will. I simply use my new Gift of 'befriending animals' to control them… I've already gotten quite good at it, in case you couldn't tell," he chuckles. Vincent growls and wiggles beneath him, but he can't knock him loose. "Although in case that doesn't work," the boy continues, "Then I shall just read your mind and pry out whatever information I desire. …I can even make it fun and make it hurt." A werewolf then bursts out of the undergrowth. He freezes, eyes wide as he sees the black dragon before him. "Stay," Hunter commands it. He remains frozen, although he looks very much like he wants to run. "Now then, Vincent, let's see what you can do... kill the werewolf."

Vincent's second stomach instantly starts rolling as he fights to disobey the command, but after only a few seconds, a stream of fire erupts from his mouth, shooting toward the werewolf and incinerating him in seconds.

Hunter laughs gleefully. "This will be fun."

PRONUNCIATION GUIDE

Asoka: Uh-soe-kuh
Beryl: Bear-ell
Demeter: Deh-meat-er
Giusto: Gee-oo-s-toe
Hausdorff: Hah-s-dore-ff
Nehru: Neh (like net)-roo
Sietta: (Like Sierra) Sea-ett-uh
Thaddeus: Thuh-day-us
Y'vette: Yeh-vet
Zilferia: Zill-fear-E-uh
Zyloff: Z-eye-loff

BOOKS BY KATIE CHERRY

The Crystal Dragon Saga

Rising from Dust: Companion novella
* * *
Crystal Dragon
Crystal Hope
Crystal Lies
Crystal Curse - June 24, 2020
Crystal Allegiance - July 29, 2020
Crystal Fate - August 26, 2020
Crystal War - September 24, 2020
* * *
Crystal Dragon Saga Boxed Set: Books 1-3

The Dragon Blood Trilogy

Dragon Blood
Dragon Soul
Dragon Heart

ABOUT THE AUTHOR

Katie Cherry is an avid reader who has been devouring books since before most kids could read, leading her to her first attempt at writing a novel in eighth grade. So far, she has most of the Crystal Dragon Saga finished, including a companion novella you can get for free when you join her newsletter. She's also completed the Dragon Blood Trilogy. Her dream is to be a full-time mother while also providing for them through her writing.

1. Find her current progress on Facebook at her profile, Author Katie Cherry, or the Facebook page https://www.facebook.com/KatieCherry-Fantasy/.

2. Follow her on Amazon to get an email ONLY when there's a new release: https://www.amazon.com/-/e/B07H3FXS7D

3. Join her newsletter to hear about free fantasy books Katie finds, sales, writing updates, and exclusive MONTHLY freebies: https://www.subscribepage.com/katiecherrysfantasyemails

4. Support her on Patreon for early releases, cover reveals, weekly sneak peeks, and eventually merchandise and giveaways! https://www.patreon.com/KatieCherry

5. Join her fan group on Facebook, Katie Cherry's Book Wyrms, to participate in weekly live videos and so much more! https://www.facebook.com/groups/1275626482623759/

6. She's also on Instagram @katiecherryfantasy and Twitter @KatieCherry818!

Made in the USA
Middletown, DE
23 December 2020